Praise for *No One's Home*

"A door creaks open. A footstep thumps on an empty floor above. A light turns on in a room left dark. In every silent room and black corner of *No One's Home*, D. M. Pulley weaves threads of hypnotic suspense with the sad strands of a family lost to one another. With an elegantly restrained hand that stops mercifully shy of showcasing the unbearable, Pulley has created a contemporary intelligent thriller that can stand with the canon of the legendary Shirley Jackson."
—Amber Cowie, bestselling author of *Rapid Falls*

"Disturbing and creepy. D. M. Pulley does a masterful job of introducing the reader to families who, at different points in time, are forced to experience life in the same menacing house. Reminds me of Shirley Jackson's *The Haunting of Hill House*, and I loved every second of it!"
—Matthew Farrell, bestselling author of *What Have You Done*

"HGTV meets Stephen King—creepy, spooky fun!"
—Mary Doria Russell, author of *The Sparrow* and *The Women of the Copper Country*

NO ONE'S
HOME

NO ONE'S HOME

D. M. PULLEY

THOMAS & MERCER

Text copyright © 2019 by D. M. Pulley
All rights reserved.

Published by Thomas & Mercer, Seattle

www.apub.com

Amazon, the Amazon logo, and Thomas & Mercer are trademarks of Amazon.com, Inc., or its affiliates.

ISBN-13: 9781542041546
ISBN-10: 1542041546

Cover design by M. S. Corley

Printed in the United States of America

For Jo and Brac

This story was inspired by the century homes of Shaker Heights, two real murders, and a rumor . . .

RAWLINGSWOOD

Rawlings family: 1922–1931
Bell family: 1936–1972
Klussman family: 1972–1990
Martin family: 1994–2016

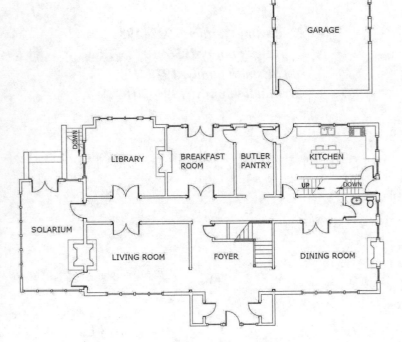

FIRST FLOOR PLAN

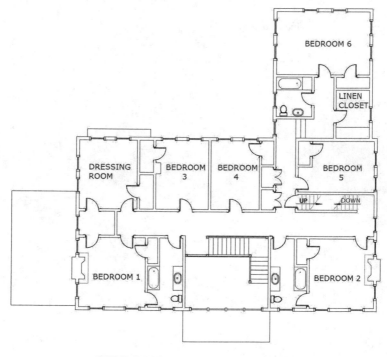

SECOND FLOOR PLAN

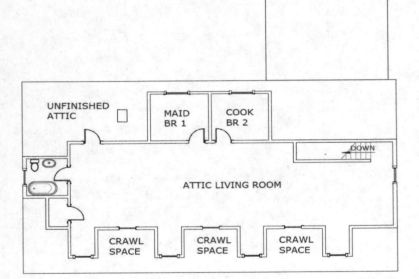

THIRD FLOOR PLAN

1

House for Sale
April 7, 2018

From the outside, no one would suspect a thing.

The three-story colonial stood on a half-acre lot shaded by gnarled oaks and silver maples old enough to remember farmland, stone mills, and the prayer songs of the Shakers. A vision of English character and charm, it lured prospective buyers in with promises of grand fireplaces, custom millwork, crystal chandeliers, and servants' quarters hidden beneath the slate roof. The builders had spared no expense back in the gilded optimism of 1922.

A middle-aged man stood at the edge of the property in a slim sport coat and Italian shoes. The stubble on his squarish jaw and the wire-rimmed glasses on his nose drew an image of an intellectual. Not short but not tall, he had wavy salt-and-pepper hair that fell strategically over his middling brow. He glanced over his shoulder at the four-lane road on the other side of the thick hedge. Downtown Cleveland lay seven miles behind it.

The pretty woman next to him gazed up at the stately brick facade, counting the leaded glass windows, imagining the view from inside. Thin and petite with deep brown eyes, she might have been mistaken for a girl if it weren't for the high-heeled boots and sharpened angles of her face. Designer sunglasses perched at the top of her head, holding back salon-blonde hair. A silk scarf draped artfully over her shoulders. Gold jewelry hung from her tiny ears and wrists. The trappings of wealth didn't quite match her uneasy gait or the apprehension on her face as the real estate agent led the couple up the winding flagstone path to the front door.

On closer inspection, the lawn was a bit overgrown, and the flower beds needed mulching. The edging needed tidying up. The paint along the eaves had begun to peel. Easy things to fix, the sales agent explained hurriedly.

A white cat darted across the entryway, stopping in front of the nearest tree to study the intruders. Its cool, appraising gaze turned the blonde woman's head. The cat wasn't wearing a collar. It cocked its head at her before sauntering around the side of the house like it owned the place.

Unnerved, the woman continued up the steps of the grand portico. A wrinkled piece of white paper had been taped to one of the windows flanking the mahogany door. It read:

NOTICE:

This property has been determined to be vacant and/or abandoned. This information will be reported to the mortgage servicer responsible for maintaining this property. It is likely this property will have its locks changed and its plumbing winterized within the next seven business days. If this property is NOT VACANT, please call the number provided below. Date: January 3, 2016

The ink had faded under the glare of the sun. The paper had curled up at the corners. Two years had passed since its posting. Behind them, the rusted chains of the *For Sale* sign creaked with a shift of the wind as the plastic shingle swayed back and forth in the yard.

"When we go in, try to reserve judgment. True, this place needs a lot of work, but for the right buyer it's an unbelievable opportunity." The sales agent fumbled with the lockbox affixed to the scrolled brass door handle and retrieved the key. "You just can't get a house like this at this price point anymore."

"I'm a little concerned about that busy road," the man said.

"You can barely hear the cars from inside," she reassured him. "You get so much more house this way. And you're within walking distance of the grocery store and the library. Besides, with the old-growth trees . . ."

The husband's pensive smile dropped when he glimpsed beyond the door.

His wife let out a startled gasp as the smell hit her.

The stench of rotting garbage and mildew hung heavily in the foyer as the man stepped over the threshold. Cigarette butts and fast food wrappers lay scattered across the quartersawn oak floors. A pile of dirty clothes and torn rags sat in the center of the formal dining room to their right. The iron radiator was missing from the foyer. Graffiti of all colors slashed the walls and custom oak paneling, shrieking warnings and epitaphs as the man wandered from the foyer to the living room.

Welcome to Hell House!

Get Out! Run!

The Evil Dead Live!

"Jesus," the husband whispered and covered his nose with a handkerchief.

The wife stayed in the doorway for several moments, her face half-buried in her scarf. She finally braved a step into the foyer to take stock. The custom features of the house competed with the smell as she surveyed the original floorboards, the huge leaded glass window over the front door, the heights of the ceilings, the custom fixtures, and the enormous fireplaces in the rooms to her left and right.

"Obviously, you will need to do an extensive remodel." The real estate agent did her best to project optimism into the two-story foyer. "But at this price, you can afford to customize every detail and really make this place your own. The bones of the house really are quite good."

A teenage boy trailed up the front walkway behind them, scanning the empty windows of the house, wary and disgruntled. Hating it already. Pockmarked and sprouting with unwanted hair and oversize bones, his body had clearly betrayed him. The baby blue eyes under his furry brow looked to be about twelve years old, but the rest of him looked twenty. Neither of his parents noticed as he stopped in the doorway, dumbstruck by the violence that had been done to the place. His mouth hung open as his gaze traveled up the monumental staircase to the second floor.

As his parents moved from the living room to the center hall to the library to the breakfast room, more insults and vandalism greeted them. With each blemish, the price fell in their minds until the house was practically free. The real estate agent held her tongue, waiting for the damage to scare them off as it had all the others.

The first floor powder room contained a cracked porcelain sink and a toilet crusted over in shades of brown. The acrid smell of sewer gas wafted up through the dry pipes from the ground below.

The agent cleared her throat of the taste and said cheerily, "The plumbing will need to be updated, of course." The house made her shift uncomfortably in her sensible shoes, and she preferred to stay close to the open front door. "I'll let you two wander around a bit. Just holler if you have questions."

The couple proceeded up the back staircase to the first enormous bedroom. A tiled fireplace sat charred and empty to the right. The walls were institutional blue, and the windows looked out over the street outside. "I think this might be the master bedroom," the husband speculated, cracking open a door leading to an attached bathroom. Dead flies and mouse droppings littered the tiny white floor tiles.

A bare mattress sat on the floor in one of the smaller bedrooms farther down the hall. A dark brown stain smeared across the center of the makeshift bed and onto the floor. The wife crinkled her nose at it. *Blood?* Crumpled tinfoil and a syringe lay next to it. "Myron," she whispered and threw her husband a look of revulsion.

"I know. Just give it a chance," he whispered back and kept walking.

The woman stopped outside a third bedroom and drew in a breath. The walls had been painted a pale pink decades earlier. Torn drapes hung raggedly from the windows, and the afternoon sun filtered in through faded linen flowers. Hand-painted butterflies flitted over the plaster between more crudely drawn satanic symbols and lewd messages.

Who's a pretty girl?

Tears swelled in the woman's eyes as they drifted from the flowers to the butterflies and back again. *Who's a pretty girl?*

The man came up behind her, his gaze darting uncomfortably between the marred pink walls and the back of his wife's head. He put a reassuring hand on her shoulder, but she stiffened. He opened his mouth to say something, but she turned on her heel and continued down the hall before the words came to him.

Bedrooms, bathrooms, linen closets—it went on and on down the central hallway and then another winding corridor that led to a wing over the garage. "Will you look at this place? It never ends!" the husband said, hoping to brighten the mood.

"It's enormous," she agreed almost under her breath. There were seven bedrooms and three full bathrooms. *Big enough to get lost in.* "I could have a studio here . . ."

One of the doors opened to a narrow staircase that led up to the third floor. The extra space sealed it for the man. Standing in the cavernous attic, he pulled out his cell phone and dialed. "Paul? This is Myron. Say, how much cash can we free up in the next thirty days?"

His wife turned a slow circle, stopping to look out one of the dormer windows down to the sidewalk below where she'd stood ten minutes earlier, on the outside looking in. Along the opposite wall, someone had scrawled in light pencil: *and we shall plant four trees, one at each corner for each Angel that speaks.* She puzzled at it.

"This place is a steal. You wouldn't believe the finishes. The mill-work alone would cost a mint in Boston . . . I know, but Margot's got her heart set."

His wife turned her head. *I do?*

"Yeah. For the right price . . . Of course. I'll let you know." Myron hung up the phone and turned to his wife. "You have to admit it's a great bargain, hon."

"But . . . are you sure we need all this?"

"Are you kidding? This place is a gold mine! They only want a hundred and eighty thousand? It would cost three or four million back in Boston, easy. We've been looking for days and haven't seen anything close to this. Admit it."

Her frown deepened to a plea. "I know, but . . . do we really have to do this? I'm not sold, Myron. Not on the house. Not on the move . . . What about Hunter? I'm not sure I feel comfortable making him leave all his friends, his school. It's his senior year. He has such a hard time fitting in."

"I know you're worried, but this could be good for him. We talked about this." Myron sighed, and his shoulders slumped with impatience and looming defeat. "We both agreed that it's our best option after everything that's happened."

Margot bit her painted lip. *After everything that's happened.*

"I can't go back, Margot. I quit. The Cleveland Clinic is the dream job I've been waiting for. You know that. We have a chance to start over here. Let's just make the best of it. Okay? We could all use a fresh start." He picked up her hand and gave it a squeeze. "This could be great for us."

Margot forced a nod, holding a brave face until he turned his attention elsewhere. Somewhere in the yawning space behind her, a floorboard shifted with a muffled creak. She turned toward the sound only to see the bathroom light glowing yellow at the end of the long empty room. She scanned the closed doors of the servants' quarters and the crawl spaces. They stared blankly back.

The taunts spray-painted on the walls below her seemed to whisper in the corners of the attic.

Welcome to Hell House!

2

The couple returned to the front foyer five minutes later. The sales agent put away her phone and flashed them a broad smile. "Well? What did you think?"

"I think we've seen enough. Can we come back tomorrow? I'd like to bring in a contractor." Myron pretended not to see his wife's distressed reaction to this.

"Really?" The woman blinked in disbelief. "That's wonderful. But. Um. If you two are serious about an offer, I suppose there's something you should know."

Margot stopped surveying the house as though she'd lost something and shot her husband another look. "I'm sorry. What?"

"This is a little awkward, but my firm has implemented a strict policy to fully disclose any potential . . . *stigma* associated with a property." She cleared her throat. "This house has a bit of a history. There's been talk about it anyway."

Myron took a step closer to his wife and narrowed his eyes. "What history exactly?"

"Well." The woman straightened her poorly tailored suit. Moments before this latest couple had arrived, she'd been on the phone complaining, *This damn house is never going to sell, Howard! Even for a foreclosure, it's hopeless. You can tell the bank to get another agent.* "There's been talk. Keep in mind Shaker Heights is really a small town at heart—that's why folks love it the way they do—but like in any small town, rumors can take on a life of their own."

Myron's expression brightened ever so slightly at the words *small town*. He had explained their situation to the woman well. They were looking for a good investment. A fixer-upper that they could make their own. Something with character. A small town with good schools. A bit of land. A real home for themselves and their teenage son, who had wandered into the room with the bloodstained mattress above them.

"None of the rumors are substantiated, mind you," she went on, with a false laugh, "but some buyers . . . they're so easily spooked."

The words *Not you two, though* were left unsaid. Myron nodded in agreement, but Margot's worry lines deepened. "What sort of rumors?"

"All kinds of urban legends have sprung up about this house. Some say the original owner, Mr. Rawlings, was murdered. Some say his wife went mad. Some claim a high school girl died here a few years back from a drug overdose." The woman waved the horrible theories away with her hand.

The couple stared at her a moment and then lifted their gaze up the carved wood staircase winding from the foyer to the second floor. The house stood perfectly still as though listening. The sound of a woman screaming threatened to break out from somewhere inside the walls above the dusty chandelier, but the house held its breath.

"That's awful," Margot whispered and silently pleaded with her husband, *We can't buy this place!*

"But none of the rumors have proven to be true. Is that right?" Myron asked, ignoring his wife for the moment.

"I haven't seen one shred of proof. But that doesn't stop the talk that the house might be . . . well, haunted."

Myron raised his eyebrows. "Haunted."

Margot let out an uncomfortable *humph*.

"You might run into an elderly neighbor or two that will try to convince you that they've seen ghosts or that the house is 'cursed.'" The agent made a point to roll her eyes and shake her head. "I wouldn't pay it any mind. Several families have lived here quite happily over the years, this latest foreclosure notwithstanding, of course."

All around them, remnants of the other families lingered—fingerprints, paint colors, nail holes, scars, stains. Margot traced their footsteps up the stairs and down the hall, settling on a far wall where someone had spray-painted words in bright red.

Murder House!

The sales agent followed her gaze. "Unfortunately, *any* vacant house can attract vandals, as I'm sure you understand. Even in Shaker Heights. There are many options if you'd like to have a security system installed, but I can assure you the police patrol the street regularly."

Margot focused on the front door a moment before turning back to the grand fireplaces, the crown moldings, the built-in bookcases, the coffered ceiling in the library, the sun-filled breakfast room, the handsome butler's pantry. Her expression softened with sympathy for the place. The house was beautiful, just horribly neglected. Lonely. Forsaken. Its broken heart resonated in the torn look on her face.

The man took a breath and asked, "So that's it? About the haunting, I mean?"

"Essentially." The agent nodded. "I just didn't want you to move in and hear the rumors from someone else. The last owners who lived here fell on some hard times, as you can see, and people are always looking for something to blame. I'm sure you see it all the time in your line of work, Dr. Spielman."

The doctor nodded. "People can be superstitious."

"Exactly." The woman smiled, looking relieved. They were still on the hook. "The housing crisis hit everyone in the country pretty hard, and ghosts certainly had nothing to do with that, am I right?"

Margot seemed far from convinced. A broken beer bottle lay in the corner where a radiator should have been. "What happened to the last owners exactly?"

"Oh. Poor Mrs. Martin just couldn't manage her expenses after her husband passed away. It happens every day. You'll find stories just like it all over Cleveland." The agent was then quick to add, "But Shaker Heights has recovered almost one hundred percent of its home values, and we're seeing a real seller's market. A house like this won't sit much longer."

Not willing to tip his hand, the doctor offered a thin smile. "We'll need to discuss the plans with a contractor and talk it over together before we consider any offer."

"Yes, of course. Take a day or two, but I wouldn't wait too long. I'm hearing from my colleagues back at the office that we have several more showings lined up later this week. Buyers out of New York." That was a lie, but the agent sold it well.

On their way out, Margot paused at the threshold. In the center of the carved mahogany door, the face of a cherub gazed out from the bronze knocker. It had been cast to resemble a little boy. On the plate below it, a faded engraving read, *Rawlingswood*.

"How did he die?" she asked softly, running a finger over the name.

"Pardon?" The real estate agent's smile fell at the corners.

"The last owner. Mr. Martin? How did he die?"

"I believe it was a heart attack. Nothing unusual, I assure you."

Her husband gave her shoulder a squeeze. "Don't be squeamish, Margot. Any old house will have seen its share of life and death. Isn't that right?"

"Absolutely," the agent agreed. "Some say it's the history that gives an old house its charm."

As they headed outside, the agent stopped and motioned back toward the house. "Uh, shouldn't we . . . Didn't you have a son with you?"

Margot sucked in air as though she'd been slapped. With all the talk of the haunting and moving, she'd lost track of him, and guilt stabbed her in the chest. *Such a bad mother.*

"Right. Of course." Myron chuckled and stepped back into the foyer, shouting up the stairs, "Hunter? We're leaving!"

The boy was standing in the middle of the bedroom with the stained mattress, facing the markings on the wall.

Natalie's a Junkie Whore!

Even as his father bellowed from the staircase, a set of pencil markings held his attention. In a small, girlish hand, it read,

> *'Tis the gift to be simple, 'tis the gift to be free,*
> *'Tis the gift to come down to where we ought to be,*
> *And when we find ourselves in the place just right,*
> *'Twill be in the valley of love and delight.*

"Hunter!"

"Yeah," the gangly boy answered, tearing his eyes away from the odd poem. He emerged into the long hall and loped his way down the front stairs, shoulders slumped in the put-upon manner of a sullen teenager. "I'm coming."

The agent closed and locked the door while the family headed down the winding stone walkway. Margot stopped to look back. The white cat she'd seen earlier sauntered out from under a bush and lay down on the front doorstep. It yawned and fixed her with a preternatural stare. She shook her head at the beast and then at the mansion behind it. It was more house than they'd ever considered possible.

She gazed helplessly at the sprawling brick facade as though it were an oncoming train.

Fifteen leaded glass eyes glared back through the tall trees.

Her mouth formed a few words out on the lawn while her hand pointed up at a third floor window. Both the real estate agent and the husband followed her gesture to one of the four dormers at the top of the house. A window glowed yellow against the gathering clouds. A light had been left on.

The agent smiled and waved a hand to say she'd take care of it, but that, of course, was another lie.

3

The Rawlings Family
October 26, 1929

"Welcome! Welcome to Rawlingswood, my dear friends." Walter Rawlings opened the door with a flourish to let in the first wave of dinner guests. His mustache gleamed with wax, and his waistcoat creaked with starch.

Andrew Carnegie's cousin Ardelia strolled in with her mincing husband in tow. She handed her mink stole to the housemaid, Ella, without so much as a glance.

The middle-aged maid stood ill at ease by the door in her black-and-white uniform and passive smile. She hated Walter's parties. So many *mahrime gaje* with such terrible manners. Ardelia's husband folded his topcoat over his arm and presented it to Ella as though it were a gift.

"So good of you to have us, Walter," Ardelia purred. She carried herself like royalty across the polished wood floor, making a cool appraisal of the imported rug, the crystal chandelier. *Pedestrian, but what can you expect from a lawyer, or whatever it is that Walter does these days?* her condescending smile said. "Now where is that gorgeous creature of yours?"

"Georgina's seeing to little Walter. Always the doting mother. She'll be down in a moment." Walter cleared his throat with almost imperceptible annoyance at his absent wife and motioned to the sitting room on the left of the two-story entryway. "See that James makes you a proper cocktail."

Three more couples arrived in short order, and soon the sitting room bubbled over with mingled voices, the clink of crystal, and the jazz record Walter had put on the Electrola. Jazz, like the liquor, was one of Walter's little social rebellions meant to lend a certain edge to the party. The conversations kept safely to golf, interior decorating, the weather, and country club board elections.

No one mentioned the state of the stock market, although the specter of the week's losses cast a shadow over the room.

It was a full twenty minutes into the revelry before Georgina finally made her appearance. Thin to the point of brittleness, she appeared ashen against the burgundy wallpaper, a ghost of herself to those who had known her before. Before Rawlingswood. Before her son. Her honey-blonde hair had grown thin and dull. The spark that had attracted Walter ten years earlier had dimmed beyond recognition. Georgina had been twenty-eight years old, hardly a girl, when they'd married, but she remained a small slip of a thing with the glassy blue eyes of a doll. She'd never managed to grow into the woman he'd expected.

The ladies' eyes whispered to each other in glances behind her back. *She's getting worse, the poor thing.*

"There she is!" Ardelia sang out loudly, already two cocktails into the evening. "Darling, you look like you need a drink!"

Ten minutes later, the bell rang for dinner. With the eight guests arranged about his table, Walter sat back, his hands folded over his pronounced belly, and beamed at the sight of his dining room. He'd demanded the oversize cavern from the architect with exactly this sort of evening in mind. Still, his smile held the melancholy of nostalgia, as if the evening surrounded by friends were a last supper.

"Is she even Christian?" The question came at him from the banker's wife to his right. Georgina had just told of how their maid, Ella, had healed a scratch on little Walter's leg with some herbs and a foreign prayer. *I'm telling you, it worked like a charm.*

Walter shrugged as though the religious beliefs of his housekeeper had never crossed his mind. "You know, I haven't dared to ask."

The woman ran an absentminded hand over her pearls. "I can't say I'd be comfortable with her as a governess, myself. Have you ever considered hiring someone else?"

"Are you kidding?" Walter laughed. "She'd put a curse on the house! I'm pretty sure her family back in the old country were gypsies!"

This titillated his end of the table, but Georgina wilted in protest.

"No, no," she murmured softly, shaking her head. "She'd never. Ella is wonderful. Little Walter just adores her. I really don't know what I would—"

Something broke her thought. A sound only she could hear. She turned her head to the phantom murmur on her right. *Is it a cry?*

"I'm sure she's quite lovely, darling. Besides, don't we all need a little witchcraft from time to time?" Ardelia arched a brow wickedly, casting sly glances around the table, daring the bourgeois collection of guests to protest.

The banker's wife ignored the quip. "Georgina? Are you alright? You look a bit peaked."

Georgina didn't answer. Her glassy eyes fixed on the far wall as though she could see through it to the timbers beneath the plaster. The wooden strands of the house strummed a silent tune, a song playing somewhere just beyond her reach.

"Darling?" Walter's voice cut through the tension gathering around the table.

Georgina blinked away the fugue. "Yes?"

Just then, Ella appeared at Walter's side and whispered, "Your guest is here."

"Ah. Wonderful!" Walter stood up and addressed the guests. "We have an unusual treat this evening, folks!"

Georgina stiffened, a finger curl falling over her cheek. Knowing Walter, it could be anyone.

He left the dining room, a hush of intrigue roiling in his wake. *Incorrigible Walter! He just loves his surprises.* He returned several moments later with an elderly woman on his arm.

"Ladies and gentlemen, it is my esteemed honor to introduce Miss Ninny Boyd. She is one of the original Shakers from the North Union Settlement. She tells me she went to grammar school not far from where we are sitting right now."

A wave of surprise and delight swept through the guests. *How amazing. You don't say? Can you imagine?*

The old woman's watery eyes scanned the painted faces of the society ladies and the boozy grins of the men until they found Georgina. "I am so sorry to have interrupted your meal. Forgive me," she said in the quavering voice of the ancient.

Georgina dropped her fork.

"Don't be ridiculous!" Walter said, pulling out the spare chair for her. "Waiters. Please get our honored guest something to eat."

The hired staff went scrambling back to the kitchen. Ninny sank her small hunched frame down into the chair, not taking her eyes off Georgina, who grew paler by the moment.

Ardelia leaned in, leering as though the old woman were an animal at the zoo. "Miss Boyd, you simply must tell us everything about the Shakers!"

"There is hardly much to say." But there was. *Please forgive me, but there is much I must tell you,* her eyes pleaded with her frail hostess. The proper words failed the old woman.

Georgina sat stricken, refusing to meet the woman's urgent gaze.

One of his golf partners turned to Walter. "How on earth did you manage to meet a Shaker, old man?"

"Georgina was clever enough to meet the dear woman the other day. Isn't that right, darling?"

Georgina's lips had gone nearly white. She took a sip of wine to stall for time and collect herself. She cleared her throat. "Yes. I met Miss Boyd in the flower garden."

Ardelia gaped in amusement. "In your flower garden here? Behind your house? What on earth were you doing back there, Miss Boyd?"

Ninny shifted uncomfortably in her seat. "I had not been back in this valley for so very long. I suppose I came to pay the past its due."

"What past, darling?" Ardelia pressed.

The old woman sat there, shrinking in the light of their collective gaze. She realized with some consternation that she would have to find the words for it. Her voice, thin as thread, rose with growing doubt. "The dead do not rest so easy here, I fear."

"The dead?" Ardelia arched an eyebrow.

An uncomfortable hush fell over the table. Georgina cocked her head at a sound no one else could hear. Only Ninny seemed to notice.

"Ha! Fascinating!" Walter said in his booming voice, slapping a loud hand on the table. Georgina jumped at the impact. "Georgina, love, why did you not tell me of Miss Boyd's mission? I love a good ghost story! Do tell us, Miss Boyd. Can we get you any wine?"

"Oh, dear." Ninny's eyes fell to her lap, her dire warning reduced to a parlor game. "I couldn't possibly."

Walter nodded. "Of course. How foolish of me. Surely these sorts of spirits were frowned upon in the old Shaker community."

"There was no drinking permitted? Even before the law, I mean?" the banker's wife put in.

Ninny folded her hands in her lap in the manner she'd been taught all those years ago. "No. Mother Ann frowned on such things, I'm afraid."

"Mother Ann?" Ardelia said with a glimmer. *Peasant witchcraft,* it said. "Who was she?"

"Mother Ann foretold Christ's Second Coming . . . her divining brought the Believers to the Valley of God's Pleasure here. They say angels whispered in her ear." Ninny's voice dropped to a near whisper itself. Nothing was going as she'd hoped.

"My. And do you believe this as well?" the banker's wife asked.

Ninny's sagging gaze settled back on Georgina's porcelain face. "I believe God speaks to those that listen." *Please, you must listen.*

"Is it true that the Shakers were opposed to marriage, Miss Boyd?" Ardelia sipped her wine, daring the old woman to discuss the lack of sex in her religion. It was common knowledge that the Shaker commune had died off largely due to celibacy.

Ninny kept her eyes on Georgina—the hostess sat stiff as a board in her seat, as though listening to whispers of her own—and then the rude question registered. *Marriage.* "We believed many things that were unfashionable at the time. I can't say this other world fits my heart better." She shook her head at the enormous crystal chandelier hanging over them. Her eyes narrowed at the ceiling as though counting the timbers hidden beneath the plaster until she'd entirely lost her train of thought. Suddenly dismayed, she frowned at her host. "Did they mill the trees here when they built the house?"

Walter looked up at this, eager to discuss the construction of his castle. "We shipped in most of the lumber, but a few of the larger beams and all the paneling came local. I had a carpenter select a few old-growth timbers from the land they were clearing nearby. You just couldn't get this type of wood for a decent price, not with all the construction going on."

A few of the dinner guests took their cue to compliment the wood carvings and grain. *It's quite lovely. Knotty oak?*

Ninny nodded, contemplating the wainscoting surrounding them, then shut her eyes a moment. She swayed ever so slightly in her seat to a rhythm only she knew—a faint singing that resonated in the wooden bones of the house.

Plant the trees round, round the cathedral.
One to the north, east, south, and west.
In the Grove, I hear angels singing
Songs of the Lord and those that rest.

Georgina lifted her eyes from her plate, afflicted. "Forgive me. I think I hear Walter Junior fussing upstairs. Will you all please excuse me?"

"Don't be ridiculous, Georgina! Ella has things well in hand," Walter said with a warning in his voice. It wasn't the first time she'd tried escaping a dinner party.

"I don't hear a thing, love," the banker's wife said and offered her friend a sympathetic smile before turning back to the guest of honor. "So tell us, Miss Boyd, what about this place brought you back? What is this about the dead?"

The old woman's eyes misted a moment, remembering the voices, hearing the warning bells. The heat of a long-forgotten fire burned in the back of her mind, mingling with the sounds of men on horseback and women and children screaming. *We are not armed! Please! Let us be! There are children here!*

Georgina lurched out of her chair. "I really must go check on little Walter. I won't be a moment." She slipped out of the dining room before her husband could protest.

"Please forgive my wife, everyone." Walter's face reddened with his irritation. "She's been a bit out of sorts these past few weeks."

"Can you blame her? After what the papers have been saying?" the long-silent doctor's wife blurted out, and the unspoken contract between them all was broken. *The papers. The market.* She glanced furtively around the room, seeking forgiveness for her faux pas.

Walter cast her a hard glance and cleared his throat, unwilling to discuss his own unease at the sudden downturn in his fortunes. His palatial home had been built on borrowed money and dubious investments. Creditors had been calling the house.

"Well, I think we would all be well served to just remain calm and go about our business," her husband said with the authority of a banker, scolding her with his eyes. "The stock market has been known to fluctuate. The last thing this country needs is a panic. Don't you agree, Paul?"

"Absolutely." The banker nodded.

Walter joined in the agreement and took another healthy swig of scotch. *Don't panic.* He'd overextended himself on several business ventures in recent years, including a small bank, and those were just his legitimate investments. *You don't climb the hill from the tenements to Shaker Heights without bending a few rules.* That's what he told himself.

"Oh, will you listen to you two? Our guest of honor certainly could not care less about the stock market," Ardelia chided them all and turned back to Ninny. "I must apologize for these bores, my dear. Please go on."

Ninny looked up from her untouched soup at the wealthy woman. Dressed in a maid's plain clothes, the old Shaker sat uneasily among the fashionable diners assembled there. "How shall I go on?"

"Please, Miss Boyd. Do tell us why the dead are restless." Walter tipped back his cup, eager to change the subject.

"I fear . . . they died the wrong way," the old woman said softly. Her gaze wandered out the window to the street beyond the trees. The same road had run through the heart of the Center Family settlement eighty years earlier. The ghost of the old gathering house reflected in her pooling eyes. It was burning. Flames ripped up into the sky as timbers cracked and fell. The floorboards above them shifted and creaked nervously.

Georgina reappeared in the doorway and hurried back to her place at the table. Her cheeks were flushed pink where she had pinched them hard and splashed cold water onto her face. "Forgive me, everyone. What did I miss?"

"We were just asking Miss Boyd about the poor souls that died the wrong way." Ardelia grinned, pleased at the intrigue. "Was it murder, Miss Boyd?"

The old woman's clouded vision fixed on the road outside as though she could see the chaos of that night. The children running. The Elders with their hands raised in protest. She flinched at a remembered gunshot.

"God left this valley years ago. He abandoned these trees, these stones, the ground beneath our feet." She leveled her eyes at Georgina trembling in her seat. "I pray you all do the same."

4

The Spielman Family
May 5, 2018

"Somebody tried to warn you, huh?" The contractor motioned to the graffiti scrawled over the woodwork in the living room. *Murder House! 666!* "We doin' an exorcism?"

The Spielmans led the fat man holding a clipboard into another room. It had been a week since they'd gotten the keys. Their all-cash offer had been so low they both were still dazed that it had been accepted at all.

The man let out a low whistle. "You sure you don't want a full gut?" he asked halfway through the tour. His voice rasped and rumbled like a chain saw. A cloud of stale cigarette smoke followed him as he circled the breakfast room. "Might be cheaper in the end."

"We're sure," Myron said with a stiff smile. He and his wife had squabbled over that very point in the foyer right before the contractor had shown up. *It's all cracked and warped, sweetie. Do we really want to spend a small fortune and be stuck with cracked plaster?*

Near tears, his wife had bit back, *You dragged us all here, Myron. You picked this creepy house. You saved all that money on the deal. Now let me make this nightmare a home, okay? Please?*

"Drywall just isn't the same quality as hand-laid plaster. Our decorator is set on keeping as much of it as possible," Margot explained for the second time and shot her husband a look. *Just be on my side for once.* Her stiletto heels clacked loudly over the floors, leaving tiny dents in the wood. Her eyes darted to the corners of each room as though expecting something or someone to jump out at her. She tightened her fists and pressed on. "The kitchen of course will have to be taken down to the studs and expanded. I want these walls down. It needs to be much more open."

She strode from the breakfast room past the butler's pantry and into the humble kitchen at the back of the house, explaining their plans for custom cabinetry, double sinks, a wine fridge, a microwave drawer, recessed lights, a massive island to seat seven, and another island for food preparation.

"Are you familiar with the Home Network show *Dream Kitchen*?" Margot turned to the fat man, who was furiously writing down his notes. In the sudden absence of her chatter, he glanced up and nodded. "Well, that's the feel we're going for. Marble and natural wood. Classic. Early American." The vision of the perfect kitchen smoothed the lines in her forehead. If they could just get the house right, everything would be okay.

The bathrooms would also be full guts, she explained. Hand-pressed subway tile, honed marble, frameless glass—she rattled off the finishes up the back stairs.

"This will be Hunter's room," she announced as the procession continued into the first bedroom. "We'll close off the access to the bathroom here and put in a linen closet to make it a true hall bath."

The contractor nodded and made a note.

Margot opened the closet door for the first time to take stock of the storage space and startled at what she found. Giant letters screamed in red crayon wax:

DeAD GiRL!

DeAD GiRL!

RuN!

A flurry of other pencil marks and crayon scarred the walls, slashing angrily over the spider-cracked plaster. Hundreds of words large and small scribbled in a childlike hand.

I KiLLeD iT! BAD BeNNy! BAD!

MusT TeLL MusT TeLL

HeLP HeR!

She drew in a ragged breath.

"What, no closet space?" Myron came up behind her with a knowing smile that dropped at the sight of the words. He opened his mouth to say something, but Margot slammed the closet door shut before he could speak. *I hate this creepy house!* her expression shrieked at him.

"What would you like for the closet, ma'am?" the contractor asked, pencil in hand.

Margot blinked away her horror and cleared her throat, visibly shaken. "Wallpaper. Old-fashioned prints. Like . . . hatboxes. We'll, um . . . we'll send you the patterns."

He nodded. After the couple stepped out of the room, he cracked the closet door back open to take a few quick measurements. "Dead girl," he muttered to himself. "That's real nice. Jesus Christ."

Out in the hallway, Margot stared blankly down the long, dark row of doors as though expecting to see the specter of a dead girl standing there. The lines of her forehead deepened, and she suddenly looked much older than her girlish hair and figure would admit.

What have we done? her face seemed to ask. Every toned muscle in her body tensed to run out the door and never look back, but it was too late. They'd paid cash for the place.

Her husband placed what was meant to be a reassuring hand at the small of her back. She recoiled as though struck.

"Hey." He tried again, holding both hands up as a peace offering. "It's just some sick kids playing games, hon. Nothing to worry about. I promise."

Her jaw tensed as she debated the wisdom of screaming, of crying, of slapping him across the face. *You did this! Now we're trapped here!*

The fat man appeared just in time. "So what's next?"

She shut her eyes and forced air in and out before rattling off the next series of instructions. *Fresh paint in every room. Reconfigure the master suite. Repurpose that bedroom. Move the master bath. Build his-and-hers walk-in closets. Refinish the wood floors.* All signs of vandalism would be eradicated. Everything would be brought up to date and rehabilitated. Every demon exorcised. Every ghost chased out.

Margot stopped their procession at the top of the narrow attic stairs. At the far end of the long, empty expanse that would have been the maid's living room, a light bulb was still burning in the bathroom. It cast a sickly yellow glow onto the dusty wood floor.

I told them to turn the light off last week. Her eyes flashed with irritation. Her upper lip curled at the porcelain floor tiles of the grungy bathroom. Dozens of filthy footprints loitered there. *Squatters, vagrants, drug addicts.* The grout lines ran black with a hundred years of dirt. She shrank from the room as though she could sense something terrible had happened there.

"And what would you like to do up here, ma'am? Paint?" He motioned to faint pencil markings on the wall—*and we shall plant four trees*—but the lady of the house wasn't looking.

She turned away from the filthy bathroom floor and straightened her back. "Not much . . . we'll just use it as storage."

The fat man clomped over to one of the half-size doors on the left and popped it open. Dust rained down from the rafters as the door slapped against the knee wall. He shined a flashlight into the unfinished crawl space under the eaves between the window dormers. "We could run our AC ducts through here," the man said and pulled a tape measure from his belt. He poked the cold metal line up and down, side to side, tearing through the cobwebs.

Margot squinted into the cavern, braced for bats or rodents to come skittering out. The roof rafters sprang from the far edge of the floor, disappearing under the plaster over her head. Orange sap beaded up on the faces of the wood boards. The beam of the man's flashlight hovered over a spot on the floor where a small leather shoe lay in the dust. From the cut of it, it was at least sixty years old. Margot frowned, debating whether to pick it up.

It had belonged to a boy.

"Can even fit the air handler, I'd bet." The contractor clicked off the light and slapped the door closed again.

Margot shook the image of the little shoe from her head. The attic left its impressions all over her face. *Unsettled. Sad. Lonely. Haunted.* The sales agent's warning rang true in that moment: *The house is cursed.* She rubbed her arms as though cold.

The contractor turned to the two small bedrooms facing the backyard. The door on the left was locked. He jiggled the handle and asked, "Anyone give you the master key?"

Margot glanced from the locked door to her husband.

Myron raised his eyebrows and said, "Nope. They sure didn't."

"We'll have to call a locksmith." Max made a note on his clipboard and moved to the next small bedroom, taking a quick inventory.

The locked pine door cast a sinister shadow in Margot's mind. She studied it warily as though she could sense something or someone on the other side of it, listening. "What do you think is in there?"

"I don't know." Myron cocked a teasing eyebrow. "Indian Head pennies? Buried treasure? Jimmy Hoffa?"

Unamused, Margot pushed past her husband and away from the mysterious door. A blemish in the ceiling over the stairs caught her eye. She squinted at the pinpoint of daylight leaking in from outside. The plaster had blistered and yellowed around it. "Is that a roof leak? Myron, was this in the home inspector's report?"

Her husband looked up from his cell phone with a defensive scowl. "No, I don't think so, but I'm sure if it was a major concern, they would've said something. Max? Can you weigh in on this?"

The contractor straightened himself and walked over to the spot the woman was pointing to with an accusing finger. He squinted at the round hole in the ceiling, no bigger than a dime. Fine cracks radiated from it like a broken spiderweb. *Bullet hole?* his face asked, but what he said was, "That shouldn't take much to patch. We'll have our roofer go up and take a look."

Myron nodded, relieved. "Good. So when do you think we'd be able to move in?"

Max flipped through his clipboard and began to talk numbers.

Ignoring them both, Margot wandered toward the first small bedroom on the right and peered into where a maid had once slept. Inside, a tiny window looked out onto the overgrown backyard. Pale flowered wallpaper still clung to the walls. She stepped into the room and ran a finger down a puckered seam. It was hand-printed paper, not machined vinyl. Clearly, the room hadn't been touched in nearly one hundred years. The sloped ceiling was slightly yellow in the corner. The pine casements and baseboards had been left unpainted. She eyed the round buttons of the antique light switch next to the door and the shadow of a narrow bed on the floorboards.

An envelope lay facedown in a corner, and she stooped to pick it up. It was a letter from Ohio University that had never been opened. The name above the address was "Ava Turner."

"Hon?" Myron called from the main living space. "You ready to get going?"

Margot emerged from the maid's room holding the envelope. "What? I'm sorry, I wasn't listening. How many days are we looking at?"

"Max here says about four months or so."

Worry knit her brow. "Really? That long?"

"Well, we could move in after the demo is completed . . . along with the work in the bathrooms. Are you willing to live off paper plates and takeout for a month or two?" Myron flashed his wife a grin that looked more like a dare.

She sighed. Her flawless makeup and manicured fingernails sent the clear message that she was not one to rough it. Her heel tapped pensively against the floor. "I hate the idea of Hunter being stuck in some hotel . . . and classes start in August." Her glance fell on the offending light bulb still burning in the maid's bathroom, then back to the contractor. "What do you think you can get done in eighty days? That's when we close on the Boston house, right, Myron?"

"July tenth," Myron said with a nod.

"I tell ya, we can focus on getting the second floor finished and the bathrooms up. But that custom kitchen's gonna take some time." The man scratched his head with his pencil and reviewed his notes again. "Cabinets alone might take two months to come in. Electrical wiring, reinforcing the floor . . . You got any plans for the basement? Rec room? Man cave?"

Margot shook her head. "Just get the laundry up out of there and update whatever needs to be updated. We never plan to go down there. Do we?" She turned to Myron for confirmation.

"Oh, I don't know." The doctor's eyes circled the attic, taking mental measurements for some plan he didn't dare share with his wife. "Maybe a game room for Hunter? A place to hang out with his friends?"

"With all this space? I'm sure we can find a place aboveground for whatever Hunter needs. Lord knows we're spending enough money, right?" This was a direct appeal to Myron's frugality, and she fixed him with those wounded eyes. *Please just make this easier for me.* She turned to the builder. "So . . . can we say we'll be done by early August?"

Max took a moment to study his notes again and let out a tortured sigh. "We can try. But there is a saying in this business, you know. You can have it fast. You can have it good. Or you can have it cheap. But not all three. I'd have to factor in an escalation fee if we're gonna push the schedule."

Myron raised his eyebrows at this and opened his mouth to protest but thought better of it. Margot's pained expression hung like a weight around his neck. "Fine. Let's just get it done."

An uncomfortable sweat had sprung up on Margot's brow and the small of her back. It was more than a lack of air circulation. It was more than the dust motes and cobwebs hovering around the yellow glow of the bathroom or the dull sky leaking in through the windows. She cocked an ear and turned as if she'd heard something. But what? The slightest chill prickled her skin despite the heat. Her fingers grazed the base of her neck, stopping at the vein pulsing against her throat.

"I think that's it," Myron said. "Right, hon?"

"Mmmm?" She turned to him blankly, then recovered herself. "Right. I can't think of anything else."

The doctor clapped a hand on the contractor's shoulder and said, "So when can we expect an estimate? I have to decide how many organs to sell."

Max laughed.

Margot ignored the two men as they tossed barbs back and forth. Goose bumps had risen over her skin. The college acceptance letter addressed to some strange girl still sat in her hand. Glancing down at it, she shook her head at either herself or the men and headed toward the stairs, not waiting for a lull in the conversation. "Could one of you do me a favor?"

The men stopped talking and turned to her. They had already said everything that needed saying anyway.

"Please get the light on your way down."

5

A crew of workers showed up three days after Myron Spielman signed the contract to gut half of Rawlingswood down to the studs.

Within a week, everything that could go wrong did. Power tools went missing in the middle of the night. Mold was discovered in all three bathrooms on the second floor. Asbestos crumbled from the boiler lines, causing a work shutdown for a week. The cast-iron waste stacks fell apart during the plaster demolition. Flashings leaked around the chimneys. The water main burst in the basement on the sixth day of the work.

"It's like this damn house is fighting us every step of the way!" Max threw up his hands every time he had to call the *Damn Doctor*. "Yes, we have contingency funds, but this is like Armageddon here. Just one thing after another. I've never seen anything like it . . . Save money? We could lose that ten-thousand-dollar refrigerator to start."

There was a long pause as he listened to the doctor on the other end of the line.

"Of course. We'll give the lady what she wants, sure, but I'm telling you . . . Yes. I know it's in the contract, but these are *hidden* conditions. Did you see me pull out my x-ray goggles when we were doin' the walk-through? . . . Lookit. I don't see through walls, and I don't have a crystal ball." The fat man blew out a stream of cigarette smoke into the gutted kitchen and listened some more. "Why don't you and the missus discuss it and get back to me? . . . Fine."

He slammed down the cell phone and threw his cigarette butt onto the exposed planks of the subfloor. "Motherfuckers!" he growled and kicked the outside wall. The floor joists creaked menacingly above him as though threatening to collapse. He took a step back and shook his head in disbelief. *Damn house.* "Shit . . . Hey, Pete?"

A head poked down through one of the holes in the ceiling. "Yeah, boss?"

"You'd better tell that plumber to pack it up today. We're waiting on change order authorizations."

"You sure 'bout that, boss? It took 'em a week to fit us in."

"Do I look sure?" Max glowered at him.

"Will do, but that's gonna slide the schedule."

"Not my problem. We can get it done fast or get it done well or get it done cheap but not all three, goddammit! And lock up the fucking tools this time. If one more circular saw walks off this son of a bitch, it's your ass. Got me?"

"Sure thing, boss."

No one said it, but the whole crew hated the house.

They refused to eat lunch inside the building. They even went outside to smoke, a rarity among contractors despite the site rules posted on the front door that forbade smoking. It hung next to a workers' comp policy and the other state laws that none of them had bothered to read. They avoided the third floor altogether when possible. When left on their own somewhere inside, the workmen could be seen checking over their shoulders and flinching at every creak and groan the wood framing let out as they ripped the house apart with their power tools.

In the mornings, they arrived on site to find some new hellish sign that they were not welcome. Fresh cracks opened up across the plaster ceilings in the night. Floor joists split at the knots. Blueprints scattered onto the floor. Plastic sheets used to control the dust fell from the ceilings. Wires pulled loose from the junction boxes.

The electrician walked off the job after inspecting the attic wiring, claiming he'd go bankrupt if they stuck to their bid. The HVAC contractor stepped on a rusted nail protruding up through the subfloor that no one had noticed the day before and had to be rushed to the ER. One of the apprentice carpenters sawed through his ring finger during the third week, claiming he'd seen something lurking in the back hallway.

And then there were the problems with the lights. The bulbs on the third floor would be burning at seven a.m. despite everyone's claims they'd been turned off. *Faulty switches,* they said, although no one seemed to believe it. One morning, Max had stood in the attic servants' quarters frowning at a small set of footprints through the construction dust. Small enough to be a child's. He studied them for over a minute before scuffing them out with his work boot and snapping off the bathroom light.

Rumors circulated among the workers, spurred on by the accidents and the graffiti they hadn't removed yet.

Murder House?

A murder happened here.

Really?

Yeah. I heard it was like fifty years ago.

Nah, man. Just some kids OD'd a few years back.

Friend of mine lives on the next block. Told me all about the last owner—said he died of a heart attack right here. Like something scared him to death.

A month into the work, Max stomped up the highfalutin stairs to the second floor, where a very disgruntled plumber was packing up his tools.

"This is bullshit, Max!" the plumber grumbled in his thick eastern European accent. "I clear my whole schedule this week to be here."

"I know it, Yanni. I'll make it up to you. We should get this cleared up in a day or two." Max lit another cigarette and offered one to the older man.

Yanni waved it away with a tremoring hand and tried to straighten the crook in his back, permanently bent from years of crouching over pipes. "Forget it. I withdraw my bid. You'd be smart to do the same. This place." He opened his arthritic arms toward the ceiling and shook his head. "It's a money pit. How much you bid on this?"

"I'll be alright." Max grinned through the smoke as if to say he'd raked the owners over the coals. He didn't mention any of his heated phone calls with his home office. *Who the fuck only figured in a ten percent contingency? You get that painter on the phone, Lois. I want crack repair included. I'm not paying unit cost on that . . . Tell Phil if he's got a problem with that, he can kiss the Salinger project goodbye! . . . Good. And throw in a pair of the Indians tickets.*

They were over two weeks behind schedule, and the Spielmans had to move in by July 13. Three weeks away. A jackhammer started back up at the other end of the hall. Max startled at the sound but immediately recovered himself. They were chipping up the tile floor in the old master bathroom. Moving the plumbing was costing a mint, but the owners didn't seem to care. The vibrations of the hammer hummed under their feet as the house quaked. A popping sound burst somewhere beneath their feet. More plaster letting go.

Max sucked on his cigarette and followed Yanni down the staircase and out the front door. In the quiet of the front stoop, he turned to the plumber. "Yanni, I need you back here tomorrow. I can't trust any of the young guys to handle a house like this. You're my man. So what's it gonna take?"

Yanni stared hard at him, then turned toward Lee Road rushing past on the other side of the towering trees. He made a small gesture with his hands, and Max promptly produced a cigarette. After five long puffs, Yanni turned back to him and said, "Twenty-five."

"Twenty, and you got a deal."

Yanni chuckled. "This is not a negotiation, Maxwell. Twenty-five. And you must bring in a friend of mine to do a smudging. This house! It wants us out."

A laugh shook Max's swollen gut. "A what?"

"Smudging. To calm the wood. There is a bad vibration here, my friend. They feel it." Yanni motioned to the three men huddled around the hitch of a pickup truck in the driveway, smoking and drinking coffee from Styrofoam cups.

"And what? This friend of yours is going to fix that?"

"It's a hundred bucks, Maxwell." Yanni patted the fat man on the cheek. "You think you can afford to not?"

6

The next morning, Yanni's friend arrived on foot, walking up from the south where the bus and light-rail stations stood on the corner of Lee Road and Van Aken. Max met her on the sidewalk, shook her hand, and handed her an envelope. The woman slid her payment into her large crocheted bag and motioned him away.

She stood in the front yard for ten solid minutes studying the face of the house, not saying a word. The sun hadn't peeked over the trees yet. A light was burning in one of the third floor windows as usual. The workmen kept their distance, laughing uncomfortably in the driveway, drinking their coffee. A white cat crouched in the hydrangea bush next to the portico. The old woman considered it a moment.

After she'd seen her fill of the outside, she approached the front door. The white cat darted away into the neighbor's yard.

"May I come in?" she whispered to the wood. She pressed her ear to the doorframe and waited for an answer. The cherub-faced knocker watched her with dead eyes as she stood there listening. The name *Rawlingswood* could hardly be read on the plate. She traced what was left of the letters with a gnarled thumb.

Satisfied, she opened the door and stepped into the foyer. Red rosin paper covered the oak floorboards. Plastic hung torn from the entrances to the living room on her left and the dining room on her right. She glanced into each room, inspecting the dust, the condition of the walls and ceiling. Walking under the grand staircase into the center hall beyond, her breath caught in her throat at the sight of the old butler's pantry and breakfast room. Gutted. Demolished. Riddled with holes. The wreckage stood like an open wound in the heart of the house.

"What have they done to you?" she whispered up through the holes in the ceiling. Her quiet voice drifted down the hallway and through the open doors above. "I'm so sorry." She placed a warm hand on one of the bare timbers for a moment.

From her bag she pulled a tightly packed bundle of dried herbs. She carefully lit one end on fire. A floorboard somewhere far above her shifted.

"No need to worry," she said softly and blew the flame out, leaving lit embers and a billowing smoke that smelled sweetly of fall and Thanksgiving dinners. She waved the smoldering bundle around the gutted expanse until the reek of men, motor oil, cigarettes, and sawdust was all but gone.

The woman walked the smoke all the way around the stripped pantry and kitchen, weaving the warm, motherly smell like a blanket. Then she carried it back to the front stairs, pausing at a window next to the front door to confirm that the men were staying in their places in the driveway.

Up on the second floor, the bedrooms stood empty and open, molested by men with hammers and snaking wires. Naked and cold. She warmed them each up with the herbs and her soft voice. "Shhh . . ."

A young boy had lived in this one. A lonely girl in that one. A soft song played over and over in the memory of the third. A lullaby. So many sleeping dreams. *I'm here, baby. Hush.* In the master bedroom at the far end, the walls ached with a sadness that gave the old woman pause. *What happened here?*

The bathrooms were autopsies. Pipes and wires and bones splayed out. The woman sucked in a breath at the sight of bubble bath songs and the patter of tiny naked feet torn out and thrown into the dumpster in the back. A filthy rubber duck had been found and set on a horizontal wood block in the wall cavity. Sewer gases seeped out through the rags stuffed in the waste stacks, hanging a sharp, acrid stench in the air. The smell of the dead. She waved the burning sage into each hollow until the sting had gone.

"It will be alright," the woman whispered. "They will make you whole again."

The long hallway split into two, one leading to the last three bedrooms on the right and the other leading to the suite over the garage. As she turned the corner, the door to the attic stood open. A welcome or a warning.

The woman stopped at the foot of the narrow staircase, transfixed. *This is the place.* The set of her face seemed certain. "*Revertere ad somnum, te volui et non es huc,*" she whispered.

She repeated the phrase as she climbed the stairs one at a time, waving the burning herbs before her now as more of a cloak than an offering. As her head emerged above the floorboards, her whispering grew softer.

The old woman felt a slight shift in the air as if the memory of a boy flitted past her on the steps. The bulb burning in the bathroom at the far end of the attic cast a yellow coffin onto the dusty floor. Behind the bathroom door, something moved.

Outside on the driveway, the aimless sports chatter of the men stopped abruptly as the light in the third floor window flickered, then went out. Two minutes later, the old witch staggered out the front door, her face blank as the sky.

"I have done all I can do," she muttered to Max, not bothering to stop or look him in the eye.

Yanni the plumber trotted behind her until he caught her on the front walk. "*Mi a baj?*"

"*Mulo!*" She shook her head and fixed him with a hard stare. "Do not linger here."

7

The Martin Family
March 1, 2009

"What are you doing in here?" Papa Martin stood in the doorway, gaping at the young girl standing sentry in the middle of the room. "Ava! Honey! What the heck is wrong with you? How many times have I told you to stay out of there?"

The room was dusty and freezing. Strange writing covered the walls.

DeAD GiRL!

HeLP! RuN!

It was one of four bedrooms that the Martins had never used in the oversize house. They kept the door shut and the radiators off to save on the heating bill.

"I'm sorry, Papa. I just . . . I find it interesting." Even though she was only ten years old, it was clear Ava wasn't quite like other little girls. There were no giggles or tea parties or dolls. The games that interested her were of a different sort. "Did you know Benny?"

"Who?" Clyde Martin hated the girl's games. Always asking questions. Always prying. Always snooping. Always acting so strange. Her little brother, Toby, was so quiet and well behaved it was hard to believe they had the same parents. He shifted uncomfortably, trying not to stare at her.

"You know. *Benny.*" She motioned to the red and black crayon etched all over the room.

BAD BeNNy! BAD!

"Isn't he the one that wrote all of that on the walls?"

"No. I do not know Benny. There probably is no Benny. This house sat vacant a few years back before we bought it. 'Benny' is probably just some silly kids trying to trick little girls like you." He led her out into the hall and closed the door. He produced a skeleton key from his pocket and locked it. "Now stay out of there, okay? When are you gonna learn to mind your own business?"

"I'm sorry." Ava shrank from him and the damning judgment in his voice. Papa didn't approve of her games, and he sometimes looked at her as though she were possessed by some demon. As much as she wanted him to love her, she just couldn't seem to help herself.

Even as his gigantic frame lumbered down the back stairwell to the kitchen, she eyed the locked door. She'd been practicing picking her own door lock for weeks using a small awl and screwdriver she'd managed to sneak out of a toolbox in the basement. Clyde was a contractor with so many tools and toolboxes that she hoped and prayed he wouldn't notice.

Left alone in the hallway, Ava proceeded to play one of her favorite games. She crept to a different closed door and tried the handle. It was also locked, so she knelt down and squinted through the keyhole into the room on the other side. Pink walls. Butterflies. Flowered curtains muted the light glowing in the windows. Kneeling there, she imagined the girl who had once lived inside the pink room. A girl with yellow hair like hers and ribbons, she imagined. A girl still trapped inside.

"What's your name?" she whispered into the keyhole. Then she pressed her ear to the door and listened for an answer.

For fifteen solid minutes, Ava sat and whispered to her new imaginary friend through the keyhole. Her name was Claudia, she'd decided, and Claudia had a terrible secret. "What did he do?" she hissed into the wood.

"What the heck are you doing now?" Papa Martin demanded from the top of the servants' stairs. He was holding a bucket and a can of paint. He slapped both down onto the floorboard, exasperated. *Why aren't you normal?* his expression seemed to ask. He often found her in the oddest places—standing in closets, crouching in cupboards, hiding in the cellar storage rooms.

"Nothing." Ava stood back up and forced a sweet smile. "Just playing."

"Mm-hmm," he grunted. "Playtime's over, Ava. I figure it is high time we get that room you like so well painted. Mama's been bugging me to do it for years, and now I finally found a reason."

He unlocked the door and set the bucket of supplies and the paint can down on the floor. In short order, he got a paint roller started and emptied half the can into a tray. "Here." He motioned her inside and gave her a quick tutorial on using the roller. "I'll do the edging. Now. You have to be careful, okay? You drip any paint on the floor, you'll have to help me sand it out by hand. Got it?"

She held the paint roller in her hand, a bit uncertain, but nodded. *Yes, sir.* The color was a terrible shade of institutional blue left over from some job he'd done around town. She looked from the tray to the secret messages on the walls, trying not to cry. *Poor Benny!* He had wanted so badly to tell her something.

RuN! RuN!

For an hour, Clyde edged the windows, floorboards, and ceiling while Ava smeared ugly blue over the words. Roll by roll the *DeAD GiRL* began to vanish from sight. She worked slowly, determined to memorize every message before it was gone.

"Jesus, Ava, you're slower than molasses in January!" Clyde dropped his paintbrush back into the bucket. "Focus, honey. We have to get this done before dinner. Got it?"

"Yes, sir," she said, keeping her eyes on the paint and the words. *BeNNy* disappeared over and over with each swipe of her roller. *Who were you, Benny? What happened to you?*

"Good. I'll be back in a little while." Papa Martin left her with the paint fumes and the half-finished walls.

The moment he was out of sight, she set the paint roller down. She poked her head out into the hallway before taking another slow tour of the room. The fireplace held a half-burnt log and several sheets of blackened paper. She crouched down to pick one up, but it fell apart in her hand. Illegible.

On the opposite wall, a closet door stood shut. Papa Martin hadn't bothered to open it. Given that there were only four of them living in the enormous house, they didn't need the storage space. Odds were good that the room would stay cold and locked long after her punishment was completed. Staring at the closed door, Ava wondered all over again why Mama and Papa had bought such a big house. Whenever she asked them about it, she got strange answers. *What's wrong with this house, sweetie? Aren't you happy here? I think it's lovely. Besides, you just never know who might come along . . .*

She crept over to the closet, checking her hands for paint before turning the handle. The light clicked on with a pull of the string, and a slow smile spread over the girl's face.

"You're still here," she whispered.

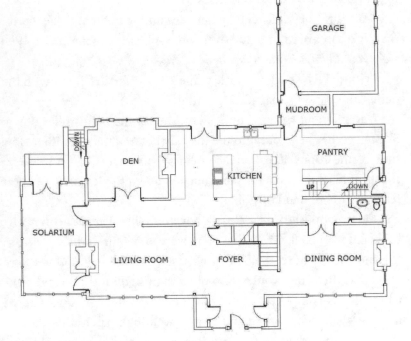

RENOVATED FIRST FLOOR PLAN

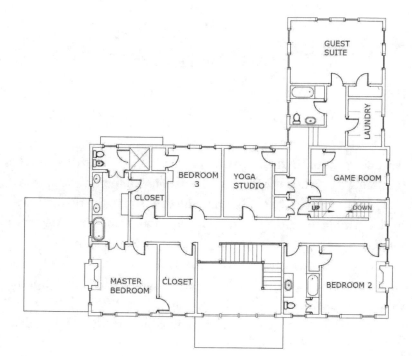

RENOVATED SECOND FLOOR PLAN

8

The Spielman Family
July 18, 2018

No one mentioned the construction accidents, the thefts, or the smudging lady when the Spielmans arrived with their moving truck.

"Not too shabby, eh?" Myron nudged his son in the ribs and held out his arms in the expansive front foyer as though he'd built the place himself.

To be sure, after a tidy sum of nearly $200,000, the house didn't at all resemble the vandalized "Hell House" they'd toured three months earlier. It stood like a revived corpse stitched together at the seams— some rooms old, some gutted and rebuilt. Scars mended. Holes filled. The obscene graffiti covered up or sanded away. The whole of it held together with new wiring and three coats of fresh paint.

The pimple-faced teenager turned a slow circle in the foyer. The morning sky rippled like water through the freshly polished leaded glass window overhead. Storkish and painfully awkward, the boy slouched his shoulders at his father's hanging question: *Not too shabby, eh?* He shifted uncomfortably in his own skin as Myron waited for an answer.

Is he disappointed? Is he impressed? Is he still devastated at the move? Will he ever be okay? Am I a total failure as a father? Myron struggled with each of these questions as guilt pulled at his face.

Margot gave her floundering son an unwanted squeeze around his shoulders. *Poor kid never wanted to move in the first place.* Worry for the boy clouded her face as she shot Myron a grim smile and clacked past him into the unfinished kitchen to take stock and steel herself for the long road ahead.

The kitchen was enormous now, three rooms combined into a giant culinary theater. The size of it stunned her as she scanned the vast expanse of newly laid marble tiles. It suddenly felt cold and empty instead of warm and homey. *What have we done? It's all wrong. All of it.* She bit back tears and searched the room for a way to fix everything that had gone wrong.

"Could we turn this into a cozy sitting room instead of a pantry?" she asked herself in the empty expanse, pacing out the idea. Fretting. None of the cabinets had arrived yet. There was still time.

Trapped in the foyer, Hunter struggled for something positive to say, squirming in the glare of his father's attention.

"So? Hunter?" Myron tried again. "What do you think?"

"I don't know. I guess it's nice," he muttered in a voice deeper than his years. Deeper than his father's, even.

"Well, take a look around, kiddo! This is home." Myron clapped him on the back and then began taking inventory. The paint in the hallway hadn't been finished. Cover plates were missing from the outlets. The workers had scrambled the day before to clear away the plaster dust, but not enough to—

"Hey, hon?" Margot called from the kitchen in a strained voice, a thin smile forced through barely contained hysteria. "Could you come here a sec?"

Myron's face fell an inch. The tension between him and his wife had tightened since their last trip to the house. "Coming, dear."

In the kitchen, Margot was pacing. "I thought they said the cabinets would be delivered last week? The appliances aren't even in yet. How the hell are we supposed to . . ."

Hunter grimaced at the sound of his mother's shrill anxiety, and his oversize feet began to climb the front stairs to get away from it. The house wasn't done. His mom was upset. None of this seemed to surprise him. A pained expression pinched his face as his mother's voice pick-pick-picked at everything.

At the landing, he paused to look out the rippled glass to the foreign street behind the trees and sighed. He'd left an entire life behind. Friends. School. Some other house in some other place he loathed to leave. The plight of all children hung from his awkward shoulders, always being dragged somewhere they'd rather not go by forces beyond their control. Like luggage.

With a deep breath of resignation and self-pity, he turned from the window and trudged up the stairs to the second floor with none of the excitement that children brought to a new house. No running from room to room. No delighting in running down the second staircase at the far end of the hall. No exploring. No planting flags. No arguing for this room or that. No brothers. No sisters. No hide-and-seek.

His mother had called the contractor a week before with strict instructions. On the door of each room hung a handwritten sign. From his left to his right, they read, "Margot Closet," "Master Suite," "Myron Closet," "Reading Room?," "Yoga Studio." Down the crooked hallway that led over the garage, there were more signs, "Game Room," "Laundry," "Guest Bath," "Guest Room." Frowning, Hunter traced his steps back to the main hall and a door marked "Hall Bath." The door marked "Hunter" was at the very end of the house across from the back stairwell. He would've preferred the guest suite over the garage, but no one had asked. He barely gave his assigned bedroom a glance.

New basket weave marble tiles gleamed up at him as he flipped on the lights to the hall bath that would be his. He scanned the new drywall, light fixtures, and frameless glass shower with grim eyes, as though he sensed the violence of the renovation. The wood timbers still hummed with the vibration of the jackhammers. A mere five weeks earlier the room had been gutted bare. Fresh towels hung from the new antiqued brass towel rods. Shampoos and miniature soaps had been laid out like it was a hotel room. Hunter flipped off the lights.

He opened the door marked "Game Room" briefly but found only a stack of unpacked boxes the movers had left there. *Anything in the attic?* one of the burly men had asked his foreman. *Doesn't say here, but I ain't goin' up extra stairs for nothin'.*

Hunter stopped at the only door without a label. The blankness of it drew him in more than any of the others, including the one with his name on it. He creaked the mysterious door open and gazed up the narrow stairwell leading to the third floor.

The smell of burnt sage still lingered there along with the sweat of the contractors who had laid ductwork into the crawl spaces. They'd demanded double pay after the old witch had left abruptly five weeks earlier. *Something's wrong up in that attic, dammit.*

The general contractor, Max, had blamed it on the heat but agreed to hazard pay to shut the two guys up and to keep the rumors from spreading. Little good it had done. Whispers still hung between the muted glow of the window dormers. *Did you see her face? Ran out of here like her hair's on fire. Spooked, downright spooked.* Yanni had walked off the job, leaving Max without a plumber for three days.

Hunter crept up the stairs one at a time with the bewilderment and uneasy wonder of a child. He'd clearly never been in an attic before. Despite his aloof shrug to his father, the house impressed him, especially as he caught sight of the long cavern under the roof. The wood plank floor was covered in traces of construction debris and hidden footprints. Dust draped itself like curtains over the four windows that protruded up through the slanted roof.

"Hello?" he called out to no one in his embarrassed baritone. He listened to the echo of his voice reverberate in the hollow of the room. The loneliness of the sound mirrored the lost look on his face.

The stairs strained under his large feet as Hunter climbed up and out into the open attic. A tiny room to his right stood empty. Hunter approached the open door and figured it for a closet—low ceiling, tight walls, tiny window. He felt trapped the moment he stepped inside it and didn't linger.

The door next to it was locked. Hunter tried the handle and pushed his bony shoulder against it for good measure, but it stuck. Frowning, he pressed his ear to the wood and listened for no reason.

The sound of approaching footsteps pulled Hunter's ear from the door. He turned and scanned the attic floor behind him. *Dad?* his eyes said. But there was no one there.

A shiver rose up on his skin. Fear flickered behind his eyes. He'd seen the graffiti on the walls, now buried under layers of paint. *Murder House!*

"Hello?" Hunter said again, this time not for the echo. "Somebody there?"

He turned to the bathroom over his shoulder. Its yellowed pine door stood open several inches, lit by the slanted light of the window on the other side. The dirty floor tiles and porcelain sink peeked at him through the gap.

He took a timid step toward the washroom, braced for something or someone to lunge at him. The pine door hung perfectly still in its frame, waiting. Untouched by the renovation, traces of so many people—the contractors, the vagrants, the past owners, the servants—still lingered in the fibers and the varnish of the wood. Fingerprints. Sweat. Cigarette smoke. Hunter pressed his palm to it slowly, as though it were alive, and swung the door open.

Nothing, except—

"Hunter?" his mother's voice called from the floor below. "Hunter, where are you?"

Hunter turned away from the empty bathroom, his trance broken by the nagging sound of her voice. "Yeah?"

"Myron, have you seen Hunter?" his mother muttered, not hearing him. "I swear we're going to lose that kid in this place. Hunter!"

As he lurched his ungainly body toward the stairs, he felt a pair of eyes on him. He stopped and faced the empty rooms again, not knowing who or what peered back.

"*Hunter!*" his mother bellowed.

"Coming," he called, dragging himself back down the steps to where his mother stood in the hallway, tapping her foot.

"I need these boxes unpacked by dinner. Okay, honey?" She motioned to the stack of cardboard bins on the floor of his room. Clothes. Books. His computer. Two gerbils sat shell shocked in an aquarium off to one side, eyes twitching.

There was no use in putting her off. Her tone made clear that she would harangue him endlessly until he did her bidding. Or worse, she'd sit down and try to have a mother-son talk to see if he was "okay."

His eyes drifted up to the ceiling and the creepy attic above it. "Yeah. Okay."

"I know it's tough, honey, but everything's going to be alright. You'll like it here. You'll see." It was more of a plea than a comfort. *Please be okay!* Her eyes bent toward him with motherly concern and buried guilt. *I'm sorry about all this. I don't want to be here either.* She gave him a pained smile and opened her arms for a hug. He returned the gesture with an awkward one-armed embrace.

"School starts in a few weeks. You'll make some friends. Right?"

"Yep." He nodded dutifully, anxious for her to leave him alone. Once she did, he closed the door and plopped onto his bare mattress. The room was enormous, big enough for two beds and then some. In comparison, he looked like a boy on a raft drifting along a dark sea of refinished wood. A stately oak mantel mocked him from the far wall with an arrangement of scented candles in the fireplace. He shook his head at them. *Scented candles. Gee, thanks, Mom.* Sighing, he gathered them up and pulled open the door to the closet he'd been allotted.

DeAD GiRL!

DeAD GiRL!

RuN!

"What the fuck?" Hunter whispered. He clicked on the light bulb and took a step back from the slashing red letters. He narrowed his eyes at the bizarre epitaphs, then glanced at his bedroom door as though debating whether to call for his mother.

The walls inside the closet had been left unfinished in the contractor's rush to complete the work and turn over the keys. The final walk-through and punch list wouldn't be completed for three more weeks, and his mother had been too distracted with the movers to notice the oversight.

She'd be furious, Hunter realized, squinting at the smaller print:

SepT 2 1990 386 cARs 2 yeLLow

AuG 8 1989 223 cARs 5 MissiNG

Hundreds of bizarre notes and stats covered the walls. Some of it was too small to read. Some of it so large he had to stand back. Most of it was crooked and written in the unsteady hand of a small child. Morbid curiosity etched over Hunter's face as he stepped inside for a closer look.

BAD BeNNy BeNNy

BAD BENNy KicK. MoM. MoM. MoM.

SoRRy so soRRy sosososo.

HeLp NeeD HeLp NeeD HeLp NeeD HeLp

DeAD GiRL. DeAD. PRetty. DeAD. DeAD.

GiRL oN tHe Bike. RuN. RuN!

DeAD GiRL!

Must teLL. MusT

Lighter markings in a much finer hand covered a few of the spaces in between the scribbled madness. Hunter narrowed his eyes to read the smaller notes:

Did you see them, Benny?
Did the old religion cast a spell?

When the dead speak, what do they say?

Benny, Bad Benny, did you see them too?
Did your dead girl come back
and haunt you?

9

The Klussman Family
June 18, 1980

"Look, Benny! Sweetie, look. See what Daddy brought you?" Frannie
stood in the doorway to his bedroom holding a small plastic tank
filled with water. A tiny goldfish flitted between her two hands.
Flashes of yellow and orange flickered between a stone castle and a
sprig of greenery.

Benny's face broke into a wide and crooked grin. He clapped his
two curled hands together to show her how much he liked the fish.
He'd never had a pet but desperately wanted to touch the animals he'd
seen on TV. The furry dogs and sleek cats fascinated him endlessly.
He often tried to pet them through the cadmium-coated glass. And
now here was another living, breathing thing. A miracle. His eyes
followed its every move, hungry for more.

The boy's broad smile almost undid his mother. Her green eyes
glistened behind her frizzled red hair. It had been weeks since she'd
seen him so happy. "So where should we put him? How about here?"

It was a rhetorical question. She'd already considered the safest
spot and carefully set the fish tank down on his desk, far from any
edges, far from his bedside, where he might flail an arm and knock
the small tank over.

Utterly transfixed by his new companion, Benny didn't consider the placement of the tank until much, much later. His mother busied him with the task of gathering a pinch of fish food between his two fingers. It was clearly another planned opportunity to strengthen his fine motor skills, but he didn't mind.

"Just a little, sweetie. Just like that."

His lack of coordination nearly dumped the entire can of food onto the desk, but he didn't mind that either. Delighted by the feathering fins and bulging black eyes, he dipped his fingers into the flaky powder and managed to shake enough into the water to make his mother proud. "Good job, Benny!" she cooed at him and smoothed his dark brown hair.

He looked nothing like his mother. Benny was a distorted image of his father, with dark hair and deep-set brown eyes. When the boy slept, his face placid and smooth, he looked so much like Hank Klussman it unnerved both his parents, but for different reasons.

Papery flecks of red and yellow floated on the surface as Benny counted them, making special mental notes of the flecks that sank, the flecks that clumped together, the flecks the fish ate first. *Red. The fish likes the red ones.*

"What should we call him?" Frannie asked. It was a dicey question. Frustration often sent Benny into convulsions if he couldn't make his mouth behave or if he desperately wanted to be understood. Gauging the boy's faltering expression, she decided to make it a game. "How about Ernie? Do you like Ernie?"

He shook his head.

"Bert? . . . Oscar? . . . Elmo?" She rattled off the entire cast of a children's show he'd stopped liking years earlier.

No. He shook his head. The name etched itself between the boy's eyes. *Darwin. His name is Darwin.* It was the name of a man that studied fish and animals in a book she'd read to him. A scientist's name. A best friend's name.

"Daw—" He tried to say it, keeping his eye on the fish. The little thing clung to the green plastic kelp as though holding on to it for dear life. Benny knew exactly how it felt.

Frannie could feel his frustration building at being unable to speak clearly but did her best to ignore it. It had been over a week since he'd smiled, and she wasn't about to ruin it. "I can tell you have a good one in mind, Benny. Whatever it is, I love it!" She kissed the top of his head and quickly changed the subject. "There are some rules, sweetie. About fish."

He tore his eyes away from the impossibly thin webbing between the spines of Darwin's tail and blinked at her. *Yes?*

"Fish don't like it when you tap on the glass. It hurts their ears."

Benny nodded. Loud noises hurt his ears too.

"You can't touch or pet a fish. It hurts their skin."

He understood. He hated to be touched.

"And he only needs to eat once a day. If he eats more, it hurts his tummy."

This one surprised him. Benny liked to eat four times a day. He eyed his mother for a moment as though calculating something important and then nodded his head. He trusted her. Almost.

"We'll feed him together, okay? Just until you're used to it." She patted his hand, knowing full well that he would most likely always need her help. The grim thought almost broke through her smile, but she didn't let it.

A few moments later, Frannie left the room. She stood outside the door for ten minutes, waiting, listening for a loud thump and the splashing of water, braced to run back in. But there was nothing. Blissful silence. Biting her lip, she debated opening the door and checking on her son but thought better of it. Instead, she crouched down and peeked in through the keyhole.

Benny sat perched on the edge of his bed, staring at the fish. When little Darwin finally emerged from his hiding place behind the green plastic, the boy clapped his hands gently as though witnessing a magic trick.

He sat like that most of the day.

For the next three weeks, Benny did little else but study his pet fish. Darwin was a source of endless data. The boy charted its every movement across the tiny acre of blue pebbles at the bottom of the tank. He noted its reactions to different colors of construction paper he'd set as gently as he could next to its bowl. He timed the number of minutes it took for the shiny thing to vacuum up all of its little paper flakes of food (7.3 minutes!). He played hide-and-seek with it to see if the fish could see him (he could!). He got up in the middle of the night to see if Darwin was sleeping (he wasn't!). He weighed and measured its growth day to day with his eyes, using the tiny castle as a ruler. He studied every scale on its skin, every spine of its fins, every movement of its eyes.

Frannie was delighted. "I've never seen him so engrossed in anything, honey!"

Hank nodded but couldn't muster her enthusiasm. He'd begun sleeping in the guest room over the garage after their latest fight. *You're not going to make me the bad guy here! I'm just saying he'd be happier in a home where he can get the care he needs. We don't have to live like this.*

Undaunted, Frannie bought Benny books on goldfish that he read voraciously whenever she would help him turn the pages. A new hope lit her tired eyes. *Attachment. Focus. Interest. Maybe the fish will help Benny connect with the outside world.* She stopped listening for the crash. She stopped waiting for the inevitable.

On the twenty-third day of Darwin's life in Benny's room, it happened.

Benny had spent the previous four days becoming more and more agitated. *He wants out,* a voice in the back of his head whispered. Worry lines etched his concerns over his forehead. *He's bored.* The fish would race from one side of the tank to the other, studying the corners, flickering its fins along the edges, testing, hoping. That was when the terrible placement of the tank finally occurred to him.

Darwin had no view. His tank abutted a blank wall, and Benny's windows were over eight feet away. The world outside was beyond the fish's reach.

Benny set his chin on the desk next to the tank and turned his head this way and that, gauging how much and how far the fish could see. Walls, fireplace, closet door, light from the windows, and maybe the shadow of a tree, but nothing else. No cars. No people. No colors. No sunsets.

He tried telling his mother. Poor Frannie stood there as he waved his arms and attempted the words. *We need to move Darwin's tank. Help me.* "Wnnrr Daaaw!"

"I don't understand, honey. Are you worried about something? How can I help you?" She picked up lamps and crayons. She offered him food. "Is it the fish?"

He nodded.

"We already fed the fish, sweetie."

He shook his head. *No. That's not what I mean.*

"Yes, we did. Remember? It was after breakfast. I came in, and we even wrote it down." She was becoming slightly panicked now, watching his body begin to curl in on itself. Muscles clenching. She pointed to the calendar on the wall and the note she'd made. "See? It says *Fed Fish.* We fed him. It's okay, honey. I promise. The fish is okay. Why don't you lie down? Alright?"

She guided him to the bed and tried to roll him onto his side. He tried to let her. He tried to will his muscles to be still, but they were screaming in protest. *MOVE HIS TANK! HE NEEDS TO SEE! HE'LL DIE LIKE THIS!*

One of his curled hands lashed out of his control and connected with the side of her face with a meaty *thwap!*

"Benny!" she gasped, recoiling from him, letting his flailing body drop to the floor. She watched him helplessly thumping his limbs against the ground as she held the side of her face, tears streaming. "Hank!" she cried out. *"I need help!"*

But Benny didn't hear her. He didn't feel the many hands pull him up off the ground or the cold stab of medication. All he could see was his fish, hiding behind the plastic kelp, gaping back at him. Trapped in his tiny prison.

The next day, Frannie woke to find Darwin's tank lying on its side beneath the window. A puddle of water and loose pebbles spread out over the floor. Benny lay on the ground next to the empty tank, frozen, staring, staring, staring.

Flecks of gold glimmered between his clenched fists.

10

The Spielman Family
July 27, 2018

Hunter Spielman gazed out his bedroom window at Lee Road at the cars speeding past, wishing he were with them, going anywhere else but the creepy old mansion. *It is so frigging boring here!* he complained almost daily to his friends back home.

His mother's voice would cut through the house with its own grating mix of concern, guilt, and desperation.

Good morning, sweetie! What do you want to do today? Want to go for a walk?

Who left the light on up in the attic again?

Have you seen any other kids in the neighborhood?

Did someone get the mail today? I haven't seen it.

Who ate all of the cheese?

Hunter, honey, please don't leave the back door unlocked. Okay?

How are you feeling today, sweetie? Are you alright? Do you want to talk?

No, he didn't.

With every helpful suggestion, nagging comment, or worried glance, Hunter grew more distant. The harder she tried, the more time the boy spent cloistered in his room with his headphones on.

It's like she won't leave me alone, he had complained to a friend on the phone. *I don't know. I wish she'd get a job or something.*

Margot tried to give her son space but couldn't seem to make it a day without bothering the boy in some fashion. She paced the house. Four thousand square feet of room and only one other person to talk to, and he couldn't be bothered. When Myron was home from work, even he seemed to be pulling away from her.

"It's like they don't even want the money, Myron!" she said, pacing across the ungrouted kitchen floor after a week of no progress on the construction project. "It's me, isn't it? They just can't face the fussy bitch from Boston, right?"

"Don't be ridiculous, hon." Myron sighed and kissed the top of her perfumed head. It was getting harder for him to act like everything was fine. "It will get done, okay? You going to the club this afternoon? I'll meet you there."

Margot, standing there in her yoga pants and indoor booties, stamped her tiny foot in protest. "Don't change the subject! When are they going to be finished?" She motioned to the boxes of unpacked custom cabinets that populated the old breakfast room and butler's pantry she'd insisted be opened up to the kitchen with a cold steel beam shoved into the ceiling. "This place looks like a goddamned warehouse! It's no wonder Hunter won't even leave his room! I'm worried about him, Myron! He's so unhappy here."

Hearing his name creep under his bedroom door, Hunter had stopped typing at his computer and listened a moment to their voices winding up the back stairs.

"He'll come around," Myron said with a gentle brush of her cheek. "It just takes time. He misses his friends."

Tears pooled against her mascara. "You don't think I know that? He's done nothing but talk to them since we got here. They FaceTime. They Snapchat. God knows what else they do on their computers all day and night. He's certainly not talking to me about it . . . I feel like coming here was a big mistake."

Myron dropped his hand from her cheek. "Let's not overreact. He was on his computer all the time before anyway. This is what they're all like now, right?" He stole a glance at the large clock over her shoulder. He was going to be late for work.

Margot lowered her voice. "It's just . . . we don't know what he's doing up there. I've been reading terrible things, Myron. These pedophiles get online and pretend to be kids. They groom lonely boys like him. They pretend to be their friend and then start to pry photographs and addresses out of them. How do we know he's not talking to someone like that right now?"

Upstairs, Hunter rolled his eyes in disgust. *Pedophiles?*

"You've got to stop reading every paranoid article on Facebook, okay? He's a smart kid. He's not going to be lured into a van with some candy. Now listen, I've got to get going. I've got a meeting at ten a.m."

Pouting, she followed him to the mudroom door. "Are you going to call Max again, or do I have to do it?"

"I'll give him a call this afternoon, okay? I'll let him know that if they don't get it done in the next two weeks, we'll void the contract and get someone else."

He'd said the same thing three days earlier. Even so, his firm voice seemed to smooth the worry around her eyes. "Thanks, honey. Call me later and tell me what he says."

"Okay. Gotta run. So will I see you at the club tonight?"

"What else am I going to do?" Her voice had the light hint of a laugh, but it wasn't funny to either of them. She hadn't made any friends in their new neighborhood. No one had visited in the ten days since they'd moved in.

"Why don't you see what that Jenny DeMarco is up to this afternoon? Harold was just telling me she's having a hell of a time finding an interior designer."

The idea soured Margot's face. "I don't know that I'm Jenny's type . . . Why don't we see if the Zavodas will join us for drinks Friday night instead? I heard Emily collects art, and I need some advice. There are so many blank walls it feels like a prison in here. Hey! Why don't we host them for a dinner party in a few weeks when the kitchen is done? It'll give me an excuse to cook again." Margot reached out and smoothed his silk tie. Her expression softened into something less tense. Less demanding. Almost girlish.

Myron smirked at her, lulled by her hand stroking his tie, ignoring half of what she'd said. "When have you ever been inside a prison?"

She arched a perfectly penciled brow. "Oh, you think you know *everything* about me?" Still strikingly beautiful even at fifty, she batted her lashes and cocked her chin. Almost a dare.

The grin fell from his lips. He dropped his suitcase and grabbed her by the waist, pulling her against his expensive suit. The two mashed their lips together with the urgency of young lovers. His hands groping her tight curves. Hers grasping the sides of his face as soft mewing sounds escaped her throat. He pushed her back against one of the boxes, lifting her bottom up onto it, grinding against her.

Margot kept her eye on the back stairwell, watching for Hunter, as she unzipped his trousers. "We shouldn't do this here," she whispered, her hand between his legs.

Leaving his briefcase sprawled on its side, Myron carried his wife straddled around his middle into their den and shut the door.

Ten minutes later, they emerged red-faced, embarrassed, and angry.

Margot was sputtering placations. "No, it's my fault. I shouldn't have started something when you're already running late. Really."

"No, don't. You're fine. You're beautiful. It's me. I've just got so much on my mind right now." Myron planted a stiff kiss on her swollen lips and grabbed his briefcase up off the floor. "I'll make it up to you later, gorgeous. Promise."

She nodded and gave her best attempt at a smile. At the mudroom door, she straightened his crooked tie as he finger combed his mussed hair. "Now, you *are* going to call Max, right?"

Margot winced a little at herself for nagging him just then.

Humiliated and off balance, Myron nodded his agreement. He hated her in that moment. His jaw tightened to keep from yelling. "I'll do it from the car."

Once the garage door opened and closed and his car pulled away, her tiny frame sagged against the boxes. She wept silently into her hands so Hunter wouldn't hear. After thirty seconds, she angrily cleared her throat and lifted her chin. *No.*

She forced herself up and slowly walked the ground floor of the house to calm her nerves. The foyer gleamed like a jewelry box. Every brass fixture and carved wood surface had been oiled and polished to a high sheen. The leaded glass over the front door sparkled like cut diamonds in the morning sun. For a fleeting moment, she tried to convince herself it was *her* foyer, *her* house.

A white cat sat curled on the stoop just outside her front door. She crouched down next to the window and tapped the glass. "Hey, you," she whispered, remembering its startling white coat and unnerving blue eyes from the day they'd toured the house. The cat barely glanced at her.

A strange feeling crept up Margot's back that made her turn and look. One of the doors in the hall above her stood open just a crack. A shadow moved behind it.

"Hunter?" she called up.

There was no answer. Upstairs in his bedroom, Hunter had cranked his headphones so he wouldn't have to listen to his parents bicker about what a social failure he'd become.

Margot's worry lines deepened as she glanced over to the glass doors to the den. *What if he was watching us the whole time?*

11

"So is your mom still a hot piece of ass?" Hunter's friend smirked from his computer screen in Boston. "I watch her yoga feed sometimes, and dayum!"

"Shut the fuck up, Caleb! Is *your* mom still a fat cow?"

"Dude. Totally." Caleb laughed. "Seriously. How's life in the CLE?"

"You know. Just slayin' these bitches." Hunter let out a defeated sigh. He hadn't seen a girl his age since they'd moved in.

"What's the school like?"

"It hasn't started yet." The pamphlet for Forest City Prep sat next to his bed. Hunter grabbed it and flashed the images of young men in uniforms at his web camera. "But I'm pretty sure it sucks."

"What'd you expect? Public school? Aren't you supposed to go to Yale and shit?"

"Fuck Yale." Hunter sulked. Myron's glittering Yale School of Medicine diploma hung in the den. "They didn't even bother to ask me what I wanted. Public schools here are fine, and the people aren't all . . . I dunno. They're normal. They're not all robots obsessed with getting into an Ivy League school."

"You mean there's chicks." Caleb grinned.

"That's not the only reason, but yeah." Hunter threw the private school pamphlet into his trashcan. "Fucking sausage party, man!"

Down the hall, Margot swung the door to her freshly painted yoga studio open and flipped on the light. She scanned the polished wood floor, the mats, the large balance balls, the free weights, and the docking station for her phone, where she played her favorite music. Her eyes stopped at her image in the enormous mirror hanging between the two bare windows. She studied her face for flaws. She turned sideways and checked the line of her buttocks, still high and firm in her tight black spandex.

Not that it mattered. Her face reddened again at Myron's flailing excuses as he zipped up his trousers. She drew in a deep breath and forced the thought from her mind. This was *her* space. This was *her* time.

She closed the door behind her and adjusted the wireless cameras—one sitting on the windowsill, one on a shelf along a sidewall. The laptop on the floor had been left open. *Odd.* Frowning, she crouched next to it and tapped a button on the keyboard. The screen flickered to life.

Once the ghostly glow lit her face, her brow knit itself into a deeper question. Her email account was open. A long list of emails scrolled past her eyes. "Unforgivable!" "Event Cancellation," "You're FIRED!" "Outpatient Follow-up." The open message read:

> Since you've elected to discontinue treatment, we highly recommend you seek out a therapist with experience in posttraumatic stress disorder and clinical depression. We can provide a referral . . .

Alarmed and exposed, Margot closed the browser window and checked her desktop for other open programs. She tilted the machine to see that she never removed the slip of paper taped to the underside with her login password and the new wireless internet passkey.

She crumpled the paper in her hand and pressed it to her lips. *Did I just leave it open?* She really didn't think so. "Son of a bitch," she hissed to herself and fought off another round of tears. *Hunter.* Gathering herself, she stood up and marched down the hall.

Knock. Knock.

"Hunter?" she called through the wood.

"I gotta go, man." Hunter quickly clicked a button on the keyboard, and Caleb vanished from the computer screen. His video game flickered back to life. "Yeah?"

"I'm coming in," she announced and, a second later, pushed open the door.

Hunter spun around in his office chair and pulled the headphones off his head.

"Sorry to bother you, honey. But . . ." She drew in a breath to steady herself. *Maybe he didn't read all of it.* "Were you messing around on my laptop?"

"Huh?" His face was a confused scowl.

"Were you snooping around on my laptop?" *Say no, say no, say no,* she silently prayed in the doorway.

"I don't know what you're talking about." He truly looked like he didn't.

Margot closed her eyes in relief, then opened them again. "Reading other people's email is wrong. It's a total invasion of privacy. You know that, right?"

"Yeah." He looked at her with teenage exasperation. *I'm not dumb, Mom.*

She tried to keep her voice steady, motherly. "Just promise me you'll stay out of my studio. Okay? My computer and my equipment are important for my work, and if you did see any of my emails, I need you to tell me right now."

"I swear I didn't." Hunter looked down at his hands to keep from rolling his eyes. Margot didn't really work. She taught three yoga classes a day using her laptop and wireless cameras to broadcast to users around the world.

She only has like ten followers. It's not even like they pay. His online friend had laughed at this. *Probably just perverts that want to see her bend over.* Hunter hadn't laughed back. *Dude. Shut up.*

Margot paused before closing the door. "Are you okay, sweetie?"

Am I not okay enough for you? Am I ever okay enough? he fumed to himself, but what he said was, "I guess."

"I know this move has been hard on you. It's been hard on all of us."

"Yeah." He didn't say more, but his sullen expression spoke volumes.

She wanted desperately to pull him onto her lap like she'd done when he was younger, but she knew he'd hate that. "Once school starts, it's going to be great. You'll see."

"Sure, Mom. I just . . ." His face wrinkled with questions he wanted to ask, things he wanted to say. He turned away from her to stare at his two gerbils. They were still too traumatized from the move to explore the maze he'd set up for them. They lay huddled together in a corner.

"You just what, sweetie?"

"Nothing."

"Do you have questions? I mean, about what happened? I know we talked to you about it a while ago, but is there anything you want to know?"

Hunter raised his eyebrows and straightened up in his chair a bit. "Um . . . I don't know." *Why did we move? What is wrong with you? What really happened in Boston?* Hunter gauged her uncomfortable posture and decided it wasn't worth upsetting her. "No. It's okay, Mom. I'm sure everything will work out."

"You sure? I'm worried about you, sweetie."

"I'm okay." He shrugged to prove it. After a moment's pause, he decided to risk one question. "Are *you* okay, Mom?"

"Uh, sure, honey. I'm fine."

Out in the hallway, Margot winced. *Are* you *okay, Mom?* She shook her head at the closed door and then at the ceiling. She debated changing her computer password and checked her watch. *No time.*

She quickly returned to her studio and set up her equipment. Computer. Cameras. Music. Tits. Smile.

"Good morning and namaste!" She pressed her palms together and bowed to the front camera. "Today we're going to be turning up the heat on our thighs . . ."

She spent the next hour talking to the tiny web cameras, bending this way and that, holding impossible pretzel poses. She did it all in a sports bra and skintight yoga pants, often pointing to her own ass or stomach to describe the tightness, the breath. "If it doesn't burn, you're not doing it right."

Forty minutes later, lying on her back, her legs spread eagled, she led her audience through a guided meditation. "You're walking along a sandy beach. Do you hear the waves crashing along the shore? Mmmmm. Smell the salt in the air. Doesn't that sun feel good?"

The soundtrack turned to ocean gulls and rushing water as Margot's voice faded until it was just her breathing. In and out. Chest up and down. The sun from the windows lit her serene face. After a full minute of silence, she sat up and smiled at Camera 2. "Doesn't that just feel wonderful? Stay still until you're ready to come back to reality. Until next time, friends, remember. The light in me sees the light in you. Namaste."

Her arm reached for the laptop and tapped a button. She grabbed a towel and wiped the sweat from her face, dabbing gently to not smear her makeup. After several gulps of water, she turned to her computer and scrolled down for feedback.

A line of text made her smile.

She clicked into a new computer screen and tapped a few keys, then turned her head back to Camera 2. "You missed me, huh?"

A husky voice answered from the laptop. "Babe, I could watch you all day. You know what you do to me."

She raised an eyebrow at the camera and gave it a slow smile. "What do I do to you?"

"You wanna see?"

She turned back to the laptop screen and stared into the fleshy glow. An embarrassed laugh caught in her throat. "Is that for me?"

"Why? You want it?"

"It doesn't matter what I want. I'm a married woman."

"I know. That's what makes it kind of hot, right?"

"How old are you again?" She glanced at herself in the full-length mirror, pushing her chest out ever so slightly. The camera sat beside it.

"Old enough to know you're the hottest thing I've ever seen."

"Is that right?" Margot gazed into the lens as though debating. Then she got up on all fours and slowly crawled across the floor to Camera 1. Gone was the worried mother and the nagging wife.

In front of the camera, she was someone else altogether.

12

The Rawlings Family
Black Tuesday, October 29, 1929

The back door slammed open at 5:35 p.m., and Mr. Rawlings stormed into the kitchen without bothering to close it. Not even glancing at the maid cooking at the stove or his son picking bits of apple off the kitchen table, he pushed past them and into his library, flushed red, reeking of brown liquor.

Ella flashed a reassuring smile at little Walter, whose face had fallen so far down he looked ready to cry. His father often had this effect on the boy. Always stern. Always demanding. Always disappointed. A fist would drop onto the dinner table, making the silver jump. *Hasn't anyone taught this child how to hold a fork properly?*

Four-year-old Walter Junior was to be seen and not heard. This phrase was repeated at least once a week when the boy attempted to interject something during the evening meal or couldn't sit still for lectures on law and commerce. *Do not speak until spoken to, young man.*

Ella would wait until Mr. and Mrs. Rawlings were out of earshot to pluck up his spirits or give him a warm hug. Just a wink from her was enough to lift the anchors of the boy's heart. They shared secrets, the two of them. Secrets little Walter would never tell his parents.

"Walter." Ella put her elbows on the table in front of him and whispered, "Did I ever show you the *dukkerin*? How to tell the future?"

His eyes went wide as he shook his head.

"There are many ways," she went on, picking up her mug and drinking her tea.

Three rooms away, Mr. Rawlings was slamming drawers and cursing to himself. The sound of papers rifling through his shaking fingers ruffled the air, and then his voice. "It can't be . . . it just can't." He rubbed his red face, nearly purple now, and collapsed into his leather chair. "That son of a bitch! We should've gotten out. We needed to get the hell OUT! 'Ride the wave,' he says! God DAMN IT!" His fist slammed into the top of his desk hard enough to make the floor quake.

In the kitchen, both Ella and Walter flinched at the sound of his voice. It was a curse on them all. The maid shot a fiery glare toward the library and slapped her tea on the counter, clearing her throat loudly.

The only response from the other end of the house was the splash of liquor into a crystal tumbler.

Rolling her eyes to the heavens, Ella muttered to herself, "*Prikaza!*" She excused herself from Walter and plodded loudly across the butler's pantry and past the breakfast room to the library door the man hadn't bothered to close. "I get you something, sir? Coffee, perhaps?" she asked sharply.

Mr. Rawlings didn't even bother to look at her. He just stared glassy eyed into his tumbler of whiskey and shook his head. In that moment, he resembled little Walter so completely she almost smiled. *Little boy. Lost.*

"I leave you in peace then." With that she quietly shut the french doors to separate whatever mess the man had made for himself from the rest of the house. She studied him through the glass for a frowning moment. *Lost wallet? Lost deal? Lost client? The man is always gruff, but this . . .*

He must've felt her staring. His murderous eyes caught hers on the other side of the glass an instant before she turned and hurried back to the kitchen, clutching her heart as though stabbed, muttering, "*Bengla!*"

Back in the kitchen, little Walter was waiting. "How?" he asked.

She smoothed the stricken expression from her face. "How what, *muro shavo*?"

"How do you tell the future?"

"Ah! Yes." Ella picked up her mug and swirled the last bit of tea before drinking it. She set the cup in front of him. "There. You see it?"

"See what?" His cherub face scrunched into a question mark.

"The tea leaves, yes?"

The soggy brown leaves sat in the bottom of the mug in a half ring with several little lumps to one side. He stared at them. "What do they mean?"

"It all depends, *shavo*. What do you see?"

"Umm . . ." The boy looked so close he nearly put his nose in the mug. "I see a cow."

"Yes. What else?"

"A . . . tree. That one there"—he pointed into the mug—"that looks like a fire."

She frowned at this, but the boy didn't notice.

"And a sword! You see it?" Walter was loving this game. "Look at the birds! In the sky. See 'em? They're flying upside down."

Ella pulled the cup a bit closer to her nose, turning it this way and that, worry creasing her face deeper and deeper.

"What does it mean, Miss Ella?" the boy asked eagerly. One look at the lines on her face tempered his excitement. His lower lip curled in dismay. "It is not *bad*, is it?"

Ella forced out a chuckle and said, "Of course not! This means great adventures for you. Pirate ships, maybe."

"Like Peter and Wendy?" The boy's face lit up.

"Maybe with a sword fight, yes?"

"Really?" Walter laughed, leaping up and pretending to sword fight an imaginary pirate.

"Good. You go practice your sword. I be up in one minute." She took the cup and the apple plate to the sink as Walter scampered up the back stairs to his playroom. Once he was out of sight, she held the cup up to the light of the window and peered in again, slowly turning the fortune over, hoping for better. The frown returned, and she quickly rinsed the leaves out and all the way down the drain. Shutting the water off, she mouthed a few words and made the sign of the cross over her chest.

She glanced back toward the office before waddling her thick frame up the back stairs. Walter's battle cries, "Take that and that . . . ," greeted her when she reached the second floor. Ella smiled at the ruckus, but the worry lingered on her forehead.

Down at the other end of the long, dark hall, Mrs. Rawlings's door was shut as usual. The woman had been in bed for days. There were never any words spoken about it in the house, but Ella knew. Ella knew from the hours in bed and the blood on the linens. Another baby lost. This was the third since Walter had been born. The maid padded lightly down the hallway to the closed door.

"Missus Rawlings?" she called through the wood.

Inside, the younger woman rolled away from the voice and gazed out the window into the treetops. She'd spent most of her time that month in bed, hoping for the baby to quicken, but it hadn't mattered. Tiny birds flitted from branch to branch on the other side of the glass. Sweet little girls she would never meet. Fresh tears burned her eyes.

"Missus Rawlings, I come and check on you in one hour. You must eat then," Ella said softly.

Georgina buried her head under the sheets as though the maid could see her through the wood. Doubled over in pain, she wept silently to herself, wondering what she had done to deserve such a curse. Somewhere from deep beneath the house, she heard a sound. She sat up with a start and listened. *A song? A cry?*

With a heavy sigh, Ella turned and headed back to Walter's room. He was lying on the floor when she opened the door. A wooden stick stood up from between his side and arm. His eyes stared lifelessly at the ceiling, his face frozen and pale. On reflex, Ella clutched her chest. "Walter?"

"Shh," he whispered, eyes not blinking. "I'm dead. Hook got me."

Ella inhaled sharply at this, still visibly shaken at the sight of him on the ground but unwilling to let on. "Aha, little *mulo*. Then you must rise up. Rise up and haunt his days and nights!"

A floor below them, Mr. Rawlings downed his second glass of whiskey and yanked open the center drawer of his desk. The crumpled newspaper on the leather desk blotter screamed its headline.

STOCKS CRASH! INVESTORS PANIC!

He pulled a silver pistol from the drawer with a shaking hand. It dropped to the desktop with the cold metal *thunk* of a dead bolt hitting the strike.

13

The Spielman Family
July 27, 2018

Myron sat in the garage, staring at the closed door. The engine ticked as it cooled. He ran a hand over his face and picked up his cell phone to read the message on the tiny glass screen again. Finally, he pressed a few buttons and put the phone to his ear.

"Paul? It's Myron . . . Yes, I got the message. I know how it looks, but you have to realize that this is a matter of professional opinion . . . I know what the Mayo Clinic says, but they didn't perform the examination. I did . . . Yes, I understand I'm under a microscope here, but that doesn't change my clinical diagnosis. Okay. I'll talk to you then."

He hung up and pressed his sweating forehead into the palm of his hand. "Jesus Christ," he whispered. "What the hell am I going to do?"

The house was quiet as Myron slipped in through the back door, locking it behind him. He was later than usual. "Hello?"

The smell of the greasy take-out dinner Margot had picked up from the local Chinese restaurant still lingered in the kitchen. Pork and steamed vegetables. She'd stuffed the leftovers in their new refrigerator, which sat dejected in the middle of a blank wall, buzzing.

Myron closed the fridge, not hungry. The flickering light of a television pulled him toward the glass doors of the den.

Margot was curled up on the leather sofa, napping to some home-remodeling show. An empty martini glass sat on the coffee table in front of her. He peeked in on her a moment. Sleeping peacefully. Blissfully silent.

He carried his briefcase up the front stairs, stopping at the top to gaze down the long hall of closed doors. A faint glow lit the bottom of Hunter's door as usual. Myron frowned at it. *Did the kid even leave the house today?* At the bend in the hallway, the attic door stood slightly ajar. The light upstairs had been left on again. He paused, considering it a moment, before shuffling past four more closed doors to the master suite at the far end.

His massive walk-in closet had its own entrance. Myron opened it and strode past the custom shelves of designer shoes and perfectly ordered suits to the door on the opposite side. Their contractor, Max, had transformed the seventh bedroom, originally designed as a dressing room or nursery, into an enormous master bath. A crystal chandelier hung in the middle of the vast expanse of brass and cold marble. The brightness of the white counters and flooring was jarring as he clicked on the lights. The floor joists strained painfully under the weight of the stone slabs and the oversize soaking tub beneath the window.

Myron flipped on the in-floor heat and headed to his half of the room with his own sink, vanity, and private cabinets. He set his briefcase down and thumbed the combination into the two dial locks on the latches. Inside lay ten white boxes, each rattling with pills. The names of manufacturers splashed across the cardboard along with flashy brand names that promised high-tech chemistry and clinical results. Stacking the boxes up, he grabbed two brown plastic prescription bottles from his medicine cabinet and popped each open. Glancing at the reflection of the closed door in the mirror, he popped two white pills into his mouth and swallowed without water. He let out a long exhale of relief.

After a quick inventory of his remaining supply, he began opening one sample box after another, prying pills from blister packs and spilling them from his palm into the half-empty brown bottles. He quickly snapped both childproof lids into place again. Once the two bottles were back in the cabinet, he gathered the torn boxes and swept them into his briefcase.

Work done, Myron straightened up and checked his own reflection. He eased the loose strands of his wavy hair back into position. He checked the whites of his eyes and pulled back each lid to gauge the color of the red meat below. Baring his teeth, he checked his gums and under his tongue. Satisfied, he picked up the briefcase and left the bathroom.

In the closet, he stopped to deposit the leather briefcase below a row of neatly arranged Italian shirts. Every shade of white hung in order as though in a clothing store. His shiny leather shoes were lined up in their steel racks like trophies. His silk ties lay neatly in thin custom drawers he and Margot had picked out together. The entire room smelled of Gucci cologne and sports deodorant.

Myron carefully hung up the suit he was wearing, shifting the hangers to avoid crowding, touching, rumpling, ruining. He threw the clothes from his gym bag in the canvas hamper Margot had insisted on keeping separate from her own. *It's just simpler this way. Besides, your workout gear stinks!* As he was setting his gym bag onto its shelf, the attic floor above him creaked.

The sound straightened his spine and craned his neck up toward the ceiling.

The white plaster over his head stared blankly back.

Another squeak in the floorboards upstairs left him no choice. Barefoot, he padded over to his closet door and peered out into the hall. The setting sun streamed in through the leaded glass window, washing the wall next to him in shades of pink and gold, shrouding the rest of the hallway in murky shadows. He squinted at the attic door, half-hidden in the back hallway.

A dark shape moved past the door.

He startled at the sight of it. Frowning, he took a cautious step out into the hall toward the attic door. "Hunter? Is that you?"

A faint laugh echoed down the crooked back hallway, bouncing off the closed doors. *Or did it come from outside? A passing car? A radio?* He stopped breathing for a moment, his eyes searching for the source, his heart pounding loudly against his ribs.

The air stood still.

"Hello?" he said louder this time. "Hunter? Is that you? Margot?" Saying their names seemed to break the spell. He exhaled. *Haunted house indeed,* he chided himself and plodded loudly down the hall.

The back corridor stood empty. He flipped on the light to be sure. He swung open the attic door and checked the stairs to find them empty as well. Up and down the back hallway, he walked a quick patrol, opening doors, snapping lights on and off. Nothing.

He stopped at Hunter's door, almost forgetting to knock.

Tap. Tap.

Inside the room, Hunter felt his father's footsteps vibrate through the floorboards before he heard the knock. He removed his headset and lowered his plastic gun. "Yeah?"

"Hey." Myron opened the door and waved awkwardly at the boy. "Was that you in the hallway?"

"Huh?"

"Just a second ago. Did you . . ." *No. That doesn't make sense.* Myron shook his head at himself. *Hunter was in his room.* "Did you hear anything just now?"

"Uh, no. I had my headphones on."

"Huh. Must've been your mother." Myron quickly changed the subject. "So . . . is that . . . that a good game?"

"I guess." Hunter shrugged.

"Is it fun?" Myron seemed to regret the question before it was out of his mouth. He wasn't a "cool" dad, no matter how much he'd like to be.

"Uh. Sort of." Hunter held up the gun. On the frozen screen behind him, a zombie's face was caught midsnarl.

"Right." His father nodded as though they'd just decided something important.

"You, uh . . . you okay, Dad?" Something in Hunter seemed to wake up, looking at the man. A sober awareness.

Myron sensed it too and stiffened his shoulders, lifted his chin. "Yeah. Just, you know, tired. Long day. You do anything interesting?"

Hunter shrugged again. He'd left the house for an hour after lunch, walking south down Lee Road toward the grocery store and library. He'd come back smelling of old books and soda pop. "I dunno. Not really."

Myron relaxed now that his son's laser focus seemed to dim. Or perhaps it was the effect of the pills he'd taken. "You gonna put together another coding club out here?"

The boy sat there slumped in his leather chair a moment, debating something in his mind. "I dunno. Maybe . . . Hey, Dad?"

The little-boy lilt in his son's voice squeezed Myron's heart. *He's still so young.* "What's up?"

Hunter stared at the plastic gun in his hand, flexing and unflexing his fingers as though working something loose. Something that was determined to stay stuck. Finally, he gave up and muttered, "Nothing."

"Okay." Myron's expression closed again, and his eyes clouded over with annoyance and unfocused irritation. He turned to leave. A faint light filtered into the hallway from the attic, casting a glow onto the dark wood floor. The sight made him pause. Hadn't he just turned it off? "Say, Hunter, do me a favor?"

"Yeah, Dad?"

"When you go up to the attic, please remember to turn off the light."

Hunter scowled at him. *But I didn't.*

Myron held up his hand as if he'd heard the silent protest. "Seriously. Every time I come home lately, that damn light is on. Now, you're the one always asking about our gas mileage and the heating bills and being 'green' and all that, right? Can we agree that leaving lights on wastes electricity?"

The man's voice had shifted just enough, his vowels growing just long enough, for Hunter to hear the difference. The boy stared at the far wall with annoyance and just nodded his head. *Drunk,* his dull expression concluded. *The man's drunk.* There was no use arguing with him. "Sure, Dad."

"Okay." Myron tapped the door. "Good night. Don't stay up too late."

After closing his son's door, he sauntered over to the attic entrance and made a show of flipping off the light switch at the foot of the stairs for no one. After he'd swung the door shut and floated languidly back down the hall toward his own bedroom, Myron stopped as if remembering the reason he'd ventured out in the first place. His eyes shifted to the ceiling again. The new paint didn't hide the waves and ripples in the plaster or the finer cracks. He glared up at them, daring the wood to creak again. Debating whether to go up there, he pivoted toward the attic door.

A shadow stood in the back hallway. It hovered twenty feet down the handwoven carpet runner from where he stood. The shape of a girl.

"Jesus!" Stumbling back, he nearly fell. The walls reeled as he caught himself. He sucked in a breath as though he'd seen the devil himself. "What the hell?" *A ghost? No. That's crazy. But—*

It was gone. There was nothing there but a shapeless darkness now that the sun had set.

"Hey." He took eight cautious steps after it, whatever it was, down the back corridor that led to the rooms over the garage. It was empty. Five steps farther and around the corner, the doors lining the hall were all shut just as he'd left them moments earlier. He stood listening a moment to the sound of his own hitched breathing. What exactly had he seen?

He cleared his throat and looked down at himself and then back toward the faint glow of the large window over the foyer. The trees outside the house shifted in the wind, and the shadows of their branches on the wall next to him moved with them. *Shadows.*

"Jesus, Myron. Get a grip."

He shuffled back into the master bedroom and shut the door.

14

Little Toby sat on the floor of his big-boy room, hugging his knees, waiting. Waiting for daylight or for someone to open the door. He hated his room. It was enormous and dark and cold and scary. And lonely. He'd been in there all alone for hours. Only seven years old, Toby hated being alone.

A sliver of moon hung outside his windows over the snowy backyard, peeking at him from behind the naked trees, watching. Pressing his nose to the frostbitten glass, he imagined the big oaks whispering to one another, their gnarled claws stretching out toward his window. One great gust of wind, and they'd be through the glass. Snowdrifts covered the patio furniture and bushes below in shallow graves, their ghostly forms rising and falling over the yard.

It was late. He should be sleeping.

A passing wind rattled the window sashes against the frame. The walls creaked above him, threatening to drop the ceiling on his head. The boy shivered, wishing he could find his way back home. Wherever that was.

His door was locked.

It's just to keep you safe, sweetie, Mama Martin had explained. *We can't have you wandering this big house at night. You could get hurt.*

She never said it, but he knew the real reason. Toby had tried to run away once. When he'd first come to Rawlingswood, he'd climbed down the back stairs in the middle of the night and slipped out the side door. He'd only been four at the time and couldn't remember a thing about it except wanting to go back home to his old house.

Mama and Papa had taken to locking his room after his disappearance. *I'll be right down the hall. You know that, honey. Just call if you need me.* But the enormous house swallowed up his voice whenever he woke with nightmares. Startled and clutching the sheets to his damp skin, he would sit up in the cavern of his bedroom, too terrified to call out. Terrified the monsters might hear.

Next to him, the closet door stood wide open to keep unwanted beasts from roosting inside. Brand-new clothes hung from the hangers, but none of them smelled like his. Many of them still had the tags.

He clutched an old flannel shirt to his chest—Bobo, his security blanket. He didn't remember where Bobo had come from; he just knew it was his. It smelled of another place he didn't remember. During the day, he kept it hidden beneath his bed. Every few weeks he'd have to rescue it from one of Mama's hampers.

Whenever he felt scared or nervous, his fingers worried along the edges of the flannel and down the long scar that ran across his forehead. Rocking back and forth there on the floor, he rubbed the bumpy and smooth and puckered skin. He'd had it the day he'd arrived at Rawlingswood but couldn't remember where it had come from. Just touching it sent waves of revulsion through him. It proved he wasn't like the other boys at school.

There was something wrong with him.

Toby heard the whispers about him through walls, through closed doors, through veiled arguments around the dinner table. The harder his parents attempted to hide something, the keener his little ears became. The overheard conversations haunted him there in the dark. *Will he ever be normal? Not "normal" but healthy? I mean, these nightmares. The discipline issues. I'm worried he'll never settle in. Surely there's something more we can do?*

It was a conversation he'd overheard between Mama and a strange woman years earlier. The stranger had tried to reassure her. *These things take time, Mrs. Martin. Toby has been through a lot. The best thing you can do for him is love him and give him time to adjust. Kids are very resilient, and I know you are doing a wonderful job. Here, call this number if you'd like to schedule an appointment, but don't lose faith . . .*

Toby hadn't understood what they were saying at the time. He still didn't understand much about it except the words *Will he ever be normal?* There was something terribly wrong with him, but no one would tell him what it might be. He'd met with counselors many times at the house, but none of them made him feel any more normal. The well-meaning young men would ask him stupid questions like, *How are you feeling today, Toby? How are you liking school? Do you want to draw a picture of your family? Do you feel worried about anything?*

I'm worried that a monster is going to come and eat me, he thought. But he never would tell them that. If he told them something like that, they would take him away someplace horrible. Of that, he was fairly certain. Boys who weren't normal got taken away.

Determined to be more normal, he clasped his hands together the way Mama had taught him and tried to pray. "Dear God," he whispered. "Don't let the monsters eat me . . ."

The faint *urrrick urrrick* of approaching feet in the hallway silenced the prayer. A shadow moved beneath his bedroom door, and he began to shake. "Ava?" he whispered inaudibly. *Is that you? Please be you.*

He unfolded his hands and legs, unsure of whether to run or hide or scream or wait. The footsteps stopped, and he could feel the weight of another person on the other side of the door.

"You okay, Toby?" a voice whispered through the keyhole.

It was his sister. He released the breath he'd been holding and whispered back, "I'm okay." He truly wished he were and wished he could see her. He had no idea how she'd gotten out but was relieved to hear her voice.

"Stay still," she whispered back. "Don't make a sound."

The *shush* and *click* of metal against metal rattled the lockset gently back and forth, and he realized what she meant to do. Biting his lip, he backed away from the door, ears perked for the sound of his parents' footsteps. Papa Martin would be furious to find either one of them out of bed.

"This is a bad idea," he hissed under his breath, his anxiety growing with each second. *We're going to get caught.* "Ava, you shouldn—"

The door clicked open before he could finish the thought. His big sister stood in the opening with a thin screwdriver and awl in her hand, grinning in triumph. She silently closed the door behind her. "I knew you'd be awake. You hungry?"

Toby was always hungry. She pulled a pack of graham crackers from the sleeve of her nightgown and clicked on the closet light. The two sat down in the yellow rectangle, munching the crackers. After several minutes, Toby began to notice something was off. His sister's eyes and lips seemed puffy and swollen, like she'd been crying.

He stiffened in alarm. Ava hardly ever cried. He was the one who could never seem to hold himself together. The strangest things would set him off sometimes, and he'd be crying for no reason, biting on his hand, desperate to make it stop. Ava was the only one who could calm him down. She would wrap his small bones in her arms and hold him fast, singing a song in his ear. *'Tis the gift to be simple, 'tis the gift to be free* . . . She made the world stand still until he could hold on to it again.

"What's wrong?" he whispered. "Did something bad happen?"

Ava pressed her lips together and brightened for him. "No. I'm okay. I just . . . I had a bad dream. You ever have bad dreams?"

Toby nodded fervently. He had bad dreams almost every night.

"What happens in your dreams, Toby? What are they about?" She blinked her eyes up at the ceiling, keeping the tears at bay. She didn't want him to see her cry.

Toby frowned at the question. "I dunno . . . it's dark, and I hear voices and noises like crashing glass. Sometimes it's like I'm in a car and there's these monsters like wolves and bears trying to get inside. It's scary."

"Do your bad dreams ever happen here, in this house?" She looked at him then with a strange expression, as though she were searching for something.

There was something big behind the question, something important he couldn't quite grasp, and the weight of it made him shift uncomfortably. "I don't think so."

"Do you ever hear strange things in the house at night?" Again, that searching stare.

The fear of monsters inched its way back into his expression. *What sort of things?* He combed his memory hard for her, wanting to give the right answer. "Sometimes the wind shakes my windows. Why? Do you hear strange things?"

"I don't know. Not really." She noticed the fearful cringe on his face, but her probing eyes had more questions. "Do you like it here, Toby?"

He shrank from her, confused and truly worried now. "Sometimes, I guess. I don't like it here at night. It's creepy."

Ava forced a thin smile and nodded. There was so much she wouldn't or couldn't say to him. As they curled up on his bed together to help him fall asleep, he sensed something dark hidden just beneath the surface of her questions.

Something terrifying.

15

The Spielman Family
July 28, 2018

A sharp knocking sound woke Hunter in the middle of the night.

He sat up in his bed, blinking the fog from his eyes. The floor-boards creaked a few rooms away. *Was that the click of a door?* He flipped on the light next to his bed and squinted at the clock. *1:08 a.m.*

"Hello?" he called out. *Mom? Dad?*

He ran a hand over his face and listened to the house. There was no answer. His gerbils, Frodo and Samwise, rustled their wood chips on the other side of the room. He looked over at the shadow of their fish tank and wondered if the strange noise had come from them. His parents had left that evening at eight p.m., telling him, *Don't wait up, honey. You know how these benefits can be.* His mother had clicked across the cold marble floor of their half-finished kitchen in her stilettos and pecked him on the cheek.

Hunter had sulked, wishing she'd hug him and wishing she wouldn't. Wishing he didn't feel so annoyed whenever she talked. Wishing she wouldn't wear so much makeup. It made the softness underneath harder to see. He liked her better in the mornings, when she looked more like a mom and less like an aging actress.

His father had flashed him a bleached grin. *Don't stay up too late, kiddo. And maybe take a break from gaming for a bit?*

Sure thing, Dad. Hunter had forced a thin smile and watched his handsome parents stroll out of the kitchen and into the garage. The Mercedes had pulled down the driveway a minute later and disappeared into the alien landscape, leaving Hunter marooned in the old house.

He'd spent the bulk of the evening watching internet porn and trolling social media under a false name. The girl he liked back in Boston had a new boyfriend. His old computer-coding club had found a new programmer. It was like his old life had never existed.

His parents hadn't come back yet.

"Why can't they just be normal?" he muttered to himself. *Why can't Margot just bake cookies for once? Why can't Myron grow a beer gut and watch the goddamn game?*

Outside his window, Lee Road lay quiet under the yellow street-lights. The huge houses across the road loomed in dark shadows. He'd been there less than two weeks, but Hunter hated his new house. He hated Shaker Heights. The malcontent pulled at his face and the hunch of his bony frame. He missed Boston. He missed the townhouse in Brookline. He missed his old school and his tiny circle of friends. The only kids he'd seen on his block so far were under the age of ten or traveled in packs more likely to kick his ass than hang out with him. The only person he'd talked to face-to-face besides his parents was their once-a-week housekeeper, Louisa, and he was pretty sure she hated all of them. He knew he would hate them too.

Louisa drove a beat-up Mazda with paper-thin doors and a cracked windshield. Hunter studied her like a tourist whenever she showed up with her bucket of cleaning supplies, wondering what she thought of his father's pretentious vinyl collection in the den or his mother's dressing room, where she'd had custom lacquered shelving built just for her shoes. Hunter kept his door shut whenever Louisa came around and insisted that she not come in there. He promised his mother he'd do his own cleaning, which was a lie, but the thought of the petite Latina woman dusting the intricate maze he'd built for his gerbils or his computer desk made him feel gross and elitist.

Hunter glanced at the layer of dust accumulating on his desk. The computer had gone to sleep, and the flat screen stared blankly at his closet door. He debated turning it on again and seeing if anyone was awake back home. At least that was what he told himself every time he sat down in front of the keyboard. Not that he hadn't spent hours video chatting with Brian or shooting zombies with Caleb, but that wasn't really what he spent most of his time doing.

A ripple of self-loathing ran through him at the sight of the balled-up food wrappers and used tissues piled in clumps on the floor around his trashcan. He really needed to stop. His father was right. He needed to get outside. He needed to meet people. *School starts in two weeks, kiddo. What are you going to do until then?* He flopped back onto his pillow at the thought.

He sighed and stared up at the cracked plaster ceiling. *Charm.* That was what his mother called it whenever they discovered a corner that the contractor had cut. They'd spent all the money gutting the kitchen and relocating their master bathroom and covering every surface in marble, but his room was still drafty and cold with a defunct fireplace on the far wall. Hunter glanced over at the shadow of it glowering in the dark, certain bats had roosted in the chimney.

He shivered and considered going back to sleep.

Hunter stood up instead. He went over to his closet and clicked on the light as he sometimes did when the house got too empty and dark for him. He still hadn't told his parents about the writing inside. It was his secret, his message in a bottle. But it felt more like a warning.

BAD BeNNy BAD BAD BeNNy

HeLP NeeD HeLP NeeD HeLP

NoNoNoNoNoNo

Hunter moved his hanging clothes aside and tried once again to find some rhyme or reason to it. His eyes went from curious to sad as he ran a finger along *Bad BeNNy.*

KiLL DARwiN

MoM MoM MoM

soRRy so soRRy

DeAD GiRL

Another creak in the floor somewhere above him broke the silence, and he froze. The timbers inside the ceiling protested as someone or something crept across the attic.

Hunter poked his head out into the dark hallway. His mother had given him the room farthest from the master suite, across from the back stairwell. The steep and narrow staircase leading down to the kitchen was built so that servants and teenage sons remained invisible. The swirling oak carvings and quartersawn treads of the front stairway cut through the center of the two-story foyer so the lord and lady of the house could make grand entrances and exits. The monumental leaded glass window hanging over the front door threw an eerie glow onto the far wall.

"Hello?" he called out for the second time, forcing his voice above a whisper. He grimaced at the wimpy sound of it. *I'm an idiot. Old houses creak. They settle. They groan. Right?*

"Mom? Dad?" At the far end of the hall, the door to his parents' suite stood open. The king-size bed was still made. The rest of the doors lining the hallway were shut.

A dull knocking sound snapped his head toward the back stairs. Then silence.

Hunter had half a mind to go back into his room and wedge a chair in front of the door. It wouldn't be the first time he'd done it. The house had been giving him the willies ever since they'd moved in. His eyes darted from dark corner to dark corner. Something was watching him. Judging him. Hating him and his parents every time they hung a picture. He didn't belong there in his sloppy T-shirt and boxers with his scrawny stork body and pimples. The house deserved better. It pined for an earlier time when servants had worn white gloves and lived in the attic.

Another footstep creaked somewhere up there, farther down the hall.

Back in his room, Hunter grabbed the souvenir Indians baseball bat his father had bought him as a bribe when they'd moved here. It had been autographed by the 1995 World Series runners-up, as if that would make him an instant Cleveland fan. *Albert Belle. Sandy Alomar. Jim Thome. Kenny Lofton.* Their sweeping pen strokes mocked him as he stood there in his underwear, scared of the dark.

The faint hint of a laugh came from somewhere above him. Hunter let out an involuntary hiss and backed away from the sound. One of the new air-conditioning vents his mother had installed hovered over his head. A scrawling white grate meant to look old fashioned covered the hole in his ceiling and, behind it, a menacing darkness.

"Hello?" he whispered at it, gripping the bat.

This is crazy, he told himself. *I can either stand here like a pussy or go up there.*

He marched back out into the hallway with the bat and rounded the corner to the servants' stairs. Outside, a police siren went screaming down Lee Road toward the smaller houses on the other side of Chagrin.

With a slight wince he refused to acknowledge, he opened the attic door.

BeNNy KiLL. The words skittered across Hunter's mind as he gazed up the attic stairs. A dim light filtered down the steep wooden stairs to where he stood. A bulb had been left burning somewhere in the attic again. Gripping the bat, Hunter climbed the creaking stairs.

"Hello?" he called into the stale air that grew warmer and heavier with each step. "Anybody there?"

The staircase led him up into the long cavern under the roof. The attic felt like a railway tunnel. The wood floorboards ran in crooked lines from the top of the stairs to the glowing white tiles of the bathroom, where a light had been left on.

Nothing moved.

Behind him, a window looked out into the darkness of the neighbor's yard. Boxes had been stacked here and there, throwing long shadows on the walls. Sweat beaded up on his upper lip. It must have been ninety degrees up there. His mother hadn't bothered piping the air-conditioning to the third floor. They certainly didn't need the room.

Hunter took a tentative step toward the bathroom. The floorboards creaked under his feet. He scanned the boxes to his left. To his right, a bedroom door stood open and dark. A nagging sensation crept up his back. *Who's there?*

He walked over to it and felt inside the wall until he found the light switch. His father had piled boxes of Christmas decorations into the corner. The one window was too small to even fit a box fan. A narrow door to a tiny closet stood open, showing two rusting metal hooks inside.

Someone was watching him.

He spun around to face the main room only to see the moving boxes and the half-size doors along the opposite wall. He'd never opened one to peer into the unfinished crawl space. He could imagine what was there—insulation, air handlers, ducts, spiders, bats, mice . . . ghosts. He shuddered, debating whether he had the guts to really find out.

Nope.

Instead, he focused on the boxes and flipped one open to find the comic books that had gone missing during the move. He rifled through his lost treasures. "Dammit, Mom!" he muttered. She'd probably been overjoyed when he couldn't find them. *Aren't you getting a little old for those things, honey?* The undertone of motherly concern and female revulsion in her voice said, *You're not going to be one of those sexually frustrated nerds that goes crazy one day and shoots up a school, are you?*

Still gripping the bat, he turned back to the offending light in the bathroom. A tiny fly buzzed lazily past the open door. Hunter crept closer to it, his mother's voice still ringing in his ears. *Hunter! Did you leave the attic light on again?* He frowned at the naked bulb protruding from the antique fixture over the sink.

He scanned the hexagonal floor tiles, the long crack running down the middle of the floor, the claw-foot tub, the porcelain sink with two water spouts. Tiny dead flies collected in piles inside the tub and around the rusted drain of the sink. They were shaped like little black hearts. One flitted under the hot light bulb. Another rested on the wall, watching.

A wooden medicine cabinet had been built into the wall over the sink. Hunter looked back at himself through its clouded silver mirror. His shaggy blond hair needed to be cut. Patches of facial hair along his jaw formed a broken attempt at a beard that wouldn't fill in for years. His eyes sat a hair too close to his big, crooked nose. Acne medication had left his skin dry and scaly.

Hunter dropped his eyes from the mirror and studied the tiles under his bare feet with growing revulsion. Dead heart-shaped flies were scattered over the grimy floor, and the grout lines varied from dull gray to patches of sticky black. A film of dust blanketed the corners. A half-used roll of toilet paper perched on the windowsill. A shallow puddle of rusty water sat inside the stained porcelain toilet bowl.

Grimacing, he turned back to the medicine cabinet and reached for the handle, not sure he wanted to see what lay inside.

The faint ring of a telephone stopped him. *The house phone?* Hunter stepped back out into the main cavern and listened as the trilling sound came again from the floor below. His parents had insisted on installing a landline for "emergencies," although Hunter couldn't remember ever hearing the thing ring. He didn't even know the number. *Who calls a landline?* he wondered. *And at what, one thirty in the morning?*

Maybe there was some sort of emergency. His cell phone ringer was off, and it was sitting on its charger in his room. What if his parents were trying to reach him? What if something had happened?

By the time he reached the antique rotary phone in his parents' bedroom, he was running. He snatched it up on the sixth ring. "Hello?" he said urgently. "Hello? Anybody there?"

No one answered.

"Hello?" He stood there gaping at the handset a moment.

The air shifted somewhere behind him. Hunter spun around, brandishing the handset like a small club. The hallway stood empty from one end of the house all the way to the servants' stairs at the other. Still, a shiver prickled up his arms.

He hung up the phone and realized he was still holding his bat. Ten steps down the hall, he stopped at the top of the monumental staircase and listened. The muffled sound of feet on carpet seemed to be coming up from somewhere below. *The living room?*

He had taken two timid steps down the stairs when the sudden whir of the garage door climbing up its track stopped him cold. *Shit.* The last thing he wanted was for his parents to catch him ghost hunting in the middle of the night with a baseball bat. He knew what they would think. He lit back up the stairs to his bedroom and snapped off his reading light.

Two minutes later, his mom and dad spilled into the kitchen, decibels louder than any phantom.

"Oh, fuck him if he can't take a joke. How many tedious golf stories can one woman take? I ask you." His mother laughed obnoxiously, the sound spilling across the kitchen floor and fading into the wood of the den. "Hon, did you leave the TV on in here?"

Hunter sat up in his bed and stared at the door. He hadn't been anywhere but the kitchen since they'd left.

"No. I can't say I did. Do you really need another drink?"

Ice clinked into glass. "For chrissake . . . do you think he got into the scotch? Will you talk to him, hon? He sure as hell won't talk to me. It's like he hates me."

"Don't be silly. He's a teenager. All teenagers find their parents annoying. Okay? C'mon . . . no more vodka. Let's get you to bed."

"You're no fun anymore, Myron. When did you stop being fun?" A glass slapped down onto a half-finished marble counter.

"And this is fun? Enough. Come upstairs with me, and we'll have some fun. Okay?"

"Mmmm . . . what kind of fun?" They shared a muffled exchange while Hunter grimaced in the dark. Footsteps stumbled up the back steps, and Margot murmured something.

"Shh . . . he's sleeping."

Hunter watched the shadows of their feet pass by in the sliver of light beneath his bedroom door. A minute later, the hall went dark.

16

Staring out at the sidewalk from his second story window, Benny Klussman sat in his usual spot, rocking back and forth in his chair. Back and forth. Back and forth. On the other side of the glass, the cars moved with him, back and forth down Lee Road. Red and shiny. Dull and black. White and dirty. A yellow one made him sit up straighter. He followed it with his eyes all the way across South Woodland and out of his windowpane. *Yellow.* That was unusual.

There were fewer cars that morning. Not as few as on a Sunday. But fewer. A dozen or two less than normal. He double-checked the calendar hanging from his wall. *Friday, September 14, 1990.* He checked it again. *Friday.* The digital clock next to his bed read *7:16 a.m.* It was seventy-five seconds fast compared to the watch on his wrist but was close enough. The morning rush should be as expected. He checked the calendar again, noting Rosh Hashanah wasn't until next Thursday. He didn't know what those words meant, just that special days on the calendar affected the traffic out his window.

He snapped his calculating eyes back to the road and watched for his regulars. White Honda with lady putting on lipstick was three minutes late and counting. Green Jaguar with angry man should've passed six minutes ago. Something was wrong. He began to count cars again. *Forty. Forty-one. Forty-two.* He checked his watch. Forty-two in sixty seconds wasn't enough. It wasn't enough for a Friday. *Is there an accident somewhere?* He traced the sky for signs of smoke. The uneasy feeling crept into the fists clenched like vises in his lap, making them want to move. To hit.

His mother hated his fists. They gripped together harder.

Benny knew he wasn't like other boys. He would never grow up and move away from home, no matter how hard he wished he might. At twenty-four years old, he couldn't tie his own shoes. He needed Velcro, and sometimes he needed help working the straps when his fingers curled into his wrists like claws and wouldn't do what they were supposed to do.

Out on the sidewalk, the brown-skinned ladies were walking to the bus. Only seven today. Yesterday it was nine. The day before it was ten. *Where did they go? The other three ladies?* One with the flowered purse, the other with the plastic shopping bag, the third with the glittery hat. *Where are they?*

The pack of boys heading to the high school from south of Chagrin Boulevard walked under his window two minutes late. Three baseball hats. Not four. Nine boys, not eleven. Something was wrong.

Benny turned to the maps his mother had taped to his wall. She'd finally gotten the one he really wanted. The one of Shaker Heights that matched the words marked on the mail labels that would come to their house: "14895 Lee Road, Shaker Heights, Ohio." Back when she'd let him sort the mail. Back before the hospital.

It had taken a long time for her to figure it out. Hours of staring at maps in books. Pointing. Smiling. Quiet. Happy. Mesmerized. *I don't know. He just loves maps! Maybe it's the colors.*

He stared at his map of Shaker Heights, eyeing the roads. Counting the streets. *Could the missing boys have gone a different way?* He squinted at the words, only recognizing some. His mother had put a big red star on it and said, *Look. There we are. This is our house, Benny. And here's our street. Lee Road. And there's the library and there's the grocery store and the gas station . . .*

She never pointed out a school. They'd tried going to school many, many years earlier when Benny was very small. It had only made things worse. He'd come home with bruises, his muscles tensed up hard as wood and the look of a caged animal. His mother would spend hours yelling into the phone and even more hours crying behind a closed door. Benny hated school.

But he'd loved his backpack. There had been a big red truck on the front, and it had been filled with paper and crayons and his favorite toy cars. He'd insisted on wearing it every time he'd left the house until it had no longer fit. He watched the larger backpacks on the boys' shoulders outside his window. No trucks. But he knew they were going to school. Only some weren't today.

Only thirty-two cars passed in the next minute, and his fists had wound themselves into hard knots. They started to pound his leg.

He yelled at them in his head. Only it was her voice yelling. *Just RELAX! Count to ten, nice and slow. One, two . . . Let go, baby. LET GO!* Her eyes would be screaming what her mouth wouldn't say: *Jesus, what is WRONG with you?*

Her voice pleading in his head felt like stabbing knives. Even though he knew she meant well, her voice dripped with helplessness and desperation and sorrow and anger and all the hate love could bring. It wouldn't stop. He tried to overpower the thought of her with his own mangled voice that he rarely heard come out of his mouth correctly. *SHUT UP! SHUT UP! SHUT UP!* "SHUUU—"

"Benny!" his mother gasped from the doorway, but only the watcher in the corner of his mind could hear it. The watcher heard and saw everything, always lurking over his shoulder, but it could never control his hands, his mouth, his body. It could only light a desperate spark behind his eyes. It could only whisper in his ear. *She's coming.*

His mother's hands fought to catch his fists. They were pounding, pounding, pounding his head. *SHUT UP!* The watcher curled up beside him, not wanting to see but unable to stop seeing. The watcher had no eyelids. No hands. No mouth. Just eyes to see and ears that heard everything.

"Benny! No. NO!" His mother caught his wrists and pressed all the weight of her 160-pound body against his arms to keep them down, to keep them from hitting her too. A dull pain beat in his head almost loud enough to stop the voices. But not loud enough. He knocked his head against the floor. *Shut up! SHUT UP!*

"Honey, stop! BILL! I need HELP!" The panic in his mother's voice made him pound his head harder. *No, Mommy. No. Don't hate me. Don't—*

He writhed to get her off him, away from him. The watcher sat in his corner helplessly recording it all. The way Benny's fist caught his mother in the chin. The way she recoiled from him in terror, backing away. Away. Away. The animal shrill in her voice as she shrieked, "BILL!"

Before his fists and feet could find themselves another target, a thick arm wrapped around his neck from behind, holding him in a vise. *Bill.*

"Now, Benny, we're gonna settle down, alright? You hear me?" The giant dark-skinned man squeezed his throat a little harder. Benny felt his fists slowly give up as the oxygen drained from his head. Bill weighed over three hundred pounds. Bill was paid by the state of Ohio to help his mother keep Benny. If Benny didn't behave, they'd take him away again. Away from his window. Away from Rawlingswood forever.

"Good man," Bill said, but he didn't let go. Instead, he made some secret gesture to his mother that even the watcher couldn't see.

Benny's mother nodded and stood up on wobbly legs. She left the room.

Wait, Benny tried to say, even though his words never came out as more than a groan. A drowning creature's voice. "Waa!"

He didn't want the needle, but the needle was coming. He wanted to ask about his road outside, about his cars and his people. *Why are they late? Is there construction on the road somewhere? Are they okay?*

"Easy, Benny. That's right. You know the rules." Bill had loosened the grip on his neck and hauled Benny up into a sitting position on the floor. Out the window, all Benny could see was sky. He was too low to see the road. He tried to get up, but Bill held him fast. "We don't have to do this every time, Benny. You know what to do."

And he did know. He knew from all the times at the hospital and all the home visits. The doctors and nurses and social workers would study him with veterinarian eyes, talking in slow, stupid words. *When Benny mad, Benny squeeze the balloon . . . Benny breathe like this . . . Benny count to ten. You know ten?*

They didn't know how much he could understand them, because Benny could never make his mouth say the words, so they figured he was stupid. Some even figured he might be deaf. He liked those ones the best because they talked to each other in front of him like he couldn't hear. Like he wasn't there. *Cerebral palsy. Nonverbal. Unknown mental capacity. Dystonia. Seizures. Spasticity. Medication. Institutionalization. Incompetence. Permanent guardianship. Severe autism?*

If he behaved himself, he was allowed to live at home. Bill was explaining this fact to him again. Bill always talked to Benny like he was a person. It made it harder sometimes. It made Benny notice how everyone else didn't. Not even his mother, even though the watcher whispered in his ear that she wanted nothing more than for Benny to be a person. The watcher saw how sad her eyes looked and the way her skin sagged gray and heavy whenever she talked to him. The watcher knew the way his father had left five years ago, even though she'd never tried to tell him.

"Here, baby." She was kneeling at his side with the needle.

Benny tried to shake his head, but Bill held him still. "Easy, champ," he said. "Your muscles are too screwed up right now. You gonna hurt yourself for real."

The watcher told him Bill was right. Every other part of Benny screamed when the cold steel bit through his skin. Then his body and mind went limp. Not a person. A jellyfish. Soft and floating in a black, black sea.

Hours later, Benny heard voices and cracked open his eyes. *1:32 p.m.,* the clock said in a gauzy blur. The room had gone pink, and his body was still washed away somewhere else.

"You sure you'll be alright?" Bill was talking in a low voice outside his door.

"Of course!" Benny's mother tried to sound cheerful, but she never really did. "Go. Go get some lunch and go to your appointment."

"I'll stop in before I head home. Around five. Okay?"

"Thanks, Bill. Really. It's been such a help having you here. I don't know what I would've done if . . ." Benny could hear the tears in her voice. *She's ready to give up,* the watcher whispered.

"You're doin' fine. It's harder when they grown, that's all. He's strong, that Benny. Just talk to him, and he'll be alright. You're a good mother. Don't forget that."

Frannie cleared her throat and said nothing.

A minute later, the door to his bedroom opened. Benny willed his eyes shut and his body still. *Don't see me. Don't see me.* But the watcher felt her eyes on him. Sad eyes. Pained eyes. Tired eyes. Broken eyes. And in that moment, Benny was glad for the needle. His body lay still, lost to the ocean. It couldn't do anything wrong.

The door clicked shut again, and he heard the *shunk* of metal on metal as the dead bolt slid home.

17

The Spielman Family
July 29, 2018

The next morning, Margot padded her way into the kitchen and turned on the coffee maker. She leaned against the counter and rubbed her eyes. Her head pounded as though being beaten with a hammer. She hadn't slept well the night before. The liquor had kept her tossing and turning as terrible thoughts pulsed through her veins. Things she shouldn't have said. Embarrassments. Worries. The idea of Hunter trapped in the big house all alone, drinking whiskey, chatting with predators. The horrifying graffiti that still lingered on the walls, buried under layers of paint.

Murder House!

The kitchen would never be finished. She scanned the white marble and boxes of white cabinets and shivered involuntarily. In the harsh morning light, it all looked so cold. Sterile. The exact opposite of the warm, wooden, cozy niche it had once been.

Margot stared out the window into the overgrown backyard. She wore her weariness on her face heavier in these private moments with no one watching. It was in the downward cast of her eye, the grim set of her lips, the fine lines of her forehead she'd tried so hard to conceal. She wasn't a happy woman. From the withered look of her, she hadn't been happy in years.

The comforting aroma of coffee lifted her spirits enough to grab a mug from the folding table in the corner and her favorite vanilla creamer out of the refrigerator. *Another day.* She breathed in her acceptance of it and poured the coffee before the percolator was done, refusing to wait a second longer. *It will be alright,* she told herself as the coffee dripped and hissed onto the exposed burner. It sizzled in protest as she shoved the pot back into its place. *Everything will be fine. Breathe. Imagine yourself on a white, sandy beach . . .*

A flutter of white silk caught the corner of her mind's eye, and Margot's head snapped around to the short archway between the kitchen and the foyer. An imbalance in the air tickled at her skin. The sense of movement just beyond the wall. Margot set her coffee down and followed it. The morning sun streaming in through the leaded glass overhead sprayed the foyer with dancing light as the trees outside shuddered in the wind. Nothing seemed still, yet nothing was really moving. Above her, a shadow drifted down the second floor hallway just out of sight. Or was it a shift in the trees?

Margot stared after it a moment, taking the time to convince herself it was nothing. Just nerves. Just the stress of a bad night's sleep. The walls seemed to tilt ever so slightly above her. She did a slow turn, surveying each room, and stopped at the sight of the white cat in the window next to the front door.

"Was that you, kitty?" she whispered.

The cat just flicked its tail.

Margot went back to the kitchen and emerged again a few seconds later with a bowl of milk. She cracked open the door, and the cat shot under the hydrangea bushes at the sudden rush of cold air from the house. She set the bowl down on the stoop while the cat watched her from a safe distance.

"It's okay, kitty." She crouched down to get a better look. Its fur was pristine white and its eyes a crystalline blue, but it had no collar. "What are you doing under there?"

Her cell phone rang in the kitchen. Margot reluctantly dragged herself back inside to see who had the poor taste not to text instead. The enormous decorative clock she'd tentatively hung on the far wall told her it was seven fifteen. She checked the name on the caller ID and let her head sag back on her neck in exasperation, debating whether to pick up. With a grimace of obligation, she pressed a button.

"Mom." Margot said the word with a mix of surprise and resentment. "I—uh—didn't expect . . . How are you?"

There was a long pause while the clock ticked.

Margot picked up her mug and took a long, exhausted drink as though the coffee would make the woman on the other end of the phone go away. "Oh, he's fine. I mean, it's tough getting used to a new place, but he's looking forward to school starting." Her gaze drifted up to the ceiling toward Hunter's room.

She held the phone an inch away from her ear while her mother continued to talk as if the sound of her voice might infect her with madness.

"He's asleep right now, but I'll be sure to tell him." Her short, terse response made clear that she wanted the conversation to end as quickly as possible. Her shoulders slumped as the strong hint fell on deaf ears. Whatever came next sent her staggering a step back against one of the enormous boxes. She furtively checked the calendar hanging in her office nook and set down her mug. *July 29.* "Yes, it is, isn't it? . . . I suppose that's why you . . ."

Margot's grip on the phone tightened, as did her face, while the woman on the other end made some sort of plea. "No. I'm fine . . . I know you think it's important, but I can't . . . You should go. I'm not stopping you . . . Be my guest! Go! Pray! Pay your respects! Do whatever you want to do . . . Of course, it's a nice thing to do . . .

"No, I am not trying to deny anything!" Her voice sharpened to a knifepoint. "I know she's dead! I was there! . . . Stop telling me how to deal with this! Every year we go through this! Every fucking year, Mom! I refuse to wallow in this and be miserable for the rest of my life!"

Margot's knuckles turned white as she strangled the phone to keep from throwing it. She closed her eyes and forced herself to take a slow, deep breath, counting silently to ten until she could talk without yelling. "I know you don't. Mom. Stop . . . Yes, I've been taking my medication. It's fine . . . I've been to therapy . . . Yes, I know, but I'm fine now . . . and I'm sorry I put you through that. I just need space, okay? Don't tell me how to feel today of all days . . . Well, I loved her too . . . Yes, but the rest of us have to keep living! Look, I have to go . . . I will." Sigh. "You too."

With that she slapped her phone back onto the folding table. Margot glanced down at her coffee a moment, then stormed off into the den. Hands suddenly more thin and frail, she poured whiskey into a tumbler and slammed it back. A slow, boozy breath hissed out of her as the angry balloon swelling inside her chest deflated down, down, down.

Margot sank down onto Myron's desk chair. Against her better judgment, she opened a drawer and pulled out a framed photograph lying there facedown. It was a family portrait. Myron with a beard and bushy hair holding a baby boy in tiny trousers and a sweater vest. Margot full lipped and rosy cheeked with a little girl on her lap. Yellow dress. Yellow curls. Blue eyes. She looked to be about three years old.

The loneliness, the constant dissatisfaction, the hollow void inside Margot matched this little girl's dimensions in every way—her shape, her smile, her twinkling laugh frozen in the resin. She leaned the photograph against her heart and slumped back in the chair. Dry tears rolled down her face. She didn't have it in her to cry. Drained of all emotion, Margot looked seventy, left with nothing but photographs of children who had vanished like ghosts.

"Hey." Myron stopped in the doorway of the den, freshly showered. He was surprised to see her sitting there. Then his eyes found the familiar frame of the photograph against her chest and fell to the floor. The days of the calendar ticked through his mind, and he nodded his head slowly. *July 29*. It didn't cut him the same way, but it hurt. He hadn't just lost a daughter. "You, uh . . . you okay, honey?"

She didn't answer. She just looked out the window. Outside, the gate between the driveway and the backyard stood open. She absently made a note of it.

Worried, but also visibly exhausted and resentful for never once being able to *not* worry about her, he tried again. Myron walked over and put a hand on her shoulder. She stiffened slightly. *Don't touch me.* "You want to talk about it?"

She shook her head just enough to say no. The distance between them echoed like a moonlit canyon.

He withdrew his hand, wondering what, if anything else, he should say. There was nothing to say, of course. *Saying things never seemed to do a damn bit of good in these situations*, he mused to himself. He debated throwing his arms around her, picking her up, and holding her like the wounded deer she was, but he didn't debate it long. From the defeated look in his eyes, it was clear it had all been tried before, and too much blame had been set at his feet for him to try again. He needed coffee. He needed a lot of things that he would be keeping to himself.

Unwilling to give up entirely, he lifted her chin with his finger and planted an unwanted kiss on her cheek almost out of spite. "I love you."

She forced herself to not recoil from the gesture and pressed her lips into a smile. "I love you too." And she did. From the other side of the canyon, she did. Her eyes softened at him as he turned toward the kitchen.

"Thanks," she said as a way of apologizing for not knowing what she needed him to say, what she needed him to do, for hating him for everything that wasn't his fault.

Myron had already turned away and didn't get the message. It was a flimsy consolation prize anyway, and she knew it. She watched him go.

After another minute held to the chair by the weight of the photograph and her abject resignation, Margot finally put the picture frame back in the drawer facedown and shut it with a hollow *tick*.

She gazed out the window at the unwieldy trees, overgrown shrubs, and neglected flower beds in the backyard. The stone pavers of Georgina Rawlings's manicured English garden lay four inches beneath the grass.

18

The Rawlings Family
January 5, 1930

Georgina sat in her sewing room, staring out the window into the back garden. The flowers and shrubs lay buried beneath a blanket of snow. The fountain sat frozen in the center of a dead white expanse.

She hadn't slept well in weeks. Her husband had been gone over two months, but the weight of his loss grew heavier with each day. She sat there listening for his footsteps, startling at every sound that rattled through the yawning expanses of the house. The memory of him standing outside her son's door the night he'd died lingered. The animal look in his eyes in the dim light of the hall still haunted her.

What's wrong, she'd whispered.

Nothing, darling. Go back to sleep.

"They're coming for us, aren't they?" she said softly into her needlepoint, as though he were still standing there. "What have you done, Walter?"

The thump of something heavy hitting the floor over her head sent her needles clattering to the floor with a muted shriek. *Walter?*

Ella raced from the kitchen up the back stairs. "Missus Rawlings!" she called as she flew down the second floor hallway. "Is everything alright?"

It wasn't the lady of the house the old maid was worried about. Ever since his father had died, little Walter had been teetering on the edge of disaster. Up all hours of the night with bad dreams, he'd wake up screaming. Ella had moved into the room above the garage so she could watch over the boy. More than once, she'd caught him walking in his sleep. He'd tumbled down the front stairs two nights before, and the entire house stood on edge waiting for the next fall.

The maid searched door after door, looking for little Walter. He was nowhere to be seen. Ella stopped outside Georgina's sewing room and spoke with measured caution. "Everything alright, ma'am?"

"Yes?" Georgina's eyes skittered wildly from corner to corner, seeing things that weren't there. "Why? Did . . . did you hear a baby cry just now, Ella?"

"Baby? What baby?" Ella glowered at her. Georgina was getting worse, frail and disconnected. "I hear something. A loud thump. Where is your son?"

"My son?" The widow shook the phantoms from her head, then scanned the room as though she'd just woken up. "I don't know. Have you seen him?"

"I keep looking, ma'am." Ella took off down the long hall. Things weren't right in the house. They hadn't been right for months. Not since she'd found Mr. Rawlings lying facedown on his desk.

Down the corridor from the sewing room, little Walter's door stood open. Nothing inside the room was amiss. Books sat on their shelves, gathering dust. Toys were in their box. The bed was still made.

"*Shavo?*" she called out and checked the closet just in case. Sometimes the boy liked to play hide-and-seek without announcing the game. She'd lost him for over an hour the week before. Kneeling down, Ella checked under the bed, making a mental note to dry mop again soon. Not that Mrs. Rawlings really noticed one way or another. Ella tried daily to see the bright side of not having a stern employer barking at her about this or that. Demanding peach pie when she'd baked apple. Running her white glove along the tops of the highest shelves the way Georgina had done her first year, back when the family hadn't been so sure about having a "gypsy" in the house. But it was unsettling the way the lady of the house had vacated the premises.

The house itself seemed vacant. Even with the three of them there at the table each night—and that was odd too, sitting at the table with them, but poor Georgina had insisted—it felt empty. Little Walter felt it. The place had gone hollow. Cold. Rawlingswood had lost its luster the moment Mr. Rawlings had expelled his final breath. The wood had begun to shrivel, and the crystal sconces had gone dull. It echoed now when she walked down the hall. Ella had taken to sneaking a nip of whiskey in the afternoons to settle her nerves.

"Walter?" Ella tried again and stepped back out into the hallway.

At the far end, Georgina's bedroom stood empty. He never hid in there. Walter hated his mother's inner sanctum, refusing to go in even to wake her after a bad dream. It had an air of madness after so many days of Georgina being bedridden with grief. Ella turned the other way and headed toward the attic stairs.

Another knocking sound sent her feet flying faster. *Has he fallen up there? Is he trapped under those old heavy boxes?* She took the steps two at a time. "*Muro shavo*? You there?"

She scanned the common room, muttering to herself in her own tongue. "*Mi duvvaleska.*"

The door to the room Mr. Rawlings used for storing his papers was shut. She tried the handle. Locked as usual. The door to her former bedroom stood open next to it. Cold air hissed through the seams of the window. It was never warm enough up there, except in summer, when it grew hot enough to steam milk.

Ella bent her stiff back to check under the mattress. Nothing was there but the suitcase she'd carried onto the steamer from Spain. She straightened herself with a small groan, keeping one eye on her luggage. Her feet itched to walk out of the house and never come back, but she was far too old for the other rich houses to take her in. Most ladies preferred young girls they could intimidate and boss around. Mr. Rawlings had only picked her because the old woman had insisted. *You have child. I take care of child. You need cook. I cook. We give it two days. If no work,* Dosta. *I go.*

She'd never received a single phone call or one scrap of mail in the four years she'd been with the Rawlings. But it was more than that. Ella couldn't leave little Walter. Not now. Not with Georgina losing all grasp of reality, Ella mused, checking the closet for the boy. *Husband gone. A big empty house. A little boy with no father.* Mrs. Rawlings was quickly growing too old to remarry. She'd been forced to go find work outside the home "decorating," whatever that meant.

Widows don't last long on their own, the accountant had warned Georgina while Ella kept Walter busy in the kitchen. *The way the country is falling apart all around us, you'll be lucky to hold on for another six months.*

Ella had taken to looking into Georgina's teacups to see what sort of future the thinning woman had left for herself at the bottom. She eyed that suitcase under the bed again but thought of little Walter.

Another knocking sound pulled Ella back out into the main room. One of the crawl space doors was cracked open. She crouched down on her aching knees and swung it wide. "*Shavo*? You there?"

The smell of mouse droppings and trapped dust hit her face as she plunged her head into the unfinished attic. She felt blindly through the cobwebs until she found a metal pull chain attached to a naked bulb. *Click.*

"Walter!" she gasped. The boy was sitting against the knee wall, rocking back and forth as though in a trance. His eyes were open but blank. His lips were moving as though chanting silent words. "*Ai, Devel*! What are you doing?"

He knocked his head against the wall stud. *Thump.* The wood board vibrated down the length of the house like a piano string. Trapped in a dream, his face contorted inside a terrible memory.

"Are you worried about the papers, Father?"

"The papers?" His father reached for his pipe, eluding the boy's probing gaze by focusing on the tobacco. Pinching and folding it, then puffing out a cloud to sit behind. He'd just gotten off the phone with an angry creditor, and his face was still flushed with panic.

"Mother seems very worried about the newspapers."

His father puffed on his pipe a moment to think, hoping the picture he drew was one of calm deliberation. Something to remember him by. "News is a bit like the weather, son. Some days it's bad. Some days it's good. You must weigh it with wisdom. As a man, you'll learn in time how to do this. Bad news never lasts. You can't let it slacken your nerve."

The boy contemplated this a moment. "So then . . . does good news ever last?"

The sad lift of the boy's brow sent a shot through his father's heart. The man gazed up at his custom coffered ceiling and blinked the agony from his eyes. How many shady deals had it taken to afford such luxuries? How many little betrayals and indiscretions? He shook his head at the alien cleverness of his only child and cleared his throat again. "I wish it did, son. I truly wish it did. You just . . ."

He sat up a little straighter and forced himself to face the boy. "You just have to make the best of the weather. And if you work hard, if you play your cards right, you sometimes get to make weather of your own. Understand?"

The boy's frown twisted to a scowl that in a second's time melted into a hopeful smile. "You mean like a wizard?"

A genuine laugh escaped the invisible noose tightening around his father's throat. The force of it nearly broke the man. "Yes. Exactly like a wizard. Now, go find Ella. I have some work to do."

It was a longer private audience with his father than he had ever been privileged. He nodded without complaint and went skipping toward the door.

"Walter?" his father called behind him.

The boy turned expectantly, his smile falling at the corners. He'd done something wrong. "Yes, Father?"

His father sat in his tufted leather chair, holding his pipe. The posture of the man looked as it always did—larger than life, commanding, demanding, unrelenting—but it also didn't. His face, though cleanly shaven and matching the dimensions of the man he knew, wasn't quite his father's face. The skin was stretched too tight, as though the lips held back a scream. The eyeballs looked ready to burst open. Fear and doubt took root inside the boy as he waited for this imposter to speak.

"Be good," the man said with a smile that was not a smile at all.

Gently, Ella shook his arm. "Wake up, *shavo!*"

Still dead eyed, he muttered, "Be good. Be good. Be good. Be—"

"Shh, shh. It is alright. Wake up, now. *Walter, wake up!*"

He sprang awake, cracking his head against a rafter on his way to his feet. His eyes shot back into focus as the pain reverberated down his spine.

"Oh, no. Oh, my sweet boy." She folded him into her arms, pressing his wail into her breast. "Ssss. I know that hurts. I sorry I startle you."

He let her hold him there as he trembled and slowly regained himself. "Where are we?" he whispered, pulling away from her.

"The attic. You were sleepwalking again, *shavo,*" she murmured, smoothing his hair. A hard lump was forming under his black curls. She held him by the shoulders and scanned his blue eyes for damage. If it weren't for the blue, he could have been her own grandson with his dark hair and heavy brow. She made a mental note to speak to Mrs. Rawlings about locking his door as he slept. The lady of the house was right that it was a fire hazard, but this was worse. She patted his cheek. "You decided to take a nap."

"I didn't decide to." He looked at her with those eyes. Ella had once told the boy that you could see a person's soul if you peered carefully enough through those windows. If that was true, Walter's soul was an ocean.

"It is no wonder," she told him. "You have not been sleeping at night, have you?"

Even from her new room over the garage, she could hear him wandering at all hours to and from his bookcase, his closet, the water closet, unable to settle down.

"I . . ." He studied his hands, black with the grime of the crawl space. "I have bad dreams."

"Hmm." She nodded. "We go and wash up. I give you some cookies, and you tell Ella about these dreams."

Walter thought about this. She could see him calculating what he might tell her. He was just learning to lie, this boy. "Okay."

"Good." She nodded. *Let him lie,* she decided, narrowing her eyes at him ever so slightly. Even liars told the truth; they just didn't know it. It came out in their faces. It hid in the things they dared not say. These things often told more than the truth. But she said none of this. "I have chocolate."

He forced a smile for her, and she loved him for it. *Brave boy,* she thought. *Brave boy without a father to be brave for him.* She waited for him to crawl out before clicking off the light. As she reached for the chain, she surveyed the floor where he'd been sitting. A piece of dull metal sat on the loose boards next to the disturbed dust. She reached for it, then stopped herself as the shape registered.

It was his father's gun.

Rolling her eyes to the rafters in a hundred unspoken curses, she squeezed her hands together, refusing to touch it. "*Prikaza!*" she hissed, and she whispered a series of chants under her breath. *Where did he find it?* She shoved it with her foot until it disappeared into the insulation between the rafters.

A gun in the house was the worst kind of luck, but little Walter was waiting.

19

The Spielman Family
July 30, 2018

"What do you mean your house is 'haunted'?" Caleb smirked at Hunter from the flat screen. The boy in Boston pulled out his vaporizer and took a long drag. "Like, full-on ghosts and shit?"

"Not exactly." Hunter took a sip of the whiskey he'd stolen from his dad's cabinet and gazed longingly at the metal tube in his friend's hand. "Just weird shit. Lights turning on by themselves. Weird sounds at night. That phone ringing. I'm telling you, man. It's not normal. This place does *not* want us here."

"What's the address again?" Caleb asked, holding another hit in his lungs.

"14895 Lee Road, Shaker Heights."

"Right." The muffled clicking of the keyboard in Boston filled the space between them for a while. Hunter took another sip and looked up at the ceiling vent over his head. The attic was quiet that afternoon, but then again, it was still early. He wanted to go back up there to get his comics, but he couldn't quite muster the nerve. As if to prove something to himself, he stood up and peered out into the hallway. His parents' room was empty as usual. His father had long

left for work, and his mother was sitting in the den staring blankly at
the television, debating what to do with herself for the day.

"Hey! You still there?" Caleb called out from behind him.

"Yeah." Hunter slumped back in his chair and took another swig
of liquor, trying not to grimace. It was more for his friend's benefit
than his own. He didn't really like the taste. "Find something?"

"That's a big friggin' house!"

"Yep." Hunter found the size of the house embarrassing, especially since there were only three of them living there. "And like a
hundred years old. Jealous?"

"Hell no. You're in fucking Ohio." Caleb leaned in toward the
screen. "Dude. I wonder how many people died in that place."

Hunter drained his glass.

"I mean, you figure that in a hundred years a bunch of people
lived there, right? Some of 'em must've died inside. People die in their
sleep and shit. Babies get that crib death, especially back then. Like,
maybe one of 'em died in your bedroom!"

"Shut the fuck up." Hunter tried to sound cool, but the thought
sent a wave of revulsion through him. His eyes involuntarily circled
the room, stopping on the closet door that hid the writing inside.
DeAD GiRl. DeAD. PRetty. DeAD. DeAD. His gerbils scurried
through a plastic tube from one fish tank to a smaller one on the
windowsill. Base Camp 1. They still hadn't figured out how to navi-
gate the full maze. Hunter shook his head at them. *Idiots.*

"Hey, listen to this. Do you know why they call it Shaker Heights?"
Caleb's eyes scanned the screen in front of him.

"No. Why?"

"There was a religious cult called the Shakers. They would like
dance and twitch and speak in tongues and shit. Check it. The North
Union Society of Believers had a commune there back in the 1800s."
Caleb paused to read a moment. "Jesus, these people were nutty. No

sex. No breeding. No owning anything. They worshipped some dead British lady they called Mother Lee."

Hunter googled the name of the group while Caleb rambled. Several articles popped up from local universities and historical societies. He opened the first and scanned it. *Second Coming of Jesus. Quaker-like discipline. Handmade furniture. Trancelike dancing during prayers. Shaking . . .*

"It gets better! They actually thought Jesus came to visit them in the 1840s. They even wrote like a whole new Bible. Then they just died out . . . I think they lived by you."

Underground Railroad. Orphans. Hunter flipped through drawings and grainy photographs of the old mills along Doan Brook, which ran through the heart of Shaker Heights only a few blocks from his house, hardly listening to his friend anymore.

"Here, I'll shoot you a map."

A second later, Hunter's computer dinged with the message. He pulled up a crudely hand-drawn diagram titled "Center Family." He traced the road lines. "Center Lee Road." "South Park." "S. Woodland." "Yeah. Our house is right there. Where the old church used to be."

"No shit?" Caleb blinked at him from five hundred miles away. "You know what that means, right?"

Hunter scowled at the shrunken video image of his friend. "What?"

"You know what they always put near the church, don't you?"

"What the fuck are you talking about?"

"The graveyard, dude! What if your house was built on top of all those dead bodies? Think about it! You ever seen the movie *Poltergeist*?"

Hunter frowned at him. "No."

"Shit, man. It's a classic! You gotta watch it. This little girl gets sucked into her TV set. Like, her whole house is possessed by these ghosts because the place was built on top of an Indian burial ground! Dude." Caleb gave him a deadpan stare. "You're fucked."

"Shut up." Hunter tried to laugh, but it wasn't funny.

"No, dude. You gotta get out of there. It's only a matter of time before some clown doll comes to life and tries to eat your face." Caleb let out a puff of vapor.

Hunter shook his head at his stoned friend. "You're an idiot. That movie's like forty years old—"

The sound of footsteps outside his door stopped him midsentence. *Irrick. Irrick. Irrick.*

"Who cares if it's old?"

"Caleb. Shut up a minute." Hunter stood up with forced bravado and stuck his head out into the hallway. It was empty. "Mom?"

There was no answer. Margot had nodded off in the den, happy to escape the day. A few steps down the hall, he noticed the attic door standing wide open.

"Dude? You there? If you can hear me, run!" Caleb called from the desktop.

Hunter walked back into his bedroom. "Yeah. Listen, I gotta go."

"Okay. Just be careful, man. Don't linger in front of TV sets. Alright? And watch that movie." Caleb leaned in toward the computer screen until he was just a pair of bloodshot eyes. "It just might save your life."

"Whatever. I'll talk to you later."

"We still gaming Saturday?"

"Like I got anything better to do. See ya." Hunter gave a halfhearted salute and shut down the chat screen.

Back out in the hall, the open attic door beckoned him closer. He stopped at the foot of the narrow stairs and looked over his shoulder toward his parents' empty bedroom. The five other bedroom doors stood like sentries, watching the hallway. Watching him. The silence pressed down on him, listening.

"Shit," he whispered.

Muted sunlight poured down the steep stairs. The door had been shut earlier. He was certain of it. He remembered coming up the back stairwell from the kitchen and fixing his eyes on it, trying to drum up the courage to go back up there and get his comic books.

He clenched his hands into fists. They felt empty without the baseball bat. He stood there with nothing but the thudding of his heart, which seemed to rise higher in his chest with each second as though it might make a break for it. Hunter swallowed it back down and cleared his throat.

He'd never seen *Poltergeist*, but he'd seen enough horror movies to know better than to go up there alone. Nerdy guys like him either got the girl like a prize for bravery or got slaughtered in Act 1. From the look on his face, he didn't have much doubt which sort of guy he'd be. He wasn't a soft-spoken hero in disguise. He was the coward who ran away from the bullies while the real hero got stomped.

Thoughts of zombie Shaker women in pilgrim clothes wandered through his mind. They flitted from room to room in his head, twitching with their dances as though possessed by demons. *Forget it.* He closed the door to the attic with his foot and went back to his room, vowing to go back up there in a day or two when the heebie-jeebies had passed.

Hunter closed his bedroom door and wished for the key that would make it lock. Every door in the place still had its original lockset. A large keyhole had been cut into the brass plates, an open slot into his room wide enough to see through, but they couldn't find the keys. His parents still hadn't called the locksmith.

I'll call the locksmith next week, his father had promised weeks ago. The only real reason to get a master key, as far as any of them knew, would be to open the one locked room in the attic, but it was a room the family didn't really need or use.

We'll get it open, Max the contractor had assured them. Of course, in the chaos of the renovation, he never had.

The air-conditioning kicked on, pouring freezing air down at him from the ceiling, the hidden machinery humming its maddening hum. Hunter shivered but not from the sudden cold. The gerbils fled through the tunnels back to the safety of their toilet paper rolls in the large aquarium. They felt it too.

"Screw this," he whispered and stormed out of his bedroom and down the back stairs. "Mom? I'm going out for a while. I'll be back for dinner."

Margot didn't answer. She flinched in her sleep when the back door slammed shut.

20

Later that afternoon, Margot slammed the door to the refrigerator and headed up the back stairs. "Hunter?"

She'd awoken on the couch around three, sticky with sweat. She shook her head at her rumpled clothes and puffy face in the hall mirror, disgusted at her own sloth. "Hunter, honey? Did you drink my protein shake? That wasn't for you."

There was no answer.

Hunter had left that morning in the direction of the bus stop, shoulders hunched, feet dragging. His lonely shape had disappeared past the intersection of Lee and Van Aken in the direction of the library.

She stopped at the entrance to his room, debating whether to knock. "Hunter?" she tried again. After a half second of silence, she peeked inside with a grimace. "You awake, baby?"

Once she found the bed empty and the office chair vacant, she flung the door wide and let out the breath she'd been holding.

The smell of sweaty socks, armpit, and Hunter's used tissues wafted up from the unmade bed and piles of laundry on the floor in a fog of captive testosterone. Margot grimaced as she furtively checked the overflowing trashcan and scanned the floor for her missing breakfast.

They'd made a deal when they moved in. *You keep your room clean, and I'll stay out of it. Laundry's on Thursday. Got it?* It was a Monday afternoon. Margot stood there for a moment taking in the dirty T-shirts and socks littering the floor. She pushed a worn pair of boxer briefs with her toe into the corner where the laundry basket stood empty and shook her head in disgust.

With a glance over her shoulder into the hallway, she sat down at Hunter's computer and moved the mouse until the screen flickered to life. "College Essay #1" read the heading of the open document. Hunter had written two paragraphs:

> What does privilege mean to me? I could give you pages of politically correct slogans about the unearned advantages I've enjoyed growing up as an upper-middle-class, cis, straight, white male, but it would be a lie to claim that I truly understand what it means. I don't know what it really means to grow up poor. I don't know what it really means to grow up black or Hispanic. I don't even have close friends that aren't privileged like me.
>
> I've spent my life living in my mother's dollhouse, playing the part I was given. I pretend to be normal. I pretend that everything in this fabricated life is real. I pretend that living in a veritable palace while others go hungry is the natural order of things. I've spent years holed up in private schools, sheltered from reality, because while my parents theoretically support public education, they don't trust it . . .

Margot blinked at the screen. "'My mother's dollhouse'? You ungrateful little shit."

She highlighted the text with the mouse. Her finger hovered over the delete button as she debated with herself, her expression shifting from anger to doubt to resignation. Indecisive, she finally minimized the screen and checked the bottom toolbar for open windows. There were none. She opened a web browser to check what websites he'd been visiting and found none. Hunter was always careful to clear his browsing history of questionable websites. She let out a skeptical grunt and stepped away from the machine.

Margot glanced at the crumpled tissues in the trashcan, and her nose wrinkled in disgust. She and Myron had staged a half-hearted fight about whether to allow a computer in Hunter's room when they'd moved him in.

You know what he's going to do up there.

Relax, Margot. He's going to do that anyway. He's a boy. That's what they do.

Stepping over to his dresser, she surveyed the detritus—cologne samples, deodorant, science fiction books, comics. Opening the drawers, all she found were crumpled clothes and an unopened pack of condoms. No cigarettes. No weed. No missing jewelry. No cash. No guns. No needles. Finished but not satisfied, she turned to his closet, wedged half-open with dirty clothes. She clicked on the light and took inventory of his one suit, his old school uniform, four pairs of pants he'd outgrown that summer, a ski jacket, a snowboard shoved in the corner, three pairs of dress shoes already too small, a Boston Red Sox jersey, and a file box of old school papers and hand-drawn comics. Nothing of interest. Except—

DeAD GiRL

She squinted at the writing on the closet walls, pushing the clothes aside. "Goddammit, Max!" she hissed, reading more and more, her pulse quickening. "I said to wallpaper the closets, you son of a bitch!"

BAD BeNNy BAD

DeAD GiRL

She shuddered before clicking off the light. *What psycho lived here?* she wondered. *And why didn't Hunter say anything about it?* She stood there contemplating the thought, tapping her foot. *What else is he hiding?*

On her hands and knees, she checked under the bed and found nothing but dirty socks and more crumpled tissues. Hiding spots exhausted, she brushed invisible cooties off her yoga pants and closed the door.

Margot padded down her $3,000 handwoven carpet runner toward the master suite. She debated lying down a moment but turned to Myron's open closet door behind her instead. Running a finger down the neat rows of suits and dress shirts, she stopped a moment to scan the shelves. The briefcase full of torn pill boxes had vanished without ever being discovered, but something in the room seemed off to her. The smell of his deodorant and cologne mixed with something else. She eyed the laundry hamper and lifted the lid to be greeted by the pungent smell of gym sweat. Frowning, she lowered it again and turned toward the master bath.

Her gaze wandered idly for a moment before locking in on an item on the counter. A bottle of perfume, lid off, standing slightly out of place. Head tilted, she walked over to it and picked up the bottle. She gave the ionizer a sniff and replaced the lid, setting it back into its proper spot alongside four other seldom-used scents.

The door to Myron's medicine cabinet stood slightly ajar. Reflexively, she pressed it closed. Then, thinking better of it, she opened it back up again and peered inside. Toothbrush, razor, deodorant, acne cream, hair-growth tonic, and three brown prescription bottles. Her eyes narrowed at the medical terms and instructions. She picked up one of the bottles and turned it over in her hand. *Levothyroxine 25 mcg—take one daily as needed.* She glanced at the other two, brow slightly bent, curious but not really concerned: *Sertraline 50 mg, Sildenafil Citrate 10 mg.* The words meant nothing to her.

She closed the cabinet with a soft click.

Bored but uneasy, she checked her reflection in the giant gilded mirror and retrieved her lip gloss from a deep drawer in her vanity on the other side of the bathroom. The drawer was filled with hundreds of dollars of magic potions meant to hide and reverse the fine lines that had collected around her eyes and mouth over the years, lines that Margot had spent a half hour studying the night before, wondering if it was finally time for injections.

Still unsettled, she strode through the master bedroom to her own closet, lined in pink damask wallpaper. Another crystal chandelier hung over a hundred square feet of custom cabinetry. It was laid out like a boutique, with her favorite shoes arranged on display shelves. On an ordinary day, Margot would circle the room, slowly taking inventory, making mental lists of what to buy next, cataloging scarves and dresses until she'd settled on the perfect thing to wear. *Sexy? Sassy? Sophisticated? Sporty?* Some days she might try on four outfits before settling into her character.

But something was wrong, and the worry line marring her forehead deepened. A shoe out of place. Hangers pushed to one side. A blouse on the floor. The expensive fabric lay puddled on the refinished wood like refuse. She snatched it up, clutching it to her chest. She turned slowly around the room. A tiny plaster cast of a child's hand lay on its side instead of in its usual spot next to a row of necklaces. A little girl's hand. She picked it up gently and held it a moment before carefully setting it back on its stand. She looked over her shoulder at the closed door that led out to the hallway.

A drawer was slightly ajar.

Pulling it open, she checked the contents. Silk and lace nightgowns, *one, two, three . . . not four.* She slammed it shut. *Not four.* She threw the blouse in her hand onto its hanger, slapping it back in place, then dumped the contents of her laundry basket onto the floor. *Not four.*

She opened the surrounding drawers—stockings, bras, socks, panties, but no nightgown.

Flummoxed, she stormed back into her bedroom and checked under pillows, then under the bed, then in Myron's hamper. It had up and vanished in a flicker of white silk.

Hunter? she wondered. *But why would he?*

Perplexed, she headed back down to Hunter's room. She searched it again, this time being careful to check each and every drawer, under his pillows, beneath his mattress. *Has he taken other things in the past?* She couldn't think of any.

"Mom?" His voice startled her out of her reverie. He was standing in the doorway with his backpack on his shoulder. "What are you doing?"

The look of shock and betrayal on his face struck her hard. She dropped the unopened box of condoms in her hand back into the drawer as if she hadn't touched or seen it. Guilt swept over her face.

"I was just looking for something. Have you seen my nightgown?" The question sounded stupid the instant she said it.

"Your what?"

"Nothing. I just . . . I want you to clean this mess up, okay?" she said, smoothing her motherly visage back into place. "Laundry is Thursday, and this place is a mess. Louisa can't even get a vacuum in here."

He glowered at her in a barely contained rage. *Get out of my room, Mom!* But all he said was, "Okay."

Margot wiped her hands on her yoga pants as though she'd just been dusting and stepped past her son out into the hall. "Okay. Good."

Hunter grabbed the door with white knuckles, eager to slam it in her face.

"So." She struggled to change tack. "Where'd you go this morning?"

He didn't want to answer. A thousand choice words died on his lips before he forced out a mumbled response. "Library."

"That's nice, honey. Did you meet anyone there?"

Her sunny, condescending voice made him cringe. To prove he could manage his own social life, he said, "Sort of. There's a guy that hangs out there sometimes."

"Really? Does he go to your school?"

"Nah. I think he goes to the public high school."

"Well. Maybe you could invite him over." She attempted a smile, but she could see the resentment bleeding off him in waves. Daunted, she tried again. "Say, why didn't you tell me about the closet?"

His eyes bulged at her, enraged she'd snooped in there as well. "What about it?"

"Max didn't finish the work. Do you want me to get somebody back here? You know, to paint?"

"I dunno. I don't care. It's just a closet, right?"

She shrugged sheepishly and left him fuming, his room tossed over like a crime scene. He slammed the door behind her and turned to the mess she'd rifled through. *His mess.* He kicked half of the crumpled clothes into the closet and shut the door, but not before reading the inscriptions again.

BAD BeNNy

BeNNy KiLL

Back at his desk, he checked his computer for signs of her snooping, then pulled a small spherical camera from his desk drawer. Hunter's face appeared on the computer screen as he plugged it in and adjusted the camera to watch over his room, his door, and the hallway outside.

21

The Martin Family
November 10, 2014

"Ava! Ava, look what I found!" Toby called out to her from one of the crawl spaces in the attic.

Ava set the yellowed newspaper down on the floor of the storage room midsentence:

> "No one but a maniac could have inflicted such wounds as I found on the boy," the coroner . . .

She carefully hid the page where her little brother wouldn't see the 1931 headline. Toby had enough trouble sleeping already without knowing the terrible things the newspaper said. The things that had happened up there in the attic. She poked her head out into the main room. "What?"

"Come here. You gotta see this."

She crossed the cold expanse of the attic to the miniature door on the other side. She poked her head into the crawl space. "What'd you find?"

In the incandescent glare of the bare light bulb, he showed her. It was a gun. He pointed the barrel at the far wall as though it were a toy. "You think it's real?"

"Oh my God, Toby! Give me that." She carefully removed the heavy gun from his hand, aiming the muzzle at the floor. "Where'd you find this?"

"Over there." He pointed to the gap between the roof rafters at the eave where the floorboards didn't reach. "It was in that fluffy stuff."

"You mean the insulation, dopey?" She popped open the chamber and saw the silver butts of five bullets. "Oh my God! This thing's loaded! Toby, you could've shot your face off!"

"Wow. What should we do with it?" he asked, crouching next to her. Ever since they'd come to the gloomy house five years earlier, they had been a *we*. He followed her around like a shadow and hated to leave her side. He would sleep in her bed every night if Mama and Papa would let him.

"I dunno. We can't exactly say where we found it, can we?"

They weren't allowed in the attic. Papa was at work, and Mama had gone to the grocery store, leaving Ava in charge of her younger brother. *Remember the rules. Don't leave the house. Don't answer the phone. Don't answer the door. No friends over. You can do that for Mama, right? Can I trust you, sweetie?*

The attic was strictly off limits, so the minute Mama Martin had left the house, the two children scrambled to the attic door. Their parents kept it bolted, but Ava had become quite proficient at picking locks.

"Maybe we should hide it," Toby said, eyes trained on the gun, both hungry and fearful. She knew what he was thinking. Ava had found him hiding under his bed the night before, convinced a monster was hunting him. *I saw it, Ava. The monster was in my room.*

"Yeah. Maybe." She weighed the metal in her hand. She didn't dare tell him the terrible thoughts racing through her mind—thoughts of how Toby could never be trusted with the gun by himself, thoughts of Papa and the trouble she'd catch if he ever found out they'd been up there snooping. Thoughts of what the gun could do.

"We can't tell anybody about this, Toby," she finally said, studying his face carefully. "Nobody at school. Not Mama or Papa. Nobody. You understand?"

The boy nodded, the gravity of their shared secret like a heavy weight in his clutched hands.

"Good. I want you to go downstairs and into my room. Okay?"

"But—"

"Go downstairs, Toby. I stashed some cookies in my sock drawer. You want them?"

The thought of such a rare treat almost made him forget the gun and what she might do with it. Any time she invited him into her big bedroom over the garage, he jumped at the chance. He scrambled to his feet and gave the gun one last glance before bounding down the stairs. "I'll save you one!"

"Thanks, kiddo!" she called back.

They would spend the next hour listening to the radio and playing their favorite game—Do You Remember? Toby hardly remembered a thing from their life before the house. Ava was his memory, and she made all the memories happy ones. *Do you remember when Mommy made you that blue birthday cake? Do you remember when Mommy bought you that big yellow truck for Christmas? Do you remember the way Daddy liked to tickle your ribs before bed?*

He never noticed the tears that would collect in the corners of her eyes as she recounted all the good times they'd never had together. He would just curl into the crook of her arm and fathom a time before the big house on Lee Road. A time when monsters didn't lurk in dark corners.

Once he was safely out of earshot, Ava set about finding a hiding place for the gun. She scanned the unfinished walls and floorboards of the crawl space, considering the loaded weapon in her hand again. Whatever thought passed in and out of her mind made her flinch. It was a bad idea keeping it. Suddenly uncertain and afraid, she looked over her shoulder. She should tell someone. She should, but then she would have to tell them everything.

Pressing her lips together in a determined line, she continued her search until she found a loose board next to the knee wall. She pried it up and buried the gun under the loose gray insulation. As she pushed the board back into place, a creaking sound behind her made her jump.

She spun to face the main room of the attic.

"Toby?" she said softly, her heart pounding in her throat. *Papa?* She poked her head out of the storage space and surveyed the enormous emptiness under the roof. The feeling that someone or something was watching her lifted the fine hairs on her arms. "Hello?"

But no one was there.

22

The Spielman Family
August 7, 2018

"Are you awake?" a voice whispered.

Warm air fluttered down the canal of his inner ear, tickling his brain. Hunter recoiled, wanting to swat at it, but his sleeping hand lay paralyzed. All he could manage was a mumble. "Mom?" The feeling of someone else in the room, a shadow hanging over him, pulled his mind toward the surface of whatever deep ocean he'd dreamed into.

Wake up.

Hunter's gummy eyelids peeled themselves open. The room was a gauzy blur of gray and blue with the sound of cicadas trilling outside and . . . *someone breathing?*

A dark shape moved.

The boy pushed himself up onto an elbow. He fumbled for the light on his nightstand. A painful burst of light sent the shadows running out into the hall. He squinted in the glare.

No one was there.

His eyes darted about the room from one corner to the next, lingering on the creepy fireplace. *Raccoon?* The gerbils were nested in the wood chips, noses twitching at whatever had woken him. He rubbed his ear, still tingling with the hot breath of a whisper and put his bare feet on the ground.

The bedroom door was cracked open. It had been shut when he fell asleep.

Gangly frame hunched and uncertain, Hunter got up and inched his way to the door. His crooked nose poked out into the dark hallway, followed by a matted nest of brown hair. He studied the open gap in the wall where the back stairs led down to the kitchen. Then he panned to the right past the split in the hallway that led over the garage, past the rows of closed doors, past the bluish glow of the front stairwell, to his parents' bedroom. The door stood open.

Mom? Was that you?

He crept toward her door one tentative step at a time, ears perked and listening for telltale footfalls, for the annoyed clearing of a throat, for rustling of sheets, but there was none.

Three steps closer, Hunter froze, muscles tensed at the top of the monumental stairs, as though expecting to find someone standing at the bottom. The leaded glass window over the two-story foyer lit part of the hall, its thin diamond stripes slashing over the awkward angles of his skin. Hunter glanced back at the dark tunnels behind him, one leading down to the kitchen, one leading over the garage.

Empty.

Turning back to his parents' room, he padded softly to the door and creaked it open three more inches. Inside, two lumps lay as far apart as possible on the king-size bed. His father was snoring in fits and starts as though trapped in some terrible dream. His mother lay on the opposite side of the mattress, facing away from the door. The duvet moved rhythmically up and down as she breathed. Hunter crept closer and closer to her until he reached the foot of the bed.

He reached out a hand as though to wake her. After a moment's indecision, he withdrew it and whispered a barely audible, "Are you awake?"

His father sucked in a breath as though startled but settled back into an uneasy rhythm. Neither parent stirred. Hunter stood over them another five heartbeats before retreating back into the hallway, silently closing the door.

He was halfway back to his room when his mother sat up with a gasp, searching the room. Margot rubbed her face, not knowing what had roused her. *Bad dream.* She curled onto her other side and fell back to the steady breath of sleep. Myron mumbled something and rolled to his back, brow furrowed.

Hunter had reached the door to his own bedroom when he heard it. A dull thump from below. *Kitchen?* He snapped his head toward the back stairs and froze, uncertain, ears cocked, waiting for a reply.

A small click answered, and strange footsteps vibrated through the wood frame of the house and up his legs.

Eyes wide, he covered his mouth and glanced down the hall at his parents' door. *Should I wake them?* The murky light of the big foyer window shifted. A dark shadow drifting over the plaster. He gaped at it and crept closer. *Is it something outside?* Out the enormous window over the entryway, he only found the same tall trees and sky that had been there moments earlier. He searched the long shadows of the foyer, but nothing was there.

His friend Caleb's words repeated in his head. *What if your house was built on top of all those dead bodies?* Hunter shook his head. No bedsheet ghosts would be found skulking around the halls, no face-eating clowns. That was ridiculous. But there was something. A feeling. A sense that he wasn't alone.

The house was watching.

The boy wiped a hand over his face and leaned against the wall, trapped in uncertainty. His lanky frame sagged with interrupted sleep. The clock next to his mother's pillow had read *4:16 a.m.*

After standing there for three more minutes, Hunter forced his feet back into his room. In his wake came a thread of song so faint he could barely hear it, if he was hearing it at all. He stopped, wide eyed, as a quavering voice wound its way up the back stairs from somewhere below.

'Tis the gift to be simple,
'Tis the gift to be free,
'Tis the gift to come down
To where we ought to be . . .

The words trailed off, leaving only a lilting hum like wind whistling in an abandoned churchyard or the creak of an empty swing.

Hunter slipped down the narrow kitchen stairs, chasing after it as it faded, not really believing he'd heard it at all. Surely, if he'd really heard it, he'd raise the alarm and wake his parents. Phone the police. Something.

Instead, he followed the sound down into the kitchen, where the light over the newly installed industrial stove cast a warm glow. The workers had nearly finished assembling his mother's dream kitchen. One of the pantry cupboards stood open.

Who doesn't know how to close doors around here? Margot had asked him more than once. Hunter instinctively pushed it closed and turned around in the cold expanse of marble and stainless steel, trying to pick up the song he'd lost.

The hint of a faint melody seeped in from beneath the shut door to the basement. Hunter spun toward it, but the refrigerator compressor kicked on, drowning it out with a mechanical hum. Inside the freezer, a tray of ice turned itself out with a cascade of falling glass, followed by the crystalline splash of water filling it back up again.

Hunter stared at the refrigerator. Was that all it had been?

A muted laugh turned his head. A blue light flickered on the polished wood floor beyond the kitchen. It was coming from the den.

Air caught in his throat. Hunter grabbed the largest knife in the wood block on the counter and crept toward the sound. Another laugh. And then the muffled sound of a man's voice came through the wall. Three high-pitched dings, and then the rippling rush of a river running over rocks. As he drew closer, the knife dropped down to his side. The rushing river was studio applause.

The television in the den had been left on.

With a big exhale, Hunter opened the glass french doors and found the remote lying on the coffee table. A rerun of some game show washed the room in flashing colors. Exhausted and embarrassed, Hunter slumped onto the leather couch. The rest of whatever his father had been drinking that night still sat in a little puddle of condensation on the coffee table. Hunter picked up the tumbler and wiped the wood with his hand out of habit. He sniffed it—watereddown scotch—and drank what was left.

"Shit," he whispered to himself.

"And what has he won, Bob?" the announcer demanded, pointing at a lit scoreboard.

Hunter clicked off the television in disgust and tossed the remote. He carried the tumbler back into the kitchen, again by habit. Not that Margot or Myron would notice in the morning. Setting the glass onto the marble counter, the hairs on his arm stood up before his brain registered why.

The basement door was standing open. It had been shut a few minutes earlier.

Still gripping the knife in his hand, Hunter crept over to it and flipped on the light. "Hello?" he called down the stairs loudly, not caring if he woke his parents. Maybe hoping he would.

He scanned the kitchen again, the two giant islands, the closed door to the newly built mudroom, the archway leading to the foyer, the long hall to the den and the sunroom they never used. Finding nothing, hearing nothing, he finally forced his feet down the open wood stair treads to the basement below.

The lower level of the old house smelled faintly of mice, then bleach with a layer of mildew underneath, and then something sweeter. His mother's perfume? Custom storage closets lined the wall to his right. The barn-style doors were all shut with rustic wooden peg locks. Clay bricks covered in flaking white paint held up the house on all four sides. Two lines of steel beams and pipe columns held up the middle. A small wine closet sat to his left with custom wine racks for his parents' growing collection. Its slatted wood door stood shut.

Hunter surveyed the space for movement—old boxes, the new boiler, the iron octopus of the old boiler covered in asbestos insulation, the water heater, gym equipment, pipes, wires, cobwebs. Rusty floor drains dotted the concrete slab. A puddle of brown water sat in the far corner under a utility sink.

The steady drip of the sink's faucet tapped out the seconds.

Another door sat at the far end. As he drew closer to it, he felt a pleasant rush of fresh air move through the clammy basement. The door's dusty window looked out into a concrete stairwell leading up to the backyard. A warm breeze whistled softly in through the jambs and a large crack running horizontally through the wood panels below the glass. He tried the handle and found it was locked. A rusted chain and sliding bolt had been added for good measure, but they both hung open. Unlocked.

He pushed against the doorframe, but it wouldn't budge. Warm air spilled through the empty keyhole as he eyed the lock below the doorknob. After a few more attempts, he gave up and rolled his eyes at himself. *What the hell am I doing?* His bare feet turned a grimy brown as he padded across the damp concrete floor back toward the kitchen.

At the foot of the steps, he stopped cold. Someone, or something, had closed the door behind him.

23

Hunter stared up at the closed door, his entire face a question. *Who's there?*

The bare bulb hanging from a wire over the stairwell went out with a dull click, plunging the steps into darkness. Hunter stopped breathing.

The utility sink behind him dripped, dripped, dripped. An inch-wide sliver of light under the door lit the stairs. Two dark shadows split the pale rectangle beneath the wood. The sight sent a shudder through him. *Feet.*

The two shadows stepped away from the stairwell, and light footfalls creaked across the diagonal planks of the subfloor next to him and then down the kitchen toward the den.

Still not breathing, Hunter began to see spots. A blanket of clammy air settled onto his skin as he stood there frozen. The faint scratch of mouse claws on concrete came from the far end of the basement and then rodent nibbling sounds. *I have to get out of here.*

Blood cold and teeth chattering, Hunter crept up the stairs, the treads creaking dryly, announcing his presence. *Ereek. Ereek.* At the top of the steps, he pressed his ear to the door and listened.

After a prolonged silence, he cracked open the door and peered around the corner into the freshly remodeled room. It looked more like a morgue than a kitchen. A bowl of apples sat on one of the island slabs, ready for autopsy.

Hunter padded silent and barefoot across the cold marble, the bare bottoms of his feet now near black with the residue of a hundred years.

The sound of footsteps in the foyer made him shrink back toward the basement. The feet shuffled closer, and Hunter squeezed the knife still in his hand, raising it to his shoulder.

A shock of white fabric and dark hair appeared in the archway. Hunter sucked in a yelp and braced his knife.

The light flipped on.

His father stood startled in the kitchen entrance, grabbing at his chest through silk pajamas as though he'd been shot. "Jesus! Hunter! You scared the shit out of me! What the hell are you doing down here?"

"I, um." Hunter lowered the blade, feeling suddenly even more exposed than before. "I heard a noise. Someone. Someone, uh . . . left the TV on, I guess."

"What the hell's with the knife?" Myron held on to the wall as though caught red-handed himself. He'd woken in the grip of a nightmare, silently screaming, *Abigail!* His hair was slick with cold sweat. "You okay, son?"

Peaked and trembling, the boy was clearly not okay. "Yeah. I'm fine." He quickly put the knife back into its wooden block and headed toward the back stairs. "Sorry. About that."

Myron just stood there anchored to the wall as Hunter loped away with his head down as if he'd broken something.

After a full minute, Myron tried to dismiss whatever thought had paralyzed him and staggered to the whiskey decanter in the den. He grabbed a tumbler and filled it to the halfway point, then stared at the crystal vessel for several beats, calculating. Some liquor was missing. Frowning, he set the decanter down and looked up at the ceiling toward Hunter's room with a mixture of anger and bemusement as he slumped onto the couch with his drink and clicked on the television. Some woman had just won a new car on a game show.

Myron let his neck go slack against the couch, and the night terrors that had roused him in the first place resurfaced. He shuddered and took another drink. "Abigail," he whispered as involuntary tears welled up. He set down the tumbler and put his face in his hands. "Please, God. Forgive me . . ."

The shadow of a girl passed behind him in the hallway. Unseen.

Upstairs, Hunter sank down onto his bed, staring at his hands, wishing he'd kept the knife. Seeing his father was no reassurance. He hadn't missed the sway in the man's frame as he'd stood there. It wasn't just sleepiness.

Are you awake? the phantom voice whispered in his ear again, and Hunter swatted the memory of it away. He glanced over at his two companions. Frodo and Samwise had trekked across ten feet of tunnels to reach the cache of toilet paper rolls he'd left in the fish tank on the dresser, but the boy didn't even smile. Instead, he got up and slid his small bookcase in front of the bedroom door with a long, high-pitched scrape. Safely barricaded, he collapsed back onto his bed and stared up at the fine web of cracks in the plaster that seemed to laugh and snarl, imagined shapes forming and unforming above him in a gathering storm.

Wait.

He shot up from the bed and clicked on his computer. After his mother's invasion of his room, he'd set up a web camera on the corner of his desk. With a few clicks of the mouse, he toggled through hours of footage of his door standing closed with scattered flashes of his own face sitting down at the computer and getting up again. He watched the hours tick by at the bottom of the screen until the video went black with the click of his bedside lamp at 1:12 a.m.

He clicked through the steady blank image to the minutes before he'd flipped the light back on, but the feed was too dark to see a thing. He made a few adjustments, shifting the exposure from black to a grainy red, slowing it down. Even then, he could only detect the faintest hint of his door swinging open. He squinted at it, tweaking and replaying the footage, until he could just make out a blurred figure moving in the dark.

24

The Klussman Family
September 15, 1990

Frannie Klussman bolted upright in her bed and glanced at the digital clock glowing red in the dark. *12:22 a.m.* The home's security system was beeping.

Benny?

Throwing on her bathrobe, she dashed toward his room, halting after three steps. His door stood open at the other end of the hallway. Down the winding staircase, the front door gaped out into the front yard, the alarm spilling into the street.

Beep. Beep. Beep.

"Benny!" she shrieked, racing down the stairs. He hadn't escaped the house in years. The last time, she'd found him seizing at the corner of Lee Road and South Woodland five feet from an ice cream truck, surrounded by a circle of children staring and whispering as they ate their popsicles. *Is he okay? What's wrong with him? Why is he shaking like that? Where's his mom? Should we call somebody?*

That was when she'd had the security system installed.

Fear stabbed her chest as she flew down the steps and out into the yard. *Bill must have left the door unlocked.* But Bill knew better than that.

"Benny?" she called. Not too loud. She couldn't bear the thought of waking the neighbors, of answering questions, of another home visit by the social worker. They'd recommended Benny be placed in a home six months earlier after he'd broken his bedroom window with his fist. That one had required a trip to the ER and stitches. *It's for his own good, Mrs. Klussman. For his safety.*

Frannie frantically scanned the lawn, running down the stone walkway to the sidewalk. Lee Road sat empty. Traffic lights blinked red in both directions with no sign of Benny. She opened her mouth to call out again, but then she saw him.

A dark lump on the sidewalk across the street convulsed violently. Groaning. Banging against the concrete. She ran to him barefoot and crouched down beside the quaking shell of a man who would always be a boy. He pounded his head against the sidewalk, eyes staring up at the starless sky, blank and frozen.

My baby!

Frannie threw a glance down each side of the street, desperate for help but also desperate not to be seen. A tall hedge hid them both from the neighbors behind it. The sidewalk stretched out in both directions empty. Benny let out a loud growl and cracked his head hard enough to leave spots of blood on the concrete.

Frannie grabbed him under the arms and wrestled his head up off the ground. He was too heavy to lift, so she dragged him foot by agonizing foot across the street, only stopping to catch her breath when they'd reached the safety of their own yard.

Partially shielded by their bushes, Frannie collapsed on the dewy grass, breathing hard. Her face splotched red with the exertion of dragging 150 pounds across the pavement. Sobs collected in her throat, breaking out in spurts.

Benny for his part had stopped moving altogether, his body knotted and his face a frozen gargoyle, twisted in a yowl. His hands had curled into stone knots. His bare heels were scraped and bleeding from being dragged over concrete and asphalt. A tuft of his hair was matted with blood from where he'd repeatedly smashed his skull against the sidewalk.

Frannie's robe blotted the blood as she held him there. Tears streamed down her face. "Benny! What are you doing out here? Why, sweetie? Why did you do that? It's not safe out here. You could've been . . . hit by a car or . . ." She couldn't even find words for the rest. Images of ambulances and canvas restraints and Benny's terrified face as they tied him to a gurney sent shudders through her. *Not again. Not again. Not again. Not my baby. Not my sweet boy.* "We've got to get you inside, sweetie. Mommy has to get you inside."

It took two hours—dragging Benny's dead weight into the foyer, shutting and triple locking the door, injecting the sedative to loosen his limbs, waiting for the medicine to smooth his tortured face into a peaceful sleep, pulling him up the stairs one by one, dragging him into the bathroom, undressing him, sponging away the blood, cleaning off the dirt, examining and bandaging the wounds, hauling him up into his bed, pulling clean pajamas onto his skinny frame, crying hard tears over all the bruises and cuts, wiping the blood from the floors and stairs, checking on him again, listening to his even breathing, kissing his forehead, crying bitter tears for the pain and injustice of his afflictions, locking his bedroom door, taking a scalding hot shower, gathering the bloodstained clothes.

Lying in bed and staring at the ceiling.

How could I have let it happen? What will happen the next time? What if they find out? What if Bill was right? What if Benny would be safer in a hospital? What if they pumped him full of the medications that dulled his mind and clouded his eyes and stole his smile forever?

By the time Frannie fell back into a guilt-ridden, heartsick sleep, it was well past five a.m. She never heard the police cars gathering on the street outside her window.

25

The Spielman Family
August 8, 2018

"What do you mean, you saw him with a *knife*?" Margot slapped her coffee mug on the marble counter, aghast.

Myron instantly regretted mentioning it to his wife. "Let's not overreact. It was late. He'd heard a noise. The minute he saw it was me, he put it away and went to bed. I just thought it was a little weird. I have no idea what his plan was with that thing. You know?"

Margot looked up to the ceiling. On the other side of the wood and plaster, Hunter was still asleep with his bookcase blocking the door. She tugged at her lip. *He's been acting so strange.* "I'm worried about him, Myron. Maybe we should get a security system."

Myron lifted his eyebrows.

"Everybody has them, right?" she went on. "Maybe it would make Hunter less nervous being here alone. We could get the kind with cameras that connect to our phones. That way we could always see what was happening down here. Even from our bedroom."

"Really? Isn't that . . . what about privacy? Shit, what about the other morning?" He motioned to the den, where he'd failed to satisfy her. "Do you really want some security company watching every move we make?"

This gave Margot pause. Her eyes flitted toward the stairs and her makeshift yoga studio. "We wouldn't have to put them in *every* room. Right? Certainly not in bedrooms or bathrooms, but the front hall? The kitchen? I hate to admit it, Myron, but I get nervous being here alone. Hunter is starting school in eleven days, and it'll just be me in the house. Alone. Christ, I can't even hear the doorbell upstairs. What's to stop someone from—"

Myron held up a hand and nodded. "Why don't you look into it? Alright? Tell me what it's going to cost, and we'll figure it out." Reduced surveillance seemed to agree with him better as he ticked off rooms that would still be safe in his head. *Bathroom. Closet.*

It was a done deal. Margot would start making calls that day. But the thought wasn't soothing enough to forget what had brought the issue up in the first place. "What about Hunter? Do you think he needs counseling?"

Myron made a show of considering it. *Counseling.* Anyone who knew him well would notice all the reasons he thought it was a bad idea ticking through his head—the stigma, the cost, the labeling, the overmedicating.

Margot pressed on, oblivious. "I'm worried about him. He just doesn't seem *normal*, does he?"

"Hey, now wait. Hon, he's a teenager. They're moody. They're antisocial. They are addicted to their phones and hate their parents. Don't you remember? This *is* normal."

"What if he's on drugs?" Her shrill voice left little cuts all over Myron. "I mean, he never comes down to talk with us. He always looks . . . I don't know. Stoned. And some things of mine have gone missing. How would we even know, Myron?"

"No. That's . . . He's not on drugs. Where would he even get them? He doesn't know anybody here." He rubbed his red eyes not unselfconsciously. A faint tremor of withdrawal vibrated in his fingers, but Margot missed it completely. "Don't get me wrong. I've considered it. I'm keeping my eyes open for the signs. But he's not losing weight. He's lucid when we talk. Shoot, even last night he seemed perfectly sober to me. Just a little spooked. Let's get the security system, okay? That way we'll know if he's sneaking out at night or anything else weird." The shape of a girl slipped through his mind. Had he really seen or heard anything?

Margot nodded, satisfied, but something still worried itself at the edge of her thoughts. *It's this house, Myron. Something is wrong with this house.* She opened her mouth to say it but caught herself.

Myron took the opportunity to change the subject. "Hey. Have you been feeding that stray cat? The white one? I keep seeing it in the yard."

"Cat? No." She avoided looking at him.

"You know if you feed it, it will never leave, right?" He sighed, annoyed and exhausted. He'd spent most of the night tossing and turning on the couch in the den.

"I'm not feeding it, Myron. I know you're allergic." She rolled her eyes at his turned back.

"You going to the club today?" he asked, putting his coffee mug in the sink and picking up his briefcase.

"Yeah. Maybe. See you there?"

"Probably around seven. I have a late meeting with the surgeons' group." He didn't face her as he said it, hiding his lie. He was out of pills, and his skin itched.

"Okay, sweetie. I'll feed Hunter something and see you later," Margot called over her shoulder as she headed toward her studio and her internet love interest. She had promised him "hot naked yoga" the day before, and her cheeks were already pink with the idea.

26

Hunter woke to the dull thump of a bass line. Music vibrated through the floor joists from his mother's studio down the hall to his room. A muffled laugh on the other side of the wall jolted him upright. It was followed by the muffled lilt of his mother's voice. Teaching again. The sound of her online yoga classes filled him with revulsion. The bookcase was still blocking his door, and the bizarre incident the night before came rushing back.

Are you awake?

He lurched out of bed. Frodo and Samwise twitched their noses at him as he sank down onto his computer chair and jiggled the mouse to wake up the machine. The two rodents quickly lost interest and continued their quest through the long tube to the tank with fresh water on the other side of the bedroom. Hunter watched them go, feeling more acutely than ever how alone he was in that enormous house without a friend within five hundred miles.

Once the monitor lit up, he brought up the video from the night before and studied it again in the light of day. The blurry shape moved past the camera over and over.

"What are you?" he whispered, squinting at it. It couldn't have been his mother or father. They had been fast asleep.

With a long, wavering exhale, he closed the video and tapped his thumbs on his desk. He slumped in his computer chair, debating whether to call the police, his father, anyone.

Caleb was online, chatting about some conspiracy involving the federal government and fluoride. Hunter sent him a DM request. A moment later his computer chimed, and a chubby face appeared on his screen.

"H-Dog! What up?" Caleb flashed the sign of the devil and grinned.

"Hey. Shit's getting weirder." Hunter relayed what had happened the night before and sent a link to the video.

Caleb let out a low whistle. "Dude. I told you. You got a ghost in your house. You gotta get out of there." His sarcastic voice and sneer made it clear that he didn't believe a word of it.

"Shut up," Hunter hissed and threw a glance at the closed door. For all he knew, the ghost was standing outside it. "I'm not kidding. What the fuck did the camera see, man? What is that thing?"

"Hell if I know. It's not like it's a fucking night vision camera, dude. It could be anything. A glitch. Did the AC kick on?"

Hunter frowned at this. "I dunno. Maybe. Would this thing pick up temperature?"

"I doubt it. What'd you spend? Like ten bucks on that piece of shit? Let it go. It's probably nothing."

"Yeah. But some weird stuff's been happening. Doors keep opening and shutting. Lights keep turning on . . . I swear I heard somebody last night. Either I'm nuts, or someone's in the house."

"Someone? Or some*thing*?" Nuts or not, Caleb still found the whole idea entertaining. "So what you gonna do? Call the cops?"

"No . . . I don't know." He truly didn't want to call the cops or talk to his parents. They would all end up blaming him somehow. "What am I supposed to say? I hear footsteps in the night? Someone knocked on my door? It sounds kinda crazy, right? It's not like I've seen anyone. I don't have any evidence except this shitty video, and my parents already think I'm on drugs."

Caleb laughed. "Are you?"

"Fuck off!"

"Seriously, how are you staying sane in that place?" As if to prove the point, Caleb grabbed his vaporizer and took a long puff. "Aren't you bored out of your mind?"

"Pretty much." Hunter rubbed his head. "But I'm telling you, it isn't just me. Here. Look at this shit."

He grabbed the portable webcam from the desk, pressed a few buttons, and clicked on his closet light.

"What the fuck is that?" Caleb's voice bounced off the closet walls as Hunter scanned the walls with the digital eyeball.

"I have no idea. Some psycho named Benny used to live in this room? Maybe he killed a girl? Then some other psycho decided to write shitty poetry about it. I've been searching all over the web to figure out who the fuck 'Bad Benny' is, but I can't find a thing." Hunter slapped the webcam back on his desk and fell back into his chair. Just talking to another person seemed to calm his nerves.

"You do a property search?"

"Yeah. It didn't turn up much. Here." Hunter opened a window to the Cuyahoga County Auditor's website. He navigated to a page labeled "14895 Lee Road Transfer History" at the top. It was a listing of all previous sales of Rawlingswood along with the property owners' names and the sales prices dating back to the early 1970s.

Transfer Date: 05/18/2018: Grantee(s) Spielman, Myron and Margaret; Grantor(s): National City Bank

Transfer Date: 05/01/2016: Grantee(s): National City Bank; Grantor(s): Foreclosure

*Transfer Date: 02/01/1994: Grantee(s): Martin, Clyde;
Grantor(s): Society for Savings Inc.*

*Transfer Date: 01/01/1993: Grantee(s): Society for Savings Inc.;
Grantor(s): Foreclosure*

*Transfer Date: 09/01/1972: Grantee(s): Klussman, Henry and Frances;
Grantor(s): Helen Bell*

"So past owners are Clyde and Maureen Martin and then Frances
and Henry Klussman and then a Helen Bell. That goes back to 1972.
The county records don't go back further than that online." Hunter
read through the list again. "Two foreclosures. Man, this place is bad
luck."

Caleb was busy typing something on his keyboard in Boston. "I
just googled Clyde Martin. What a dull fucking life. On the board
of the Shaker Country Club. Ran a company called Shaker Family
Construction. Not much else. Here."

Hunter's screen dinged as a few links came through. He clicked
through several pages of dead ends, thinking. Frodo and Samwise
were halfway across the windowsill over his desk. He studied them a
moment, then had an idea.

Typing quickly, he navigated to the website of the Cuyahoga
County Public Library and scrolled through their pages until he
found what he was looking for—*Plain Dealer* e-edition. It was a digital archive of the newspaper. With a few clicks, he opened a search
engine and tried typing the name "Clyde Martin" again. This time
fifteen articles came up. Hunter scrolled through them one by one
until a series of obituaries flashed onto his screen.

Muttering under his breath, he read, "Martin, Clyde—Shaker
Heights. Clyde Martin died yesterday in his home. He is survived
by his wife, Maureen. The family asks that all donations be made to

the Shaker Historical Society, where Mr. Martin sat on the board of trustees. No services or calling hours."

The date of the newspaper was December 6, 2014. Hunter tracked back to the previous screen. The bank had foreclosed on the house eighteen months later. He did the math, then returned to the obituary, reading the names of the survivors again. *No children. No Benny.*

"Died yesterday in his home?" Caleb repeated through the speakers. "Jeez. Where do you think he croaked?"

Hunter pushed his chair away from the computer. "That's not funny."

"I'm not laughin', asshole. What about the wife?"

They repeated his searches but this time for Maureen Martin. A newspaper clipping flashed onto Hunter's screen. "Shaker Heights Widow Arrested, Forced to Vacate Foreclosure."

Caleb read out loud, "'After months of notices and warnings, Shaker Heights widow and Case Western Reserve University professor Dr. Maureen Martin was arrested yesterday morning by the Cuyahoga County Sheriff's Office for trespassing on a foreclosed property. Martin was reportedly admitted to a local psychiatric hospital for observation later that day.' Blah, blah, blah. 'Sheriff will not seek to press formal charges. The university would not comment on the case.'" Caleb paused a moment to let the words sink in.

"She went crazy," Hunter said. It didn't bode well. A poor woman barricaded there in the house, by herself, haunted by . . . what? Benny? His *DeAD GiRL*?

Next, Hunter typed "Frances Klussman Shaker Heights" into the search engine. The results were a bizarre smattering of court records and restaurant advertisements, none of which matched the full name. He tried the *Plain Dealer* search next and came up empty except for the public foreclosure notice that matched the county auditor's records. He read through it, searching for anything that might help, but the legal notice listed nothing but the barest information—the address, the owner's name.

"So Clyde drops dead in 2014, and no children are mentioned in the obituary. I can't find shit on the Klussmans except a foreclosure in 1993. Before that, who knows?" Hunter shifted uncomfortably in his seat. He needed to use the bathroom, and he was losing patience. "So who the fuck is Benny and this dead girl?"

"Hmm . . . Benny. That'd be short for Benjamin, right?"

"I guess."

"Let me grab a search from a newspaper aggregator. Maybe something in the criminal database." Caleb began typing furiously. "You do a search for dead girls in Shaker Heights?"

Hunter leaned into his screen, wheels turning. "No. Not yet."

"Well, it's like a rich suburb, right? Hoity-toity?"

"Yeah."

"Can't be too many then, right? I'll cover the online search, but you might need to hit the library. Call me back?"

"Yeah. I should get the hell out of here for a while anyway."

Hunter disconnected and cleared his browser history, then took an inventory of all the embarrassing details of his life strewn about, looking for items an intruder or ghost might steal. He grabbed his wallet, his phone, his backpack. Shoving the bookcase out of the way, Hunter stepped out into the hall.

It was empty.

Down the corridor, loud music thumped through tiny speakers, creating a wall of sound in the yoga room. A hot breath hissed through Margot's laptop. "Baby. Baby. Baby. That was amazing."

Margot lay naked on her side, flushed pink and sweaty, smiling dreamily at Camera 2. Eyes shut, she looked more relaxed than she ever did patrolling the house in her designer shoes. Even sleeping— her eyebrows furrowed together, teeth grinding with the fitful dreams and anxieties simmering under her lids—she wasn't this peaceful. She stretched like a cat in the warm sun of the three cameras. The eyes behind them watched her every move, caressing her, cradling her. Revering her like art.

"When can I see you again? In person this time?" His voice came through as heavy pants, his lips too close to the microphone.

She chuckled and opened her eyes. "Don't be ridiculous."

"No. I'm serious. We should meet. I promise I'll make it worth your while."

This brought another laugh and a feral gleam to her eye. "I'm sure you would, but Kevin . . ." She rolled toward Camera 2. "I told you. I'm married."

"So what? What's he gonna do about it?"

She shook her head at the thought, probably imagining Myron whipped into a rage. Myron—a man who hardly had the nerve to raise his voice to her. "I'm sorry, hon. It just wouldn't work. I'm sure you understand."

"Oh, do I?" He grunted a laugh into his microphone.

Annoyance crept back into her forehead, the familiar lines creasing the skin. "Kevin, please. Don't ruin this. I like chatting with you."

"I like chatting with you too. Want to see how much?" The face on the computer screen next to her slid up and out of view as his camera panned down.

Margot let out a small laugh, gratified by his full attention. "Well, that's very nice."

"It's for you. Let me come over there and give it to you."

"Hmm . . ." She batted her eyelashes at him. "I wish you could."

"I don't live that far away. Your husband isn't home."

She shook her head at his persistence. This wasn't the sort of fun she was after—and then his words sank in. *I don't live that far away.*

"You don't know where I live," she said, sitting up.

"I know more than you think, baby." His voice sounded menacing now. "I know he leaves you alone all day. I know he lets you broadcast your ass all over the internet and doesn't do a damn thing about it. So when can I come over?"

"Will you keep your voice down?" She turned down the volume on her laptop and shot a glance at the door. *Did Hunter hear that?* The face on her screen had turned mean. The eyes pointed in a glare. Suddenly aware of her nudity, Margot grabbed her silk robe and pulled it on her shoulders. "I think that's enough play for today, Kev."

"Like hell it is! You think you can just tease a man to the breaking point, then walk the fuck away?"

"Yeah." She smiled viciously at Camera 1. "Yeah, I do. That's the whole point, you moron."

"What did you call me?"

"A moron. Look it up, Junior. This session is over." She reached for her mouse.

"Bitch, I'm gonna find you and your fucked up husb—"

The voice stopped with the click of a button.

Margot pressed her lips together in a hard line while the tremor in her hands made its way up her arms. "Damn it," she hissed at herself. It was the first time she'd ever gotten into a fight with one of her viewers. Her eyes circled the room as though trapped for a moment, and then she slapped her laptop shut.

Hunter was halfway down the front stairs when his mother emerged from her studio in her pink bathrobe, flushed. She startled at the sight of him. "Hunter! Hi! I mean, good morning. You, uh, going out?"

"Yeah. Library." He hardly looked at her as he made his way down the stairs.

"Again?" *What did he hear?* she wondered. "What've you been doing over there?"

If he had heard anything, he didn't let on. "Research, I guess. Walking around."

"Research on what exactly?"

He sighed his impatience. "Dead people."

Her eyes widened, and she tightened her grip on her bathrobe. "Dead people? What dead people?"

"The people that used to live here." Feeling her worried eyes on him, he decided not to reveal his acute interest in Benny and his dead girl. "Like, a research project on the area. Did you know they buried a bunch of the old Shakers just down Lee Road next to the grocery store? There's a plaque and everything."

"Really? I've never seen it."

"It's hidden behind these overgrown hedges. The gravestones are all falling over and hard to read. Some are dated before the Civil War. But they didn't used to be there. They used to be buried in another place along Shaker Boulevard or something, and the city dug them up." His eyes wandered up the stairs toward the attic.

"Wow. That's . . . pretty interesting." *Dead people?*

He shrugged and trudged out the front door, leaving his mother staring after him.

27

The Rawlings Family
January 19, 1931

Someone was there.

Ella felt it before their fist pounded on the front door. She set the teapot back down on the counter and headed into the foyer. No one ever knocked on their front door. Not in weeks.

She studied the strange man on the front stoop through the side glass and reluctantly unlocked the door. He had the look of a scoundrel—unshaven face, bloodshot eyes, rumpled cheap suit.

"I am sorry, but Missus Rawlings is not receiving guests today." Ella kept her grip on the handle, only opening it a crack. Her foot and knee braced against the wood.

"I ain't here for Missus Rawlings." The man's breath reeked of grain alcohol. He motioned to the laundry bag on his shoulder. "Big Ange sent me with a delivery."

The large woman sighed. "Deliveries are to come in the back only. Yes? Go round." Then she slammed the door in his face, shaking her head. *This bad business is out of control,* her expression said as she waddled through the foyer into the kitchen and to the side door. *The neighbors will begin to suspect.*

Unfortunately, better choices had run out on Mrs. Rawlings.

By the time Ella arrived at the back door, the unsavory man was waiting, his yellow grin an inch from the window.

"You." She pointed a fat finger in his face. "You must tell this 'Big Ange' that all these comings and goings will get noticed. You should have uniform for laundry service."

"I'll pass along the message." He pushed his way past her into the kitchen. A pot roast sizzled in the oven, filling the air with the welcoming smell of a proper home. He drew in a long breath and glanced longingly at the oven but kept walking. "Where should I put this?"

From the awkward bulk of the sack on his back, she knew what he carried. "The sugars go up, up to the attic. Here, I show." She led him up the back stairs, pausing in the second floor hallway long enough to make sure little Walter's door was closed and Mrs. Rawlings was out of sight. When Ella had struck this bargain with Mr. Rawlings's creditors, the accountant promised the boy and lady of the house wouldn't be disturbed.

Keep everything out of sight. Don't draw any attention from the neighbors. Only accept deliveries in the back of the house. Everything must look as though a respectable family still lives here, understand? The boy mustn't know a thing. The less Georgina knows, the better.

She carefully unlocked the attic door. Halfway up the steps, the smell of burning sugar hit her face. The company man, Felix, poked his head out of the spare bedroom. "Ella? That you?"

"Yes, Felix. We have visitor." She didn't dislike Felix as much as she'd feared she might, but his presence in the house was still utterly unacceptable. Unfortunately, it couldn't be helped. Mr. Rawlings had left too many debts to pay. She lifted her eyes to the rafters at the memory of him. It hung over the house like a curse.

Ella had found Walter in his office that frightful night. The smell of urine and vomit still lingered in the floorboards no matter how many times she scrubbed them. The police had ruled it a heart attack. *Thank the angels,* she thought, as she did most days. The insurance policy she'd found under his head made it clear that suicide would negate the contract.

None of the policemen or the coroner found the vial of belladonna he'd taken from her cupboard; she'd made sure of that. His dead eyes had followed her when she crossed the room and picked it up from the desk blotter next to his empty teacup. From the feel of the bottle, he'd consumed the whole thing. Ella had tucked the brown vial into her apron and his pistol back into its drawer before calling the police. Her hands still shook with the memory. The tremor of it would be with her the rest of her days.

Damn you, Walter, she cursed his ghost, standing in the attic. Even with the insurance money, Felix had shown up ten months later with the illegal still and instructions from a man known only as Big Ange.

"You got any hooch ready?" The scoundrel plunked the sack of sugar down without a care for the mother and child a floor below.

"Couple gallons." Felix motioned to the bathroom, where brown jugs and mason jars sat on the tile floor in haphazard rows. "Ange want it today?"

"Just a few for the boys. Truck is coming tomorrow for the full order. Twenty-five gallons. You'll be ready?"

Felix whistled through his teeth. "It'll be close." Behind him the makeshift still steamed and bubbled with the erratic ticking of a mad clock. The heat of the boiler steamed the windows. A black pipe stretched from the still through a hole in the bedroom wall to the chimney in the crawl space on the other side.

Ella shifted uncomfortably in her worn shoes. They had taken over her former bedroom with sacks of sugar and glass tubing and empty jugs and apple crates. The two men continued discussing the orders and the latest news from the underworld. The distillery kettle in the next room sweated and belched wretched fumes as they chatted. *Tick. Tick. Tick.* It was only a matter of time until something blew up.

When they had concluded business, the maid led the unsavory man back down the stairs with his three mason jars of liquor and locked the attic door behind him.

Little Walter's voice stopped them both in the hall. "Miss Ella?"

She turned toward him, doing her best to block the intruder with her girth. "Yes, Walter?"

"Who is your friend?"

"He is a plumber. He come to check the pipes for us. But all is well, yes?" She turned to the man holding the jars.

"Uh. Yes. No leaks here." The man straightened himself into a modicum of respectability. "Thank you kindly, ma'am. I'll just see myself out."

"Let us make sure we pay for your time. Walter? You stay. I be right back." Ella smiled and nodded at the boy too vigorously to be believed.

Still, Walter obeyed and stayed put in the hall, watching with his father's dead eyes as they descended the back steps. Once they were out of sight, the boy's gaze shifted up to the ceiling, where footsteps creaked from one end of the house to another. Slipping silently into the back hallway, the boy stopped and pressed his ear to the attic door.

The sound of Felix singing an Italian folk song drifted down through the keyhole. The boy squinted into the lock, seeing nothing but stairs and the warm yellow glow of the attic lights. The smell of cigarette smoke mixed with something else, something darker.

Down in the kitchen, Ella fumbled in the pantry until she found a burlap sack. "Here," she hissed. "You put jars in there." She handed him a bag of rubbish. "Take this too. You must look like serviceman."

He reluctantly grabbed the bag of trash and headed to the back door. "Big Ange's got a friend coming. She needs a safe place to stay."

"A friend," Ella repeated, her fists clenched by her sides.

"Yeah. A friend. Carmen somethin'. I dunno. It ain't like you folks don't have the room, right?" He motioned to the seven bedrooms over their heads. "Just for a few days. That's what I'm told."

The man's eyes circled the kitchen once more, looking for things to steal, no doubt, and then he left. Ella locked the back door behind him and let out a long sigh.

Upstairs, Georgina lay in her bed, reading an old book. *The Divine Book of Holy and Eternal Wisdom* was dated 1849 and had been written by the Shakers, by Ninny Boyd's Believers. Inside, angels whispered of the end of days and the Rapture soon to come.

The wood inside the walls whispered back.

28

The Spielman Family
August 8, 2018

"Mom?" Hunter called out as he opened the front door.

There was no answer.

The door swung into the vacant foyer without a sound. The hot buzz of the summer night followed him in as Hunter surveyed the front of the house for signs of life. An unkempt young man in a black T-shirt and ripped cargo pants pushed past him and inside.

"Damn. You weren't kidding!" His unfamiliar voice echoed in the two-story foyer. "This is the place. I can't believe you actually live here. When'd you move in?"

"Like three weeks ago," Hunter answered as he closed the door behind him. The teenager slouching in front of him was nearly the same height and had the same scruffy chin—a member of the same awkward species.

"Man. I used to come by this place all the time, you know, when it was empty. We called it the 'murder house.' Kids used to break in and stuff." The kid spun around and stared up the monumental staircase toward the sound of a shower running. "I partied here once or twice. My older brother smoked his first joint right upstairs."

Hunter tried to keep his voice light. "Why'd they call it the mur-der house?"

The kid turned with a devilish gleam in his eye. On closer inspec-tion, he was not exactly the same species as Hunter. Better looking and a better liar, he had the swagger of a salesman. "A girl died here, brah. She wasn't the only one either."

Hunter's new friend sauntered into the kitchen and opened the fridge without asking. He pulled out two beers and offered one to Hunter, who took it quickly and directed his entitled guest up the back stairs. "We should take these to my room. You know. The folks." Hunter had caught the glow of the television in the den and heard a rush of water through the pipes above him.

"You the boss." The kid shrugged and followed him up to his room. "I dig these servant stairs, man. My house has a whole apart-ment over the garage for maids and shit. Wouldn't that be amazing? Some hot little maid living under your roof?"

Hunter ushered the kid into his bedroom with a nervous glance at his mother's closed door. Once safely out of the hallway, he popped the cap off his beer and took a long swig. "I don't know. We have a maid that comes once a week, and she's not hot." Hunter shivered at the thought of fifty-year-old Louisa naked.

The kid chugged half his beer as a show of dominance and nod-ded. "Yeah. But don't you think about it sometimes? What it was like to live in this place when it was new with like butlers and shit?" The kid plopped down into the desk chair, relegating Hunter to the edge of the bed. "If I were the king of this castle, the maids would be hot."

Hunter let out a nervous laugh. "So, um . . . what did you mean? A girl died here?"

"That's the rumor. A buddy of mine swears you can see her face in the windows at night. He's kind of an asshole, but that's what he said." The kid pulled a plastic baggie out of one of the pockets in his cargo pants. It was filled with clumps of dried herbs. He pulled a large bud out and breathed in the skunky smell as though sampling ambrosia. "Want some?"

Hunter's eyes shot to the door but tried to play it casual. "Like to buy?"

The kid gave him a deadpan look. "Yeah, dummy. To buy."

"Uh, sure. An eighth, I guess?"

The kid nodded as though he'd expected the answer and laid the tiny pine tree on Hunter's mouse pad along with a second one. "You need a baggie?"

Hunter studied the contraband a moment, uneasy, before the question registered. "Yeah. That'd be great."

The kid pulled out a roll of silvery plastic bags and tossed one to Hunter, not missing the slightly constricted look on the boy's face. "Jesus, don't worry. Cops don't give a shit about weed anymore. Not in this part of town. Now, pills and powders are a different story. That there's fifty."

Hunter nodded and pulled out his wallet.

The kid in his chair jostled the computer to life. "Nice system, man. You game?"

"Yeah. A bit."

The two went on to discuss their favorite video games for the next five minutes while Hunter tried desperately to relax. He squirreled his newly purchased weed into his pocket and watched apprehensively while his new buddy rolled up a joint on his desk.

"You got a spot we can blaze this thing up?"

"Well . . ." Hunter shifted his jaw in consternation. Would they get caught? Would his parents even notice? "The attic, I guess."

"Sweet. I cannot wait to tell Jamie I smoked up in the murder house! This is bonkers." The kid tucked the joint behind his ear and bounded out into the hall. Hunter's heavier feet followed him.

Margot's door was still shut. There was no sign of movement downstairs. Hunter quickly figured the risks. His father was probably working on his laptop somewhere, and his mother would've had a cocktail by now. An uncomfortable guilt weighed him down as his gaze lingered on her door. They didn't trust him, and he was about to prove them right.

"You comin'?" the kid chided from the attic doorway.

It was an initiation of sorts, and Hunter knew it. If he and this kid were going to be friends, he'd have to prove himself worthy. And right then, Hunter needed a friend.

"Yeah," he said and closed the attic door.

29

"It's hot as balls up here." The kid sat down cross-legged on the attic floor and passed the lit joint over to Hunter.

"Yeah. I guess my mom didn't see the point in piping the AC in." Thoughts paced back and forth through Hunter's mind as he took the tightly rolled joint. Would his mother smell the smoke? Would she put him in rehab for one joint? The weight of the alpha male's stare stiffened his back, and he took a shallow toke, holding more in his mouth than his lungs.

"We could have some hellacious parties in this place, man. Do your parents go out of town much?"

"No. Not really." He took another hit of the joint and coughed out a cloud of smoke. "They don't trust me enough to leave me alone for a whole weekend."

"They sound like assholes."

Hunter laughed dumbly and nodded. He was secretly glad they hadn't left him there overnight, picturing himself wandering the big house alone with whatever or whoever had slipped into his room the other night. He closed his eyes to block out the unwanted thought of it.

Are you awake?

His lids flew back open, and a shudder jarred his head, now a lead balloon on his shoulders. This had been a bad idea, he realized as the

Cheshire grin of his new friend widened to show more teeth, but he was trapped now. Staggering to his feet, he mumbled, "We should . . . open a window."

After a moment's fumbling and tugging against a hundred years of paint, the dormer window slapped to the top of the frame, and a blast of air shot into the room. Hunter sucked it in like a drowning man and then opened the other one, praying the smoke would clear out before his parents noticed.

The kid on the floor chuckled and handed him the warm, sticky roll of paper.

Hunter waved him off. "Nah, dude. I'm good. Thanks."

He waved it at him again. He seemed like the sort of boy who would poke a dog in the eye with a stick for entertainment. "Don't leave me hangin', man."

"Dude. I'm baked." But Hunter obeyed and took the joint. "This shit is kicking my ass."

Eyes burning red, the kid nodded his approval as Hunter hit it one more time. "My cousin brought this shit back from Colorado. Those dirty hippies know how to grow, man."

Hunter did his best to not inhale any more as he sucked the smoke into his mouth. He waited for what felt like a month before blowing it out and handing the thing back. The brown paper had burned his fingertips a bright red, but it took several seconds for the pain to register. Squinting one eyeball, Hunter examined the pads of his fingers. Swollen swirls and ridges and creases. It was the hand of an alien.

"Hey!" The kid knocked him in the arm to snap him out of it. "Don't you want to know about the rest?"

"Huh?" Hunter looked up at him, blank as a newborn baby.

"The murder house, man! The dead bodies."

Nausea bubbled from Hunter's stomach to his slackened brain. *Too high. Too high. Too high.* His voice came from down a long tunnel, slow and foreign. "What dead bodies?"

"So check it. Last summer, on a night kinda like tonight actually, these kids broke in here to party, right?" The kid gauged Hunter's swaying expression before continuing. "Business as usual, whatever. But then the next morning there's all these ambulances out front and police cars. Two of those kids turned up dead. The cops said they overdosed on something, probably fentanyl, who knows. Some junkies just can't handle their shit . . . but I talked to one of the guys that was with 'em, and he had a totally different story." The kid's expression flickered from amusement to reverence.

Hunter stopped swaying and gripped at the floor with his palms. "Wait. Wait. What? They died here. That's . . . you're bullshitting me, man."

"The fuck I am! Were you here, Boston? I don't think so."

Hunter tried to blink moisture back into his gummed-up eyes and see straight. "No, but . . . there was nothing in the papers about it. I checked."

"You checked? That doesn't mean shit. This is Shaker Heights, brah. Families here make sure certain shit doesn't get in the papers. Google Niles Gorman and Natalie Cain. They each got tiny obituaries and their numbers quietly added to the opioid crisis." The haunted expression on the kid's face didn't match his grin.

"Sorry, man." Hunter held up his hands in surrender. "That's seriously fucked up. Did you like know them?"

"Sort of. Not really. I knew one of the guys that was with them, and man . . ." The kid shook his head. "His parents had to send him off to Hopewell Farm for like six months."

"What the hell is that? Like a mental hospital?"

"Yeah. Kinda. The poor bastard couldn't stop going on and on about something they saw. Like a ghost or demon or some shit." The kid wasn't smiling anymore.

Hunter's face went slack. "What ghost?"

The kid shrugged. "Fuck if I know. But the kids in the neighborhood all think this place is haunted."

White silk flickered in the corner of his mind's eye. Hunter swatted at it and scanned the attic for a sign of it. Was it listening?

"You ever see her?" The kid took another deep drag.

"Her?" Hunter's stomach dropped.

"Yeah. The ghost. You ever see it?"

Hunter blinked at the kid a moment before shaking his head. *Did he say* her *or* it?

"I still can't believe you live here, man! It was kinda dope you invited me in." The kid stood up with what was left of the joint. "There a bathroom up here?"

"Uh. Yeah. Over there." Hunter pointed at the bathroom door, hanging open only an inch. A shadow loomed on the other side of the slab of wood, a gathering sense of dread. The light was off, he realized, gazing into the sliver of darkness. The light was never off.

The kid swung the door open and turned the sink on, then off again. He came back to where Hunter sat dumbstruck and handed him the wet joint he'd just put out. "You want the roach?"

Hunter slowly shook his head.

"So." The kid set the roach on a windowsill and turned a slow circle around the room. "Thanks for giving me the tour, man."

"Sure." Hunter wobbled to his feet on scarecrow legs. The blood rushed from his head, and a kaleidoscope of dead teenagers flashed and blinked. "Shit."

The kid clapped him on the shoulder. "You want more, you know where to find me, right?"

Hunter nodded blindly and waited for the spots to clear.

A wide grin split the kid's face in two. "You might wanna take a minute and get yourself straight. I'll see myself out."

Before Hunter could collect his voice, the kid had bounded down the steps. "Wait," he called after him weakly. He staggered to the stairwell, his head floating two feet above his shoulders.

His friend was gone.

He hardly knew him, and now the guy was wandering the house and possibly talking to his parents. *High as a kite.* "Roger?" he hissed into the empty stairwell.

At the bottom of the steps, he saw his mother's door standing open at the far end of the hallway. He scanned the front stairs, the foyer, the front door—there was no sign of Roger. Hunter caught a glimpse of his own face in the hall mirror and thought better of talking to his mother in the state he was in. He turned toward the back steps and headed down to the kitchen.

Margot was standing in front of the refrigerator, holding the door open.

"Oh . . ." Hunter said, taking a step backward, fretting dizzily that he reeked of smoke. "Hi, Mom."

"Hi." She hardly glanced at him, keeping her eyes on the fridge, trying to hide the fact that they were swollen from crying. "Did you eat dinner?"

He paused a moment, waiting for more questions. *Who's your friend? Have you been smoking drugs?* If he hadn't been in a panic of his own, he might've noticed the stilted tone of her voice, the broken lines in her face. "No, I'm not really hungry." He lurched past her toward the front door as casually as he could. "Have you seen Dad?" *Or my high friend?*

"Your dad? Oh. I think he's napping in the den."

Hunter wasn't listening. The foyer was still empty. He spun back toward the den on the other side of the kitchen, the walls rushing past in a blur. The television was still flashing blue and green images. Creeping a bit closer, he could see the open bottle of bourbon on the coffee table and his father's cashmere feet propped up on one end of the couch. Over his shoulder, Margot was still staring into the refrigerator, letting the cold air soothe her swollen face.

There was no sign of Roger anywhere.

A door slammed at the top of the steps.

A lanky figure rushed down the stairs and out the front door in a startling blur.

Dazed, Hunter stumbled after it to the open doorway. Roger's black T-shirt vanished behind the trees, and Hunter ran out onto the front sidewalk after him. "Hey! Where the hell are you going?"

After a gaping pause, he scrambled back into the house and shut the door.

"Somebody here?" his mother asked from the edge of the kitchen.

"Uh. Yeah. A friend stopped by." He kept his back to her so she wouldn't see the unfocused panic distorting his face. *What was Roger doing up there?*

"Oh, that's great, honey. I want to meet him sometime." Margot gave a little nod and shuffled back into the kitchen.

Relieved she didn't want to discuss it further, Hunter followed the trail of pot fumes back up the front stairs to his mother's bedroom. The feeling something was terribly wrong twisted inside him. The walls seemed to undulate in and out with his breath.

In his mother's bathroom, he found both medicine cabinets flung open and pill bottles scattered over the marble vanity.

"Shit! Roger?" he hissed, grabbing one bottle after another. Empty. Empty. Only one rattled in his hand. Frowning, he frantically shoved them all back into their proper places. Closing his dad's medicine cabinet, he caught a glimpse of something or someone in the mirror. A flash of white silk.

When he spun around to the closet doorway behind him, it was gone.

You ever see her?

He started after whoever or whatever it might be, but a flash of red in his mother's soaking tub caught him midstep. The room reeled as he took in the color. A small splatter of red puddled near the drain. Next to it, an open straight razor gleamed silver in the light.

Blood.

Hunter grabbed the counter to steady himself as the walls breathed in and out. It was the old-fashioned type of razor that no one used anymore. Except in horror movies. A cold sweat broke out on his forehead.

Whose blood? Roger had taken off down the street with his pilfered stash of pills. His mother was in the kitchen.

With an unsteady hand, Hunter turned on the tap and watched as the water in the bathtub swirled red and pink until it ran clear. He slid the razor into the hot stream using a shampoo bottle, not daring to touch it until it had been rinsed clean. Then he picked it up, folding the blade against the handle. The weight of it in his hand focused his bloodshot eyes.

He shoved the razor into his back pocket and hurried down the hall to his room. After barricading the door, he paced the floor. He picked up his cell phone and began to dial and then set it back down again. *What would the police do? What if it's Mom's? What if she tried to . . .*

He shook his head violently at the idea.

He sank down onto his chair and picked up the phone again. He scrolled through the numbers saved on the screen until he found the right one. After a full minute of listening to the other line ring, he got voicemail. "Hey, Roger! What the fuck just happened, man? This is Hunter. Call me."

He took a minute tapping out the same message into a text, then clicked on his computer. A search engine popped up, and he typed in Roger's name. Nothing came up except a few defunct social media accounts. *No police record,* Hunter mused, *but how old is Roger anyway? What the hell am I going to tell my parents about the pills?*

Hunter considered calling the police again. *No. The weed. I'm stoned. Shit.*

To busy his twitching fingers, Hunter entered one of the names Roger had rattled off, *Niles Gorman Shaker Heights.* A series of results flickered onto the screen. Football stories. A Facebook page. A story in the high school student paper titled "Opioid Crisis Hits Shaker." Hunter clicked on it.

> Families mourned the loss of SHHS senior Niles Gorman and junior Natalie Cain last week. Both students died of what appeared to be a drug-related overdose . . .

> The bodies were found in a vacant house on Lee Road known to be a nuisance property. Police are working now to secure the house . . .

Hunter scanned the article for any mention of a ghost or foul play and found nothing but teachers remembering what sort of students they'd been and friends insisting that neither of them had had a real drug problem. The rest of the article cited recent statistics of the opioid crisis in Cuyahoga County, a crisis that had left families in ruins and children stranded in the overcrowded foster care system.

Hunter rubbed his chin, pulling on the sparse hairs, then spun in his chair to face the door. He wasn't sober enough to face either of his parents. He pulled the razor out of his pocket and studied it again, wondering if maybe his father had inherited it from his own father or bought it at a shop, or . . .

The floor creaked outside his room.

The electric current of another person only twelve feet away charged the air, creeping up his back as a shadow hovered on the other side of his door. The feel of it strummed his nerves as he sat there waiting for something to happen.

"What do you want?" he finally asked, his voice barely above a whisper.

There was no answer.

Hunter could feel something or someone squinting at him through the keyhole. Reflexively, he gripped the razor tighter.

The shadow creaked away toward the attic steps, and the sensation of being watched released its grip. He stood up but stayed put. Jumbled thoughts flashed behind his eyes. *This is stupid. I should call the police. If it's a person, they're trespassing, and if it's a dead person . . .*

But his head was still not properly attached. He squeezed his eyes shut and blinked them open again. The whites still burned red. He couldn't call the police in the state he was in. He couldn't even talk to his parents. He might've imagined the whole thing. Then a more coherent thought flashed through his mind.

The camera.

Hunter spun back to his computer and enlarged the feed from the webcam to see his own face gaping at the screen. Then he rewound the footage to earlier that day, not sure what he was hoping to find. His doorway stood empty on the screen. He sped up the recording. Nothing. Nothing. *Wait.*

He backed up until he found it. His door swung open on his screen. The hallway outside was dark and grainy, but something moved—a slip of white fabric. He backed up the video feed and slowed it down. A shoulder. A white nightgown. A strand of blonde hair. Then nothing. No face. He tried adjusting the exposure but got nowhere.

"Shitty camera!" he hissed.

It could've been his mother; that was what everyone would say. But staring at the frozen profile, his nose an inch from the screen, he knew it wasn't.

30

The Martin Family
February 15, 2014

Ava woke to the sound of footsteps coming down the crooked hall-way toward her door. She could hear the heavy footfalls even over the whirring box fan next to her bed.

"Ava, honey? You awake?" Papa Martin whispered through the open door. "I thought I heard you crying."

She didn't answer. Silently, she slipped from her bed and crept on cat feet toward her closet in the far wall, not breathing.

The key rattled in the lock. The noise gave her cover as she closed the closet door behind her. In the breathless dark, she pushed through the hanging clothes to the laundry door set two and a half feet above the floor. The wood panel opened into a laundry chute. The shaft of cold basement air chilled her skin as she reached through the wall chase to push open the laundry door on the opposite side. It swung into the adjacent walk-in linen closet with a faint squeak. Ava cringed at the sound.

The door to her bedroom creaked open, and she felt Papa's foot-steps shake the floor as he lumbered into the room. "You okay, girl? Mind if I lay down here awhile? The bed is so empty when Maureen's out of town . . . Ava?"

The laundry door was just wide enough for her tiny frame to squeeze through, and she silently thanked God she'd stayed so small. Even at nearly sixteen years old, she was often mistaken for a much younger girl and kept her curves hidden under loose clothes and a self-conscious slouch. As silently as she could manage, she pulled herself across the twenty-foot drop to the basement and into the oversize linen closet on the other side. The shelves of folded sheets, towels, and blankets muffled the sound of her body spilling headfirst onto the floor.

The closet door behind her swung open before she could pull the laundry door shut. *Too late.*

"Ava? What the hell are you doing?" Papa Martin's voice boomed through the closet. Hangers screeched as he shoved the hanging clothes aside. A meaty arm thrust through the laundry door and nearly caught her nightgown as she slipped out of the linen closet and took off running down the hall.

"Ava!" he hissed after her.

She didn't look back. Her feet flew down the hall to the back stairs. Outside, the snow was falling, and her feet were bare. She wouldn't get far, she realized, running down the steps and into the kitchen. She opened the side door anyway and peered out down the driveway. The snow fell in big flakes, melting on the dark pavement. *Good. No footprints.*

She grabbed her shoes and coat from the rack and left the door standing wide open. Then she slipped down the basement stairs as quietly as she could. Papa Martin wouldn't have heard her anyway over the furious thump of his feet or the angry huff of his breathing.

"Dammit, Ava!" he bellowed down the back stairs. Mama Martin was out of town, so there was no one to wake except Toby. The thought of the boy locked in his room and wondering at the commotion sent a knife through her as Ava ran down into the basement.

But Papa has never raised a hand to the boy, she reassured herself as she stashed her coat and shoes in one of the storage closets and herself in another. *What the hell am I doing?*

Papa lumbered through the kitchen and crashed open the storm door. "Ava?" he called down the driveway. Waking the neighbors wouldn't do at all, he realized and closed the door. "Jesus Christ!"

He stormed back into the kitchen and picked up the phone. His voice traveled down the basement stairs to Ava's hiding spot, where she cowered next to his coveralls and tools. "Al? Yeah, this is Clyde. Listen, could you send a car by around here? Ava snuck out of the house . . . Hell if I know! I think it's some boy from school . . . Believe me, she's gonna be grounded for a month. Just have the fellas keep an eye out for her . . . See you Saturday at the range? Okay. Thanks." He hung up the phone.

Ava sagged against the closet wall. *Now what?* His police buddies would surely believe Clyde's version of the story. She didn't know if she'd even have the nerve to tell anyone the truth anyway. She'd had chances.

In the musty air of the storage closet, she listened as Papa Martin pulled a beer from the fridge, then slammed the door shut hard enough to shake the floorboards. His angry feet stomped away from the kitchen. The television clicked on in the den, and the muted sounds of a game show filtered down to where Ava crouched, debating what to do next. *Run? What about Toby? Call someone? But who?*

The endless questions and dead ends swirled around her in the suffocating darkness until she lost all sense of time. Consciousness wound out of her head as she descended into a nightmare of terrible possibilities. Ava trapped in the backseat of a police car. Toby lost in the woods. Papa Martin's hands squeezing her neck until she couldn't breathe. Ava drowning in a black, black sea.

Hours later, a sudden rush of air and a burst of light woke her like a slap. She blinked her eyes in the sudden glare to see the barrel chest of Papa Martin standing in the open door.

"There you are," he said.

31

The Spielman Family
August 8, 2018

Bleary eyed, Myron studied himself in his bathroom mirror, searching for jaundice, weighing his thoughts. He really needed to stop. He knew this but opened the medicine cabinet despite himself. *Tomorrow.* He'd do better tomorrow, but today of all days . . .

He picked up a brown bottle and shook it in his hand. The bottle that had been full of white pills of various sizes two days earlier was now nearly empty.

"Damn it! Who's been in my things?" Myron spun around in the empty room, looking for someone to blame. The small digital clock by the sink blinked *11:27 p.m.*

A floor below, Margot was asleep on the couch thanks to the two martinis she'd had with dinner. Home Network reruns lit her face in tasteful shades of sage and mushroom. He didn't have the nerve to wake her or risk rousing her suspicions.

Red faced, he stormed down the long hall to Hunter's bedroom and threw open the door without knocking. "Hunter!"

The boy jumped in his computer chair and fumbled to get the article he'd been reading about poltergeists off the computer screen. "What?"

"Don't *what* me." Myron brandished the near-empty pill bottle at his son. "Have you been stealing my meds?"

"What?" He shrank from the accusing look on his father's face, eyes darting from the bottle to his father's bloodshot face. *Dammit, Roger!*

"I said. Have you. Been stealing. *My pills?*"

"No!" Hunter's face went pale. The pot he'd smoked with Roger the Thief had mostly worn off, but he panicked anyway.

Myron charged forward and clamped a manicured hand onto the boy's arm. Hard. "Don't lie to me. Did you take them?" He searched the boy's face for signs. *Obfuscation? Intoxication? Addiction?* "If you have a problem, you need to tell me, son. Taking other people's meds is dangerous. It can ruin your life. Even kill you. Do you hear me?"

"Yes, sir," Hunter said, trying hard not to show his terror at being discovered. The small bag of marijuana was tucked into his box of gerbil food.

"Do I need to get you drug tested?"

"What?" Hunter's mouth hung open, aghast. *Oh, God!* "No! Dad! I'm not on drugs!"

And he wasn't really. Not normally. Hunter's only addiction was glowing behind him with the lurid promise of everything his fevered brain wanted to see and plenty that he didn't.

Myron probed the boy's eyes like the doctor he was, looking for the telltale signs. Pupils. Skin color. Balance. Eye movement. Not trusting him for a second.

Hunter sat there squirming under the microscope until his father finally released his grip.

The man straightened himself, perhaps realizing how this might look from the boy's point of view. The slight tremor in his hand, which he quickly concealed by shoving both fists and the bottle into the pockets of his bathrobe, was a dead giveaway. Myron fumbled for the voice of an exasperated father. "I don't like you spending so much time in here. The first couple weeks? Fine. But this is getting ridiculous! Your mother and I are both worried sick."

The boy's gaze immediately turned inward. His father's disapproval wrote its damning words all over Hunter's face. *Failure. Weak. Disappointment. Loser.*

"I want you to get out of this damn room tomorrow. Go outside. Walk around. Meet some people your own age. Stop haunting this place like Eddie Munster. Alright?"

The condemnation cut the boy in places no one would ever see. Hunter nodded, not looking at his father. He didn't bother arguing that he'd spent the whole afternoon outside the house or that he'd met a friend who had turned out to be a thief.

The shame he'd just inflicted made Myron grimace. More furious at himself than Hunter, he didn't bother parsing the two feelings. He reached past his son and grabbed the boy's wireless keyboard. "I'm taking this until you can show me you're responsible enough to have it back. Got it?"

Hunter gaped at the keyboard and then his father. Anger overtook the humiliation of his father's dressing down. "Hey! That's mine."

"No, son. It's mine. Who do you think pays for all this, huh?" Myron waved his hand over the room with its posters, books, creepy fireplace, and gerbil maze. "We have a deal, remember? You do your job, and I'll do mine. And right now, my job is to get you the hell out of this room. And your job is to stop frying up your brain. Now, get some sleep! And stay the hell out of my medicine cabinet!"

Hunter narrowed his eyes at his father as the man stomped out of the room. Once the door was closed, the boy stood and rummaged through his closet.

DeAD GiRL BAD BeNNY

BAD BAD BAD

He found his old wired keyboard in a crate, buried under discarded video games and a photograph of a little boy perched on the lap of an older sister. He paused a minute at the photo before shoving it back in its box. He plugged the keyboard into the back of his machine and sat back down with renewed determination. *Fuck him.*

In the search engine, he typed, "Signs of pill addiction."

Down the hall in the master suite, Myron took what was left of the white pills, then stashed his son's keyboard in the back of his sock drawer. He wouldn't discuss the altercation with Margot. He scowled as if he could hear her nagging, *Are you sure taking his computer was the best thing to do?* Her doubting voice cranked so many gears inside him that he nearly sprang apart. He collapsed onto the bed and waited for the pills and cable TV to wash his guilt and tortured thoughts away.

An hour later, a sound nudged him awake. "Margot?" he mumbled, but her side of the bed was empty.

He heard the sound again and sat up, woozy. It was coming from his bathroom. Myron put his sweaty feet on the cold wood floor and padded silently in the dark toward it.

In the ghostly glow of the white marble, a figure stood at his sink—the shape of a girl. Myron stopped breathing, frozen in the doorway. Bare legs. Long pale hair. White gauzy slip. A wisp of smoke. "Margot?" he whispered.

He squinted at the female shadow and took a cautious step into the doorway. The shape of her slipped into his closet with the softest laugh he'd ever heard. A breath escaping through the slightest of smiles.

Not Margot.

"Hey!" He fumbled for the light switch that wasn't there. It had been installed on the other side of the wall, but his foggy brain couldn't manage the math. "Who's there?"

He followed the shadow to the other end of the bathroom, peering through the doorway of his closet. Walking in its wake, he caught the scent of Margot's perfume and something else. Something sweet and smoky.

"I'm not kidding." Myron took an unsteady step forward in the dark, feeling the wall for the light switch. "Who are you? And what the hell are you doing in my house?" His voice slurred with sleep and the pills he'd taken.

He tried to blink his eyes clear in the faint light streaming in through the window sheers behind him. A shape moved between his suits. Closer. Then gone again. Vanished into the shadows.

"Who are you? What the hell are you doing in here?" he asked, still fumbling along the casing for the damn light switch.

The door at the far end of his closet creaked open into the hallway. The shape of a girl caught in silhouette in the doorframe stopped and turned to Myron. He froze, transfixed. *Is this a dream?*

He found the switch and snapped it on in a painful burst of white. The sudden brightness stabbed his eyes, forcing them to blink and focus and see. There was nothing there.

Margot's voice jarred him fully awake. The sound of it was coming from her yoga studio, and she wasn't talking to him. Myron stepped out into the hallway to find the door to the yoga room standing open and a soft blue glow beckoning him closer. He stumbled toward it, and her voice grew louder.

"Feel the stretch from your shoulders all the way to your feet," she said softly. "Doesn't that feel good?"

He stopped in the doorway to find his wife's laptop open in the center of the room.

"It's important to breathe," Margot cooed at him from the computer screen with her knees knotted over her head. "Breathe from your spine, letting your muscles go on the exhale. You're doing well. Two more breaths . . ."

Myron scanned the room for the intruder, not quite convinced he'd seen one at all. *Margot?* Then his eyes shifted back to his wife on the screen as she curled into another uncomfortable pose. He crouched down and examined the video and found another link open. Clicking on it, Margot's flushed face appeared larger on the screen.

"Is that for me?" she asked him, smiling coyly.

"Why? You want it?" Another voice came from somewhere off camera. Myron sank down to the floor, transfixed at the image of his wife smiling that smile at some stranger. Batting her eyelashes like she did when she wanted something from him. Whatever he'd seen in the closet slipped away as her naked body filled the screen.

"It doesn't matter what I want," she purred. "I'm a married woman."

32

The next morning, Hunter heard his father's phone ring down in the kitchen. He sat up in bed and listened.

"This is Dr. Spielman . . . No, I haven't had a chance to look at it . . . I'm sure it is convincing . . . Of course, a jury is going to be moved. Listen, aren't you the one that told me a sad story isn't enough? . . . Look. I'm heading into my office. Let me call you back."

Hunter grimaced at the sound of his father's agitated voice. He'd stayed up half the night, debating what to do about his father's accusations, Roger and the stolen pills, and the dead girl in his house. He packed up a backpack stuffed with his weed and a few changes of clothes and threw it onto his shoulder. *He's going to kill me. I can't stay here.*

A scratching noise behind him stopped him at the door. Frodo and Samwise were clawing at a toilet paper roll. The frayed cardboard rustled against the wood chips. Their tiny claws scraped the edges.

"Shit," he whispered. He grabbed the box of gerbil food and deposited it in several piles throughout the maze of tubes and the three aquariums. Enough food for a week. "Sorry, guys," he said and ran a finger over each of them through the glass. "I'll be back once I figure out what to do."

Down in the kitchen, Myron muttered softly to himself over his morning coffee. "They can't prove malpractice unless they prove acts outside the standard of care . . . The nurse said she checked the stitches, dammit!"

He didn't notice his son slip out the side door and down the driveway with a backpack on his shoulder. He drank his coffee at the sink and then headed to work.

Two hours later, Margot padded into the kitchen half-asleep and hungover. She stood in her robe, glaring at the dark rings Myron had left on the marble next to the coffee maker.

In the middle of her annoyance, there was a knock on the front door.

"Are you Margaret Spielman?" a delivery man asked from behind an enormous arrangement of red roses. Two dozen at least.

Margot set her coffee mug down on the table by the door, her face flushed in the glow of the bright petals. "Yes?"

"Then these are for you." The dark-skinned man handed her the flower vase.

"My goodness!" She marveled at the size of them, the thick stems, the opening blooms gathered in a heavy umbrella the precise color of blood. She set the heavy arrangement on the table next to the staircase, a table selected specifically for large flower arrangements. There wasn't a card. *Are they from Myron?* She dismissed the thought as quickly as it came to her. Grand gestures weren't his style. *But who?*

"Can you sign here for me, ma'am?"

Margot bristled at the word *ma'am* but offered a thin smile. She grabbed the pen and clipboard. "Is there a card?"

"Not that they gave me."

He held his hand out for his clipboard, but she held on to it a second, scanning the form for any name but hers. "Are you sure there isn't some sort of name at least? Those must've cost a hundred dollars! I can't imagine anyone would go to such trouble without at least leaving their name. Can you?"

The man shrugged. "I dunno. Can't really predict what people will do though, right? I've seen some weird stuff on this job."

"Can you call someone back at the shop for me?" She batted her eyes at him ever so slightly and crossed her arms to push her breasts together just so. "I'd hate not knowing who to thank."

"I don't know what good it'd do. We just get the orders off the internet. People don't leave a name, they don't leave a name." He lifted his chin at her cleavage, assessing. He knew this game and didn't feel like playing. He pulled a worn business card from his back pocket. "You can call the number there if you want."

She took the card with a sigh and closed the door.

The enormous bouquet threw a red shadow on the wall as she stood there alone in the foyer. The longer she stood there looking at it, the more uncomfortable they made her until she finally grabbed her coffee mug and headed back to the kitchen, where her pink phone was waiting on a cold marble slab. She glanced at the business card in her hand again before tossing it in the trashcan. Then she dialed a number from memory.

"Yes. Good morning. Can I please speak to Dr. Moriarty? . . . Yes, I'll hold."

She set the phone on the counter and turned on the speakerphone. Classical piano music spilled out of the pinholes in the plastic and onto the floor. Chopin. The eerie notes curled up the stairwells and down the hallway upstairs to where Hunter's bedroom stood empty.

Margot drummed her fingers nervously, then went to the pantry and grabbed a jar of organic peanut butter. While the ominous funerary played, she ate two guilty spoonfuls and refilled her coffee.

Finally, a deep voice broke through the speaker. "Moriarty."

"Alan? It's Margot."

"Margot? What, ah . . . How are you?"

She snapped off the speakerphone and picked up the receiver. "Fine. Listen, Alan. You didn't"—she tapped her heel against the ground and winced—"send me flowers. Did you?"

There was a long pause as he answered from wherever it was he worked.

"Yeah. I know. I just got these roses and thought. I don't know." Her face burned pink.

Another pause.

"Of course. No. I won't . . . You take care of yourself, okay? Thanks." She tapped a button on her phone irritably and dropped it three inches onto the counter as if it were hot. She shook her head at herself and put away the peanut butter. "Stupid," she whispered. "So fucking stupid."

After all of the breakfast dishes had been put away, Margot circled the kitchen feeling guilty, restless, worried. *I don't live that far away.* She shuddered to think "Kevin" knew her address. There was no way some stranger had found her address online. She'd been so careful.

Two full laps later, she picked up the phone again. Two buttons. Three rings. "Myron? . . . No, everything's fine. Um . . ." She glanced back toward the flowers in the foyer, debating whether or not to ask about them. "Yeah. No, I'm sorry. I know you're working. It's just . . . I *am* taking care of myself! Jesus, I'm not an invalid! I'm just going stir crazy here in this house . . . I know quitting my job was my decision. It's just—"

Myron's voice could be heard through the earpiece, loud and agitated.

Margot squeezed the phone harder, angry. Calling him had been a mistake. "Okay. Fine. We'll talk later!"

She slammed the phone down and stormed back out into the foyer. The flowers hadn't moved but seemed even fuller than before. Impossible to hide. Bleeding red on the walls. She tugged her lip at them, debating. Standing in the two-story foyer with her ponytail and bare legs, she looked tiny, girlish.

Lost in thought, she trudged up the oppressively grand staircase and padded barefoot into her room to run a hot bath. The house stood still as the bathroom clouded with steam. Once Margot had sunk down deep into the hot water, she shut her eyes and listened to the sound of the street outside. The way the warm wind slapped the window sashes back against their frames in her bedroom. The hum of a lawn mower a block away. A silvery drop of water hitting the still surface of the bath, sending ripples toward her neck. Margot lay there rigid, willing her muscles to relax, darting from one thought to another.

I don't live that far away.

A loud crash of a box hitting the attic floor jolted her upright. She climbed out of the tub, barely pausing to grab her towel. Racing out into the hall, she called, "Hunter? Is that you?"

Down at the bottom of the grand staircase, the front door was closed. *Did I remember to lock it?* she wondered. The roses still waited for an explanation from their perch in the foyer.

"Hello?" she called out again.

The silence of the house answered.

Margot shivered in her towel, unsure what to do next, taking three steps forward. The door to her studio gaped open. She puzzled at it a moment. She never left it open. When she poked her head inside, everything seemed to be in order.

Peeking into the dark corridor that led over the garage, she saw the attic door was shut. Even in daylight, Margot hated going up there. Rumors and graffiti seemed to circle her thoughts as she climbed the stairs, swatting at imagined cobwebs. Smells of the contractors and the half-dead squatters who had once slept there still lingered in the air—sweat and cigarettes and chemical poisons. A pile of old blankets had been left in the corner. Margot eyed them, making a mental note to complain to Myron.

The bathroom light at the far end had been left on again.

"Hello? Anybody up here?"

Hair still dripping, Margot inched her way across the floor of the long attic cavern toward the bathroom. To her right, doors to both the attic bedrooms hung open. She blinked at the second one. It had been locked since they bought the place. Max's voice the day they'd toured the house came back to her. *Anyone give you a master key?*

No one had, but there the door was, standing wide open.

A dusty box lay on its side in the middle of the mysterious room, toppled over. *Was that the bang I heard?* She puzzled at it. It wasn't one of theirs. It was too old and grimy, lying there in the rectangle of daylight streaming in through the tiny window. Outside, tree branches waved lazily in the wind.

Unnerved, Margot quickly finished her search of the attic. The mystery room of old boxes, the room full of her Christmas decorations, and the main living room were empty. She clicked off the bathroom light after checking the tub and behind the door. A large shadow on the bathroom floor gave her pause. A place where the grout had been stained darker than the rest. Margot didn't want to consider what had spilled there and made a point to step over the stain with her bare feet.

Satisfied the attic was empty, she sighed in frustration at her ruined bath. "This creepy fucking place," she muttered to herself and headed back to the stairs.

The stairwell felt darker than before, and it took her a moment to figure out why. The door had swung shut. A jolt of fear shot through her. She scanned the empty room for some sort of weapon. Not a baseball bat or a golf club in sight.

"Shit," she hissed and crept down the stairs as quietly as she could. *I don't live that far away.*

She pressed her ear to the door and listened for an intruder. Nothing. With a deep breath, she turned the handle and pushed the door. It didn't move. She tried again, pushing harder. The dead bolt slapped against brass strike with a loud *tick*.

It was locked.

33

Margot pounded on the door until her fist was raw. "Hello? Hunter? God dammit! Let me out of here!" she bellowed, her voice echoing off the bare sloped ceilings and hard floor of the attic. "This is it, Hunter! I've had it! Let me out of here now, or I swear to God . . ."

She could never finish that sentence, not even while pounding and kicking hard enough to crack one of the panels of the door. The crackle of cleaving wood startled her enough to stop her banging. Squinting in disgust, she ran a finger over the joint between the panel and the style. *These doors alone are worth a fortune!* the interior designer had exclaimed, sauntering around during his tour. *Fifteen hundred dollars apiece, easily!*

Margot collapsed on a step. *Is he even home? Did I see him leave? Do I know him at all anymore?* The thought of awkward, lanky Hunter locking her in a room left her gaping with disbelief. *But who else?* "Hunter? Are you there?"

Her hands were trembling. The bath towel had fallen onto the steps in her fury. She looked down at her naked torso, then up at the attic ceiling. It would be hours before Myron returned home from work. And that was if he didn't stop off at the gym, or wherever it was he went. "You've got to be kidding me!"

An electronic trill of music made its way under the locked door. *The cell phone.* She'd left it down in the kitchen. She leaned toward the sound. *Hunter? Myron?*

The song abruptly stopped. She waited with shallow breaths for it to begin again, but there was nothing. A hostile silence radiated up through the floorboards. She shrank back against the steps, sweating in the stale heat of the third floor. The sun had drifted higher in the sky, beating down on the dark slate of the roof, cooking the wood and plaster. She swallowed hard.

Finally, she stood up and crept back up the stairs to take stock. Out one of the front dormer windows, cars rushed past on Lee Road down below the trees. A delivery truck rumbled past. Each window dormer created a useless but charming alcove not quite big enough for a desk or a reading chair, just the frustrated possibility of one. She opened a window and called out, "Hello? Can anyone hear me?"

Cars kept passing by.

In the crawl space, the air-conditioning kicked on, filling the air with the hum of the electric motor and the waterfall sounds of the air rushing through the ducts buried behind the knee walls. A bead of sweat dripped down Margot's back.

Out the bathroom window, the view was entirely trees and the shadow of the house next door. The sash opened without a fight. Several cigarette butts sat piled in the windowsill, and a smattering of ashes blew into her face along with a blast of fresh air. Margot recoiled, spitting and wiping her face. "Max! You son of a bitch!"

Once she'd cleared the ashes from her face and mouth, she pressed her forehead to the sash and yelled, "Hello? Anybody? Help! I need help up here! Hello?"

The only answer was the rush of the cars and the screech of brakes from a commuter bus. The house next door sat quiet. The Spielmans had never invited the neighbors over, never said hello or called them. The people next door worked late and traveled a lot. The only sign of life from the other house was the team of gardeners who came to groom the lawn every week.

"Hello? Anybody? Help! Ple—" Her voice cut off as she caught sight of a strange man walking along the sliver of sidewalk between the trees. She stiffened and glanced down at herself standing there. Nude.

"Shit." She stepped away from the window and sank down on the toilet seat. The dark stain in the grout lines spread out before her in a dried puddle. *Mold? Raw sewage?* A wisp of cool air blew in through the window.

"What the hell am I going to do?" she whimpered, stepping over the stain and onto the wood floor outside the bathroom.

The ceiling rafters above her creaked as they stretched in the heat of the August sun. Margot lurched at the sound and spun around as though expecting to find someone standing there. Hunter brandishing a knife. Myron with her phone, pointing to some private message he wasn't supposed to see. "Kevin" holding the roses.

There was no one there.

Her bare skin prickled with the feeling of being watched. She turned another slow circle, debating her options. No phone. No neighbors. No key. No Hunter. Louisa wasn't due to come for another day. *Alone. Alone. Alone.* Her only hope was to pick the lock or break down the door.

She stormed into Ella's old room, searching for a tool of some kind. The only item in the room was a bare curtain rod. Margot pulled the rod off the wall and searched it for springs, screws, anything. It was just a steel rod, but as she weighed it in her hands, she realized it might be enough to break the door or pry off the jamb. She set it against the wall as a last resort and continued her search into the other room.

The box that had toppled over with a loud thump lay on its side, waiting for her to right it. She tiptoed across the dusty floor and crouched down. Loose twine sat in a puddle around the flaking cardboard.

She scanned the other six identical file boxes stacked up in the corner. None were labeled. There was nothing else in the room besides an ashtray with six cigarette butts that looked recently smoked. Margot narrowed her eyes and added them to her inventory of complaints to the contractor. On the wall above her, a round hole the size of a salad plate punctured the plaster. She stood up and peered into the darkness behind it to find unfinished attic space and the shadow of a brick chimney. She picked at the torn wallpaper around the edges, wondering. It was too neatly cut to be an accident. Soot darkened the edges of the hole. *Woodstove?*

She gave up on the mystery and tipped the fallen box back upright. Yellowed newspapers spilled out the top. Margot let them go, lifting several more out of the box, searching for a screwdriver, an awl, a skeleton key. Evening editions of the *Cleveland Press* and the *Plain Dealer* fell to the floor. They were all dated from the late 1920s and early 1930s.

Under the papers, she found a large brochure for the Van Sweringen Company. She opened it to find hand-printed etchings and calligraphy promising a life of tranquility away from the bustle and grime of the city.

To Where, Beyond the City, There Is Peace.

Margot gazed forlornly at the 1920s notions of grandeur and wealth. White servants. White gloves. White pillars. White Anglo-Saxon Protestants. *What would they think of a lapsed Catholic and nonpracticing Jew living here now?* she wondered with a smirk.

Still, the land-company brochure was a sort of quaint notion to Margot—the idea of a utopia just outside of Cleveland, Ohio, of all places. Her friends back in Boston would get a kick out of it, she decided and set the brochure aside.

The bottom of the box contained a slew of unopened mail all postmarked between 1929 and 1932. Most envelopes were addressed to Walter Rawlings. A few letters were addressed in a beautiful hand to Georgina Rawlings. Unpaid bills. Christmas cards. Birthday cards. With guilty hesitation, Margot opened one postmarked January 5, 1930. It was a handmade card with a praying angel in cream and gold. Inside it read,

> *Dearest Georgina,*
> *We were heartbroken to hear the news. May the new*
> *year find you well and keep you better. May God have*
> *mercy on us all through this terrible winter.*
> *Much love to you and little Walter,*
> *Mr. and Mrs. Herbert Cline*

Margot tossed the card back into the bin and shoved a few more aside. Amid the cards and bills, she found an old wooden cigar box. It felt unusually heavy in her hands as she pulled it out and set it in her lap. She flipped it open and drew in a sharp breath.

A gun. Four bullets rolled loose next to it.

Horrified, she slapped the lid closed and shoved it back under the bills as though the box contained a live snake. *A gun. In the house. Not acceptable.* Shaking her head, she gathered the old newspapers into a pile, having mental arguments with Myron as to when and how they'd get rid of the thing. It wasn't exactly the sort of thing you donated to charity. They didn't have a permit or a license or whatever it was one needed to even transport the thing.

Her nervous hands stopped moving as her mind took a moment to catch up to her eyes. The headline on the paper in her hand read:

WIDOW KILLS SON AND SLASHES SELF
Sickness and Money Troubles Blamed
for Rawlings Suicide Attempt

She read the name again. *Rawlings.* Margot picked up the paper and continued to read:

> The attempted suicide of Mrs. Georgina Rawlings and the body of her murdered son, Walter Rawlings Jr., 6, were discovered last night at 14895 Lee Road, Shaker Heights. That the child made a struggle against his mother's insane attack was indicated by numerous deep cuts on the boy's hands and fingers, according to Coroner Pearse.

> "No one but a maniac could have inflicted such wounds as I found on the boy," the coroner said . . .

"My God," Margot whispered, reading the story for a second time under her breath. "The boy was found lying facedown on the floor of the servants' washroom."

Murder House!

Her gaze shifted toward the bathroom and the dark stain on the bathroom floor behind her. Breathing shallow sips of air, her heart drummed in her ears as she realized what caused it. *My God. It's blood.*

A muffled voice wormed its way through the seams in the floorboards from down below. Margot stopped breathing to listen. It was singing.

. . . where we ought to be,
And when we find ourselves in the place just right,
'Twill be in the valley of love and delight . . .

The voice drifted away with the almost imperceptible shifts in the wood framing as footsteps moved along the second floor hallway. The paper in her hand dropped. Someone was in the house, and it wasn't Hunter.

The vibration of another human being walking down the hall below her inched its way up Margot's stricken spine. She bolted up and closed the door to the storage room, then slid the stack of heavy boxes in front of it. Grabbing the gun from its wooden cigar box, she backed herself into a corner. The gun trembled violently in her fingers as she trained it on the door. Panicked, she realized she didn't even know how to work the thing. *Is there a safety? Are there even bullets in the chamber?* She was shaking too hard to check and realized she might as easily shoot herself as anyone else. She set the thing down and stifled a sob.

Myron will be home in a few hours, she told herself, squeezing her eyes shut, praying whoever it was wouldn't find her up there naked. *Just a few more hours.* Margot hugged her knees to her chest, the gun by her side, her mind curling into itself. *A dream. This is all a terrible dream. The voice. The song. The blood. The murder.*

The stifling heat of the storage room kept climbing above ninety degrees as the afternoon sun beat down harder on the roof. Margot lay there, baking with the old newspapers as scenes from 1931 played in her head again and again. *He was just a little boy.*

Ten feet below her, a shadow wandered from room to room, humming softly to itself.

34

The Rawlings Family
January 24, 1931

Georgina Rawlings woke to the sound of singing. She sat up in bed and held her breath, listening. It was coming from the backyard.

Standing at the window, she pressed her nose to the cold glass and looked out over the blanket of snow that covered her garden. The roses had been cut back to dead twigs. The tulips and daffodils lay sleeping beneath the snow. She searched the perfect plane of white for signs of life, footsteps, or shadows and saw nothing. With her eyes open, the singing was almost impossible to hear, so she shut them, her lids squinting to catch what wasn't there.

Under the inaudible melody, the steady rhythm of marching feet vibrated deep in the ground, up through the stones in the foundation, through the hewn wood. Eyes shut, her face went slack as though seeing it all laid out before her. The chanting of the Believers as they marched in their circle under the stars, pleading with their angels to deliver them a message. The Shaker schoolhouse and gathering house burning.

They died the wrong way.

She opened her eyes with a start as if expecting to see the Believers marching in their slow circle down in the garden. Her skin glowed pale in the light of the full moon. It gazed down at her with the unblinking eye of heaven. There were no clouds to hide what had happened there, and she stared back into the light until her eyes watered. "I'm so sorry," she whispered.

A faint laugh burst somewhere above her beyond the ceiling, and Georgina woke from her trance. A pair of footsteps padded lightly overhead. The lady of the house stumbled away from the window, clutching her nightgown to her chest. The laugh came again, clearer now, mocking her.

The old Shaker woman had warned them. *The dead do not rest easy here.*

It all made sense to Georgina now after hearing Ninny's stories. After her husband's horrible death and the financial ruin that followed. After all the babies she'd lost. After reading the beautiful Shaker tales of the angels that sang and the Second Coming. The truth had come to her in waves of recognition one after another as she'd sat and read and let the fever open her mind.

She put a hand over her mouth to keep it quiet. "They're here . . . they've come for us," she whispered into her palms, backing herself into the corner, searching the darkened room for signs of them.

At the opposite end of the house, little Walter sat up in his bed. He'd stopped sleeping through the night when they'd found his father dead in his office. Wide awake at 2:15 a.m., he sat there in the dark and listened too.

Georgina opened the door to her bedroom and peered out into the hallway. The fear on her face mixed with anticipation as she searched the darkened foyer below for signs of Ninny's dead or her husband's hulking shadow. Puddles of moonlight collected on the stairs and on the polished wood floors of the foyer. The carved railing threw long dripping shadows onto the walls.

The laughter fell from the ceiling once again, deeper now. Sinister.

Georgina shrank against the wall, her heart rattling her ribs. The deep timbre of a man's voice sounded in the dark, its words muffled but the intent clear. *Listen. Obey.* Her eyes widened. *Walter has come back from the grave.* Heavy footfalls thumped over her head, and what blood she had left dropped from her heart to her feet.

"Dear God. What do you want from me?" she whispered and stifled a sob with the back of her hand. Then, breathing deep, she recited a verse from the Shaker prayer book sitting by her bedside. "The dead come unto me so that I might see. His angels bear golden fruit from the tree of paradise and word from the kingdom of heaven . . ."

She took a brave step down the hallway. Drifting toward the attic door, Georgina appeared to be a ghost herself. Floating past Ella's back hallway in her white nightgown, pale skin drawn tight over her thinning frame, her eyes were two hollows peering out from the bone.

The maid didn't stir. Exhausted from a day of worry and secrecy spent waiting for the hard fist of the law to pound on the front door, Ella simply rolled over in the middle of a dream and continued to snore in a low and even saw.

Little Walter stiffened at the sound of footsteps outside his bedroom door and slid down from his perch on the pillows. Squinting through his keyhole, he glimpsed a shroud of white and his mother's thin hand as it turned the corner to the attic. The ring his father had given her caught a sparkle of moonlight.

Ella had locked the attic door as usual that evening, leaving the key resting on the casing above it. Georgina felt the ledge over her head before even trying the handle. They'd kept the door locked ever since Ella had found Walter hiding in the crawl space with his father's gun.

Behind the door, low voices whispered to one another. She pressed her ear to the wood, listening to the dead as they conspired together. Angry. Vengeful. *What do they want from us?*

They went silent when she rattled the key into the lock. They held still as she swung the door open and mounted the steps toward the yellow glow of a single incandescent bulb burning at the other end of the attic.

Georgina didn't notice the small face of her son appear at the bottom of the stairwell. His worried eyes peered up the steps after her. *Mother?*

35

The Spielman Family
August 9, 2018

Margot woke with a start. Hot air rushed into her lungs, thick and soupy. Her naked body muddy with sweat and dust, she gaped at the unfamiliar walls until it all came back to her. The attic. The murder. The song. The intruder. The gun on the floor.

Horror and confusion lined her face. *Have I lost my mind?* She pulled herself to her feet, eyeing the barricaded door. *Is someone still out there?*

Myron's muffled voice came from two floors down. "Hello? Margot? . . . Anybody home?"

Her entire body went slack. *Thank God.* She pushed the boxes to the side and flung open the door to the storage room. "Myron! Myron, up here!"

She ran across the attic floor to the stairwell, nearly tumbling down the steps. When she reached the door, she pounded it with her bruised fists. "Myron! Help! I'm up here! I'm locked in!"

"What?" The sound of feet rushed up the back stairs, then pounded into the hall. "Margot?"

The knob turned, and the door flung open with ease. A rush of cool air hit her in the face. Her mouth fell open, and her naked body recoiled in surprise. *It was unlocked?*

"What the hell were you doing up there?" Myron looked dumbfounded at her sweat-smeared face and naked body and picked her towel up off the stairs. "Jesus. Are you okay?"

He looked at her as though she'd sprouted another head. Her eyes had gone feral. Her hair was a matted mess. Her hands were blackened with dust and newsprint. Margot snatched the towel from his hand and struggled to recover herself. Utter relief twisted into abject fury.

"No! No, I am not fucking okay! Someone locked this fucking door! I've been trapped up there for hours!"

"But . . ." Myron pointed at the doorknob, which had clearly not been locked, and raised his eyebrows at her.

"But what?" she shrieked. "Are you suggesting that I stayed up there for hours for no fucking reason? Are you *insane*?"

Myron didn't answer, but his face made clear he doubted her sanity altogether.

Apoplectic, Margot stormed down the hallway back to her room. Myron reluctantly followed. The bathtub was still filled with water that had long gone cold. She pulled the plug and tapped her foot to keep from kicking something.

"Someone was here!" she seethed. "I heard them in the house! Someone locked me in the attic."

"Whoa. What are you talking about?" Myron held up his hands as though approaching a loaded gun.

"Someone was here!" she barked. "Someone must have found the skeleton key for this fucking place. Did Max say anything about the key?"

He just stared at her as though she were speaking in tongues. "No. He didn't. We haven't been able to find the key. You know that."

"And! That real estate agent lied to us, Myron! She fucking *lied*. This place isn't just *rumored* to be haunted or cursed. The first owner *killed* her son! She killed him in the attic! There's still a bloodstain on the goddamn floor! No wonder no one wanted this goddamn place!" She pointed an accusing finger at him. "You just had to have it. Such a great price. What an investment! Fuck, Myron! A six-year-old boy died up there! Six!"

Her face had gone red, and she was shouting so loudly he could barely follow what she was saying. *Murder? Boy?* All that was clear was that she blamed him for it somehow. It was all his fault.

He finally gained control of his slackened jaw and managed to speak. "Hey! I don't know what the hell you're talking about, but you need to calm down."

"I need to calm down?" she shouted. "I—fuck you, Myron! Just . . ." She began to shake. Her towel dropped to the floor, and her body followed it, sliding down against the wall.

"Hey, hey." His voice softened. "Take it easy. Let me look at you." He tipped her red face up toward his. The doctor in him examined her. Dried, cracked lips. Dilated pupils. Flushed skin. Incoherence. "You're dehydrated, and probably starving. Here." He stepped over to the sink and filled a glass of water for her.

She took the glass and spilled tears into it as she held it up to her lips. The feel of his doctor's eyes watching and making notes as she talked, his ears perked for any sign of lunacy, delusion, or schizophrenia, undid her. The glass tumbled from her hands.

Utterly disarmed and dismayed, he picked it up. He found a place on the bath mat next to her and put an arm around her shoulders, pulling her to him. She didn't have the energy to resist. "Okay. Just breathe. Let's start from the beginning, okay?"

By the time Margot had told him the whole story and had taken a hot shower, Myron was the one coming unhinged.

"Glenda? Hey, this is Myron Spielman. The house on Lee Road? . . . Yeah. Listen, we have a problem." Myron poured himself a scotch and took a long swig to keep himself from yelling. Margot sat on the sofa behind him, nursing a drink of her own. She'd decided it would be best for him to make the call. *I'll just start screaming. Besides, people prefer to talk to a man.*

After a moment's listening, he continued, "Well, the problem is that you sold us a murder house. Those 'rumors' you alluded to? Turns out a kid was killed in our attic . . . When? Does it matter? . . . 1931 . . . Yes, I realize it was a long time ago . . . I don't give a shit what your company's policy is, we should have been informed! There've been some odd disturbances . . . No, I'm not claiming ghosts, damn it . . . My wife just found a bunch of newspapers about it up in the attic along with a goddamn gun, for Christ's sake! A gun! . . . No, I don't suppose you can be held responsible for the contents of the house, but what kind of 'great investment' is this if we can't sell this damn place, huh? . . . We also suspect that there's been an intruder here. Someone with a key . . . Of course we changed the locks, I mean a skeleton key for the doors inside . . . I want to contact the last owner . . . Well, you'll be hearing from my lawyer!"

He hung up the phone, slamming it onto the coffee table.

"What'd she say?" Margot asked numbly.

"What do you think she said? 'Not my problem! It was almost a hundred years ago!' Blah, blah, blah." He pounded the rest of his drink. "She can't give out any information on the last owner besides what is in the contract . . . Didn't Max say something? During the reno, didn't he talk about some issues?"

"I have no idea." Margot stared into her glass, her face blank. *We're screwed. This is a murder house, and now we're trapped here.*

"It doesn't hurt to ask, right?" Myron, determined to be a man of action for his distressed wife, picked up the phone again.

"Max? This is Myron. Spielman. The house on Lee Road in Shaker? . . . Yeah . . . No. Everything is working just fine. Thanks again for putting in all of the overtime, we're really happy with how it turned out . . . Right. Listen, we've run into a bit of an issue with the house itself. Nothing to do with you, but do I remember right that there were some problems, rumors among the guys about bad luck or something? . . . Did the guys ever see anyone on site? Like a trespasser? . . . No? Well, we just found out about a murder up in the attic back when it was built. That ring any bells? . . . Really? What was her name? Can you text me her number? I think we'd like to chat with her . . . Okay. Thanks!"

The conversation lifted Margot's eyebrows. *What?*

Myron plopped down on the couch next to her and let out a stream of frustrated air. "I was right. Something had spooked the guys. He brought in some sort of psychic to take the curse off the house." He let out a forced laugh. "Can you believe this shit?"

"No, I can't . . . So he sent you her number?"

Myron picked up his phone and scrolled through his messages. "Not yet. Says he'll send it when he gets into the office tomorrow. In the meantime, what about that security system? Did you make some calls?"

"Yeah," she muttered, shutting her eyes. "They can't get here until Monday."

"You call anyone else?"

"No, Myron. I did not call anyone else," she spat. "If you want to call someone else, be my fucking guest. Okay?"

Her venom made him flinch.

"You're just upset," he said more to himself than to her. "Don't worry, honey. We'll figure this out. I'll take tomorrow off so you don't have to be here alone. We'll get a security system installed and the locks changed. It'll be fine. I promise."

"No. It's not going to be *fine*. What are we going to do about this house, Myron?"

"Hey. According to Glenda, stigmas on properties usually vanish after a few years. It's going to be okay. All of that is ancient history."

He patted her knee, and she gave him an unconvinced smile for the effort, which fell the instant he looked away. She stared blankly out the window into the backyard and saw the white cat perched on a fence post.

It was watching the house.

36

Later that night, Hunter still hadn't come home. Myron fed his wife another martini and headed up the back stairs to investigate what she'd found and ferret out any intruders—real or imagined.

There was no sign of damage to the attic door hardware. There was no sign of anyone lurking in any of the rooms or closets. Myron studied the attic lockset again, wondering if Margot was being entirely honest about what had happened. *Is she taking her meds? Is she losing it?*

Still, he called a locksmith and left a message. "We need an estimate to change out the locksets for a 1922 house. Please give me a call so we can schedule something in the next few days. It's urgent."

The newspapers up in the attic proved Margot wasn't being hysterical, at least about one part of her story. Myron stared at the dark stain on the bathroom floor where little Walter had died and shook his head. *Six years old.* Memories of Hunter at that age ran through his mind. Hunter laughing. Hunter playing with toys. Hunter beaming with all the golden starlight promise of the very young. Heartbreaking in every way.

Myron found the gun right where Margot had promised it would be. Lifting the silver-plated pistol into his hand, Myron aimed it at the far wall, squinting one eye down the sight, imagining what it would be like to pull the trigger. The chamber turned out to be empty. He counted the four loose bullets and put the gun back into the cigar box. He'd promised Margot he'd "take care of it." All she'd done was nod. It was an act of wifely submission so rare he'd blinked twice.

As he stood there at the top of the attic steps with the cigar box in hand, a faint melody drifted toward him. It came from two stories below. He followed the phantom sound down to the front entryway, but it slipped away from his ear.

"Hon?" he asked softly.

There was no answer.

The muffled voices of the television in the den muttered softly back and forth. He turned a slow circle and noticed the bleeding roses on the hall table, their perfume thick and heavy. He flipped on the chandelier overhead and examined the red petals more closely.

Margot sat curled in a corner of the couch, nursing her drink, ignoring the home-improvement show glowing in front of her. *Hunter, where are you? Are you okay? We have to get you out of here before something happens to you. My God, that poor little boy . . .*

Myron set the cigar box and the gun inside it down on the built-in mahogany shelf and poured himself another scotch. After downing half of it, he pulled open one of the drawers and placed the box inside. *Until I can figure out what to do,* he told himself.

He settled down on the other end of the sofa and patted Margot's knee. "So . . . who were the flowers from?"

The haze cleared from her eyes. "What?"

"The roses. In the hall. They're pretty. Secret admirer?" He raised his eyebrows at her. He didn't mention what he'd seen on her laptop or any of his suspicions. He kept all that hidden as he waited for her answer.

The question gave her a moment's pause, but there was no knowing twinkle in his eye to tell her he'd sent them, just a vague sadness and a touch of something else. *Jealousy?* she wondered, then quickly dismissed the thought. She let out a cheerless laugh. "I wish. My mom. I guess she felt bad for not sending us a housewarming gift."

"That was nice of her." He smiled for her benefit. If she'd been paying closer attention, she would have noticed his jaw tighten ever so slightly.

"I guess." She downed her martini and set it on the coffee table. With her other hand, she disarmed him of his drink and then buried her face against his neck. "Will you hold me?"

He opened his arms and kissed the top of her forehead. She nestled in where she couldn't see the hard line of his mouth or the anger flashing behind his eyes along with images of Margot's naked flesh on a computer screen. *I'm a married woman.*

After he'd locked all the doors, after he'd assured her that Hunter would come back, after Margot had passed out from her third martini, after Myron had taken the last of his white pills and drifted into the abyss, a shadow crept into their bedroom. It hovered over them, watching them sleep.

Margot's brow furrowed, but the alcohol kept her from waking.

Myron didn't feel a thing.

37

The Klussman Family
September 15, 1990

Frannie Klussman slept through the flashing lights that came in the early hours that morning and the sound of police cars gathering across the street. The sounds bled into the white noise of the ambulances and buses that passed along Lee Road day after day.

Hours later, she sat at the kitchen table with Bill, drinking her morning coffee. Her eyes were red and swollen from the night before. The fine lines of her hands and the gaps under her fingernails were stained red and black with Benny's blood and dirt from the front yard. The memory of her son banging his head against the sidewalk outside replayed itself in her tired gaze over and over.

He had a pretty bad seizure last night, was all she'd told the home health aide. She'd said nothing about Benny's escape from the house.

Bill had assured her when he arrived that morning that stitches weren't necessary, but he'd recommended she take him to the hospital just to be sure. Frannie's lips had pressed together at the advice. The hospital would ask questions she didn't want to answer. *Let's see how it looks tonight.*

After a few prolonged moments of silence, Bill said, "I'm real sorry I wasn't here last night. I should have stayed."

"Oh. It's not your fault." He would surely have called the social worker if she'd told him the whole story. "He just had a bad dream."

"You don't have to do this alone." Bill patted a spot on the table next to her hand. "There's places he can go. Places that will keep him safe, Ms. Klussman."

She shook her head violently. "They'll keep him drugged up like a vegetable. They'll keep him in restraints. That's what they did to him the last time. You've seen what they do. I can't just let him live like that . . . what kind of mother would leave her baby in a place like that? I can't! I just—"

A knock at the door cut her words off. She stood up, and so did Bill.

"You want me to answer it?"

She wiped the tears from her swollen eyes and shook her head. "No. You drink your coffee. I'm fine."

On weak legs, she staggered through the kitchen to the dusty foyer and looked out one of the tall leaded glass windows flanking the front entrance. A police officer stood on the other side. Frowning, she opened the door.

"Good morning, ma'am." The officer flashed an apologetic smile and his badge. *Shaker Heights Police Department.* His name was a blur. "Do you mind if I ask you a couple of questions?"

Frannie reflexively glanced over her shoulder at the stairs behind her before stepping out onto the front porch in her bathrobe. Benny hated strangers and loud noises and any disturbance to his daily routine. A barking dog could send him into a seizure. She quietly shut the door behind her. "What's this about?"

Several police cars were gathered out in the street beyond the trees and bushes that shielded the house from the outside world. Frannie's gaze fixed on them a minute and then the officer on her doorstep.

He took out a clipboard and made a note of her house number. "Are you Frances Klussman?"

"Yes?" She swallowed hard, surveying the flashing lights with a growing sense of dread.

"I just need to ask you a few questions."

"What's this about?" she tried again. Panic took root in her stomach. She squeezed the door handle to keep her knees locked.

"I'm sorry to tell you that a young girl was killed last night."

Her back pressed against the door, the cherub face of the bronze knocker cold and hard between her shoulder blades. "Oh my God! Here?"

"Across the street." He motioned to the large house on the other side of the road. Yellow tape had been strung across the sidewalk. A team of police officers had scattered throughout the yard, behind and in front of the tall hedge. "Did you hear anything unusual last night between the hours of eleven and one a.m.?"

She shook her head slowly. *Benny. Benny outside on the sidewalk.* Across the street, a policeman was hunched down over the spot where she'd found him slamming his head against the concrete. *Dried blood.* "No. Not that I can think of."

"No screaming? No loud noises?"

A young girl was killed last night.

Her hand gripped the long cast-bronze door handle harder. "No. I was asleep. The television was on in my room, but nothing woke me up."

The policeman made notes on his clipboard. "Anyone else live here?"

"Just my son, but he's . . . he's mentally disabled. He, um." Her voice broke with fresh tears at having to say these things out loud. "He can't speak. He doesn't really leave the house."

The officer didn't look up from his clipboard. "Can I speak to him, Ms. Klussman?"

A trickle of blood seeped out of her palm onto the scrolled bronze door handle. A burr had dug into her skin, keeping her upright, keeping the shriek out of her voice and her legs steady. "He's asleep, I'm afraid. He, uh . . . Sorry, it's been a tough night. He had another seizure last night. We had to sedate him. You can get his medical records from the Cleveland Clinic. Benjamin Klussman. He's twenty-four years old."

The officer looked up from his notes, his expression softening. "I'm sorry to hear that, ma'am. Were both of you home all night last night?"

"Yes."

"Did you see any strange people or strange cars around here in the last week?"

"Not that I can think of." She shook her head again and kept squeezing pain into her palm. *A young girl died here last night.* "My God. Who? Who was she?"

"High school student. From the Fernway neighborhood a few blocks over. We can't release specifics just yet. Have you noticed a young girl riding her bike around this neighborhood late at night in recent weeks? Thin. Pretty. Ten-speed bike?"

Frannie turned her head ever so slightly toward her house and its many eyes looking out over the street. Benny's window sat just over her shoulder. "I can't say I have, but we go to bed pretty early here."

"Is there a Mr. Klussman I can talk to?"

She let out a breath of a laugh. "No. He left five years ago. I think he's over in Lakewood now? You could try to reach him, but . . . he doesn't come to visit Benny."

The policeman nodded, making another note. He took a respectful pause before asking, "I noticed a second car in the driveway?"

"That's our home health aide, Bill. He comes to help out with Benny."

"Was he here last night?"

"No. He comes in the mornings to help. He got here around eight. Would you like to speak with him?" She shifted her weight against the door as casually as she could manage. Her heart pounded against the wood. Bill might talk about what had happened the night before. The blood. The laundry. Benny's violent streak. *It can't be Benny's fault. Can it?* The bruises on Frannie's ribs sent an almost imperceptible shudder through her. Benny had kicked her three days earlier. Her body was a map of old wounds.

What if someone saw me dragging Benny into the house? The thought hung like a gasp in the doorway.

Bill sat in the kitchen, doing the crossword puzzle. He didn't like to meddle in Frannie's business. That's what he'd told his wife on the kitchen phone that morning while Frannie had slept. He'd found the bloody laundry and hadn't known whether to call someone else. *She doesn't want the social worker to come . . . I can't do nothin' about it. Isn't my business . . . they don't pay me enough for that.* But then he'd hung up and lowered his head in prayer for her and poor Benny.

Frannie motioned toward the house and Bill, a limp offer to open the door for the policeman.

"No. That shouldn't be necessary right now. We may have to come back to talk more. Would that be alright?"

No. No. NO. "Of course. Do they know who did this?" Her eyes wandered across the road again to where the forensics team was hard at work collecting samples of Benny's blood.

He took the horror in her voice as a natural reaction to the news. "Not yet. But don't you worry, ma'am. We've got Shaker's finest on the case. We're bringing in forensics from the county. Whoever it was won't get away with this. I can promise you that." He flashed a toothy grin that older women like her were meant to find charming. He couldn't have been more than twenty-five years old. The fact that he was the same age as her son made his smile almost unbearable.

She bowed her head and nodded, hiding her face. A drop of blood fell from her hand onto the sandstone stoop. The boy cop didn't notice.

"Thank you for your time, ma'am, and I'm sorry to hear about Benny. You know they say the good Lord never gives us more than we can handle. You have a good day now."

She didn't dare move while the young man strolled down the front walk. She didn't move as he crossed the sidewalk past the bushes and tall silver maple to the next house. She didn't move as he knocked on the door a hundred feet away.

"Good morning, ma'am. Mind if I ask you a few questions . . ."

She listened to the interview, still gripping the door. The same questions came one by one. Her next-door neighbor's response was, "Oh my God! You have to be kidding me! Was it gangs? Oh, those poor parents!"

Frannie didn't move until she heard the answer to the next question: "No. We didn't hear anything. Hon? Did you hear anything strange last night?"

They hadn't seen anything either.

Only after the policeman had moved on and out of earshot did Frannie let go of the bronze door handle. The scratch in her palm ran in a jagged line. She cupped the pooling blood and headed back inside.

"Who was that?" Bill asked, looking up from his puzzle. He cared about her despite his best efforts. *Ms. Klussman is the loneliest person I've ever seen.*

"What?" Frannie grabbed a paper towel for her cut hand, keeping her back to Bill so he wouldn't see the blood. Bill would find out. They'd all find out eventually. She just couldn't face it yet.

"At the door. Who was it? Cops?"

She nodded into the sink.

"I saw them when I pulled up this morning. What'd they want? There a car accident out there or something?"

"No. It . . . some girl died. They're knocking on all the doors in the neighborhood."

He stood up at the odd sound in her voice and walked over to her, studying her shock-white face with a nurse's eye. The paper towel in her fist was turning red at the edges. "You don't look so good. Maybe you should go lie down."

"Yes. You're probably right. I should."

She headed up the back stairs. *This isn't happening. It can't be.* Benny's fists swung at her in her mind. Her hand flew to the scar, the puncture along the side of her neck where he'd inadvertently stabbed her with a pencil. He'd been hospitalized for almost a year after that incident. *They'll take him away forever now.* The blood rushed out of her head.

"Whoa." He caught her as her knees buckled from under her. "Take it easy. You're just tired, Ms. Klussman. Let's get you to bed."

Bill helped her up the stairs and into her room.

Down at the other end of the hall, Benny's brow furrowed in his sleep. His face screwed up in terror at the nightmare playing in his mind and memories of a girl screaming somewhere outside.

38

The Spielman Family
August 9, 2018

A little before midnight, a key slid into the side door of the house next to the basement stairs. The lock pins turned until they landed with a metallic click. Hunter stood outside and listened for a solid minute to the hum of the refrigerator and the sound of his own breath against the wood.

Still not trusting the house, he pressed his nose to the glass and scanned the dark basement steps in front of him and the sliver of kitchen he could see through the basement doorway on his right. The lights were off. Turning the handle with the faintest of squeaks, Hunter nudged the door open just a crack and waited. Then an inch. Then a foot. His mother's enormous kitchen stood empty.

He waited another minute before closing the door behind him and sliding the bolt back into place.

Leaving his size 13 shoes on the basement landing next to the door, he padded out in socks onto the cold marble tiles, then froze. *Is that a footstep upstairs?* The rainfall cascade of water down a pipe in the wall told him someone had just flushed a toilet upstairs. Then more footsteps. Then nothing.

It was his mother shuffling back to bed, half-asleep. Margot crawled under the covers for a few more fitful hours. Next to her, Myron lay curled up on the far edge of the bed, his back to his wife. *Roll over, Myron. You're breathing on me again.*

After the toilet stopped running, Hunter found the courage to move. He opened a pantry cupboard and grabbed one of the plastic shopping bags Margot hoarded there and began to fill it with granola bars, chips, juice pouches. Like a good thief, he was careful not to empty any box, lest it be noticed. Once his bag was full, he risked opening the refrigerator. In the white glow of the appliance, he stuffed whole slices of cheese and ham into his mouth, barely leaving enough room to chew.

A creak in the floor directly above him caught him midswallow. He slowly closed the door to the fridge and backed away, studying the ceiling as though a specter might float down through one of the recessed light fixtures Max had cut through the plaster.

Another rush of water came through the pipes overhead, this time closer to the bedroom over the garage. Hunter frowned up at the ceiling. No one had slept in the guest suite since they'd moved in. *Who's there?* he wondered. The sound of running water stopped.

Spooked, Hunter grabbed the bag of stolen food off the floor. Chips rustled. Plastic baggies crackled. Cringing at the sound, he slipped into the basement stairwell and closed the door to the kitchen with the softest of clicks.

Imaginary feet pounded across the ceiling toward the back stairs. The phantom intruder rushed through the kitchen, reaching for the handle, flinging Hunter down the basement steps right onto his back. Teeth at his neck. Claws through his shirt.

But the house stood still.

Next to where he stood on the basement stair landing, the side door flanked the driveway. He pulled aside the lace curtain. The driveway was empty. The house next door was dark. He flipped on the light bulb at the foot of the basement stairs.

Carrying his looted plunder and shoes, he staggered down the flight of steps into the cold air pooling over the cement floor. He set his bag down inside his parents' pretentious wine room. Several lower-cost bottles sat in an open case on the floor. *Thanks for the two-buck chuck,* his father had laughed into his phone when the gift had come in the mail.

Hunter grabbed a cheap bottle and unscrewed the cap. He took a whiff of the acrid, thin wine, then a large swig. It went down like acid, but he drank another gulp anyway. It had been a long, terrible day. After a few more sips, his shoulders loosened a bit, and his heart rate slowed to a more manageable pace.

Exhaustion hit him with the buzz of the wine. He slumped against the wall of the cellar and ate a granola bar. He pressed his forehead to his knees. He'd come back despite his father looking at him as though he were a drug addict and a thief, despite the intruder his camera had caught in the hallway. He had nowhere else to go.

He lifted his head and stared at the far wall as though he could see her standing there. Whatever she was.

"I don't believe in ghosts," Hunter whispered.

He put the cap back on the wine and stood up. Over in the storage closets on the other side of the stairs, his mother kept skis and camping equipment that looked as though it had never been used. He pulled out two sleeping bags, unrolling one on top of the other onto the wine room floor. It felt safer in there, he decided. Four walls and a door. Out of sight from anyone or anything that might come along while he slept.

The thought made him glance back at the far door at the other end of the basement. Clenching his teeth, he crept over to it and looked out the window into the backyard six steps up. Blue shadows of trees and a sliver of moon hung beyond the dirty glass. A flash of headlights lit between the houses as a car turned down South Woodland a hundred yards away. In the bloom of light, Hunter saw something behind the trees. *The shape of a person? A deer?* He squinted, but the car had passed, leaving everything darker than before. He grabbed the loose, rusty door chain, forcing it into its track with a rattling scrape. He gave the empty yard another scan before walking back to his makeshift bed.

Inside the wine cellar, Hunter closed the slatted wood door, wishing it had a lock. Slivers of yellow light streamed in through the open gaps between the boards, and he was glad he'd left the light burning out in the main room. Still scared, he placed the half-drunk bottle of wine at the foot of the door as a makeshift booby trap. He had no idea what he would do if the intruder tipped it over in the night, he realized.

He pulled the old-fashioned straight razor from his pocket and opened the blade. For good measure, he grabbed another bottle of cheap wine to keep at hand just in case he needed to bludgeon something to death. He tested the heft of the bottle in his hand with little to no conviction. With nothing left to do but wait, he lay himself down and dropped almost immediately into the abyss of sleep.

Hunter didn't hear the approaching footsteps or see the light go out with a sharp click.

39

The Martin Family
August 12, 2016

"What are you doing in here, son?"

A flashlight blinded poor Toby, curled up in the corner of the basement storage room. The voice belonged to a police officer. "Everyone's been looking for you."

The small boy recoiled from the light and the man holding it. His face was smudged with dirt. His clothes were filthy. He'd been hiding in the basement for the past two days. He'd been running from the authorities ever since the strange woman had delivered the horrifying news.

We've found a new home for you, Toby. A really nice family can't wait for you to come and meet them.

But this is my home. I want to stay with Ava! Where is she?

Of course, it wasn't up to him or the policeman. It was up to the computers. It was up to the teachers at his school and the rules and regulations about children in unsafe homes. Not even Mama Martin could save him. An eviction notice from the bank had been posted on the front door in January.

The policeman grabbed the boy by the arm. "C'mon, son. Let's not make this harder than it has to be."

"But I can't leave. Don't make me go." The boy began to cry big ugly tears as his heart crumbled in his chest. "This is my home. I live here."

Papa Martin had died a year and a half earlier, and nothing had been right since. Mama Martin had stopped eating. She'd stopped getting the mail. She'd stopped going to work. She'd stopped washing Toby's clothes and making his lunches. She had taken to spending hours up in the attic, talking with herself. *I don't know what to do anymore, Clyde. God, please tell me what to do. It wasn't supposed to happen like this . . .*

"Mrs. Martin isn't here now. She doesn't own this house anymore. The bank does. You know this. She's going to the hospital, where she can get the help she needs, and she wants you to be safe."

Toby had heard her screaming upstairs when the police broke down the door.

"It's against the law for you to be here. A boy like you needs a home and supervision." The man was losing patience, and Toby could hear the bomb ticking in his voice. It was the third time they'd come to collect him from the house. "You're trespassing here, son."

The man wasn't wrong. The house wasn't safe for a child his age anymore. The doctors had given Mrs. Martin pills to cope with her grief. Medicated, she'd slept all the time. She'd locked him in his room once and forgotten about him for an entire day. Then there was the night the ambulance had come for her, and the next day, social work ers had come for him. That was over a year ago.

He'd returned to Rawlingswood three nights later under the cover of darkness, shaken and bruised, looking for his sister. Every few months, he came back.

"But I belong here. I want my sister. I want Ava," he whispered, even though he knew it wouldn't do any good. "Why can't I stay with her?"

Nobody had been able to officially locate his sister, but the officer didn't say that. "We have to go, kid. You can't stay here. Now, we can do this the hard way or the easy way. Your choice." The policeman kept his flashlight trained on the boy's fallen face. A pistol hung at the man's side along with a pair of handcuffs.

The wavering light in the boy's eyes went out. They'd never listen. He pulled himself to his feet and let the large man drag him out of the cellar and up the stairs. Toby debated yanking his arm free and running away but thought better of it. He'd find a way back, he told himself. He always did.

Behind them, in the farthest corner of the basement, a shadow stood hidden, watching, trembling with tears. It was the shape of a girl.

40

The Spielman Family
August 10, 2018

The dull *tink tink tink* of a glass wine bottle sliding against the concrete floor pried open Hunter's eyes. The room was cold and dark. Too dark.

He bolted up and blinked to get his bearings. He was in his parents' wine cellar. The events of the previous day shuffled back into place. He'd run away. Sort of. No one knew he was there. As he squinted in the dark, a rectangle of gray stood against the black. The door to the wine room was open.

The feeling of someone hovering nearby sent him shrinking against the wooden wine rack to his left. His mouth dropped as if to speak, but nothing came out, not even air. A shadow moved into the open door. It was the shape of a girl. A wisp of white fabric.

DeAD GiRL.

Rabbit eyed and drained of blood, he shook his head. *I'm dreaming,* the wish whispered between his ears, along with a jumble of others. *Please. Away. Don't. Not me. Go.*

Her shadow slipped into the corner of the wine cellar, where her shape blended with the walls until it had all but vanished.

Hunter struggled to see in the dark. The wine buzzed around his head as he strained to hear the thing breathing, but there was nothing but the dripping of the faucet in the next room. Still, he felt it. The magnetic pulse of another being stood there, three feet away. He felt the cold concrete for his razor and came up empty.

"Who are you?" he whispered into the dark. *What are you?* "Are you . . . real?"

A soft breath of laughter fell through the silence.

The connection between his mind and body severed at the sound, and the boy sat there trapped in his own quaking skin. *Help! Somebody! Help us!* His rabbit eyes focused on the open door. *Run.*

The thing picked his booby trap up off the floor and unscrewed the cap. Wet gulps followed. Obscenely loud and threatening in the dark, the sounds sent thrills of terror through the cornered deer that was Hunter. *Blood. Vampires. Teeth.*

He was stunned still.

Neither fight nor flight could move him. He could barely breathe. Backed against the wine, tangled in a sleeping bag, blinded in the dark, what could he do? The thought of his razor finally sent his numbed hand fumbling over the concrete again. Slowly, slowly, so the poltergeist wouldn't see.

His fingers finally connected with cold glass, winding themselves around the neck of a bottle. Bash. Bludgeon. Kill. Die. *Am I going to die?* His eyes drifted on their own toward the ceiling with a hopeless hope. *Mom? Dad?*

The warm smell of his mother's sugary vanilla perfume drifted down to where he cowered on the floor, holding his bottle. But it wasn't her. His mother would've turned on the light. His mother would've yelled.

"Wh . . . why are you here?" he breathed.

The feel of a soft hand brushed against his cheek and sent his bottle clanking to the floor. "I need your help." The voice warmed his ear, soft and female.

He jerked away from it. "My help?"

The shadow moved over him, hovering. "I want to be friends. I've been watching you, Hunter. You could use a friend like me."

The scent of wine on her breath and the warmth of her skin only inches away from his brought him back to his senses. He raised a finger and connected with the solid flesh of her arm. Thin and soft. *Not a ghost.* "Who are you? What are you doing here?"

The shadow of her nestled down onto the sleeping bag beside him. "Are you going to drink that?" She tapped the bottle on the floor.

Fumbling, he offered it up to the shape of a girl sitting there in the dark. She took it and cracked the seal on the top, slowly unscrewing the cap. The sound of her drinking came much quieter now, softer, prettier. The glass bottle then pressed back into his hand, and he accepted it. Dry mouthed with terror, Hunter took a long swig. Blood rushed back into his limbs. *Vampires don't drink wine. She's just a girl.*

A new fear took hold. *This girl will think I'm a total pussy.*

"Seriously," he said, desperate now to sound like a normal teenager confronted by a total stranger. An intruder. "What the fuck is going on? How'd you get in here?"

"I live here," she whispered, taking the bottle back.

"What do you mean, you *live* here?"

"I mean this is my home."

"But . . . *we* live here."

A little laugh twinkled in the dark.

"What's your name?"

The shape of a girl turned toward him, revealing a silhouette of her face, fine and delicate. "Does it really matter?"

"How are we going to be friends if I don't even know your name?"

She sighed. "Ava."

"Okay, Ava. Nice to meet you. What the hell are you doing here?"

"What is anyone doing here?"

Hunter let out a frustrated stream of air and took another gulp of wine for courage. "Enough with the fucking games! Why are you here?"

"Waiting. Like you."

"Waiting," he repeated. *Waiting to leave? Waiting to go off to college and start your life?* "Waiting for what?"

"You wouldn't understand."

He frowned at the shape of her next to him. She suddenly seemed so small and young. "How old are you? Does anyone know you're here?"

She exhaled another laugh. "Don't bother calling social services, okay? I'm nineteen."

"How long have you lived in this house?" Hunter measured his words. He took another swig of wine. No sudden movements. No accusations. Just friendly questions. He shifted ever so slightly, wishing he could pull out his phone and record her.

"Since I was nine years old."

"But the Martins lived here. They bought the house in 1994. I've seen the property records." He was going to piss her off, he realized, and he tried to ease up. "I mean, I didn't think they had kids."

The shadow of her moved and shifted. A cigarette lighter flared up, casting half her face in a flash of yellow light as she lit a cigarette, and then it was gone. He got a good glimpse of her eyes, dark and lifeless as a shark's. After blowing out a plume of smoke, she said, "That doesn't mean kids didn't live here."

"What do you mean? Did they"—*what?* He cringed slightly— "kidnap you?"

"Not exactly." The ember of her cigarette glowed red in the dark. "You smoke?"

"No. Thanks. What happened to your parents?"

"What happened to yours?" Her voice drifted lazily, a little drunk.

"What do you mean?"

"They're a mess. Aren't they?"

"Yeah." Hunter stiffened. "Yeah, I guess they are."

"What happened to your sister?"

"Huh?" The unexpected question made him shrink.

"Your sister. What happened?"

"She, uh . . . she died. Lymphoma." He blinked back a swell of tears he hadn't even known were there. "She was eleven."

"I'm sorry." Ava went silent a moment. "That's why your mother is so sad. And your dad."

"I guess. Yeah." A shiver ran through him. She'd been watching them for weeks, snooping in corners, listening to their every word. *It was her,* he realized. She had broken into his mother's laptop that day. The shape of her sat in a puddle of white silk. *Mom's nightgown.* Margot's face the day she'd ransacked his room flashed in the back of his mind.

"Did Myron really kill that girl? Abigail?" Another cloud of cigarette smoke blew toward him. "The one in Boston?"

Stunned, he sat there a beat before answering. "He didn't *kill* anyone. A patient died of complications. It's really sad, but it happens."

"He's being sued for malpractice, you know. Is that why they moved you all the way to Ohio?"

"I don't know." Hunter felt his agitation building, but he needed to keep her talking. "My dad got this new job. People move all the time."

"You know something's wrong with him, right? He's hiding something." She let that hang in the air a moment and then said, "Your mom is too. What's her story? Besides your sister, I mean."

"Fuck you, okay?" he barked, furious now. "Why are you still here? Clyde Martin died of a heart attack. Maureen went to a hospital."

"You mean she went to a nuthouse."

The wound in her voice softened him just a little. "Yeah. Is she still there?"

"I dunno." Her voice had dropped to almost a whisper. "I don't care."

"Why are you here?"

She ignored the question. "It wasn't a heart attack, you know."

"Who? Mr. Martin?"

"This place killed him."

Hunter's anger fell into confusion. "What?"

"This house is bad for men, for boys. They all die here. Almost every single one. And the women go mad. Did you know that?"

Hunter's mouth went dry. He took another sip of wine before trusting his voice. "I, uh . . . well, Walter Rawlings died here."

"Yeah. Both of them."

"And Clyde. And Niles Gorman."

"Benjamin Klussman disappeared. Did you find anything about him yet?"

"Benny?"

"He disappeared the day after a girl named Katie Green died. Strange, huh?"

DeAD GiRL. BAD BeNNy.

Hunter thought on this a moment. "Did Benny do it?"

"You've seen the writing in the closet, right? The girl was murdered right outside this house. He disappeared the day she was found."

Hunter struggled to string his thoughts together through the buzzing wine and the intoxicating smell of her next to him. "How do you know so much about all of this?"

"I told you. I've lived here for years." She paused a moment and considered him from the shadow beneath the wine rack. "Did you know the Shakers used to speak to the dead?"

"The Shakers?"

"This whole place was a religious commune or cult or whatever. They believed it was heaven on earth. 'The Valley of God's Pleasure.' They'd dance outside in the moonlight until they had visions."

"That's pretty weird."

The ember of her cigarette glowed in the dark. She traced the air with it, making circles. "They believed if you sang and danced inside a ring of trees, you could hear the dead speak."

Pilgrim women twitched through his head. He shook them away. "That sounds like a bunch of bullshit."

"No. It's true. You read about it yourself at the library. I saw you there." The cigarette tip pointed at him.

"You followed me?" He took a breath. "Why? Why do you care about any of this? Why are you here? Why are you stalking us?"

Ava went quiet a minute and finally said, "What if they were right?"

"Right about what?"

"About speaking to the dead."

Hunter held his breath a moment. *She's insane.* "Do, um . . . do you speak to them?"

The shadow of her didn't answer.

"What did you mean earlier? When you said you were waiting? Waiting for what?"

The uncomfortable silence stretched out between them. A deafening sadness that left Hunter utterly disarmed, heartbroken, and then angry. He shifted awkwardly, wondering whether to call the police. Trespassing. Larceny. *Assault?*

"Did you . . . cut Roger? In my mom's bathroom? There was blood. And a razor." He felt the floor again for the razor as he said it. It wasn't there. "He had a bandage on his hand last time I saw him outside the library."

"He cut himself when he tried to grab it from me. He'll be fine." She let out another breathy laugh. "I think I scared him."

Hunter imagined Roger turning at the sight of a strange girl watching him in the mirror, grabbing at the blade, and slicing his skin. *It could've happened like that,* he decided, not wanting to envision the alternative. "He wouldn't tell me what happened."

"You do know he robbed you, right?"

"Yeah. He's an asshole." Hunter furrowed his brow. *Didn't you rob me too?* "Does anybody know you're here but me?"

"No."

"This is messed up, Ava. You shouldn't be here, okay? You need to go. You need help."

"Help from who? They won't believe me." She angrily stubbed the lit end of the cigarette out on the floor. He watched her do it, realizing that he would be blamed for the burn mark and the lingering smell of smoke in the air. "They never do."

"What won't they believe?"

The silence that came in the wake of his question filled his ears and lungs. Resentment gathered around her. She finally said, "Listen. I need your help." A small hand dropped onto his thigh, scattering his thoughts.

"Help? With what?"

Her breath came closer, sweet with wine, falling on his cheek as though she might kiss him. His pulse quickened.

"Can you keep a secret?" she asked.

The heat of her body next to him set every nerve on edge. He breathed in the sweet, smoky smell of her and made a wish. "Maybe."

"You can't tell anyone you've seen me."

Hunter pulled away to consider it. "For how long?"

"Until you leave. Your family needs to leave this house. It doesn't belong to you."

"What do you mean, it doesn't belong to us?"

She ignored the question. "You have to convince them to leave, Hunter. Before it's too late. Tell them you want to go back home to Boston."

"Oh, right. I'm sure they'll just pack right up. What the fuck makes you think they'll listen to me? I've been saying that for weeks. I never wanted to come here." He felt furious and helpless and bewildered all at once. *Before it's too late?*

She stood up, taking the warmth of her body with her. The white silk lit in the doorway. Then a shimmer of long hair. A slim silhouette. "Come home tomorrow. They're worried about you."

"Wait." In all this time, his parents hadn't noticed this strange girl living in the house. They just blamed him for the missing food, the lights being left on, the missing clothes. All along it was her. "If you're gonna stay here, could you maybe . . . stop doing things to get me in trouble?"

"When have you ever been in trouble?" she asked with a bitterness that shamed him. "Get some sleep. They'll be up soon."

Too stunned and confused by their conversation to move, he listened to her light footsteps on the basement stairs. The faint threads of a song drifted down the steps behind her.

An angel whispered in my ear.
The dead, they know, they know you, dear.
Their moonlight sees just like the sun
Nowhere to hide, nowhere to run . . .

41

The Rawlings Family
January 24, 1931

Georgina's ashen face emerged from the stairwell.

Two strangers were smoking cigarettes in her attic. They sat in the rectangle of light outside the bathroom door on cast-off chairs. The strange woman wore only a slip, and the man sat in an undershirt and shorts. Not the specter of her husband. Not the restless dead the old Shaker woman had warned her about. Just strangers.

The sight of them knocked her breath out and nearly sent her tumbling down the steps. She clutched at her neck to find it bare. She was herself wearing nothing but a nightgown.

The hot smell of sweat and smoke chased any thought of ghosts from her mind. There was nothing otherworldly about either of the two people sitting there. Was there? She squinted at them and then at the door to the maid's old bedroom. *Ella,* she thought to herself. *Ella with the keys. Ella let them in.* All the knocks she'd heard at the back door and all the footsteps at night took on a new color in Georgina's mind. Ella had kept it all from her, she realized, and now Ella was sound asleep one floor down.

"Who are you?" Georgina whispered.

"Evenin', ma'am," the sweaty man finally said with a tip of an imagined cap. "Apologies for the noise. We was just talkin.'"

The woman beside him didn't speak. She just smirked at the ghoulish lady of the house and puffed on her cigarette.

"What are you doing here?" Georgina demanded, her feet hovering on the steps, ready to run. "Who are you?"

"Name's Felix. Ange has me watchin' over things. You know, Big Ange?" the surly man asked with a broken grin. He looked more likely to rob the house than watch over anything. "I believe he was a friend of your husband's?"

Georgina's shock and indignation wilted noticeably as she stood there trying to remember. The accountant had referenced "certain creditors" when they'd talked three months earlier, sitting in the parlor. This was after the notice from the bank had come, explaining in cryptic terms that the insurance money had run out. The letter had sat on Walter's desk for weeks with the other unopened bills and invitations. Georgina had refused to read it.

Walter always handled that sort of thing, she'd explained helplessly when the stern-faced accountant showed up at her door.

Walter isn't here now. Is he?

"Forgive me, but I did not know Walter's friends very well. Or his business partners," she said, her voice thin and brittle. Georgina climbed the last two steps on unsteady legs. The warm yellow light beckoned her closer. The water boiling behind the storage-room door bubbled at her ears. She puzzled at the sound and then Ella's room full of crates and boxes she didn't recognize. "What are you doing here?"

"Tendin' the still." The man motioned to the closed door.

"The 'still'?" she repeated.

He stood up in nothing but his unmentionables and opened the door to reveal a complex network of pipes and kettles. A makeshift smokestack had been cut through the far wall. "Ain't exactly legal, but no one's gonna bother it in a nice house like this. Are they?"

Georgina stared at the Frankenstein apparatus churning and steaming. Sacks of sugar were stacked on the floor along with a collection of mason jars filled with homemade liquor. "How long have you been up here?"

Felix took in the full view of the high-society lady in nothing but a thin shift of a nightgown and then forced himself to avert his eyes. "A couple of weeks, I guess. 'Cept this one came along two days ago."

The strange woman flashed a guarded smile at Georgina. Her legs were bare and crossed like a harlot's. The thin shoulder strap of her slip drooped down to her elbow. Georgina immediately assessed her station in life. *Not even proper enough to be a maid.* "You were a friend of Walter's as well?"

"I might've met 'im once or twice." The harlot's lips curled into a slow smile. After a cool appraisal of the older woman standing stiff and thin as an ironing board before her, she added, "Don't take much wonderin' why now, does it?"

Color flushed into Georgina's cheeks for reasons she couldn't quite identify outright. It wouldn't do at all to ask more pointed questions. She could barely form them in her own mind, much less say them out loud. The thought of Walter and this woman together in any context left her speechless. "Well, that's . . . he is not here. Anymore. So I cannot imagine what you are doing here."

Georgina didn't hear little Walter creep up the stairs behind her, peeking over the edge of the floor.

"The boss thought it'd be best if I laid low for a bit." The woman shot her male counterpart a look and puffed on her cigarette until the red coal had burned down to her fingertips, then tossed it into a rusted can. She stood up and pulled her drooping slip strap back onto her shoulder. "Where's the gypsy?"

"The what?" Georgina took a step back. Little Walter ducked into the shadow.

"The old gypsy. The one that locks us up here day and night. Where is she?" Carmen arched a penciled eyebrow.

Felix shifted uncomfortably on his stool. Their argument still lingered in the smoke, hanging thick in the air above them. *I don't care what Ange says. He ain't here, is he? What's to stop us from just takin' that cash over there and catchin' out on a train, huh? Let the gypsy deal with him.*

Carmen's wrist was still red where Felix had grabbed it. *Where exactly we gonna go? Who you think you're coppin' from? Big Ange's got eyes in every town, and I ain't about to get fixed for some little tart.*

She'd slapped him then.

Emboldened, the harlot took a step toward her hostess. "The gypsy sleepin'? How about the little one? He asleep too?"

Georgina lost all color along with her breath. *Little Walter.*

The horrible woman produced a straight razor from her garter belt and snapped it open. "Whattaya say we let 'em sleep, doll? You stay nice and quiet, and they won't be disturbed one bit. Got it?"

The half-naked man took a step toward her. "Take it easy, Carmen."

"Shut up, Felix," she said without even looking at him. She'd figured him for a fool the first moment she saw him sitting there slack jawed, watching the still bubble. *No imagination,* she'd said with a roll of her eyes. "This is between me and Missus Walter here. Ain't it."

Georgina's wild stare darted from the open razor to the brazen grin on the woman's face. She pressed her lips together and nodded.

"Give us the key to the door, hon." Carmen held out her hand.

Georgina looked dumbly down at the brass key in her hand. She'd forgotten it was there at all. With a plea in her eye, she handed it over. *Not Walter. My sweet baby Walter.* The phantom sound of a baby cried deep inside the house. No one heard it but Georgina.

Key in hand, Carmen nodded at her. "Good. Now you tell Big Ange I had to leave. Okay?" With that, she grabbed her bag off the floor and sauntered into Ella's old room. Felix and Georgina watched dumbstruck while she loaded her bag up with cash from the apple crates until it was near bursting.

"Hey. Hey!" Felix barked. "What the hell are we supposed to tell Big Ange about the dough you're takin', huh?"

Georgina turned to him, hopeful that he would know what to do, but it became clear from the sway in his step and the slur in his voice that he'd been sampling the mason jars heavily all night. His foot knocked an empty one over as he staggered toward the harlot, red faced.

Carmen chuckled at him. "What do I care what you tell 'im? Tell 'im you got too drunk to stop me. Tell 'im you were asleep. Tell 'im whatever you gotta tell 'im. I ain't stayin' here no more."

"You know damn well I can't do that." He raised a heavy fist at her, but she easily ducked to the side, where Georgina stood petrified and gaping.

With rough hands, Carmen grabbed the smaller woman by the neck and pressed the blade against her throat. "And you know damn well what will happen if you don't butt out, Felix. Whattaya think Big Ange will miss more? A few thousand or this little safe house? Huh?"

The cold steel against her neck sent Georgina's mind plunging into shock. Locked out, she watched the room as though from outside the attic window. None of it was possible. The harlot in her home, the drunk henchman stumbling around as he tried to contemplate his options. Her detached gaze drifted to the boxes of cash just sitting there in her attic. Enough to pay back all of her husband's debts and then some, she thought, all there right under her roof.

"Just take what you want," she heard herself whisper. All feeling left her limbs as her bones dissolved inside her. *Is this how it feels to die?* she wondered. *To stare up at the world from beneath the ground?* Her mind slipped further down the hole.

"Whoa. Take it easy, girlie. Think. Okay? Think." Sweat had broken out over Felix's forehead. His options were grim. His gun lay in his trousers in the next room. She'd been so clever, so very clever, removing him from them. "This ain't gonna work out for you. Not like this."

Carmen pressed the razor deeper against the poor woman's neck. The sharpened blade broke the surface of Georgina's skin in a shrieking line of pain and a thin trickle of cold blood. "Thanks for the thought, Felix. Now you do what I say or kiss our lady here good night."

"No!" a small voice shouted. Walter bolted out of the stairwell, his little fists flying. "Stop! You leave her alone!"

"Wal-ter," Georgina choked, nearly swooning at the sight of him. Her voice failing, her body falling. Carmen dropped her to the floor and grabbed Walter by the arm.

He swung and kicked and shouted, "Ella!"

"Ain't you a feisty thing?" Carmen wrestled him closer with one hand gripping the razor. Small cuts slashed his flailing hands.

Georgina watched the horrifying scene unfold before her in broken time, her nose pressed to the glass of the moment, unable to move or even speak. *Not my baby. No. NO!*

"Listen, lady, I'm gettin' outta here." The thrashing limbs of the little boy bucked wildly as she talked. "Now, I want you to tell me wh—"

Tenacious little Walter stomped the harlot's foot. He dropped his weight violently to escape from under her arm and caught the sharp blade square in the neck.

Walter!

The boy's eyes went wide as the steel sank into his skin.

"Oh, Jesus!" Felix hissed. "Carmen. What have you done?"

42

The Spielman Family
August 10, 2018

The attic window glowed yellow against the pale morning sky. The servant's bathroom peered out from its perch below the gabled roof at Hunter standing in the driveway.

He backed himself across the pavement until his backpack hit the neighbor's fence. A shadow moved across the ceiling. A shape shifted in the corner of the window. The invisible strings of someone watching followed him all the way to the front door.

The wine he'd drunk the night before pounded in his temples. The memory of her shadow in the doorway, the sound of her laugh, and her hot breath on his neck twisted through his addled brain.

Can you keep a secret? her voice repeated as he opened the front door.

"Hey, Mom? I'm home!" His voice drifted up the front stairs and down the empty hallway. No one answered. "Mom?"

He found her sitting in the den, eyes glazed with her hangover. Myron had gone out an hour earlier to look into a home security system. *Will you be okay for a bit while I'm out?*

"You're back," she said flatly, not looking at him.

"Uh. Yeah. Sorry, I was just . . ." He hadn't thought of a good explanation. *I was just what?*

She stood up and floated past him toward the kitchen. "You must be hungry. Have you eaten?"

"No. I'm starving." *Am I?* He couldn't feel his stomach. Following her, he made a concerted effort not to look toward the basement door. He dropped his backpack at the edge of the kitchen as quietly as he could. He sank onto a stool at one of the enormous marble slabs in the middle of the room and waited for the yelling to start.

Margot went through the motions of making a sandwich as though in a trance. The rage and fear she'd felt trapped in the hot attic the day before were nowhere to be found. Relief and exhaustion took their place as she pulled ingredients out of the fridge. Her baby was home just like she'd prayed in her head. But was he? The filthy teenager at the counter was more a stranger than her baby. She stopped to look at him.

Hunter tensed. *What?*

Her little boy was gone. The sad realization struck her as it had every single time she'd noticed a change in him. Every inch he grew and every facial hair that sprouted were reminders of the boy he could no longer be. *Lost. All of it just slipped away.* She turned away again to grab the bread.

The yelling didn't come. It was too easy. Hunter's muscles unwound one by one as it seemed more and more that the whole thing would blow over. His eyes roamed the kitchen awkwardly as the silence between them widened and deepened.

The calendar showcasing their ski trip to Aspen last year hung by itself on the bulletin board over the "home office" desk next to the refrigerator. Margot looked flushed and vibrant in her hot pink parka against the snow. The month of July had come and gone, but it still hung there forgotten. No one in the family really used the calendar.

Not with their computers and phones constantly at the ready. Hunter had nothing to put on a calendar anyway. Nothing except . . .

Oh.

His eyes darted from an empty square on the calendar to his mother's back. *July 29.* It had been the previous week, and he hadn't said a thing. *I'm a terrible son.*

He wished desperately that he knew the right thing to say to her. The thing that would tell her, *I'm sorry she's gone. I'm sorry it wasn't me. I'm sorry I can't fix it. I'm so, so sorry . . .* But a part of him wasn't sorry. A part of him was sick to death of having to feel sorry all his life. A part of him hated her for not just loving him instead and for the shame he felt for living. The story wrote itself over his face. His storkish frame sagged with it. *It should've been me that died. You wish it had been me.*

"You have fun last night?" His mother's voice fell dully against the marble.

"Sure," he answered, and then he remembered he'd run away. He was in trouble. He was a bad son. "Yeah. I, uh, met up with some friends. I'm sorry . . . I should've called."

Margot looked up at her perfect mosaic backsplash at the word *friends.* Her eyes fell back to the bread on the plate. "Yeah. You should've."

She turned and slapped the plate in front of him. Ham sandwich, cheese, no mustard. The way he'd liked it when he was little.

"Thanks," he said and tried to catch her eye with a smile. *Is she okay?* he wondered. Fear lurked around the edges of his face—a wariness, like something bad had happened, a shoe had dropped. "Hey, Mom?"

"Hmm?" Margot looked up with feigned interest from the other side of the island. Her eyes were bloodshot and heavy.

"Do you, um . . ." He lost his nerve and changed tack. "Do you know anything about the people that used to live here? You know, before us?"

"Not really. Why?" She narrowed her eyes at him, wondering what strange things he'd seen and heard in the house. The memory of the intruder and a voice singing inched up her back. *Has he heard it too?*

"Just something that kid Roger said." He tried to sound casual. "I did some hunting through the county records and found that the last owners were Clyde and Maureen Martin. Do you think they had kids?"

"I have no idea, honey. The contractors found some unopened mail . . . I think your father put it somewhere. Let me go check."

Her brow furrowed as she went into the den. *Should I say something about the intruder?* she wondered. *No. No need to panic or over-react. It will just upset him, and besides . . . I didn't actually see anyone.*

Myron had tried to calm her nerves again that morning. *The security system will be monitored by a twenty-four-hour service. We'll be fine.*

"I want to leave this house, Myron," she whispered to herself.

A scrap of paper on the desk blotter caught her eye as she rifled through the files in the drawer. *Max's Smudging Psychic Lady—Madame Nala* and a phone number scrawled in Myron's agitated hand. She picked it up and read it again before putting it in her pocket.

Hunter had managed to swallow half his sandwich before she came back.

"Here," she said, handing him a manila folder. "You can look through this if you'd like. What's with this interest in the house all of a sudden? First the dead Shakers and now the last owners?"

He shrugged as nonchalantly as he could. "I dunno. Just curious. This place is kinda weird."

"Yeah. I suppose it is." She didn't say more about her own thoughts on the house. The newspaper stories of the little boy murdered in the attic turned her stomach. *How could a mother do such a thing?* She put on a brave smile for her son's sake and said, "Since you're doing all this research, maybe you could write one of your college essays about it."

"Yeah. Maybe . . . I think I'm going to go shower." He needed one, no doubt. If Margot had been paying attention, she would've noticed the grime of the basement staining his hands and clothes and the guilt dirtying his face.

"Okay, sweetie."

Relieved to be away from her and the specter of his dead sister and the weight of his lying, Hunter grabbed his backpack and headed up the stairs. He paused in the hallway, listening, scanning the dark corners, eyeing the closed doors. *She could be anywhere.* In a house big enough for twelve people, it was no wonder they'd never noticed.

Your family has to leave this house . . . before it's too late.

Down in the kitchen, Margot didn't move. She stared at the half-eaten sandwich as though in a trance. The sound of water raining down a hidden pipe broke the spell. She glanced up the back stairs and then to the empty barstool, opening her mouth to shout at her son, then shutting it without a sound.

Hunter's shower drummed the floor above her.

She dumped the sandwich into the sink and wandered into the foyer. The grand staircase loomed over her, somber and still. It felt like a funeral parlor. The blood red roses bloomed lasciviously from their table. Taunting her. Displaying a glimpse of pollen here, dropping petals there. Stripping naked, slowly, slowly, slowly.

The phantom voice of a man breathed in her ear. *I don't live very far.*

With an exhale of utter disgust, she grabbed the fat bouquet by the throat. Yanked from their vase, the stems dripped dirty water onto the floor as she stormed back into the kitchen, slapped open a cupboard, and shoved the inexplicable roses into the trash. Thorns ripped at the plastic liner as she shoved the display down to the bottom of the can and slammed the door shut.

Drops of red hit the gleaming white floor. *Tap. Tap.*

Margot stared at the color blooming on the marble tiles dumbly until it registered that it was blood. Blood dripped from her torn palm down to the floor. She watched it fall with an unhealthy fascination. She squeezed her fist into a ball of pain, eyes bright and clear for the first time that morning. The pain felt good. So good. So much better than before. She opened her palm and studied the punctures as though wishing for more. A block of sharp knives sat on the marble slab three feet away, waiting for their chance. She let out a long hiss of breath and shook her head.

Staggering back to her feet, she grabbed a paper towel and watched the white fibers turn brilliant crimson in her palm. The blossoms of red on the floor kept spreading into the crystalline depths of the marble, finding the minute cracks in the grout, seeping down to the wood below.

The shadow of a girl watched from the back stairwell, but when Margot turned her head, she was gone.

43

Hunter ran the hot water until the bathroom clouded over with steam. After a full minute's debate, he cracked open the door and listened for his mother's footsteps. Satisfied, he stepped out into the hallway and tiptoed across the carpet runner to the attic stairs.

Down below, his mother's feet padded away from the kitchen toward the den, and he took the chance to creak open the attic door. One excruciating step at a time, he made his way up to the third floor. His head slowly emerged between the rails into the empty room. "Hello?" he whispered.

The morning sun streamed into the long expanse through the dusty windows. The bathroom light at the far end burned yellow through the open door. But there was no one inside. He reached the top of the steps and scanned the main room for signs of life. One of the crawl space doors stood ajar between the window dormers. Fixated, he crossed the room and swung it open.

"Hello?" he whispered into the rafters and the insulation. "Ava?"

Insulated ducts ran under the rafters, carrying cool air to the rooms below. A pile of rags sat a few feet inside the crawl space to his right. To his left lay a little boy's shoe. With its cracked brown leather and moth-eaten laces, the shoe looked nearly as old as the house. He leaned in for a closer look. It belonged to a small child, a boy of maybe five or six years old.

His body was halfway into the crawl space when he heard the attic door close behind him.

He cracked his head on the roof planks, hard. Vision blurred, he extracted himself from behind a knee wall and spun around to face the empty room. "Hello?"

Nothing.

Frustration mixed with the pain as he staggered back to his feet and down the steps. To his relief and near surprise, the door wasn't locked. He swung it open hard, determined to not let some crazy girl frighten him.

The second floor hallway stood empty.

Behind him, the back hall wound around a corner to the guest suite, silent and dark. Along the main hallway, all seven doors were shut. All except the master suite. He crept toward his parents' room. The sight of his mother standing at the front door pushed him back into the shadow of the far wall. He was supposed to be in the shower. He was supposed to be a lot of things. As his mother turned his way, he slipped back into his bathroom and out of sight.

Margot scanned the foyer, the dining room, the entrance to the kitchen, the stairs, the hall above. Someone was there, watching. She was sure of it. But the only sound was Hunter's shower and her angry feet pounding across the wood floor toward the kitchen.

Hunter closed the bathroom door without a sound and rubbed his bruised head. "There is no such thing as ghosts," he said to the clouded shape of himself in the mirror. "Crazy girls? Yes. Ghosts? No."

He defiantly stripped down naked, despite the prickly sense of being stalked, and stepped into the scalding shower. Broad shoulders. Long, gangly legs. Four chest hairs and counting. A smattering of pimples across his back. Patches of dark hair where his limbs met his torso. He ran a bar of soap over all the parts of his body that suddenly seemed foreign to him. As though someone else was watching.

A wisp of cool air fluttered against his back, making him shiver. Outside the steamed glass, a small form stood in the corner next to the sink. Hunter could see nothing through the clouded door. Still, he felt it. On instinct, he smeared the condensation with his hand.

Nothing was there but his own ungainly form in the mirror. The bathroom door stood open an inch. The chill set into his skin as the cold air leaked in.

He shut off the water, grabbed a towel from the rack, and darted out into the hallway.

Still empty.

He raced across the hall to the attic door and listened at the bottom of the stairs for footfalls, for breathing. He heard a cupboard slap closed down in the kitchen. Taking the back steps down two at a time, he hit the cold marble tiles with wet feet to find the room vacant. The glow of the television flickered from the den. His mother, he figured. The ham sandwich sat dejected in the sink.

Red drops of blood dotted the floor.

His breath caught, shocked not just at the red color but that it had been left there to mar his mother's pristine marble. He knelt down and touched a drop with his fingertip. It was still wet. Thin and cold, the blood soaked into his skin, staining it. He lurched up, alarm spreading over his face.

"Mom?" He took off for the den. "Mom? You okay?"

The television glowed from the built-in bookcase where house flippers picked out bathroom tiles on the screen. The couch was empty. The crystal stopper of the liquor decanter lay on its side on the coffee table. The whiskey had been drained.

"Mom?" he called out again, turning toward the front stairs. Sprinting now, he dashed up the red carpet runner to her bedroom.

The door was shut. He pounded on it with his fist. "Mom? You in there?"

There was no answer.

He pressed his ear to the door and heard water running in her bathroom. Alarm turned to panic. *July 29. Blood on the floor.* He pounded again.

"Mom!"

44

The Martin Family
June 13, 2015

"911. What's your emergency?"

"We need an ambulance. Please! She's bleeding!"

"Who is bleeding?"

"Mama Martin. Maureen."

"And what's your name, miss?"

"Just come. She's bleeding to death!"

"Are you in danger?"

"No. Please! Hurry!"

"Is there anyone there with you?"

"No . . ." Papa Martin had died a few months earlier. That had been a 911 call as well. *We need help! He's not breathing!* Ava's voice echoed off the white subway tiles. "It's just us."

"What is the address?"

"14895 Lee Road. Just hurry!"

"I'm sending an ambulance now, hon, but the more you tell me, the more we can help. Understand? Where is she now?"

"The bathroom. Upstairs."

"Okay. Where's she bleeding from?"

"Her wrists."

"Did she cut her wrists?"

A choked sob echoed in the cold, hard room. "I don't know."

"Is she awake?"

"I—um—I'm not sure. No. I don't think so."

"What was the weapon?"

"I'm not sure . . . wait . . . a razor."

"Does she have it with her now?"

"It's on the floor."

"Listen carefully. I need you to kick that razor out of her reach. Okay? Do not pick it up. Understand? Don't touch it."

A tinkling of metal over tiles was followed by a shaky breath. "Okay."

"Now, I want you to see if you can stop the bleeding, alright? The ambulance will be there in five minutes, but we need to try and help her right now. Can you find some towels?"

"Uh. Yeah. Here's one."

"We need two. Okay?"

"Yeah."

"Good. I want you to wrap a towel around her right wrist, tight. Try to tie it into a knot. Alright?"

"Oh, God. It's bleeding so fast. Um . . . okay. I wrapped it, but it won't knot. It won't. It's too thick."

"That's okay. Just tuck the ends under as tight as you can. Okay. Now do the left wrist."

"Okay. Okay. Okay. Oh, Jesus. I don't think she's breathing."

"The ambulance is coming. I want you to elevate her arms over her head. Get them higher than her heart, alright?"

"Okay."

"Good, sweetie. You're doin' good. Is the front door unlocked?"

"Um . . . I don't know."

"Are any doors unlocked?"

"I don't . . . maybe the back door?"

"Okay. Where are you in the house?"

"The second floor. In the bathroom. On the left."

"Alright, you just sit tight, sweetie. They're almost there. You hear them?"

The sound of approaching sirens sent a shudder through the house.

"Yes."

"Okay. Good . . . now I need you to tell me your name, hon."

There was no answer.

"Hello? Are you there?" the operator chirped through the speakerphone sitting on the floor next to the tub. "Hello? . . . Are you okay?"

The tinny voice drifted out the open door and down the long hallways of Rawlingswood.

Two minutes later, men in uniforms burst into the house in a thunder of voices and pounding feet. The girl listened to them come and go as she lay curled inside a closet next to her brother. She whispered in his ear, "Shhh . . . it will be okay. Mama's just not feeling well . . ."

45

The Spielman Family
August 10, 2018

"Mom!" Hunter called again, banging on the door. "Are you okay?"

Margot turned her head toward the sound. She didn't want to see him. Not like this. She swallowed a sob and called out, "Stop! Just stop, Hunter! I'm fine!"

Hunter quieted at the muffled sound of her voice. He slowly lowered his fist but hesitated to leave. She didn't sound fine. He reached for the doorknob but stopped himself. She'd be furious if he barged in.

Margot turned back to her pale reflection in the bathroom mirror and opened her cabinet to get bandages for her hand. Beige tape and ointment and wrappers scattered over the counter as she wrapped her wounds. A small brown bottle marked "Benzodiazepine" sat on the top shelf. She reached for it and gave it a shake. *Empty.* She popped the lid and stared into the empty bottle, not remembering the last time she'd taken them. *Yesterday? The day before?* She looked up at the dark circles under her eyes from lack of sleep or too much vodka or both. Scowling, she tossed the empty bottle into the wastebasket and shuffled into her bedroom. Another brown bottle lay tucked in her nightstand. She popped a large dose and closed the drawer.

The tears in her palms had already bled out to the edges of the bandages.

"Why?" she whispered, glancing up at the now-silent door. She hoped Hunter had just taken the hint and left her in peace. *The roses.* She had to stop the roses from coming again before something worse happened. Before Myron found out. Before . . . she didn't dare guess.

I don't live that far away.

Margot padded into her closet and shut the door. Sinking onto the soft beige carpet with her phone in her hand, she didn't know who to call. The closet held a host of strangers—someone confident, someone glamorous, someone fun, someone flirtatious, someone younger, someone who still had her daughter. But all those people she longed to be were missing, hacked apart, shuffled together in a random, grotesque collage of silk and wool and cotton.

Margot lost a breath as the realization hit her. Someone had been in there. Someone had rearranged her clothes. Blouses hung out of sequence. Skirts had been shuffled. Shoes had been toppled over.

It's a message, she thought, gaping at the rumpled mess. It said, *Get out!*

Ten feet away, Hunter stood outside her door, debating whether he should go in and talk to her. Somewhere above him, a board creaked. He turned and wrapped his towel tighter around his waist, scanning the hallways and doorways.

The house held still, waiting, waiting, waiting.

The air-conditioning whirred to life, and the hairs stood up on his arms and legs in the sudden cold draft. Exposed and naked, he pressed his ear one more time to his mother's door. The water had stopped running. He heard her voice coming from the closet to his left.

"Myron," she said into her cell phone. "I need you to come home. Okay? I'm freaking out . . . I know. I will. Okay."

She hung up and staggered back into the bedroom, voices buzzing in her head. The dead boy in the attic. Her dead daughter. Myron's
dead patient. Her dead marriage. Myron's odd expression the day
before. *He knows something.*

Relieved his father was on his way home, Hunter shuffled to his
room. He slid his bookcase back in front of the door, then did a quick
search for the strange girl. Under the bed was clear. The closet was
empty, and he scanned the creepy writing once again, wondering if
the finer notes belonged to her.

When you see the dead, do the dead see you?

"This is nuts!" He wiggled the mouse and pinged Caleb.

While he waited for a response, he opened the folder of lost mail
his mother had given him. Expired pizza coupons, lawn services, paint-
ing ads, a cable bill addressed to Clyde Martin—he sorted through the
junk until he found something useful. An Ohio University admissions
letter addressed to an "Ava Turner." He opened it.

> *Dear Miss Turner,*
>
> *It is our distinct pleasure to welcome you to Ohio
> University. Based on your early application . . .*

It was an early admissions letter dated December 1, 2017. Hunter
read the name again and opened a web browser. As he was typing the
name "Ava Turner," Caleb's grinning face appeared in the corner of
his screen.

"Hey, dude! You get axe murdered yet?"

"Not yet, but almost." Hunter filled him in on Roger, the two dead
teenagers, and the girl in his basement.

"Dude. Either you've got a ghost, or there's a squatter in your house." Caleb's glib laugh made it clear that he didn't believe a word of it. "Is she hot?"

"Shut up," Hunter hissed and threw a glance at his closed door. "I'm not kidding. I think she used to live here. She said some pretty weird shit about how the house kills people and drives them insane. She really wants us to leave." *Before it's too late.*

"Whoa. Are you shitting me?" Caleb's smirk fell a bit. "So what are you gonna do? Call the cops on her?"

"No." Maybe it was the loneliness of the house or the town, but he wanted to talk to her some more. He wanted to know who she was, this girl. The only girl Hunter had talked to face-to-face in months. He shuddered slightly at the memory of her warm breath on his cheek. "I think her name is Ava Turner. I'm googling right now . . ."

Random girls named Ava came up with profiles in various social media sites, but none seemed to match.

Caleb began clicking away on his computer as well. "How old is she?"

"She said she's nineteen."

"If she has a record, it's probably sealed." Caleb kept tapping away at the keys. His father was a lawyer, so he figured himself an expert on most things. "Why was she living with the Martins?"

"I don't know. She didn't really say. I asked if they'd kidnapped her, and she said, 'Not exactly.' What the hell do you think that means?" Hunter scanned the next page of searches and tried another thread. No luck.

"Was she adopted?"

"Maybe."

"Hmm . . . according to this website here, adoptions are closed records, really hard to trace without a court order."

"But wouldn't she have been listed as a next of kin in Clyde's obituary if she'd been adopted? Wouldn't she have changed her last name?" Hunter eyed the letter again.

"Yeah. Probably. What about . . . could she have been like a foster kid?"

"Maybe. That would make sense, right?"

"Yeah. I just saw some FML article online about foster kids turning eighteen and ending up homeless because they age out of the system. They have no family . . . no money."

Hunter began slowly nodding. "Oh my God. She's nineteen."

"Exactly! It fits. But foster care is some pretty touchy shit. I don't think you're going to find those sorts of records online or in the newspapers. You may have to call social services and see if they'll talk to you . . ." Caleb's voice trailed off as he kept typing. "Hey, check it. I think I found her. I'm sending you a link."

The message blipped onto Hunter's screen. It opened a missing persons database from the website of the Ohio attorney general. A photograph of a waifish blonde girl with a nose ring appeared under the name "Ava Turner."

Missing since October 29, 2015. Missing age: sixteen.
Current age: nineteen.

"Is that her?" Caleb asked, leaning in. "She's kinda hot."

"I'm not sure. Maybe." Hunter squinted at the girl's face. Her light eyes avoided the camera, wary and watchful. There was a phone number to call for the Cleveland Police Department. "She said she was here because she was waiting for something."

"Waiting for what?"

"Got me."

Hunter sank back from the girl's face on the screen, digesting it all. Foster care. Runaway. Homeless. *Poor Ava.*

"So do you think she's nuts?" Caleb asked, cocking an eyebrow.

"I don't know." Hunter fought the urge to check the hall outside his room. "She says some pretty strange stuff about hearing the dead speak."

"Dude. What if she's like a schizophrenic? Don't they see and hear stuff?"

"Yeah. I think so." Hunter tapped a few words into his keyboard, and a new web page came up. "Auditory hallucinations are common. 'Teenagers are most likely to develop symptoms in times of severe stress.' Here, I'll send you the link."

Is she crazy? Hunter frowned and shook his head. He didn't want her to be.

Caleb's eyes scanned the article. "Uh-oh. Says here that marijuana can bring on the first psychotic break, so *we're* fucked."

"Shut up." Hunter rubbed his face and tried to take stock of what he knew. "Clyde Martin died at the end of 2014, and Maureen Martin got hauled off to a psychiatric ward for refusing to vacate the property in 2016. If Ava was staying here like alone with a crazy woman for over a year, it might've messed her up. But it would mess anyone up, right? I think this girl is smart. She got into college." He held up the acceptance letter for Caleb to read.

"Early admission. Impressive . . . Wait. You *are* just fucking with me, right, dude?"

"Nope."

"You mean you actually have this chick holed up in your attic right now?" Caleb eyeballed Hunter a moment. "Holy shit. This is crazy! You need to call the cops before this bitch like slits your throat in your sleep."

"Shh! Fuck off, Caleb." Hunter glanced over his shoulder at the closed door again. "I don't think she'd do that."

"How can you know what the fuck she'd do, huh? She's hiding in your fucking house, man. This is *not* normal."

"No shit. But maybe she needs help. Shouldn't I try to help her?" Hunter clicked back to the footage from his webcam and scrolled through the hours until he found her. A girl in a white nightgown slipping past his room. He stared at her frozen on his screen a moment with morbid fascination, until Caleb's voice snapped him out of it.

"You fall asleep?"

"No . . . I was just thinking. I mean, if she wanted to kill me, she would've done it by now. Right?"

"If you say so, dude." Caleb tapped the webcam with an annoyed finger. "Hey. Don't you even want to hear about the other one?"

"What other one?"

"Your boy, Benny. I found him."

Hunter straightened up in his chair and minimized the image of Ava on his screen. "You found him? How?"

"Benjamin Thomas Klussman, age twenty-four, checked into St. Dominic's Hospital in El Paso, Texas, October 15, 1990. Severe lacerations to the face, whiplash, unresponsive. His mother, Frances Jane Klussman, was pronounced DOA. Car accident."

"Damn. How'd you find that out?"

"Newspaper search. My dad has a subscription."

"So he was in the hospital in 1990. Then what happened to him?"

"It was kind of a big deal. They didn't know what the fuck to do with him, right? His mom was dead. They couldn't locate a father. He couldn't talk. They said he had cerebral palsy and a bunch of other shit wrong with him." Caleb rattled off the facts through the speakers. "They couldn't find any family or friends in the area. It looked like Benny's mom was making a run for the border. They found suitcases and cash in the car. They ran ads in the paper and over the wire for a few weeks."

"No shit." Hunter slunk back in his chair and shifted his gaze to the closet door. *DeAD GiRL.* "I wonder if he really killed her."

"Killed who?"

"Katie Green. That's supposed to be the name of a girl that died across the street. You know, if we believe anything Ava says."

Caleb tapped out the name on his keyboard and scanned an article. "Katie Green was stabbed to death on September 14, 1990. Shit. That's pretty fucking gruesome. Girl sneaks out of her house to visit her boyfriend and is found dead in the bushes . . . Dude!"

"What?"

"It says here they never found her killer. And we've got Benny and his mom speeding out of the country with all their shit a month later. It doesn't look too good, right?"

Hunter shook his head. "Do you know what happened to him?"

"Last article I found said that some special home in California offered to take him in. A place called Golden Heart Ranch in Pasadena."

Hunter wrote it down.

"You gonna call?"

Hunter stared out the window, Benny's window, at the bushes across the street. *This house is bad for men, for boys. They all die here.*

"Yeah. I need to know what happened."

46

"Golden Heart Ranch, can I help you?"

"I don't know. I hope so." Hunter cleared his throat. "I'm looking for Benjamin Klussman?"

"Which unit would he be in?" the woman asked in a pinched voice. "Long-term care? Daycare?"

"I'm guessing long term?"

"Let me transfer you. Please hold."

Hunter kept his cell phone on speaker and set it on his desk while the synthesized Muzak piped into his room. On his computer screen, he continued typing in search engines for Ava Turner, finding nothing.

"Hello?" a man's voice boomed through the phone.

"Yeah. Hi. I'm looking for Benjamin Klussman?"

"Benny? You're lookin' for Benny. Oh my gawd! This is unbelievable! Do you know he's been here almost thirty years without a single phone call or visitor? How on earth do you know my sweet, sweet Benny?"

"I don't. Not really. It's sort of . . . complicated. I live in his old house back in Cleveland. I found some notes he'd left on the walls, and I've been trying to find him. Is he really there?"

"Well, yes, he is. But you are not family. Is that right?"

"No. I'm not."

"And he doesn't know you at all?"

"No." Hunter winced. The whole thing sounded nuts.

"So . . . why do you want to talk to Benny?"

"It's just that he used to live in my house. He, um, left some strange messages about a girl." Hunter didn't say the rest. *A girl he might've killed.*

The phone stayed quiet a moment. "Lord, Benny. I'm not sure this is such a good idea."

"Is he . . . allowed to talk on the phone?"

"Well, of course he is! This is an assisted living facility, not a prison. It's just he doesn't do so well with surprises. He has troubles."

"He has cerebral palsy. Is that right? Is he . . . mentally disabled?"

"I'm sorry, but I can't really discuss a patient's issues with you, HIPAA and everything. I'm sure you understand."

"Okay. Well. What should I do?"

"Why don't you give me your name and number, and I'll get back to you in a few days."

Hunter provided the information.

"And you said this is something about a girl?"

"Yeah. A girl in Shaker Heights. Katie Green? I think maybe he knew her."

As Hunter hung up the phone, he heard a creak outside his door-way. He silently rose from his chair and crept toward the door as quietly as he could. Crouching down, he put his eye to the keyhole to peer out.

A pale blue eye stared back at him.

"Jesus!" He fell back onto his ass, heart pounding. It took several ragged breaths to regain his nerve and stand up. *She's just a girl. She's just a girl.* He shoved the bookcase aside and opened the door.

She was gone.

"Ava?" he hissed after her. "Where are you?"

Halfway down the hall, he stopped at the sound of his mother's door opening. Margot emerged haggard and red eyed. "Who are you talking to, sweetie?"

He studied his mother's worried expression. *Can you keep a secret?* "Uh. Just a girl. On the phone." He pulled his phone out of his pocket as proof. "We sort of had a fight."

Margot puzzled at him a moment but decided to let it go. "What do you say we get out of here for a while? Any place you want to go? I'll drive."

Hunter thought for a moment. A pale eye stared at him through a keyhole in his mind. "Yeah. I'd love to get out of here."

47

The Klussman Family
September 15, 1990

Hand aching, Frannie studied the bloodied bandage on her palm where she'd cut herself that morning. It took her a moment to remember how it had happened. She'd scraped it on purpose while talking to the boy cop. About the girl. The dead girl.

She sat up in bed and stared at the far wall toward Benny's room. Remembering she'd locked his door, she bolted out of bed with the guilt only a mother could feel. *How many hours has he been locked in there? How could I leave him alone like that? How could I let him get out of the house?*

When she reached Benny's room, she fumbled with the key, calling, "Benny? Benny, Mommy's here. I'm sorry you were left alone. Are y—"

Her words dropped away when she opened the door. Angry black marks slashed across the walls. Giant, crooked letters screamed.

GiRL! BiKe! DeAD! BusHes!

Black and green crayon and pencil scratchings attacked every solid surface. Even the windows. Girls rode across the walls on bikes.

"Benny!" She breathed in the word as though it were a noxious gas. "What are you doing?"

Benny was standing with the side of his face pressed against the far wall. He dropped the crayon in his hand and turned to face her. His mouth opened to explain and then shut again. The words would never come. Instead, he pointed out his window at the police cars gathered across the street and groaned loudly, his eyes rolling desperately in his head. *Tell them! Tell them!* "TEEAAWW!"

Frannie took a step backward, her face slack. "What have you done, Benny?" Tears blurred the words screaming over the walls as she backed away from him. Terrified.

Benny's eyes widened as she backed out of the room. *She's afraid of you,* the watcher in the back of his mind whispered. He stumbled after her in protest, forcing his legs to move, forcing his arms open. *No. No. NO.*

She slammed the door before he could reach her and threw the dead bolt.

All the life drained from Benny's gaze, leaving nothing but the spasm in his optic nerves. His muscles seized one by one in a slow-motion attack, and his body fell against his bed and then onto the floor.

Out in the hallway, Frannie backed away from the dull *thump thump thump* of Benny's poor head on the floorboards, stifling her sobs with the back of her hand. She gazed out the two-story leaded glass window at the police cars across the street. No doubt the officers were running the blood samples from the sidewalk to a lab at that very moment. Samples that would link her son to the scene. She looked back at the bedroom where he'd scribbled his confession on the walls.

"Everything alright up there?" Bill called from the kitchen.

Frannie wiped the tears from her cheeks and put on a smile. "Everything's fine. He's just . . . you know. A bit upset."

Thankfully, the thumping on Benny's floor had stopped. The searing pain in his skull from the previous night quieted all the voices.

He lay frozen, staring up at the ceiling with dead eyes, brain bruised, hearing everything and nothing at once.

"Why don't you head on home?" she said to Bill now at the bottom of the stairs. She forced a lightness into her voice. "Benny and I will be fine tonight."

Bill raised an eyebrow and studied her. He'd seen boys like Benny hurt by those who were supposed to love them most. He'd seen kids like him nearly strangled to death. *These kids, they take it out of you, Ms. Klussman. Believe me. I've seen it. Sometimes the best thing is to walk away a bit and cool down. Don't go in there unless you ready.* He'd given her this caution a few times in the last twelve months. But he'd never seen Frannie lift a finger against her child. Not once. "You sure about that? It was a pretty long night last night."

She nodded again. "And thank you for letting me sleep. That nap made all of the difference. Please. Go home to Jackie and give her my best."

Bill nodded slowly. The timbre of her voice no longer had a shake in it. He watched her walk steadily down the winding front stairs. Her eyes, still swollen from crying, were crinkled in a warm, motherly smile. "Really, Bill. I'm fine."

He let out a long sigh. "Alright. But I'm gonna keep my pager on me. You have any problem, any problem at all, I want you to call me." He gave her a practiced look, hard enough to mean business but not so hard as to scare a white lady. "For real. Any time of night. You call."

She nodded slowly, pressing her lips together, almost losing her composure. "I will. I promise." She placed an awkward hand on his shoulder and gave it a squeeze far too familiar for his taste. "Thank you so much, Bill. Really. Thank you for everything you've done these past few months. I don't know what I would do without you."

It was a goodbye, and part of him knew it. It registered in the slight softening of his brow and the stolen glance up to Benny's bedroom. "Just my job," he said, taking a step toward the door. "I'll see you tomorrow? Same time?"

She nodded. "That would be great. See you then."

Frannie watched the home health aide leave before heading back up the stairs to her son.

Benny lay still on the other side of his door, head throbbing, waiting for the needle to come, waiting for the ambulance. For something. This time was different. The watcher knew. His glassy eyes drifted from one horrid image he'd drawn to the next. The terrible markings on his walls looked down at him in judgment. *The girl. The girl. The girl.* Her memory raced by him on her bicycle, swerving her way past his window forever. He didn't dare move.

Frannie stared at his closed door a moment. It had been her playroom door. Decades earlier, when she'd only been six years old, she'd played with her dolls in there, sung songs, and screamed at Matthew, her older brother, when he'd beaten her at Go Fish. The shadow of the girl she'd been skipped past her down the hall to her old bedroom. She followed it, as though in a trance. The sounds of her mother baking cookies in the kitchen below—pans clanking, bowls hitting the counter, the wall oven ticking—echoed in the walls beneath her.

She passed the bedroom where her mother had died eight years earlier, back before Frannie's husband had given up on her and Benny, before he'd moved into the guest room over the garage, back when they were still a family of sorts. She paused and looked in at the sad twin bed under the window to the backyard. Her poor mother, Helen Bell. Breast cancer had reduced her to nothing but gray skin and hollow bones by the time it was done.

This can't be good for Benny, her husband had complained.

What am I supposed to do, Hank, just dump her in a nursing home? She gave *us this house. It's the least we can do.*

That of course had sparked another fight. Hank had never wanted to live at Rawlingswood in the first place. If he'd been anything other than a midlevel accountant for some midlevel company, he might've insisted on moving elsewhere, but as it was, they'd inherited a veritable palace in a good school district. A school district they'd never had the chance to use in the end.

Frannie sank down onto her mother's deathbed and gazed out at the bird fountain in the backyard. They'd tried for years to fill the bedrooms of the house with children. So many doctors, so many fights, and finally Benny.

A tear slid down her cheek as she saw the girl she'd been out there in the yard, planting her pet flower patch, digging in the dirt with her mother trying to get carrots and tomatoes to grow. The dried well of the birdbath gazed up at the sky, empty.

Back out in the hallway, she passed the door to her old bedroom, still painted pink with flowered curtains. She'd always hoped to fill the room with a little girl of her own. Her favorite books and dolls still lined the shelves, waiting for her phantom daughter to come along. Now at the ripe age of fifty-nine, she'd stopped waiting. She'd stopped hoping after Benny's yearlong stay in the hospital. She'd stopped hoping the day Hank had screamed, *Are you married to me or Benny? Because I'm tired of coming last!*

It had taken him another ten years to get the guts to actually walk out the door for good, but he'd already left them both. He'd left them the day the pediatrician declared that nothing could be done.

Frannie stopped outside her brother's old room and hesitated before opening the door. It was just as he'd left it all those years ago. Hank may have been a bastard, but he'd never pushed her to repurpose the room. Dust covered the photographs, the baseball trophies, his bed. At just eighteen years old, he'd been one of the last American soldiers to die in World War II. She was fourteen when he'd enlisted against their parents' wishes. *Such a goddamn waste! If the stupid son of a bitch had just waited six more months!* Her father had slammed his fist into the wall of the foyer when the notice came. The folded flag delivered with the news sat on the shelf over his bed.

She'd always been afraid to touch it. Even at that moment, she couldn't bring herself to hold the last memento of her brother.

Do you really have to go? She'd sat at the edge of that very bed, teary eyed, gazing at her hero and savior the day before he left. She sank down onto the same spot and imagined him sitting next to her.

Yeah, I do. He'd slung an arm over her shoulder. *This life, this house, this town . . . this isn't the real world, Frannie. Don't you ever get that feeling? That this is all just a pretty picture we're living in, that this is all make-believe? People are dying out there. People are starving out there. I'm not going to sit here in this playhouse and drink tea.*

Four months later, there had been a knock on their door.

Her eyes circled the room, and she whispered, "This is all make-believe."

Her mother had left the original hand-printed wallpaper on his walls. Beneath it hid the plaster, the stone wool insulation, the wires, the pipes, and the wooden bones inside the walls. This building, this "childhood home," was just a pile of wood, a carefully constructed lie.

She buried her face in her hands and stifled a sob, rubbing the tears back into her eyes. Her brother, Matthew, had known it at eighteen years old. Surely she could face the same truth at fifty-nine. It was just a room. It was just a house. She grabbed a small framed photograph of her brother—it was his last picture from Shaker Heights High School—and tucked it under her arm.

Back out in the hallway, she didn't bother with the other rooms. The guest room where Bill sometimes spent the night was just a shell. She hated the suite over the garage where Hank had slept bitterly for those last few years, too guilty and too cowardly to leave. His voice still hovered in there. *You're not going to make me the bad guy here!*

She stormed past the memories of her ex-husband to the attic door. Her father had never allowed any of them up there. *It's just not safe. You've got exposed wires, loose floorboards . . .* The one time he'd caught her and her brother up there exploring, he'd taken the strap to them both.

Back in 1936, when her father, Marcus Bell, bought the place, he decided to keep the home's bloody history to himself. He never told Frannie's mother about the murder in the attic. *Why look a gift horse in the mouth?* he told himself when the bank handed him the keys. He'd bought a mansion at pennies on the dollar.

Of course, all the neighbors had been too polite to bring up the subject of the murder to his wife's face. Helen Bell was left to wonder why her invitations for tea or dinner parties were always politely declined. When she complained to her husband, Marcus just brushed it off. *You know how the snooty types can be. Don't like Catholics. Don't like Jews. Don't like new money. You just keep your chin up, sweetheart. They'll come around.*

Marcus was one of the few to have come out of the Great Depression ahead. He'd bought up a bankrupt tool-and-die operation down in the Flats. His wife's family was as Irish Catholic as they came, and Helen and Marcus had spent the next twenty-odd years trying to prove themselves to the neighbors.

Frannie pulled the key to the attic down from the top of the door-frame and considered it a moment. She glanced back at Benny's room and listened for him to stir.

He didn't move. He just lay there counting her steps, listening to the way they sounded in different rooms, wondering when they'd come back for him.

She turned the key, and the dead bolt gave way with a wiggle and a nudge. The stale air from the attic fell down into the hallway as she opened the door—mothballs and dust and trapped sunshine and dried tree sap and death. Her footsteps creaked up one step at a time, and the dust motes swirled in the air. She hadn't set foot up there in over ten years. There had never been a need, and she still feared her father's wrath even after all those years.

Marcus Bell had abandoned Frannie and her mother two months after her brother had died. All her mother would ever say on the matter was, *He was a good man. He took care of us, Frannie. He paid off this house and paid the taxes on it every year until you were married.*

At the top of the stairs, Frannie let her eyes roam the main room of the attic. A tin can sat on the floor outside the bathroom, filled with ashes. In the two smaller rooms a few tattered remains lay strewn. A torn silk slip. An empty apple crate. Filing boxes. Mouse droppings littered the corners of the floor. The windows gazing out over the yard were muddied with cobwebs and soot.

Frannie's tracks through the dust mingled with her brother's and little Walter's as she stood among the footprints of the past. *What do you think is up here? Wanna play hide-and-seek? What if they catch us?*

Turning back to the main room, she eyed the closed door at the far end. It was the door to the bathroom. After a moment's hesitation, she crept over and turned the stiff doorknob. The door swung into a tangle of spiderwebs lit by a small window. Rusted porcelain fixtures lined the walls, and a foul odor hung between them. She stepped back with a hand over her nose and mouth to block the smell. The room hadn't been opened in decades, not since the police had found little Walter facedown on the floor.

The caretakers the bank had hired back in 1932 had drained and winterized the attic bathroom along with the others, and her father had never dared to recommission it. Dust, plaster debris, peeled paint, and dead flies littered the room. A large stain darkened the grout lines between the porcelain floor tiles.

Frannie grimaced and backed away from the abandoned washroom. She didn't know what she'd expected to find up there. Buried treasure? Answers? Her brother's ghost? There was nothing to take with her. After fifty-three years living in the house, there was nothing she really wanted besides her brother's picture.

Her gaze fixed on a crawl space door. They'd never told a soul about the gun they'd found. The shock of holding it, so cold and heavy in her hand, had felt like a crime. Fifty years later, she still felt guilty.

The gun must still be there, she realized. All these years, it had waited in the back of her mind as a last resort. A door she'd never open unless . . .

A floor below, Benny stared up at the ceiling as though he could see her standing above him. Frannie grabbed the handle of the crawl space door and closed her eyes a moment as though in prayer.

I won't let them lock him up.

A tiny shoe lay on the ground just inside. A little boy's shoe. She froze, undone at the sight of it. A little boy scampered across her mind, a little boy with a broken smile clutching a yellow truck. A little boy without a cruel bone in his body. She slammed the door and ran back down the steps with nothing but her brother's picture in her hand.

Benny heard her feet racing to his door and her hands fumbling with the key and braced himself for the needle, for her horrified face, for whatever terrible thing was coming.

Falling to her knees next to him, Frannie lifted his bruised head into her arms and kissed his forehead. "Benny, oh, my sweet, sweet boy. Whatever you did, I don't care. It's going to be okay. We're going to go someplace new. Someplace nice and warm where we can see the ocean. Won't that be nice? I'll find you a really big window, sweetie. I promise. One way or another, it's going to be fine."

Benny couldn't move or respond. All he could do was stare over her shoulder at his scribbled drawings of the girl. She glided past him on her bicycle again and again. All he could do was watch.

48

The Spielman Family
August 10, 2018

An hour later, Myron lurched in through the back door, stopping in the cramped mudroom off the garage with his phone pressed to his ear.

"What do you mean, they want another deposition?" he demanded, glancing into the kitchen and relieved to find it empty. He dropped the shopping bag in his hand. "How much more information could they possibly need? The mortality and morbidity hearing was eighteen months ago, George. I was cleared . . . No. My leaving was voluntary. You know the board, damn it. It was political, that's all . . . What do you mean, there's new evidence? What evidence? . . . Oh, for fuck's sake. They're just looking for a bigger payout, okay? . . . Do I need to find better representation? . . . No, I'm asking you to do your damn job!"

He hung up and ran both hands over his red face, then punched the wall hard enough to leave a dent. The burst of pain in his knuckles cleared his head. He stood there silently talking to himself, coaching, calming, and straightening until he'd regained the better part of his composure. He checked his hand for signs of fracture and saw none. Only then did he set foot in the kitchen.

"Anybody home? Margot?" It was more a privacy check than a greeting.

No one replied.

Relieved, he staggered to the den and the liquor cabinet. The empty decanter on the coffee table was the first thing to catch his eye, then the fact that someone had left the television on. Frustrated and mildly concerned at the missing whiskey, he walked with greater purpose into the foyer and shouted up the stairs. "Hey! Anybody home? Margot? Hunter?"

The house answered with cavernous silence.

"Thanks for leaving me a drink, you bastards," he muttered under his breath.

A flash of white in the living room turned his head. Then it was gone, but the air buzzed with movement. A thump to his right sent him running into the dining room.

A white cat was standing on the buffet.

"How the hell did you get in here?" he hissed at it.

It took a few quick maneuvers to catch hold of its tail. The beast bared its teeth and scratched his arm.

"Ow! Dammit!" He grabbed it by the scruff of the neck, catching two more swipes of its claws. He marched it to the front door and tossed it out. An empty bowl sat on the front stoop. He snatched it up and muttered, "God damn it, Margot."

Back in the den, Myron dug out another bottle of brown liquor and didn't bother to decant it into a more decorative container. He'd never cared for the formality anyway. It was all Margot's doing— setting up the silver tray, displaying the crystal. Myron slapped the bottle down on the table and slammed back a double. *It's not like we ever have guests, Margot.*

That's not true, the Margot in his mind argued back. The fight from a few days earlier replayed itself in his head. *We're having a dinner party next week. You didn't forget, did you?*

Next week had turned into tomorrow night. The last thing in the world he needed at that moment was to entertain guests. "Fuck the Zavodas!" he muttered, examining the thin lines of blood leaking from his forearm.

He poured another three fingers' worth into a glass and slumped into the leather chair behind the desk. Then he noticed the gun.

Walter Rawlings's silver pistol lay casually on the leather desk blotter as though it were an afterthought. Myron set down the drink and picked up the gun as the shock of it buzzed through his veins. He stood up slowly and walked, trancelike, to the drawer where he'd hidden it, yanking it open to find the cigar box right where he left it. But now it was empty. *The bullets.*

The color rushed from his face as Myron carefully opened the cylinder. The butts of three bullets stared back at him from their chambers. Not four. One was missing. Hands trembling now, he dumped the remaining bullets out into the box. He quickly shut the drawer and turned around to survey the room. The books were still in their places. The lamp wasn't broken. The television was fine. No holes in the windows. No blood on the floor. The desk—

He froze, looking at the desk with fresh eyes.

Papers had been strewn about, papers he hadn't noticed because of the gun. Moving closer, he saw that they all came from the same file. The manila folder read *Allison Lordes Spielman* in a doctor's hand. Myron sank into the chair again and took stock of all the medical bills, the death certificate, the paperwork from the funeral home, the death notice with his little girl's picture that Margot had insisted on clipping from the *Boston Chronicle*. Myron ran a hand over his face, grabbed his tumbler of whiskey, and drained it.

"Jesus, Margot. What were you doing?"

Shaking his head angrily, he gathered up all of her papers and stuffed them back into their file, pounding the edges of paper together on the desk until he bent a corner. He studied the damage he'd done, running his finger over the edge, smoothing it, staring into the dead space between the desk and the floor. Then it hit him.

He shot up from the chair and took off running. "Margot!"

He flew up the front stairs, shouting her name. He flung open the door to their bedroom to find the bed made. In the bathroom, spots of blood marred the tiles on the floor. Blood in the sink. Drops of blood on the carpet in her closet. "Margot!"

He ran down the hall, checking room after room. Each empty. Hunter's door stood open, displaying his usual mess. The boy had left his dirty clothes lying on his bathroom floor, but there was no sign of him. Or her.

"Margot? Where are you?"

Myron's face had gone nearly purple with exertion and panic, his lips white and thin as he yelled her name over and over. Up the attic stairs two at a time, he rushed into the hot room, a cold sweat dripping down his back. The rooms were empty, empty, crawl space empty. The bathroom light was on again. *That ridiculous stupid fucking light.*

In a rage, he slapped the switch off and unscrewed the hot bulb, burning his fingers. The bulb smashed into the sink, shattering the onionskin glass in a tinkling cascade.

"God damn it!" he bellowed loudly, then caught a glimpse of himself in the mirror. The late-afternoon sun out the window cast half his crazed face in shadow. He looked like a wild-eyed maniac. It had come to this.

Adrenaline seemed to plummet from his bloodstream as something heavier and far more permanent took hold. A sense of doom. His wife wasn't there. She hadn't really been there in years. *But where . . .*

Out in the main attic, he lurched toward the stairs. The dormer windows projected the low sun in glowing golden rectangles onto the far wall, and Myron in his state didn't see it at first.

A small figure stood in the shadow at the top of the stairs. It was the shape of a girl. Her white slip of fabric stood luminous against the dark wall.

"She left," the girl said. "They both left. You should leave too."

He gaped at her, stunned still.

"If you stay, this place will kill you," she whispered, then vanished down the steps.

"Hey!" he screamed after her. "Who the fuck are you?" He stumbled blindly across the floor to the stairs. The heat of the attic pressed down on him, quickening the liquor. He nearly fell. His shaking hands caught the railing just in time.

A faint melody came from somewhere below.

Myron lurched up and ran down to the second floor and then the back steps into the kitchen, then the den, the dining room, the living room, and back to the kitchen. The basement door beckoned him down into the bowels of Rawlingswood. He stopped at the top of the steps and listened.

Silence.

"What are you doing in my house?" he shouted down into the cold.

He flipped on the light switch and scanned the unfinished space from the top of the steps. Nothing moved. Climbing down slowly, he stopped again at the foot of the stairs, listening to the sound of the slop sink dripping. No one was there.

A few bottles sat on the floor of the wine room, empty. Myron frowned at them and closed the door.

A tickle at the back of his neck sent him spinning around only to find another blank masonry wall, the white paint flaking and sweating off the blocks as the damp earth on the other side seeped through. He ran a trembling hand through his hair and surveyed the exposed pipes and beams overhead. No one was there. Not Margot. Not Hunter. Not the strange girl.

But she had been there. He was sure of it.

He climbed back up out of the ground and ran to the mudroom, where he'd set down a shopping bag. He dumped the contents out onto the floor. Security cameras. Wireless alarms.

"I'm going to catch you, whoever you are," he muttered under his breath.

He spent the next sweaty, frantic hour setting up four wireless cameras to watch over the first floor. They connected to his smartphone, and he checked each one twice. Every creak of the house made him jump and brandish the butcher knife he'd grabbed from the kitchen. It was Hunter's knife, and he looked like a lunatic holding it.

At the fifth jump, he finally stormed into the den to get the gun. Could he bring himself to use it? he wondered, weighing the pistol in his hand. Could he really shoot a young girl? A girl who looked so much like . . . her.

No. He couldn't.

He put the gun back in the desk drawer and glanced down at his watch. Surely, Margot would be home any minute, wondering what the hell he was doing with a knife and why his hands were sweaty and shaking. The nausea creeping up into his gut finally eclipsed the fear, twisting it in another direction.

He couldn't let Margot or Hunter see him like this—sick with withdrawal. He couldn't call the police like this. *Call the police and tell them what?*

"What did you see, Myron?" he whispered to himself. "What can you prove?" He checked the cameras again with his phone. Nothing yet.

Myron climbed up the stairs and down the long hallway to the inner sanctuary of his closet. He needed medicine. Just a small dose would set him straight. Closing the door behind him, he sat down on the wood floor of his closet and pulled his gym bag out from behind the hamper. He'd run out of pills days ago, and it appeared that no more sample boxes would be coming. Someone must've noticed.

He pulled out a small zippered leather case. Inside it lay a syringe, a spoon, a lighter, and a little plastic bag of brown powder. With clammy white fingers, he prepared the injection, dosing out the brown powder, tapping the air bubbles out of the needle. *How much is too much?* He contemplated the milliliters. Sweat beaded on his upper lip as he worked. His ears stood sentry over the hall outside, the foyer, the garage, the front door. He removed his left sock and stuck the needle into a fat vein on the top of his foot.

Then everything slipped away. Too far. Too fast. Too much. His expression went slack as the heavy dose flooded his brain. His body sank to the floor. *Breathe. Keep breathing,* he told himself as his eyes rolled in his skull.

From deep down in his stupor, Myron felt a shift in the air. He heard a click of a door. He felt a shadow moving nearby, but his eyes couldn't focus. His lips mumbled something as he heard the *zuzz* of a zippered case winding shut.

Long hair dusted his face, and the shadow of a head loomed over him. A cold finger pulled his left eye open, letting in a painful blast of white light. Then his right eye. The dangling hair and the smell of sugar swept away from him. As he lay there, not asleep but not awake, he heard a voice singing softly.

> *. . . And when they lie upon your grave*
> *The leaves will fall, the trees will wave . . .*

Myron lay pinned to the floor as Ava wandered down the hall toward the guest wing over the garage with the zippered case in her hand.

"Poor Hunter," she whispered to herself, pausing at the sight of his open door. He had no idea how bad things were about to get.

She turned the corner and headed to the part of the house no one used. No one but her. The contractors had left the plumbing access door in the guest bedroom untouched, not considering the space behind it was large enough for a person to stand in, unseen. No one had noticed the plumbing chase leading up into the attic over the garage, not even the home inspector.

The girl opened the half-size door and retreated into the narrow space, pulling a flashlight from her pocket. If she had been any larger, she wouldn't have fit. The back of the cast-iron tub sat behind a network of pipes. Dried plaster bulged and dripped between the wood slats. The two-by-four blocking between the wall studs formed a makeshift ladder that creaked as she climbed up next to the cast-iron vent stack and onto the makeshift floor of the unfinished attic over the garage. Piles of rags, clothes, and stolen food sat to one side of the plumbing chase and a makeshift bed to the other. She sank onto the pile of cast-off blankets and sleeping bags and considered the zippered case in her hand.

The wood shifted on the other side of the house, and she shined her flashlight into the framing of the main attic. The beam of light shimmered through the dust and cobwebs, through the forest of rafter ties and braces, to the unfinished sides of the main attic walls. She scanned the two access doors that led to the servants' rooms beyond, holding her breath and listening.

"Toby? Is that you?"

49

The Murder House
August 5, 2017

"What's the story with this place?" a teenage boy asked as a pack of kids crept through the overgrown backyard. They scanned the houses on either side, listening for the slam of a door or the shout of a neighbor. *Who's out there?*

"I dunno. It's been empty for over a year. Heard the last owner died or something."

One of them, the one smoking a cigarette, led the group to a side door with a broken window panel. He reached inside the cracked pane of glass to unhook the chain and open it.

"Watch your step," he whispered, pointing to a drop in the floor. "Those stairs go down to the basement."

One of the girls curled her lip. "It smells terrible in here! Are you sure this is a good idea? It's so dark."

"You scared?" the leader teased her. The whole expedition was a dare.

She didn't answer. Instead, she turned to the only other girl with pleading eyes. "Do you think this is a good idea?"

The girl with dyed-black hair just shrugged. Her ears were pierced multiple times, and her lipstick was blood red. "Let's check it out."

Six intruders stumbled past the basement steps and across the kitchen floor. Two used their cell phones as flashlights to guide the way. One tried the light switch, which clicked back and forth dumbly to no effect.

They made their way to the living room, where the streetlights along Lee Road lit the floor in long rectangles beneath the windows. The previous owners had left a couch and a few straggling chairs that someone had dragged into a circle by the fireplace. Pieces of a broken dresser sat half-charred in the firebox.

"Whoa. Look at this place . . . Is someone living in here?" One of the kids pointed to the abandoned fire.

"Nah. People just come here to party." The leader smirked and lit another cigarette. He dropped his backpack to the ground and plopped onto one of the couches.

"Niles," the nervous girl whined. "I don't want to get jumped by some homeless junkie. This is crazy."

Niles pulled a bottle of whiskey out of his bag along with a six-pack of beer and offered her one. "There's like six of us. You really think a drugged-out dude is going to jump all of us? C'mon. Relax, Sammy. I was just here with some friends the other night."

Sammy sank down onto one of the splintered chairs and opened her beer. The other girl distanced herself from the worrywart by plopping down next to Niles. The three other boys scattered around the room, reading the graffiti on the walls, pounding their beers. Their voices echoed off the bare plaster and up the front steps to the second floor.

"Looks like somebody stripped the house. All the radiators are gone. Wonder if they took the pipes too."

"Hey. Somebody wrote *Murder House* in here! Check it out."

"Someone got *murdered* here?" The boy let out a Halloween cackle.

"Knock it off, Steve! You're going to give Sammy a heart attack."

"Fuck off, all of you!" Sammy protested, sipping her beer.

"Who brought the party favors, man?" one of them asked as they wandered back to the dead fire.

Niles pulled a plastic baggie from the front pocket of his school-bag. He produced a tightly rolled joint and lit it up, passing it to his right, and then lit another and passed to the left. "Cheers."

The kids took turns puffing and coughing out skunky clouds of smoke. After a few minutes chatting idly about the origins of the weed (it had come from a friend of Niles's brother), the quieter boy asked, "So where do you think the guy died?"

Sammy blew out another shallow hit and made a face. "What guy?"

"You know. The last owner. Do ya think he died in here?" The kid spun around slower than a sober person might, studying the walls and ceiling. "I heard you totally shit your pants when you die."

"That's real nice, Cliff," the girl with the piercings said, taking a swig from the whiskey bottle.

"That's nothing. Wanna know what I heard?" Niles said, pausing for maximum effect. "I heard a kid died in here. Got murdered by his parents."

"No. You made that up," Sammy protested.

"Swear to God. I heard they killed the kid upstairs in the attic, like in some sort of sick ritual where they tried to conjure the devil. He bled to death all over the floor." He took another deep swig of whis-key and then continued his ghost story in a hushed tone for effect. "Supposedly, every kid that's lived here since has died. They got sick. They killed themselves. None of them made it out of here . . . alive."

The taller boy started laughing. "Bullshit! You saw that in a movie or something."

"Okay. Maybe . . . but don't you want to go check it out?" Niles raised both eyebrows and stared down the three other boys.

The tall one glanced over at Sammy, who was sitting rigid on the edge of her seat. "Shouldn't one of us stay here and keep watch?"

Sammy's shoulders went slack with relief. "I'll stay if someone stays with me."

"Whatever, pussies." Niles laughed. "The rest of you up for some exploring?"

"Sure," one answered.

The other shrugged.

"How 'bout you, Natalie? You game?"

The girl with the piercings nodded slowly, stoned, and pulled herself to her feet. "Sure. I love haunted houses."

"Alright. We'll catch up with you bitches later." With that, Niles led his expedition through the foyer and up the front stairs.

Sammy watched them leave, chewing on her lip. Her worried eyes darted to the street outside and then to her newfound partner on the couch.

"So." The tall guy flashed her a grin. "You gonna sit all the way over there?"

She blushed at herself perched on the edge of her seat and went over to the empty cushion next to him. To prove she wasn't a total loser, she picked up the whiskey bottle and took a long drink.

He cocked a half grin at her and helped himself to a shot as well. "You likin' Mr. Aldridge's class?"

"Hmm?"

"Chemistry. I sit three rows behind you."

"Oh. Yeah. It's fine, I guess." Her eyes wandered back to the foyer, where her other friends had vanished. She tried not to stiffen when the boy next to her draped his arm over her shoulders.

"You know. I always thought you were sort of pretty." He smiled at her lazily, his eyes drifting from her mouth to her chest and back up again.

Upstairs, the four others wandered down the long hallway, opening door after door. One room was empty. One was half-filled with boxes. One had a dirty mattress on the floor. Smatterings of graffiti scarred the walls. The door at the break in the hallway led up to the attic.

"Hey, guys," Niles called to the others. "Go check it out up there. There's something I want to show Natalie here."

"Yeah. I'll bet," Cliff muttered under his breath. He pulled out his cell phone, turned on its high beam, and headed up the stairs with the other kid.

Niles wrapped an arm around Natalie's waist.

She turned to him with a smirk. "What do you wanna show me?"

"I brought something special, just for you," he whispered back, pulling her toward the room with the mattress.

"Wow. You really think it's that easy, huh?" She took a step back and crossed her arms. The smile dancing on her lips combined with the short cut of her skirt suggested it just might be.

"That's not what I'm saying, okay?" He held up both hands. There was a small plastic bag in one of them. "I just figured you might be interested in taking this party up a notch."

She eyed the little bag and then him. "Is that what I think it is?"

"Only the best."

She followed him into the room with the mattress and closed the door.

Niles sprinkled the powder onto a crumpled piece of foil he'd pulled from his pocket and handed her a glass tube. Natalie took in a shallow puff of smoke while Niles held a lighter against the back of the foil. "Go easy. They promised this was some good shit."

Within two seconds, Natalie's muscles went limp. She sank down onto the mattress as the acrid smoke rushed her brain.

"It's good, right?" Niles chuckled before inhaling his own hit.

Up in the attic, the two other boys pointed their phones at the walls, where someone had written words in light pencil.

And we shall plant four trees, one at each corner for each Angel that speaks.

"What the fuck is that?" The writing was smudged and hard to read in places. "Cliff, come look at this."

"I have no idea, man. But there's more of it." Cliff pointed his cell phone at the opposite wall.

Prepare a Stone to set at the head of the Fountain.

In the Grove, we shall sing unto thee . . .

"It's like they really were up here casting spells or something. You think this is where that kid died? You know. In that ghost story?"

"You mean if Niles isn't completely full of shit?" Cliff laughed. "Probably just junkies or kids. Like the graffiti downstairs and the radiators."

"Right." His friend surveyed the rest of the attic with the light of his phone. "Still pretty creepy . . . Well, I'm bored. I'm going back down. You coming?"

"Yeah. In a sec." Cliff finished the beer in his hand and shuffled into the bathroom to take a leak before heading down the steps.

He didn't notice the crawl space door silently swing open behind him.

Downstairs, the kid stopped outside the bedroom where Niles had led Natalie. He stood next to the closed door and listened to the gasping breaths coming from under the door. Niles let out a muffled grunt. The boy in the hall wrinkled his nose and laughed.

A panicked shout cut the air.

It was followed by running feet pounding the length of the house and down the attic steps. A door slammed open in the hallway. "Run!" Cliff shouted. "Somebody's here! Guys! We gotta go! Now!"

Cliff blew past his friend and thundered down the front stairs. *Somebody's here?*

A figure appeared next to the attic door. It stood there, a hint of white against the dark shadows of the hall. It was the shape of a girl.

The kid in the hall stumbled back and then went careening down the stairs after Cliff. "Holy shit! Holy shit! What was that?"

In the living room, Sammy pushed the boy on top of her away and sat up, pants unbuttoned, as Cliff burst in.

"Get up! Somebody's here!"

The tall kid pulled his hand out from under Sammy's shirt. "What?"

"I saw someone. In the attic. We gotta go. Where are the others?"

"I thought they were with you."

The other boy barreled up behind Cliff, spooked sober. "I saw it, man! Jesus, I saw it. Niles can fuck straight off. I'm out. You comin'?" He didn't wait for an answer. He just took off for the back door. The rest followed in a fumbling blur, leaving Niles and Natalie behind.

Ava approached the stair railing as the four teenagers dashed out the side door and into the night. The sound of Niles retching pulled her toward the closed bedroom door. She opened it to find two teenagers sprawled on the mattress, twitching ever so slightly.

"What did you do?" she whispered.

She pushed into the room as the couple convulsed and seized from whatever they had smoked. Ava hovered over the pair of them a moment. Their breaths grew shallow and thin. Blood had drained from their faces. Vomit collected in the girl's hair. The foil and glass tube had tumbled to the floor.

The boy's cell phone lay next to his trembling hand. Ava reached for it, and a moment later, a shrill voice came through the speaker. "911. What's your emergency? . . . Hello? Are you there?"

"Come right away." Numbness buzzed through Ava's veins. *Not again. Not again. Not again.* "Two kids. They're dying. It's an overdose."

"Overdose of what?"

"I don't know . . . some sort of powder."

"Stay on the line. We're tracing your phone," the disembodied voice announced into the mattress. "Can you give me an address?"

"14895 Lee Road."

Ava ignored the rest of the questions. She wiped the phone of fingerprints and set it back down next to Niles. The boy's pinpoint pupils lolled to the back of his skull as she hovered next to his ear.

"What do you see?" she whispered. "Can you see them?"

His answer was nothing more than a hitched gasp for air. A gurgle.

When the sirens came, Ava hid in the trees at the back of the lot, watching as heavy boots shook the walls and flashlights darted across the ceilings through the shuddering windows. Out on the street, flashing red and blue lights shrouded the house and bruised the sky.

50

The Spielman Family
August 10, 2018

The walls flashed blue and green at the end of the center hall.

Margot dragged her tired feet from the kitchen toward the convulsing lights of the television to find Myron passed out on the leather couch in the den. She glanced down at him, relieved to find him unconscious, and headed up the stairs.

Hunter's door was shut, but she could hear his muffled voice talking with someone. He'd returned home on foot an hour earlier and gone straight to his computer.

Margot shut her bathroom door and pressed her forehead to the wood, forcing air in and out of her lungs through the lump in her throat. In the unforgiving glare of their white master bath, she stripped off her clothes and buried them in her wicker hamper. They reeked of cigarette smoke, spilled vodka, and someone else's sweat. In the shower, she scrubbed her skin raw as though trying to remove an entire layer and examined a small welt on her left breast. Her head shook at it, tears pooling. *It was a mistake. All of it. A terrible mistake, and now . . .*

Her lip trembling, Margot pushed her face into the scalding water, hoping to wash it all away. Why? *Why?* She let out the sob she hadn't been able to muster the week before while holding the photo-graph of her lost daughter. She ripped the bloodied bandage off her palm and forced the wound into the water, letting the white shot of pain blind her. She dug her fingernail into the pale silver line of a scar on her left wrist as though hoping to rip it open. She crumpled to the floor of the shower and wept.

The hot water eventually ran out. She pulled herself up and set about erasing what had happened. She scrubbed the bloodstains from the bathroom floor, the sink, her closet. A strange leather case caught her attention as she rinsed the sponge. It sat on the marble counter, between her sink and Myron's. She dried her hands before opening it.

A syringe. A spoon. A small baggie of powder.

"Oh my God!" she breathed, staring at the contraband. She spun around as though expecting to find Myron standing there and then turned back to the case. Panicked, she picked it up, shoved it into one of Myron's drawers next to his shaving cream, and slammed it shut. "Myron?" she whispered to herself.

She surveyed the large bathroom with suspicion and began opening and closing cabinets and drawers. She turned to his closet behind her and stormed inside, shoving suits and shirts aside, check-ing shelves, emptying the hamper, opening drawers. In the bottom drawer, under his spare gym clothes, she found a stack of files.

The first was a collection of his clippings and articles, showing a much younger Myron back when he'd first been named a head sur-geon at Boston General. He had been a fellow at Johns Hopkins and published articles with the *New England Journal of Medicine*. The last clipping was from a much smaller newspaper article.

Local Doctor Questioned in Patient Death

Margot set aside the clippings to view the files underneath.

Malpractice Suit—Abigail Marty

Mortality-Morbidity Report—Abigail Marty

Patient Record 372-XX-8444

Margot's gaze darted between the file labels. She knew about the pending lawsuit, but seeing the actual files was different. One was stamped "Confidential." She flipped it open.

Medical charts. Hospital reports. She paused at the words "Cause of Death" and read more carefully.

> Hemorrhage from surgical site and aspiration into lungs. Uneven sutures resulting in dehiscence . . . Possible surgical error, further review recommended.

She flipped to the next page.

> Comments: Even more troubling than the possibility of surgical error, the board finds the diagnosis of chronic tonsillitis to be ambiguous at best, and the subsequent surgery likely unwarranted. Further investigation has shown statistically anomalous rates of tonsillectomies in this department, indicating inordinate use of surgical intervention and the possibility of unethical medical practice. Inflated profits have been a direct result of the high rate of invasive procedures. The board recommends the suspension of Dr. Myron Spielman's practice until further investigation can be completed, effective immediately.

Her jaw dropped as she read the words again, trying to make sense of them. "Myron," she whispered. "What did you do?"

Fresh tears burned her eyes as she shoved the papers back in their place. Her breath came faster as the house of cards fell in her mind. The patient death, the lawsuit, the move, the drugs, her marriage. *Hunter.*

She stumbled back into the bathroom to splash cold water on her face. As she dried off, a flash of pink caught her eye on the marble counter. A plaster handprint lay next to her bottles of perfume. It was the handprint of a little girl, her daughter. She spun around, certain it hadn't been there before.

The door to the hallway stood open.

She ran through it and into the hall. The empty foyer gaped over the railing. She pushed open doors one after another until she reached Hunter's room. She banged on it with her fist until she heard him call back. "Yeah?"

"Hunter, honey? Were you in my bathroom just now?"

The door opened just a crack. "Mom? What's wrong?"

She looked a fright. Skin red, eyes swollen. She studied his mussed hair and startled expression for signs of guilt and found none. "Nothing. Just . . ." *Did you see your father's drugs? Were you in my closet? Have you heard an intruder?* "Your father must've moved some things around. Can I come in?"

He shifted his weight uncomfortably and opened the door.

Margot sat down on the edge of his bed and glanced over at his computer desk. A newspaper article filled the glowing screen. It was about the death of a boy. "What are you reading about?"

"Nothing." Hunter clicked off the image. "Just more research."

"About the house?"

"Yeah. Kind of."

"Listen, Hunter—"

The sound of the toilet flushing in the hall bathroom next door stopped her cold.

She narrowed her eyes at him. "Is someone here?"

Hunter's jaw dropped to say something, but before he could utter a word, a girl appeared in the doorway. Blonde and petite with an unsettling feral look in her eye, the girl was wearing Hunter's T-shirt and a pair of leggings. "Hi, Mrs. Spielman. I'm Ava."

"Ava?" Margot threw Hunter a glance that was a mix of confusion and relief. The name ruffled something in the back of her mind she couldn't quite catch. "Well, hello."

"Uh, yeah. Mom, this is Ava." Hunter tried to hide his alarm by glaring at the girl wearing his T-shirt. *What are you doing?*

Ava ignored him and smiled at Margot from the doorway, performing her best impression of a normal girl. "We met at the library a few weeks ago. I hope it's okay I came over. Hunter didn't think you'd mind."

"Oh, no. Not at all." Margot straightened her robe and stood up, suddenly aware of how terrible she looked. She shot her son another glance, checking his face. The boy seemed petrified in the presence of a girl his own age. "It's really nice to meet you, Ava. Call me Margot. You're welcome to stay as long as you like. I mean, assuming your parents know you're here?"

Ava nodded demurely and settled into Margot's spot on the bed.

"Okay. Well. I'll let you two visit." Margot turned to Hunter with a half smile. "Just leave the door open, okay?"

"Uh, sure, Mom."

Margot turned on her heel and left the room, feeling foolish and exposed and utterly out of sorts. On her way back to her bedroom, she caught sight of the attic door. It stood open, mocking her as she passed.

That damn door!

She stormed back to her bedroom and shook the contents of her purse out over the bedspread until she found a small paper bag from a locksmith's shop. Inside rattled three steel skeleton keys. She tried each one in her own bedroom door until she found one that worked. With a breath of triumph and relief, she slipped back down the hallway and locked the attic door with a satisfying *click*.

The soft voices of Ava and Hunter lilted back and forth at the far end of the hall. Margot held still and listened.

"Are you sure this is a good idea?"

"I don't know why I didn't think of it before. It's better this way. You'll see. I'm so tired of sneaking around. Now we don't have to worry so much," the girl cooed.

Margot blinked in disbelief and then amusement. *Hunter has been sneaking around. Hunter has a girlfriend.* All inklings of an intruder in the house took on a different shade in her mind. *How long has it been going on?*

She looked down at the key in her hand, suddenly feeling paranoid and hysterical. Perhaps there was a reasonable explanation for her getting locked in the attic the day before. Faulty hardware. Swollen wood. But someone had moved her things. She was sure of it. *Had Hunter given this girl a tour of the house?* she wondered. Had the two of them rifled through her closet the way she had rifled through his bedroom? She debated grilling the two teenagers about it but couldn't bear the thought of embarrassing her son in front of the first girl to ever set foot in his bedroom.

Exhausted, Margot returned to her own room. Sinking down against her pillow, she glanced over at Myron's empty side of the bed. *Myron.*

"Damn it," she whispered and got up. Back in the bathroom, she grabbed his drug case from the vanity and carried it into her closet for safekeeping.

A floor below her, Myron shifted on the leather couch. Brow slick with sweat and face contorted, he muttered to himself, lost in a dark and fitful dream. Walter's pistol lay on the coffee table by his side. It was loaded.

51

Ava lay next to Hunter on his bed, staring up at the cracks on his ceiling. The heat of her skin sent electricity down his side, but he did his best to ignore it.

"So. Are you ever going to tell me why you're here?" he asked timidly. He decided not to mention the article he'd found online or what he'd learned that day in his research. "What are you waiting for in this creepy old house?"

Ava didn't answer. Instead, she rolled off the bed and walked over to the closet. Clicking on the light, she scanned the writing that Benny had left. "I can't believe he's still alive."

"Who?"

"Benny. I wonder what he'll tell you." She traced the crayon markings with her fingertip.

DeAD GiRL.

She bent down and picked something up out of a box and carried it back to the bed. "Is this your sister?"

Hunter looked over at the photograph in her hand. A little boy sitting on the lap of a girl with blonde curls. "Yeah. That's Allison."

"What did you do when she died?" Ava sank onto the bed next to him, studying the girl in the photograph and then Hunter's cherub face.

"What do you mean?"

"I mean, did you do all the things you were supposed to do?"

"What was I supposed to do?" He propped himself up on an elbow and frowned at her. He didn't like where this was going.

"You know. Did you cry for everyone at the funeral? Did you tell the child psychologist *all* of your feelings about it? Did you go back to school right away and act like nothing was wrong? What did you do?"

His face darkened. "I'm not sure what the hell that has to do with anything."

"Did you believe she was really dead? Or did you look for her . . . at school? On the playground? At the store?"

Uncomfortable and exposed, he looked down at his bare chest, bony with ribs and dotted with a few embarrassing hairs. He'd been getting ready for bed when she'd shown up unannounced and uninvited. "Fuck you, okay? I was just a little kid! What the hell is your problem?"

"Do you still try to talk to her?" Ava looked up from the photo at him. A tear had escaped one of her pale, lifeless eyes. He wanted to touch it. He wanted to wipe it away.

"No. I haven't done that in years. I guess I used to, though." He sat up. The sight of her quivering lip made him forget he was angry. It made him want to hold her. "Ava. Are you okay?"

She looked away from him and set the photograph next to his bed. "I'll see you tomorrow," she said and left the room.

52

The Rawlings Family
January 24, 1931

From the sidewalk, the house stood dark and serene against the night sky. The only sign of the trouble within could be glimpsed in the moving shadows that darkened the yellow glow of the attic windows. The ominous shapes shrank and swelled violently across the ceiling. A muffled scream caught on the wind and got lost in the rustling of the bare trees, falling silently down to the blanket of snow in the yard.

The streetlights up and down Lee Road kept burning. The final sleeping hour unwound in silence. Not a soul could be seen wandering the sidewalks in the still moments before the first streetcar of morning would appear and the milkmen and the paperboys started on their routes. The houses to either side of Rawlingswood slept soundly, windows dark. A fat raccoon crept through the backyard, sniffing around the birdbath, scratching over the stones.

The back door burst open, sending the raccoon scuttling for cover into the trees.

Ella Rady, ashen and wild eyed, sprinted her heavy frame across the yard. Her ragged voice shattered the still air, echoing off the trees and the backs of the houses. "Help! Help us!" Her green robe flapped.

Her bare feet cut a jagged line through the snow to the neighbor's yard.

The back door to the house gaped open in a silent scream.

A half-dressed man appeared in the mouth of it, staring after Ella as she vanished through the trees. "Shit!" he muttered, taking off after her.

The stutter of a wooden window being opened rattled three stories up. A woman stuck her head out and hissed down to him. "Felix! Forget it. We have to go. *Now!*"

He stopped and turned to see Carmen toss a small object out of the window. He stared dumbly as a thin piece of metal fell with a flashing glint of steel, cutting through the snow, staining it red. *The razor.* Not daring to touch it, he trudged back into the house.

Two minutes later, Felix and Carmen appeared again but in coats, their arms loaded with apple crates full of cash. Felix pulled open the garage door, and the two of them climbed into his truck, dumping their spoils into the back.

"Why?" he barked at her as he revved up the engine. He slammed his hand against the steering wheel. "Why'd you have to go and do that? Big Ange is gonna kill us. He's gonna find us and fix us for good."

"He will if you just sit there, you idiot! Shut up and drive!" she barked back. A splatter of blood stained her skirt. She looked down at her hands and grabbed a rag off the floor to wipe the red from her fingernails.

"Sweet Jesus. That kid! That poor kid!" Felix stared blindly out the windshield into the backyard.

Georgina lay on the attic floor above them, locked in the bathroom with her dead son, her throat slit but not deeply enough, bleeding out but not fast enough. Little Walter's lifeless face lay trapped in the glass of her eyes as her mind tore itself apart.

The prostitute bared her teeth and pressed the barrel of Felix's own gun to his temple. "Felix. I swear to God, I'm gonna kill you myself if you don't drive this damn car!"

The truck squealed out of the garage, taking the turn down the driveway so fast he almost hit a tree. With a screech of the brakes, the brown Ford swerved down the driveway and out into the empty street. They headed south away from the city.

The house shuddered in the cold. Its garage gaped, mouth open. The back door wailed hot air into the night sky as the biting wind rushed through the kitchen. The attic windows gazed out with an empty glow into the night. Not a single shadow moved.

Ten minutes later, a sheriff's car glided its way silently up Lee Road. No sirens. No lights. Nothing to shatter the calm of Peaceful Shaker Village. A second car followed, and both vehicles stopped in front of Rawlingswood. The grand house cowered as Ella led the policemen up the driveway to the open back door.

"Let's go through it again."

The detective sat across from Ella in Mr. Rawlings's office an hour later and took notes.

A terrible sun had come up over the trees. They'd carried Georgina out on a stretcher. Ella had glimpsed the scream in the woman's eye, the shocked stare of an animal in a slaughterhouse, as they bundled her into the ambulance with bandages around her neck, her nightdress clinging to her bare legs, drenched in red. Even if they managed to save her body, the poor woman's mind was gone.

They covered little Walter's face before they carried him out.

"Miss Rady?"

Ella shuddered with revulsion, her own mind nearly broken. *My baby. My sweet shavo.* A hard tear slid down her cheek as she shook her head numbly, not believing, replaying it all over and over in her head, searching for a way to stop it. All the way back to the moment she'd found the boy lying on the bathroom floor. Back to the moment she'd heard the scream. The barrel of Felix's gun pointed at her again and again, and the woman behind it snarled.

"Miss Rady? We really must continue."

Her glazed expression fixed then on the man in the wool suit. The suit itself was telling. Tailored well. Custom cut. Far too expensive for an honest lawman. Two stories above them, a team of three deputies was busy collecting evidence. Loading the illegal still and empty crates into an unmarked truck parked behind the house. Ella followed them with the corner of her eye as they loaded the contraband out the back door and past the office windows. Out the back door, not the front.

"Mrs. Rawlings was living on her own, then?" he continued.

"Yes. Mr. Rawlings passed away. Eighteen months, I think." She didn't recognize her own voice. Dry as a husk. Lifeless as the rest of her.

"Did she mention any money trouble to you?"

"No. Not to me. But to the accountant. He came and explained. We had to pay back money to Mr. Rawlings's investors, the people he swindled. A man named Big Ange. He brings these terrible people. He put that machine up there. If we don't cooperate, the accountant said Missus Rawlings and . . ." She couldn't say the boy's name. She swallowed it. "He said they lose the house."

The man had stopped writing. He studied the vacant expression on her face and the calluses on her working-class hands. "Did you ever meet this 'Big Ange'?"

Ella shook her head.

"So as far as you know, this man may not even exist. Correct?"

Ella just stared at him. The twitch of a smile at the corner of his mouth matched the glint of the gold pinkie ring on his finger. She looked down at his notepad and how little he'd written, and it was clear.

"I understand that Mrs. Rawlings had a friend staying with her?"
Ella lifted her eyebrows at this but said nothing.

"A Miss Eveline Prentice, I believe?" he continued. The name had been chosen by someone with a plan. "She says she's been staying here for weeks. I can bring her in if you'd like me to refresh your memory."

Ella squeezed her hands together until the knuckles turned white.

"Miss Prentice has given us a written statement as to Mrs. Rawlings's erratic behavior as of late," he continued. "Had you noticed Mrs. Rawlings acting strangely?"

Ella lowered her eyes. It was true. Georgina had not been herself in months. But it was becoming quite clear that the truth was irrelevant here. Whoever this Big Ange might be, he had the detective in his pocket, and the fix was in. She glanced up at another load of crates slipping out the back door and into the driveway.

"I also understand that Mrs. Rawlings left a note." The detective pulled a piece of paper from a leather folio. "Her instructions to her brother state here that the house and all of its contents be auctioned and the proceeds given to charity. Do you recognize this handwriting?"

Ella nodded, not even bothering to look at the paper he brandished at her. He wasn't collecting evidence anymore, and she knew it. He was just demonstrating his weapons and making clear the part she would play.

"Now, I don't see any arrangements here for a severance package for you, her trusted housekeeper, for all your good service. But that hardly seems fair in my opinion. I'm sure that your dear employer would want to make sure you are well provided for as you recover from this tremendous . . . shock."

She watched him lay out a stack of hundred-dollar bills, her heart a stone. Her gaze drifted through the open doors of the office to the foyer where they'd carried Georgina out on a stretcher. There was no saving her. Not now. No matter what she told the newspapers or the judge or the governor. None of it mattered anymore. None of it would bring the boy back. The only thing the truth would do was get Ella killed herself.

She gathered the money without looking her new owner in the eye. Instead, she contemplated the spot on the desk where she'd found Mr. Rawlings sprawled out in a puddle of his own urine. *The coward.*

She shifted her gaze back to the windows beyond it, and her breath caught as though she saw Ninny's restless dead. As though the specters of two men, a young woman, and a baby stood there just outside the glass. The mother's and baby's throats had been slit open.

"When the *mulo* come," she whispered, "I hope they come for you."

"Pardon?" The man sat up a bit straighter.

She leveled her eyes at him. "You tell your Angelo to burn this house."

With that, she stood up and left the detective in the office with his forged letters and incomplete notes. She plodded down the center hallway and up the back stairs to little Walter's room.

Once inside, she ran a hand over his bed, his books, saying a prayer in her own tongue, knowing they would never heed her advice. The house, built on lies and stolen money, was worth too much, even tainted with murder.

Closing her eyes, she imagined another boy in this room. Another Walter, but not hers. Above her, Walter's blood soaked into the gaps in the bathroom tile, through the wood and the wool fibers of the insulation down to the dead space between the floor and the ceiling. She crossed herself and let her tears fall.

God protect the poor souls who come next.

Ella Rady left Rawlingswood with her small suitcase in her hand. The empty eyes of the house watched her shuffle slowly down Lee Road, heartbroken.

53

The Spielman Family
August 11, 2018

The next day, a bent old woman knocked on the front door.

Margot nodded at her through the side glass and unlocked it. "Good morning! You must be Nala. Thank you so much for agreeing to come back."

"You have the money?" the woman asked.

"Of course!" Margot shuffled back into the kitchen and returned with two fifty-dollar bills. "Please, come in. Can I get you some coffee or tea?"

"No need." The crone made the sign of the cross before stepping over the threshold. She eyed the ceiling high above her warily. "What is it you want?"

"Would you join me in the living room?" Margot motioned the woman into the impeccably decorated sitting room to the left of the staircase. Silk drapes, custom upholstery, imported rug—Margot had fussed over the room for months but had only sat in it twice. She chose a spot on the long sofa, hoping the woman would join her there.

Madame Nala took a seat at the edge of the chair closest to the door instead, clutching her large purse to her chest, hunched like a buzzard. The woman's thick accent sounded eastern European, but Margot couldn't quite place it.

"Are you sure I can't get you anything?" Margot tried again.

"No." The old woman let her eyes circle the elegant room and wander back through the cased opening into the foyer. She caught sight of Hunter peeking through the railing upstairs, the bulk of him hidden in the shadow of the hallway. The old woman gave him the slightest nod and turned back to Margot. "What is it I do for you, Mrs. Spielman?"

Margot's smile faded ever so slightly, but she kept her voice light. "Our contractor, Max Tuttle, tells us you were of some assistance during the renovation."

"Yes. I come. I try to help. It did not do much good, I see."

Margot nodded as though this was what she'd expected to hear. "I understand there were some disturbing incidents." She took a breath, searching for the right thing to say. "We've come to realize some pretty disturbing things about the house ourselves."

The old woman said nothing in the pregnant pause that followed. She just stared at Margot with her dark eyes and withered face, waiting.

Shifting uncomfortably in the silence, Margot continued, "It seems as though the real estate agent left some things out about the history of the house. There was a murder here. In 1931, Georgina Rawlings murdered her son."

This news didn't seem to faze the old fortune-teller; she simply nodded. *The attic. It happened in the attic.* "And how do we know this?"

"We found some old newspapers. A mother killing her only son made some headlines, I guess."

"Hmm." The crone looked up at the ceiling. "You are a mother. Do you believe a mother would do this?"

"Do I . . . I don't know." Margot winced and tried to imagine holding a knife to Hunter's throat. *No.* "The newspaper said she'd gone mad."

"The stories people tell to newspapers, even the stories they tell to themselves, are not always the true stories. No matter. What is it I do for you?"

Margot held her palms open to the ceiling, feeling foolish. "I guess I was hoping you might be able to help us."

The old woman narrowed her eyes. "Help us how?"

"Get rid of the bad luck, I guess. It just feels wrong here. It feels like someone is . . . I don't know." *Watching us. Judging us.* "It's just not a good feeling. I can't help but think the house needs an exorcism."

"I have no magic for this house. I try smudging. I try coaxing the calm back into the wood. This house, it has a memory that goes back. Back to the earth it rests on."

"What do you mean, the earth it rests on?"

"We Roma, we have stories. We pass them down. Some get lost. Some change. After I fail Yanni, I go back. I ask my *Bibio.* I ask *Baba Natalia.* We have stories of this place. An old *drabarni* lived here once, so the story goes."

Margot drew in her chest at this revelation. "What story?"

"This place, it is *mahrime*, unclean. Haunted by many *mulo.*"

"Mu-lo?" Margot repeated.

"How you say? Ghosts?"

"Ah." She fought not to roll her eyes at herself or the old woman. Hearing it out loud made her realize how ridiculous it sounded. But still, this was the reason she'd called the woman in the first place. "How do we get these *mulo* to leave? Can you do something? We'd pay, of course."

Margot told herself the sheer lark of it would be worth the price. Perhaps she'd invite some would-be friends over to watch the old witch work. She'd turn it into a cocktail party with Ouija boards and dry ice.

"This is no *bujo*, no swindling trick. I have no cure for you. These *mulo* very old. Stories say there are bones here. Deep in the ground. From before house was built. *Mahrime!*"

"What?" Margot gaped at her. "What bones?"

"The dead were laid here. Beneath the stones." The old woman pointed toward the back of the house.

"What dead?" Margot shifted in her seat to stare at the wall behind her.

"I cannot say. I do not know. The story is just a story, but I felt it. I saw the shadows moving. I felt them in the wood. This house . . ." The old woman reached out her gnarled hand toward Margot. "You must leave this house."

54

"Who was that at the door, hon?" Myron asked. His hair was dripping from the shower. He kept his back to her as he fixed himself a coffee so she wouldn't see the sickly pallor of his skin or the twitch of his hands. He hadn't been able to find his gear that morning, even after an hour of searching his closet. He didn't want to think where it might've ended up. *Just hold it together. It will turn up,* he told himself.

"That crazy witch Max hired. I called her." Margot poured another cup of coffee and avoided looking at him. *Is he high right now?* she wondered. She'd hidden the drug kit she'd found the night before, but he could have more stashed around the house. *What the hell am I going to do?*

"Was she any help?"

"Hardly. You wouldn't believe the crap she was peddling. She made it sound like this place is *The Amityville Horror.*" She retrieved the creamer from the fridge and took a sip of coffee long enough to change the subject. "Don't forget we have the Zavodas and DeMarcos coming tonight."

"That's tonight?"

"Yeah, hon. I put it in your calendar over a week ago." Margot rolled her eyes. *Maybe you were too busy shooting up to remember.* She shook the thought away. *Myron would never use heroin; he's too smart for that. Isn't he? There has to be some sort of explanation. Is he injecting B vitamins or something?* She couldn't bring herself to ask. "I'm having the club do the catering. I'm just not up to cooking for six."

"Six. What about Hunter?"

"What about Hunter? I'm sure the last thing he'd like to do is sit around with a bunch of middle-aged parents discussing tennis. I'll fix him a plate. Don't worry. Oh, and get this. Hunter has a girlfriend."

"Really?" Myron brightened at this. "Who?"

"I don't know. Some cute little blonde girl named Ava. I guess he's been sneaking her into the house. Have you seen her?"

Cute little blonde girl. Myron's face furrowed with recognition. *The girl in the closet. The girl at the top of the attic stairs. Oh, Jesus, what has she told Hunter?* He cleared his throat to steady his voice. "Uh. No. I haven't. Do we need to have a talk with him?"

"A talk? I thought you'd be happy he was socializing."

"Of course I'm happy about that, but sneaking girls into the house? Are we okay with that?"

"I have no idea what the hell we're okay with anymore. We're living in a goddamn murder house, Myron! I would like to sit down and seriously discuss what we're going to do about that. That gypsy woman thinks this place is going to kill us, for God's sake!" A million things Margot wasn't quite ready to say simmered at the edge of her voice. "I just really wish we never came here."

"Jesus, Margot! Are we going to have to have this same goddamn fight every goddamn day?"

Neither one of them could sense the boy standing on the back stairs listening to them bicker. Hunter turned and crept back up the steps to his room. Once inside, he locked the door and pinged Caleb on the computer. It was only ten a.m., and when his friend appeared on the screen, he was bedraggled and yawning.

"What the fuck, man? It's like the crack of dawn!"

"Sorry. But you are not going to believe this." Hunter filled his friend in on the old Romany woman and the talk of bones buried somewhere in the yard.

"I told you, man! Did I tell you, or did I tell you? Fucking burial ground! Unbelievable. What are you gonna do?" Caleb's pimpled face lit with perverse glee. "Are you gonna go like digging for them?"

"Why the fuck would I do that?" Hunter gaped at him. "Are you insane?"

"That's how they lifted the curse, dude. In *Poltergeist*. Or one of those movies anyway. You have to like find the bones, and the spirits will rest. Or some shit. Aren't you at least curious?"

"I dunno. The lady seemed totally off her head, and we found the ghost, remember? Girl in the attic?" Hunter glanced at his closed door, wondering if she was outside it, listening. He'd woken that morning to an empty room.

"Well, you found one of them anyway. I've been looking for more info on Ava Turner and can't find her anywhere, man. Have you thought about asking around? Like at the schools and stuff? Or . . . what about that asshole? The guy with the weed?"

Hunter shrugged and checked his phone. Roger hadn't texted back. Hunter didn't say so, but he was relieved. "I doubt he knows anything."

He didn't mention the article he'd found about the dead boy or his worst fears about Ava.

"I still say you get a shovel, man."

"Shut up."

"Fine. Have it your way. But what are you going to do about the girl?"

"I'm not sure." Hunter turned to his closed door. The sound of his parents arguing crept in through the seams, swelling louder and louder, ready to burst.

"What aren't you telling me, Myron?"

"What the hell are you talking about? Are you off your meds again?"

His eyes drifted to the photograph of him and his sister sitting next to his bed. *Allison,* he thought. *I really wish you were here.*

To Caleb, he said, "I have to get out of here."

55

"Hello there! Come on in. Welcome to Rawlingswood!" Myron held the front door open with a flourish for their guests. "So glad you could come."

"Rawlingswood?" the man chuckled.

"Check the door knocker, my friend," Myron said with a snarky grin. The screaming argument he'd had with his wife that morning only showed in the red tinge around his eyes. He'd stormed out of the house, happy for an excuse to leave and go find what he needed elsewhere. "This is a bona fide estate."

"Well, shoot. If I had known, I would've worn my tux."

"Oh, shut up, Harold." Harold's wife waved a dismissive hand at him and strolled into the foyer with a smirk on her face. "Myron, thank you so much for inviting us. Where's your better half?"

"She'll be down in a sec. You know how you ladies can be . . . Mark, nice to see you! Thanks for coming." Myron gave the other gentleman a handshake and nodded at his wife. "Emily, good of you to drag the old man out. Can I get anyone a drink?"

"Chardonnay?" Harold's wife did a slow turn in the foyer, calculating the relative cost of every fixture. "I'm dying for a tour of this house. Myron, it's stunning!"

"Why don't you two run up and find Margot? I'll grab the drinks." He waved the women up the grand stairway and led the men into the kitchen, where he'd assembled a top-shelf selection on one of the marble islands.

The ladies twittered up the stairwell, commenting on the chandelier, the woodwork, the paint color. "I'm so glad that they stayed true to the original architecture."

"I love that they left the wood trim unpainted."

Margot heard them coming and hastily dabbed at her eyes, trying to erase all traces of her hellacious fight with Myron. *What do you mean, you have to go back to Boston next week? You're just going to leave us here in this place? What about Hunter? . . . I don't care what the lawyer said. You told me the lawsuit was all but settled. Are you hiding something from me? . . . Why are you acting so nuts?*

She didn't mention finding his leather case in the bathroom the day before. She didn't mention the needle or the powder or the confidential files she'd found in his closet. Saying the words would make them real. *Maybe I overreacted. There must be a reasonable explanation for all of it*, she told herself, checking her makeup. There just had to be.

Margot greeted her guests in the hall with a practiced grin. "Hey, ladies! Thanks so much for coming."

Gales of forced laughter and swooning followed as she gave her new friends a tour of the second floor. The master suite brought high-pitched approvals. "Gorgeous! I love the marble!"

"You must've spent a fortune!"

The other rooms were dispatched more quickly. Margot had made a point to check them all that morning in the light of day. She paused at the door to the guest room over the garage, eyeing the rumpled duvet. *Hunter? That girlfriend of his?* she wondered as she smoothed the bedding back to perfection. She didn't feel the weight of a girl standing behind the plumbing access door as she guided her ladies through the suite and adjacent laundry room.

Hunter's room was avoided altogether. "You know how teenagers can be about their privacy," she chortled with a wave of her hand.

"What did you do with the third floor?" Harold's wife asked. "We turned ours into a media room and just love it!"

"I wish," Margot mused. "We left it untouched for now. With just the three of us here, we decided to spend the money in the kitchen. Emily, I'm dying to hear your thoughts on the dining room. We have so many blank walls . . ."

She led her guests down the servants' staircase to where Myron was waiting with drinks. None of them noticed the footsteps in the back hallway over the chatter in the kitchen.

"Will Hunter be joining us for dinner?" Emily asked a half hour later as they settled into their places at the table.

"Oh, I think he's still out with friends," Margot said with a knowing wink even though she had no idea where her son had gone. He'd slipped out during her fight with Myron. She held up a bottle, eager to change the subject. "Who needs more wine?"

Conversations separated themselves by gender as they ate. The women discussed art, decorating, the coming school year, and the struggle to find proper extracurriculars to pad college applications. The men kept their conversation to golf, boating, and work. It was the talk of the hospital that sent the evening reeling in the wrong direction.

"You know, I've been meaning to ask you. How is that legal matter progressing back in Boston?" Harold asked.

Margot's ears perked up at this.

Myron took another drink of wine, hoping no one noticed the slight tremor in his hand. He'd managed to score a fix that afternoon somewhere outside the house, but it wasn't quite enough. "It's coming along. You know these things can drag out. It can take years."

"I hear you. Apparently, the board has received a few phone calls from Boston. You may want to follow up."

This revelation tightened Myron's jaw, but he managed to lift an eyebrow sardonically. "Really?"

"Just thought you should know."

"Well, I guess some lawyer is really trying to earn his fee. Vultures." He forced a laugh, but it rang false. The other two men nodded for his benefit, and Myron downed his glass of wine. "Shall I open another? You won't believe this rosé we found the other day."

Myron pushed away from the table and tried to look casual strolling into the kitchen. Alone, he ran a shaking hand through his hair before taking stock of the wine fridge.

"Fucking Margot," he muttered to himself. He'd never wanted any of it. The dinner party. The guests. The questions. He just needed some space to figure things out, to breathe, but no one ever considered what *he* needed. Certainly not his wife. He threw the wine key into the sink. "I could kill her."

Movement caught the corner of his eye, and he turned to see a blonde girl standing at the foot of the back stairs. He nearly dropped the bottle in his hand. It was *her*.

"Hi, Dr. Spielman," she said.

"Uh. Hello?" Myron stared at her a beat. She was wearing one of Hunter's T-shirts.

"I'm Hunter's friend. Ava. He said he'd meet me here." She gave him a little wave, harmless, but something was off about her smile. It didn't match the dark look in her eyes.

Myron fumbled with the wine cork. "Nice to meet you, Ava. Hunter's not here right now."

"I know. He said he'd be back soon. Um. Are you okay?"

"Excuse me?" His face had gone red with the exertion of being polite to this strange creature that he was certain he'd seen before skulking around his house. He glanced over at the block of knives on the counter as he ripped the cork from the bottle with a faint pop.

"Are you alright? You seem . . . I don't know." She stared at him with a deadened gaze that did not belong to a teenage girl. Her eyes had seen too much.

"I'm sorry, but I think you'd better leave, Ava. We have guests." Myron barely kept the bite out of his voice. "I'll have Hunter call you when he gets back."

Ava gave him a small nod and one more probing look before slipping out of the kitchen to the mudroom and then the backyard.

He was heading back to the dining room with the open bottle of wine when Hunter came in through the side door. Myron, lost in his own agitation, snapped at him. "Nice of you to show up. Your friend Ava was just here."

"What?" Hunter stopped in his tracks.

"Ava. She was here. And by the way, I'm not so comfortable with you sneaking your girlfriend into the house or letting her hang out here when you're not around. We're going to talk about that later. Listen, your mom invited over some friends, so you are going to be on your best behavior. Understood?" He motioned to the dining room, where the chatter had lightened to a dinner party shade. "If you're hungry, grab a plate."

"Sure, Dad." But Hunter wasn't interested in food. He bolted up the back stairs to his room.

His father's gaze trailed after him a moment, helplessly disconnected. *What is up with that kid?* Myron straightened himself and sauntered back into the dining room. "Wait until you try this wine. It will change your life."

Margot had been studying her plate for the last several minutes, replaying Harold's comments about Boston.

After the table had complimented the new wine, Emily started a new topic. "So tell us more about the house. It's gorgeous! Was it like this when you bought it?"

"God, no. It was a mess!" Margot had downed several glasses of wine, and it showed. "The copper was stripped. The radiators were missing. The place had been utterly vandalized."

"Wow. That must've been a bit unsettling."

"Ha. Yeah. And it just keeps getting better. Right, hon?" Myron dropped his fork and glared at her.

"What do you mean?" Emily and the others were staring now.

"It's a murder house. The words were spray-painted on that wall over there. *Murder House!* But we didn't mind that much. Did we, Myron?" Margot fixed him with a vicious smile that said, *I will never forgive you.* "The price was just too darn good to pass up."

A murmur rippled around the table.

"What do you mean, it's a murder house?" Harold asked.

"There was a murder here like a hundred years ago. For some reason, my lovely wife thinks that means the house is cursed." He tipped his glass at her in a mock toast. *Fuck you, babe.*

"Really? A murder? Here?" Emily gaped at them both. "That's unbelievable."

"Why? Is Shaker Heights too fancy for murder?" Margot laughed, sounding more than a little tipsy. "A six-year-old boy was killed in the attic. How *fancy* is that?"

"Margot," Myron warned. "You're being rude and ridiculous."

"Why don't we change the subject," Harold suggested uncomfortably. "Do you two have big plans this winter? You wouldn't think it, but the skiing just south of here is really something."

Margot talked right past Harold. "I'm being ridiculous? How am I being ridiculous?"

Upstairs, Hunter sat at his computer and booted up the screen. His face was a worried frown as he pulled several books from his backpack, including a 2015 Woodbury Elementary School yearbook stamped *Property of Shaker Heights Public Library.* He flipped it open to the back and a picture of a young kid. *Toby Turner.*

The sound of his mother's voice from downstairs made him stop and listen.

"What's ridiculous is you leaving your wife and son in this *murder* house alone to go back to Boston for a week! Why are you going back there, Myron? Harold, what are these phone calls to the board about, exactly?"

"Margot, I think you've had a little too much wine." Myron shook his head in disgust at her, eager to deflect her questions. "I'm sorry, everyone. This move and the house renovations have been a bit of strain. Margot just hasn't been herself lately."

"Perhaps we should go," Mark suggested, frowning at both of them.

"No. Stay." Margot's face burned red with rage and embarrassment. She straightened herself and drank some water. "Myron's right. This move has been hard . . . It's hard to be taken from all of your friends and neighbors when you're not even told the truth about why you're moving. But obviously, I'm being ridiculous."

"No, I'm the ridiculous one." Myron held up both his hands, seething at her. "I'm the one that can't even send my wife *flowers* without her struggling to figure out which of the guys she's fucking sent them."

Her jaw dropped. *The roses.* She quickly shut it again. *You son of a bitch.*

"Other men, Myron?" she said coldly, narrowing her eyes. "You sound paranoid. Harold? Mark? You're doctors, right? Isn't paranoia a sign of drug addiction?"

Myron stiffened ever so slightly and then fixed her with a murderous glare. "You're drunk, Margot."

Harold spoke for all of them when he said, "I think we'd better get going. It was a lovely dinner, Margot. Perhaps we'll catch up some more another time . . . Myron."

Within two minutes, all four guests had left in an embarrassed shuffling of feet and placations.

Once the door shut, Margot turned on him. "I cannot believe you pulled this shit in front of them! You have to work with those men, for God's sake!"

"Mark is a nurse anesthetist, and Harold doesn't even work in my building! If you actually paid me one bit as much attention as you do your little internet fuck-boys, you would know that!"

"My what?" She gaped at him. "Whatever, Myron. I want you and your pills and your needles and whatever else you're doing out of this house. Tonight!"

"This is *my* house. Why the hell should *I* leave?" he bellowed back. "I'm not the one running around screwing twenty-two-year-olds!"

She didn't dare let her mask slip. "I have no idea what you're talking about!"

"Oh, really? Well, let's see." Myron pulled out his phone and queued up a video stored there. The screen came to life with an image of Margot bent over in her yoga studio, slowly counting to ten, naked. "What do you call that, huh? That's real educational, hon. I think I just saw your tonsils!"

"You've been *spying* on me?" she hissed, internally calculating how much he'd seen and how he'd tapped into her system. "What did you do? Set up your own little camera?"

He ignored her. "Exactly how many of your yoga fans are you sleeping with?"

"Keep your voice down!"

"Why? You worried your teenage son might find out you're screwing his classmates?"

"Fuck you, Myron!" she seethed, storming into the den. With trembling hands, she poured brown liquor into a tumbler.

"That's real nice, hon. Have another drink," he taunted her from the doorway.

She downed the glass and took a breath before turning back to him. "Like you're one to talk. How long, Myron? How long have you been using? Huh? Were you doing it back in Boston? Were you *high* when that poor girl died in the recovery room? I saw the files, Myron. Unwarranted surgery? Unethical medical practice? Did they suspend your license? Is that why we had to move all the way the fuck out to Ohio? Is that why you took a hospital *administration* job?"

"Don't be ridiculous," he muttered, but fear flashed in his eyes. "I followed hospital policy. Always, dammit!"

"Was it hospital policy to perform unnecessary surgery?"

"Whether to operate or not is a matter of fucking *professional opinion!*" he shouted at the top of his lungs. "I couldn't take the risk of letting something suspicious go! Could I? I saw irregular tissue! What if the lesions were malignant? What if they metastasized? How could I take that risk that I might miss something? That some poor little girl might . . ." His voice caught in his throat.

Margot stared at him, stunned, watching tears leak from his eyes. "This is about Allison, isn't it?"

He turned away from her and struggled to put the tears back in his eyes and the words back in his mouth. *What did I just say?*

"Myron. What happened to Allison wasn't your fault. Her cancer wasn't your fault." A wave of sadness threatened to knock her from her feet. She gripped the edge of the desk. "Jesus, how many little girls have you cut open trying to fix this?"

"Don't be ridiculous!"

"Ridiculous? *I'm* being ridiculous! A girl is *dead*, Myron! She's dead because of you!" Her voice and hands were shaking. *What if that girl is dead because of me? I didn't see the signs. I didn't make him get help.*

Margot yanked open a drawer in the desk. She pulled out the leather zippered case she'd found in the bathroom. The gun lying beneath it hardly registered. "Is this me being ridiculous?"

She unzipped the case, shaking the needle, spoon, and powder onto the desk blotter. Seeing it all sent another shock through her system, one she couldn't ignore. "I cannot believe you brought this *filth* into our house, Myron! What if Hunter found it?"

Myron's eyes flashed from Margot to the drugs and back again, registering a diffuse terror at being discovered and then rage. *I will not be berated by* you. *I will not. Not ever again.* "What if Hunter found it? Ha! Where do you think I found this stuff in the first place?"

Margot just gaped at him. *Hunter?* Her missing pills, her missing nightgown, her shuffled closet all tumbled through her mind.

"I didn't want to tell you." The lie smoothed the fraying edges of Myron's face, giving his rage direction. "I thought it would put you over the edge. You've barely been maintaining since we got here, and Lord knows the boy doesn't need to live through another one of your fucking breakdowns, Margot. He's got enough problems. But here we are, aren't we?"

As he regained the upper hand, the divorce filing took shape in his fevered brain. *History of mental instability. Alcoholism. Infidelity.* He might even get custody. Margot seemed to realize it too.

"You're saying you found heroin in Hunter's room?" The adrenaline buzzing in her ears muffled the sound of her own voice. It was the sound of her losing everything. *Not my baby. No.*

His malpractice suit all but forgotten, Myron kept driving his nails. "You're always worried he might be on drugs. Well, there you go, Margot. I guess you were just too drunk yourself to notice."

"What?" Hunter, who'd crept down into the kitchen to listen to the argument, appeared in the doorway.

"Admit it, son." Myron turned on his boy with an iron stare. "It's okay to admit it. You have a problem. And we can help."

Hunter shook his head. The baggie of weed buried inside the gerbil food loomed in the back of his mind, but then he saw the hypodermic needle. "No way! That's not mine! I'm not shooting up fucking *heroin!*"

"Watch your mouth." Myron took a menacing step toward him. He wouldn't lose his life, his career, his son. He couldn't. He'd make it up to the boy somehow, he told himself. Someday, Hunter would realize that this was the only option. Margot wasn't fit to be a mother. She hadn't been fit in years. "We know you've been sneaking around here with that junkie girlfriend of yours, stealing things. We know you locked your poor mother in the attic. The first step in recovery is admitting you have a problem, son."

"But I don't! This is bullshit! You're the one with the pills, Dad. You're the one. All the articles say when the pills run out, heroin is what addicts turn to next . . . Mom," he pleaded with his mother, but Margot was lost in her own nightmare.

"Did you?" she whispered, shaking her head. "Did you do this?"

"Drug test me! Okay? You might find a little weed, but you won't find fucking heroin. And then drug test *him!*" Hunter shouted, pointing a finger at his father.

Myron cracked the boy across the face with an open palm. "Don't you dare point a finger at me. You have no idea what the hell you're talking about. You're just a kid. And you have a problem, and so help me God . . ." He grabbed Hunter by the shoulders with the look of a man holding on to the edge of a cliff. "You're not going to lie your way out of this!"

"Myron! Let him go!" Margot shouted.

"No. You're always babying him, but he has got to learn." Myron pushed the boy against the wall. "Just admit it, son. There is right. And there is wrong."

"Myron! Stop!"

"I want to hear him say it, god dammit. Just say, *Dad, I—*"

The crack of a gun shook the room.

In the utter shock of the blast, Myron lost his grip.

"Let him go, Myron." She pointed the gun she'd found in the attic at his head. "I don't believe you. I don't. Look at you, for God's sake. Look at your hands. They're shaking."

Hunter stumbled back, stupefied at the image of his mother with the gun. *This isn't happening.*

"Hunter!" a small voice hissed from the kitchen.

He turned to see Ava standing in the kitchen. She was holding his cell phone. The numbers *911* glowed on the screen.

Myron shifted his cornered gaze and saw the girl. *The girl. Oh, Jesus. The girl.*

"Come on!" Ava shouted. She grabbed Hunter's hand and dragged him into the kitchen.

Dazed, the boy followed her three steps, then turned back to his mother, who was holding the gun in two shaking hands, tears streaming down her face. His father, with his palms up, took one step toward her and then another. "Calm down, Margot. Let's think this through."

Ava kept pulling.

"Hunter, get out. Get help!" Margot choked out the words, following him with one eye as he slipped out the back door. *Run!*

Outside, a patchwork of incandescent lights from the windows lit the yard. Ava dragged him beyond the reach of the house.

"The police are coming," she whispered, retreating back into the trees.

He followed her, legs numb and stumbling, not believing any of it. The gun. The fight. His father's fingers digging into his arms. The red welt on his cheek. From a distance, the house no longer seemed real. Shadows danced violently in the den windows, and he watched them with detached fascination.

Ava was crying. "It's happening again."

"What's happening again?" he whispered.

Another gunshot made him jump.

56

The Martin Family
December 5, 2014

A door slammed like a shot.

"Ava? Ava, honey, where are you?" Papa Martin's voice called out in the hallway below, shaking the timbers of the old house. The hour was late, but her foster mother was out of town at another academic conference. Mama Martin traveled a lot, leaving her husband and foster children to their own devices.

Ava held her breath in the attic crawl space, praying this would be the time he didn't find her. Her shadow huddled under the rafters. All the other doors in the attic were locked. He'd made sure of it.

The weight of the man's footsteps vibrated up through the walls. Another door slammed open beneath her. The sound of Papa Martin's voice chilled her blood.

"Hey, buddy. I'm looking for Ava. Is she in here?"

She couldn't make out Toby's response ten feet below her.

"I think she ran away. I can't find her anywhere, champ. Did she say anything to you about it?" Papa was talking loud enough for her to hear. Deliberately loud. "I'm afraid she's never coming back."

Her brother's muffled answers became wails. "Ava!" the boy cried out, terrified. "Where are you?"

Ava covered her ears, shaking. *No. No. No.*

Mr. Martin had never hurt Toby before. He'd never raised a hand to him, and that had been Ava's only consolation. Her brother had been safe. Hearing him crying through the floor, hearing him convinced she had abandoned him, was unbearable.

She squeezed the skeleton key she'd stolen from a junk drawer in the kitchen and set it along the top of the knee wall. Hands trembling, she felt the floor blindly for the loose board.

Toby cried out again. "Ava, don't leave!"

If he cried hard enough, he would start choking. His asthma would tighten his airways down to nothing. She could already hear the rattle in his voice.

Unable to stand it a moment longer, she pounded the floorboard with her fist and called out. "Toby! It's okay! I'm up here."

The house went still. Listening.

"I think she's hiding, Toby. You stay here. I'll go find her."

The door to the boy's room clicked shut and rattled as Mr. Martin locked it again. Ava's numb fingers ran along the boards of the crawl space, scrambling for a plan. The social worker wasn't due back for months. Plenty of time for bruises to fade and broken bones to mend. There was no telling what he might do. The last time she'd run from him, he'd squeezed her neck so hard it left marks.

Her hand hit a loose board near the knee wall. *There it is.* She pried it up and dug into the stone wool insulation below until she felt it. Metal. She fumbled the gun into her sweating palms as the weight of the heavy man pounded down the hallway to the attic door.

The lock gave way. The door slapped open.

He took the steps two at a time as Ava righted herself. The weight of the gun in her hand still hadn't fully registered in her mind when he crested the stairs.

"Ava, honey. What are you doing up here?" the man said in a sickly-sweet voice. He stood there, all six feet five and 270 pounds of him, in his undershirt and boxer shorts. "Toby's worried sick."

The blood drained from her face at the thought of her brother sick and alone and what was coming next. His eyes focused on her mouth, her neck, her breasts. Not her hand. Not the gun.

His fists clenched, he took a step toward her and then another. "What are we going to do with you?"

The coming scene played out in his pitying smile and the hard set of his eyes, one ugly image after another—his hand cracking her across the face and slamming her into the floor (*Why do you make me do this?*), hands petting her bruised cheek (*Why can't you behave, honey?*), hands slipping under her nightgown (*Let me hold you*), his soft voice muttering consolations in her ear as he took what he wanted (*It's okay, baby, it's okay*).

Ava shook her head at his smiling face, tears spilling from her eyes. She braced herself and raised the gun. *It's not okay.* She squeezed her eyes shut.

BAM!

The blast exploded from her hand. The deafening sound reverberated up and down the attic. The world swelled around her, every atom screaming. Then it vanished, taking her with it.

Then nothing.

The ragged sound of someone struggling to breathe slowly brought her back into her shaking bones. Air hissed in and out of her throat.

When she dared open her eyes, she found herself in the diorama of a crime scene. A thin wisp of smoke hung in the air. Sensations registered in the corner of her mind. The smell of something burning. Her shoulder aching as though it had been wrenched loose. Her hand stinging with the burn of gunpowder. The glint of the pistol lying at her feet.

Clyde Martin lay on the ground two feet away from it.

He's dead. Her eyes lolled in and out of focus, refusing to see, unable to not see. *I killed him. He's dead.*

Down below, a small voice screamed through the plaster and wood, "Ava!"

As if in reply, Clyde rolled onto his side and coughed. His face had swelled to the point of bursting. His arms shook as though with seizure. But there was no blood. No blood pooling on the floor. No urine. No vomit. No bullet hole.

Ava numbly surveyed the spectacle of him convulsing there, searching for fluids, with a detached fear he'd spring up and attack her and also that he wouldn't.

He clutched himself under his arm and shuddered again, sucking in air. "A-va," he gasped, his face puckering in pain. "Call 911. Call . . . ssss. Heart. It's—"

Morbidly curious, she scanned the floors and walls until she found it. A tiny hole had punctured the ceiling over the staircase several inches from where he'd been standing. *I missed.* Emotions failed her. Relief? Despair? She dropped her empty gaze back down to the man on the floor.

As the shock of the blast dissipated, his words began to make sense. *Heart. Heart attack.*

It took several moments for her to think to pick up the gun and keep it out of his reach. She drifted through her next motions as though in a dream, grabbing the gun at her feet, wandering to the hole in the ceiling, picking up a chip of plaster from the floor, squinting at the puncture she'd made out into the night sky. A whistle of cold air fell onto her face like rain.

The man rolled again, his large belly heaving for air. His face purple now. His lips working the shapes of words but unable to make a sound. *Call. Help.* She studied him with detached fascination. His

heart seizing in his rib cage, his lungs gasping, his arteries bursting—
the shape of a man but no longer a man.

Call. Help.

Ava slowly considered the gun in her hand, what it meant and
didn't mean, and then her eyes circled the room. How many times
had she hoped for a scenario just like this? How many hours had she
prayed? A story began to form in her head, a script she would read
later. *I was asleep in bed and heard a terrible noise . . . Please send an
ambulance! He's not breathing!*

Her foot scattered the plaster dust below the hole she'd made
until it was gone.

She went back into the crawl space to retrieve her stolen key
and carried it into the tiny storage room on the right, next to Ella
Rady's old room. Glancing back at the man writhing on the floor,
she unlocked the door and stepped into the closet-size bedroom. She
carefully wiped her fingerprints from the gun like she'd seen done on
TV shows and shook out the bullets. She placed it all inside an old
cigar box, burying it under the crumbling newspapers about poor
little Walter. She then dusted all traces of herself from the top of the
box and the floor. She closed and locked the door once more, taking
her time to wipe the doorknob with her nightgown.

Giving Mr. Martin a wide berth, she drifted past him to the attic
stairs, to her brother. She could hear the boy crying, "Ava! Ava, where
are you?"

Toby would need comforting. They would need to get their stories straight. *It's not our fault. There was no gun, sweetie. You never
saw or heard a gun, right?* She would unlock the doors and return the
key to its drawer and wait.

"A-va," the man behind her choked.

She turned to him one last time, committing the sight of him
helpless on the floor to her memory, declawing him, defanging him.

Crouching down next to him, just out of his reach, she whispered, "It's okay, Papa . . . I won't tell anyone. I promise."

His skin darkened to a deeper shade of purple.

As she headed down the steps, she caught a sensation that stopped her cold. A shadow stood in the bathroom doorway at the other end of the attic, just out of reach of the light.

"Who's there?" she whispered, eyes darting from the shadow to Clyde lying on the floor and back again. The man's purple face followed her gaze, searching the bathroom for help and finding nothing but an empty doorway.

She stared another moment at the apparition, blinking her eyes until it was gone, then headed down the stairs.

57

The Spielman Family
August 11, 2018

The sirens came two minutes later. Hunter sat on the ground at the back of their lot and watched through the windows as two police officers entered, guns drawn. Ava sat at his side, silently weeping and holding his numb hand.

This isn't happening.

The thought wrote itself over Margot's face as the two officers shouted from the foyer. "Mrs. Spielman. Are you alright? If you can hear us, put the gun down and your hands on your head."

The sulfur and smoke of the gunpowder burned her nostrils. *The gun.* Margot searched for it in slow motion, her brain unable to catch up, and found it lying on the ground next to Myron. A puddle of blood was spreading over their carefully selected oriental rug, blood from a small hole in his foot.

The blast had knocked all thought from her head and left her nearly catatonic, watching from a safe distance as Myron yowled in agony, as Myron screamed at her to call an ambulance, as Myron chewed the insides of his mouth raw to keep from fixing a hit for the pain.

When the paramedics came, they found him in a shocked stupor, gazing up at the ceiling, unable to comprehend the exact moment when things had taken a turn in this terrible direction. Was it the day Abigail died in his recovery room? Was it the day he found relief in a little white pill? Was it the day he found Margot bleeding from her wrist? Was it the day his daughter, Allison, passed away? Was it the day of her diagnosis? Was it the moment he realized that even with his medical degree, he couldn't save his own daughter? The dominoes fell over and over in his mind's eye. So many lost moments when he might've stopped it all went careening past him.

He caught a glimpse of Margot's slackened face above him. *Margot.* But then she was gone. A blinding penlight shined into one eye and then the next. Hands checked his pulse and lifted his screaming foot. *Can you hear me, Dr. Spielman?*

Morphine, he whispered. *I need morphine.*

Hunter watched through the window as the paramedics carried his father out on a gurney. The boy's body nearly collapsed in relief when his mother stood up and walked out with the police officers. *She isn't dead.* He forced a breath past the stone in his throat.

"He won't press charges. We won't let him," Ava whispered. "It'll be okay, Hunter."

Two flashlights darted through the house, into closets and under beds, searching for him. The back door opened, and a high beam scanned the yard.

"Hunter? Are you out there? Everything's going to be okay, son. We just want to talk to you . . ."

The two teenagers crouched behind their tree and waited for the light to pass them over.

"They'll give up in a minute," Ava whispered.

And they did. After a ten-minute search, the police cars left them in the darkness of the yard.

Hunter stood up and scanned the back of the house, then squinted down at the girl standing next to him in the slanted dark. She looked more like a faded memory than a girl, a pretty heartache, a bird in a storm.

"What did you mean, 'it's happening again'?" he asked, wiping a stream of tears from her face. "What happened here, Ava?"

She didn't answer.

"What happened to your brother? His name's Toby, right? He's the one you're waiting for, isn't he?"

She avoided his eyes and gazed up at the house. The attic light was still burning.

"You can tell me. It's okay." He wanted to fold her into his arms and hold on for dear life. Instead, he squeezed her hand.

"Toby left. After Papa Martin died . . . they took him away. And, um." The house wavered in her tears. "He was so messed up by everything, you know? He just wanted a home, but they wouldn't let me keep him . . . they said I couldn't take care of him, that I was too young, and, uh . . . the family they found for him didn't want me. I was too old. But they didn't get it. He just kept running away. He kept coming back here to find me."

"What happened to him?"

She wiped her face with a shaky hand, unable to say the words out loud.

"I found an article about a boy in the paper. A boy named Toby. Was that him?"

She didn't answer.

"I'm so sorry, Ava." Hunter kept his eyes on the ground.

"They wouldn't let me see him, not even at the funeral . . . they treated me like we weren't even related, like I was nobody to him." Her words jumbled into sobs. "I should've run away with him. I should've stopped them from taking him. It's all my fault . . . I should've called the ambulance sooner. If Papa Martin hadn't . . ."

Hunter went quiet as her voice trailed off, afraid to speak. Swallowing hard, he put an arm over her shoulders. To his utter amazement, she let him. She curled into his chest, and he wrapped himself around her as the grief racked and shook her.

"It's not your fault," he whispered. "There's nothing you could've done. They had police and courts and social workers, and it wouldn't have worked. You were just a kid. It's not your fault."

Eventually, he felt her stiffen and go quiet. She pulled away from his arms and wiped her face. It took several more minutes for him to build up the courage to finally ask, "Why are you still waiting for him?"

"Because I am. I always am." She squinted up at a nondescript shadow hovering in the attic window. If she tilted her head just right, it was the shape of a boy.

Hunter followed her gaze but saw nothing.

"This place. They built it from Shaker wood and stone. Did you know that?" she said. "They believed if you stood in the right spot, if you sang just the right song . . . you could talk to the dead."

"Do you talk to him?"

She shook her head and let out an aching laugh. "I try. I really do . . . Sometimes I think I even see him. Sometimes I think I'm just seeing things because I want to."

"I know what you mean. I used to try to talk to Allison late at night. I used to imagine her lying next to me in bed, listening. But . . ." His heart broke for her. "Do you think Toby wants you to stay here like this?"

"I don't know. He hated to be alone, and I feel like I left him when he needed me most. It's all my fault. If I had just let Papa . . ." She couldn't finish the rest.

"It's not your fault, Ava. It's not." He searched the sky for what to say and what to do. "Do you have any other family?"

She shook her head.

"Yeah. Me neither." The gunshots reverberated down his spine again, making him flinch. The terrible sequence of events replayed again in his mind. His head snapped to the side as though slapped. "What are we going to do?"

"I don't know. This is all my fault. It is." She pushed herself away from him. "I should've left you and your parents alone. I just . . . I wanted to scare you. All of you. I wanted you all to go away and leave my house alone. I'm so sorry. I didn't mean for any of this to happen."

"What do you mean? What did you do, Ava?"

More tears slid down her face as she confessed to him all the things she'd left out for Myron and Margot to find and all the ways she'd exposed their secrets and lies.

"I just thought they would leave and go back to Boston. I thought Margot would get therapy or something. I wanted Myron to go to rehab before he hurt another patient. I shouldn't have done it. I never thought it would end like this."

Hunter sat silent, digesting everything she'd said and done, unfelt emotions crashing against his numbed brain. She'd locked his mother in the attic. She'd stolen his mother's nightgown. She'd left out the drugs for Margot to find. She'd led Myron to the naked videos. She'd been haunting the house ever since they bought it.

After what felt like an hour of buzzing silence, he said more to himself than to her, "It's not your fault. You didn't make him a heroin addict. You weren't in Boston when that girl died. You didn't make my mom troll the internet for attention or validation or whatever the hell she was looking for. You didn't hit me or fire the gun. You didn't do any of those things, Ava. It's not your fault. They've been fucked up for years." He stared up at the three stars that managed to shine through the light pollution of the city. "You know, my mom tried to kill herself a few years ago. I'm not supposed to know about it, but she went away for a few weeks back when I was fifteen . . ."

"I'm so sorry, Hunter. I didn't know."

"I think they thought this house would make them normal again. Funny, huh?"

"It's not funny," she said in a dull voice. "Maybe it would've worked if I'd left you all alone."

"No. There's something wrong with this place. It's ruined every family that ever lived here." Hunter sat up a bit straighter. "Do you think that old fortune-teller, Madame Nala, was right?"

"Right about what?"

"About there being bodies buried here? About this place being haunted?" He'd begun to tremble as the aftershocks set in. His hand went to the welt on his face where Myron had hit him.

She didn't speak for a moment, and then she said, "What do you think they want?"

"Who?"

"The ghosts."

"I don't know. Maybe they want us to leave. Maybe they want us to die here too." Hunter kept his eyes on the house and imagined all the past owners staring out through the windows, trapped inside. He could see his own face framed behind a pane of glass.

What is going to happen to me? he wondered. *Will I end up homeless or in foster care like Ava?* His mind reeled with images of his mother in a jail cell and his father in a hospital bed and the sound of the gun firing again and again.

"Fuck this," he said and took off for the garage.

"Where are you going?" Ava called after him, suddenly terrified of being left alone. "Hunter?"

He didn't answer. Instead, he typed in the code to the garage door and watched it roll open. Inside, he flipped on the overhead light and grabbed a spade. He marched back over to the spot where Ava stood. "Nala said bones were buried here, right? Under the stones. That means no proper burial, no proper resting place."

"So?"

"So maybe Caleb was right. Maybe this *is* fucking *Poltergeist*, and these bones need to be found. Okay?"

"That sounds kinda . . . crazy." She cracked half a smile.

"Yeah. Well. We could burn the house down instead." Hunter drove the shovel into the ground. It felt good to tear into something. It felt good to make a hole. He knew he should be calling the police and finding out where they'd put his mother. He knew he should be going to the hospital to check on his dad. But that would make everything that had happened real.

He threw a shovel full of dirt onto the grass and looked up at his only friend within five hundred miles. "Do you have a better idea?"

58

The Rawlings Family
October 3, 1929

The Believers wouldn't recognize this valley, Ninny Boyd mused, counting her steps through the backyard of the enormous brick mansion. On the other side of it, Lee Road ran in the track of the old road that had once cut through the Center Family village. The home before her was big enough to house twenty of the lost children they'd once taken in as their own. It was an island unto itself, an isolated monument to individualism, capitalism, materialism, and modern American success. Mother Ann's dream of a holy utopia had borne out something else entirely.

Ninny walked much more slowly now. Huddled under a red woolen coat, she inched her way across the site of the old gathering house. Her thick body, hunched and limping slightly to the left, dwarfed the girl she'd once been. That girl still looked out through her blue eyes, but they were much darker now, with heavy lids, the skin creased by time and weather. It had been over seventy-five years. She'd outlived them all, but more importantly, she'd been right. The Elders hadn't seen what she'd seen that night in the Grove. They hadn't seen the ruin coming. They hadn't seen this future without a trace of them left.

Ninny stopped and looked back toward the three remaining trees of the Holy Grove for a bearing and then gazed down at her feet. They were still there. The four bodies, just bones now, lay there beneath the garden, watching the sky. The headstones she'd made for them were missing. An elaborate birdbath sat inches from them. A stone patio had been laid across the graves, and an iron lattice bench had been set above them to ponder the enormous house Walter Rawlings had built seven years earlier.

Too old to kneel, she lowered her brittle frame onto the white iron bench, keeping her eyes on the ground. Tulips and daffodils would sprout in spring over their bodies. Ninny studied the dried flower stalks trapped in a nest of English ivy. The garden had been laid out in an attempt at an English style—flower beds lined with hedges, stone pathways, and staged moments of country repose. Ninny studied the artifice, noting the lack of a vegetable garden, fruit tree, or berry patch, and shook her head. None of the plants were of any practical use. Scanning the backs of the houses lined up in a row made it clear that none of them made much use of the fertile ground so prized by the Believers. None of them would survive a day on their own.

Settling her eyes back to the ground, she let out a long sigh and began, her voice as crinkled and worn as crepe paper. "I still don't know your names. Isn't that something? After all these years. I still don't know."

Her eyes swam with tears penned in by drooping lids. "I suppose it's too late now to do anything about that. It's too late for a lot of things. For all I know, they moved you somewhere else when the builders came through."

She laughed then even though she didn't find it funny. She clasped her hands in prayer, suspecting that the stones she'd laid over the graves had been moved by the Elders long ago. "No. You're still here, aren't you. They couldn't face what they had done and failed to do. They left you here. Those builders didn't dig deep so far from the house."

She gazed up at the undisturbed trees that dotted the back of the garden. They'd been saplings when she'd left. She closed her eyes and listened. Underneath the rumble of the streetcars and the singing birds, she strained to hear the faint squall of a baby crying. Ninny hummed the song she'd heard coming up from the root cellar those many years ago.

When this world comes raining down
I shall build a home beneath the ground.
And when the storm breaks the sky
I shall shelter you where I die.

The song broke her heart all over again. Ninny went quiet a moment and then whispered to the ground, "I pray that you may finally rest in peace. Your people are free now."

It wasn't quite the truth, and she knew it. Her shoulders hung heavy with the truth. Not a single dark-skinned man, woman, or child had set foot on that piece of land since the runaways had been murdered all those years ago. She shut her eyes as the violence of that night echoed between the trees.

"Are you familiar with the Fugitive Slave Act, ma'am?" the man asked one of the sisters. He didn't wait for a response. Instead, he announced for all to hear, "The Fugitive Slave Act states here that we have the right to search these premises for runaway slaves. It also states that anyone harboring runaway slaves will be prosecuted to the fullest extent of the law. Now, we've heard some pretty disturbing things about you folks. Heard you have injuns and harlots livin' here like they was proper folks. That true?"

The sound of doors being kicked in and children and women screaming broke out through the trees. The sky lit up like the sun had risen. Ninny fell back on her rump and gaped as the roof of the school caught fire, the wood shingles burning like kindling. The gathering house was next. The heat of the climbing flames warmed her face from a hundred feet away. The crackle and roar nearly drowned out the screams and cries of the Believers out on the road. The sound of feet running through the dried leaves pounded past her fifty feet away, and young Ninny pressed herself to the ground, hoping her shape stayed lost in the shadows.

With her ear to the grass, she could hear the voices hidden there in the root cellar. A baby crying, and beneath it, much softer and sweeter, a mother sang a frightened lullaby.

"Be still," she called into the ground. "They are coming!"

Through the brush, she saw the silhouettes of three men with rifles against the hot glow of the burning buildings. They scanned the grounds, no doubt looking for the poor souls hidden beneath her. With a whispered prayer, Ninny pulled herself to her feet and darted into the tree line.

The men with the rifles heard the squalls of the baby from beneath the ground.

Elder Samuel and the other Believers backed away in horror as the slave hunters began digging through the loose dirt. In short order, they uncovered the hatch door. Shotguns trained on the entrance to the root cellar, and the leader of the raiders threw it open, ready for hell to break loose.

"Well, I'll be damned," the slave hunter muttered, recoiling from some gruesome scene splayed out below. Ninny lifted her head in horror as she realized that the baby had stopped crying.

"Jesus," one of them whispered.

"You all owe me twelve hundred dollars. Got that?" the leader barked at Elder Samuel. "That's what they's worth! Twelve hundred."

Samuel fell to his knees, head hung low. "If money is all you wanted, we could have settled this quite easily. This blood is on your hands now. You will be the one to answer for it when His judgment comes."

"His judgment, huh? Well, I don't go in for your religion, old man. I've got my own church, and I'm sitting just fine with God." As if to prove

it, the man stomped down into the cellar. "You think God really cares about these ones down here? Cuttin' and stabbin' themselves like this?"

A muffled scream burst out of the ground. A large dark-skinned man in Shaker clothes took off running up and out of the hole before the others could react. A knife was in his hand, and blood darkened his shirt. His feet pounded the earth, making six long strides toward the trees before the first bullet hit his back. It took three more slugs to bring him down.

He hit the ground at the edge of the tree stand to the sound of men shouting and the lone high-pitched scream of a girl hiding in the underbrush. The man died staring into her blue, blue eyes, her pale face half-hidden by a tree. As the killers came running, she crumpled to the ground ten feet from his fallen body.

They didn't see her lying there in the undergrowth.

"Darn it, Jeb! Why couldn't you just shoot 'im in the leg?" one of the men called out after inspecting the kill. He kicked the side of the dead man as though he were a horse. "We can't do nothin' with him now. Dammit!"

Ninny lay there petrified, staring into the dead man's face until the Elders came to drag him to his unmarked grave. His black eyes stared into hers, the eyes of God gazing right into her soul. Why? *they asked.*

They hadn't buried the four victims of the raid that night in the North Union graveyard. Instead, all evidence of them in the Valley of God's Pleasure had been buried along with their bodies in the bloodstained ground. *We can no longer harbor fugitives of the law,* Elder Samuel had decreed. *The fires set against us are a warning, a warning we must heed.*

And now it was too late.

Ninny gazed up at the fifteen windows of the house above her. A young woman's ghostly face gaped back at her from a second floor room. Her features contorted in a mask of outrage at the strange old crone trespassing in her garden.

It was no use to try and scuttle away. Ninny couldn't move that fast, and besides, no policeman would arrest her. Not an old woman like her. Not for sitting on a bench. Ninny sighed and waited.

Inside the house, a startled Georgina wished her husband were home from work. Walter would know what to do and say, but he wasn't there. Making her way down the hall, she made a concerted effort not to bother Ella or the boy reading stories in his room. Walter Junior had been having such nightmares lately, waking up screaming two or three times a night. She paused at his door and listened to him sounding out the words in his storybook.

"Good, *shavo!*" the housekeeper cooed when he'd finished. "You read me the story about the monkey now. That one makes old Ella laugh."

Georgina slipped past them and down the servants' stairs to the kitchen and then out the back door. "Excuse me," she said loudly, approaching the stranger on the bench. "This is my home. May I help you?"

Ninny gazed up at the woman with tired eyes. "Forgive me, ma'am. I did not mean to disturb you."

Seeing clearly now the woman's age, Georgina relaxed ever so slightly. "I am not disturbed, but you are on my property. Are you lost?" The younger woman looked toward the street, wondering how the old woman had wandered back there.

"No. Not lost. I know exactly where I am." Ninny smiled, flashing three missing teeth. Her face was a map of everywhere she'd been: the scars from the war, the years of hard labor, the children she'd borne.

Georgina studied its contours, growing more curious by the minute. "Do you live nearby?" She straightened herself, silently cataloging her neighbors and their relatives.

"No. Not for a long, long time . . . but I went to grammar school right over there."

Georgina lifted her carefully plucked eyebrows and turned in surprise toward her neighbor's house.

"It was a long time ago." Ninny nodded. "This all used to be farmland. I must say it is awful strange to see it now."

Figuring the math of the woman's face, Georgina slowly nodded. "I imagine it is. You were one of them, then? The Shakers?" Another broken smile made the younger woman shift her gaze uncomfortably.

"I suppose. But we never really called ourselves that. That was more what the outside world thought of us. You can't really tell much of anything looking in from the outside though, can you?"

The turn of phrase charmed Georgina into a rueful smile as she gazed up the back of her stately home. "I suppose not."

Ninny studied her then, with the younger woman's focus shifted elsewhere. Thin. Too thin. Pale. Brittle. Far too brittle for her age. The young lady appeared haunted.

The moment the thought crossed the old woman's mind, Georgina flinched as though she'd heard something.

"I think you ought to know something about this place," Ninny whispered. She forced her creaking body up from the bench. "A long, long time ago, four people died right where we're standing. They were murdered, you know."

"I beg your pardon?" Georgina stiffened and swung her attention back to the old woman in her garden.

"They were buried right here." The old woman tapped the ground beneath their feet with her cane. "Two men. A young woman. And..." The words *a baby* died in her throat, too cruel to say out loud.

"What?" Georgina backed away from the invisible graves. Her mouth fell open. "I am sorry, but—I think you had better leave."

"You are quite right, I'm sure. I will go. I just . . . I thought you ought to know." Ninny hung her head and began her limping shuffle toward the street. It had been a mistake to come. It didn't solve a thing. She had nothing to offer the dead or the living.

As she gazed up at the house one last time, the feeling of it gazing back stopped Ninny in her tracks. Fieldstones lined the chimney caps and the flower beds. Sandstones held the corners of the foundation, the same size and shape as the ones the Believers had used to build the millhouse and the foundations of the school.

"They took the stones," she whispered to herself.

"Excuse me?" Georgina demanded. She'd been following the old woman out to the driveway.

Ninny cleared her throat. "Your builder. Where did they get the stones?" The image of three headstones formed in her head. *Mother and Child*, one read.

"Why, I have no idea." Georgina cowered under the chimney caps and windowsills as though they might fall on her head. "Why on earth do you ask?"

"Perhaps it is nothing." Ninny shook her head and kept limping down the driveway.

"Wait!" Georgina called after her, her peace of mind utterly upended.

Ninny stopped walking.

"What is your name?"

"Ninny Anne Boyd. Forgive me for disturbing you."

"Mrs. Boyd, I'm Georgina Rawlings. Please forgive my rudeness. You just gave me quite a shock. I want to ask my husband about what you said. How can we reach you?" Georgina stood like a wraith in the driveway, nearly translucent.

The old woman gave the name of a rooming house.

Georgina made a mental note of it, not certain whether to thank the woman for her time. Proper etiquette for the circumstances failed her.

Ninny stopped at the sidewalk and gazed up once more at the towering mansion behind the trees. An electric light burned in the attic window, casting a yellow glow onto the reflection of the midday sky.

Little Walter, having escaped his reading lesson for the day, pressed his nose to the glass and waved.

59

The Spielman Family
August 12, 2018

"Hunter?" Margot whispered from the doorway.

The clock by his bedside table read *3:15 a.m.* She'd crept into the house a few minutes earlier, her eyes black with smudged mascara and red from crying. She sank onto the edge of his bed in the dark, not daring to turn on the light, not wanting him to see what the last few hours had done to her.

The boy stirred from a heavy sleep.

"Are you okay, sweetie?" She patted him on the arm.

"Mom?" He sat up and studied the shape of her in the dark. "You're back. What time is it?"

"It's late. Don't get up. I just wanted you to know I made it home. I'm so sorry, honey. I'm so sorry for everything that happened." She swallowed to keep her voice from cracking. "Your father is going to be fine. I talked to the doctor, and he's okay."

"Okay. That's good." And it was, but there were no words for what he felt toward his father. His cheek was swollen. He had bruises on his shoulders from the man's grip.

A small figure lay next to Hunter in the bed, listening but not moving. Margot noted the shape of a girl there under the covers but said nothing. "I didn't want you to worry. Everything is going to be alright. I know it doesn't seem like it right now, but we'll figure it out. Go back to sleep, honey. We'll talk in the morning."

"Okay." Hunter sank back down to his pillow, his arms stiff and sore from hours of digging in the backyard. He'd have to explain it all in the morning. "Hey, Mom?"

Margot stopped in the doorway. "Yes, sweetie?"

"It wasn't me, you know. Those drugs you found. It wasn't me."

"I know it, Hunter. I know. You're a good kid. I really don't know what I would've done if anything had happened to you." She sniffed and collected herself. "Now, go back to bed."

Hunter rolled over, and Ava curled into the crook of his arm. Neither of them said a word as his mother staggered away and down the hall. He pressed his lips to the back of her neck. She stiffened but made herself kiss his arm back. *Hunter* is *a good kid,* she told herself. *He's nothing like* him.

As Hunter drifted back to sleep, Ava lay there petrified. The boy's tender affections unearthed so many feelings she needed to keep buried. The bone Hunter pulled from the ground earlier that night resurfaced in her mind. *Dead. He's really dead. I'll never see him or talk to him or hold him again.* Her lifeless eyes stared blindly into the dark, listening to the heartbreaking silence of the house.

Margot collapsed onto her bed without bothering to undress or close the door. She lay there catatonic, trying to not think and to think at the same time. What would they do? Where would they go?

A soft mewing sound caught her midthought. She bolted upright and flipped on the bedside lamp to see a white cat curled on the upholstered bench at the end of the bed. The hand clutching her chest dropped, and she slowly exhaled.

"Kitty, you scared me."

Crawling over the duvet, she lifted the cat up onto her lap and held it until her blood pressure had fallen to an almost normal level. "Who let you in here, huh?"

The feral cat just fixed her with its sphinx eyes.

Margot chuckled and buried her face in its fur. "Well, I'm glad you're here, sweetie. I'm really, really glad."

For the rest of the night, the house stood still, and the attic lights stayed dark.

60

Late the next morning, Hunter woke to an empty bed.

He sat up and felt the spot where Ava had been sleeping. It was cold. He surveyed the room, hoping to see her sitting in his computer chair or reading the closet walls. His gerbils, Samwise and Frodo, shuffled through one of the long plastic tubes toward Base Camp 1.

"Where did she go?" he asked them.

Frodo just twitched his nose.

Hunter ran a hand through his rumpled hair and grimaced at the pain in his shoulders. His fingernails were still black with dirt. He fell back against his pillow as the consequences of the previous night hit him all over again. He'd have to explain what he'd done to the backyard. He'd have to call the police about the bones he'd found. He shuddered and rolled under the covers.

Where did she go?

His cell phone pinged with a new message. At first, he couldn't bring himself to look. He just lay there, wishing sleep would take him far from that moment, from that house, from that life. The cell phone pinged again.

He grabbed the phone and scrolled through the messages. One of them made him sit up and dial the phone.

"Good morning. Golden Heart Ranch," a voice said over the speaker.

"Good morning." Hunter cleared his throat and head. "Can I speak to Maurice in long-term care?"

"I'll put you through."

Digital music filled the silence.

Hunter climbed out of bed and woke up his computer. The article about Toby Turner's death filled his screen. He glanced back at his empty bed and skimmed the words again. Toby had been found in an abandoned car in a Cleveland Metropark by the lake. He was described only as a runaway. The paper had published Toby's last school picture. A smiling twelve-year-old boy gazed out from his computer screen. He looked no different than any other boy in the yearbook Hunter had stolen from the library. From the outside, no one would suspect a thing.

Hunter's heart broke for Ava all over again.

"This is Maurice," a musical voice chimed from his phone.

"Yeah. Hi. This is Hunter Spielman. You left me a message."

"Yes, Hunter. How are you doing this fine, fine day?"

Hunter minimized the news clipping on his screen and tried to shake Toby's hopeful smile from his head. "Okay, I guess. How's Benny?"

"Well, he is just beside himself! He cannot wait to talk to you! It's gonna take us a few minutes to get it set up. Do you Skype?"

"Uh, yeah. I can."

"Give me your email address, and I'll patch in a link to you. He can't really talk due to his disability, but once we got him his modified keyboard, we could not shut him up!"

Ten minutes later, the face of a scruffy older man appeared on Hunter's screen. Scars drew deep lines over his forehead and down one cheek. At fifty-two years old, his spiky hair had gone gray, as had the stubble on his chin, but Benny's eyes lit up like a five-year-old's at the sight of Hunter on his screen. Benny waved at him with a slightly curled hand and a crooked grin.

Hunter waved back. "Hi, Benny!"

Gripping a pencil in his hard fist, Benny began typing on an oversize keyboard.

Ben33: Hello

Ben33: How are you?

"Okay. How are you?"

Ben33: Happy to see a new face. What is your name?

"My name is Hunter. Hunter Spielman."

Benny's eyes drifted to the ceiling as he checked his memory for any such name.

"Yeah. You don't know me. My family moved into your old house on Lee Road. I think I'm in your old bedroom." Hunter picked up the webcam and gave Benny a sweeping view of the room. Then he opened the closet door and scanned the writing on the walls, lingering on the words *DeAD GiRL*.

When Hunter sat back down, the older man had stopped smiling. His face screwed into a spasm, and his fists lifted off his keyboard. A nurse rushed to his side and talked in his ear a moment. Benny shook him off. *No. No.* After a few moments collecting himself, Benny slowly uncurled his arm and started typing with his pencil again.

Ben33: Benny didn't do it. But I saw. I saw her through the window.

"What did you see, Benny?"

61

The Klussman Family
September 15, 1990

He wasn't supposed to be awake.

Benny knew it the moment he looked at the clock. It was past midnight, and the house stood silent. The only sound was the ticking of the clock in the hallway—a heartbeat that never matched his own no matter how hard he tried. Under the ticking, he could hear the unwinding of a spring, the unevenness of the motion of the second hand. Every other second hung a synapse longer than it should before the wheel turned. There was a small burr in the gears. The unevenness grated on his nerves, but he didn't know what he would do without it. The *tick tack* of it comforted him like the sound of his own breathing in his ears.

The downward pull of the sedative his mother had given him had let go, and he felt his body resurfacing from the depths of the sea back onto his bed. He sat up. Yellow light from the streetlamps streamed in through his window.

The nighttime world was his favorite world. Quiet. Slow. Benny's body worked better at night with no one watching. His muscles stayed smooth and even. He was more himself at night. The bright, blinding lights and deafening sounds of daytime pinned him against the wall of his mind, a squirming insect. The watcher did more than helplessly whisper in his ear at night. Alone in the dark, he was the watcher and the watcher was him.

Benny sat up and listened to the clock in the hall and, under it, the creak of the wooden bones of the house, straining to hold up the ceiling above him and the floor beneath him.

Careful in the silence, he stood up and went to his desk. Papers had been taped down onto the wood for him to draw and write. Under his mother's pained watch, he could hardly hold the pencil. *Let's try again. This is an* A, *Benny.* A *is for* apple. He wanted so much to do it correctly that he'd break the pencil in his hand. His failures registered in the darkening flecks of her irises. *Hopeless.* But she'd smile at him. *That's okay, sweetie. Let's try again.*

It was better when she read. On a good day, lessons abandoned on the desk, she'd sit next to him with a book and read him the pages, hoping against hope that he was following along as her finger traced the sentences set in small, even typeface. He was indeed following her words and reading and rereading the ones that came before and after. Reading at a pace far faster than hers. He wanted to show her. He wanted her to know that he could do it, but no words would come from his mouth except a barbaric groan that convinced her he was in pain. She would put the book down and gaze at him with that smothering concern and anguish that made him want to beat his brain against the wall. And sometimes he did.

She hadn't read to him in weeks.

Benny grabbed a pencil from the desk and scanned the papers covered in torn letters. The paper was always too thin to hold up for long. Chalkboards were better, but he couldn't bear the shrieking, and the chalk always broke in his hand. He turned away from his tortured markings to his closet door. She'd get angry if he wrote on the walls. He knew this, so he wrote where she wouldn't see.

Inside his closet, there was nothing but a few hanging garments he would never wear. All his regular clothes were free of buttons and zippers and snaps and anything that could be swallowed or used to scratch or cut or maim. A dress shirt and pants hung there, three sizes too small. There were outgrown shoes with no laces in a pile on the bottom; each new size had brought his mother new despair. His mother hadn't opened the closet in months.

He pushed aside the sparse items and clicked on the bare light bulb by awkwardly pulling its string. He liked the buzz of the filament. He liked the yellow light hanging over him like a tiny sun. It belonged to him, unlike the sun outside that reeled over the sky, too bright, too loud, making him shudder as he waited for it to fall. Sitting on the closet floor, he wrote in a crooked hand:

SePteMBeR 14 1990:
two LADieS MissiNG toDAy.
oNe HAt. two Boys.
18 cARs.
soMetHiNG is wRoNG

It felt better getting the words out of his head. Putting his worries onto his walls got them all the way out where he could see them. He scanned his notes from the last month, searching for a pattern. The green car had been missing for four days in a row. It had reappeared looking cleaner, and he decided that it must've been taken to the shop, like Bill's car the month before. He didn't know exactly what a shop was, but Bill had said his Toyota was "like new" when they were done. The green car looked like new too.

The lady with the flowered purse had missed the bus seven times in the last month. He worried she might be sick. His own mother had left for eight days once the year before. Bill and the night nurse, Faye, had said she was sick, but she'd be better soon. No one had said the word *hospital*, but he knew his mother wasn't home. The watcher could tell by the sound of the floor, the smell of the air, and the tilt of the walls that she was gone. His muscles had knotted with worry she'd never come back. They'd had to give him the needle every day until she returned home.

Benny scanned the notes again, comforted by the proof that he existed. A part of him wanted to show her, wanted her to find his notes and see what he could do, but the other part was terrified. The watcher could see it gave her some comfort to believe he couldn't really feel or really know what was happening to him. In a way, thinking he was still a baby inside made her happier. She could hold a baby. She could rock a baby. She could love a baby.

Benny clicked off his light and slid his feet silently and slowly along the floorboards to his window. Outside, Lee Road stretched out into the night in both directions, empty. The streetlights blinked red at the South Woodland intersection. Benny counted the intervals between the lights and the ticking of his clock. When they converged, a jolt of satisfaction tightened his fists. Fifteen cycles until the patterns intersected. He counted off again.

A movement down the street caught his eye. A bicycle. Benny pressed his nose against the windowpane and watched, mesmerized, as the thin line of the ten-speed traced a long sine wave along the sidewalk, weaving and gliding. Then it stopped.

Benny jerked back from the window.

A figure got off the bike. It was the shape of a girl with a long ponytail. In the streetlamp he could see her red sweater and brown hair. Pretty. Like so many girls he'd seen walk past in packs and sometimes alone. The alone ones worried him. *Where are her friends? Where is her mother?* Girls never walked under his window alone at night. Almost never.

He squinted at her through the glass. It had been months since he'd seen her. Screwing up his face, he strained to remember the date. It had been spring. *April fourth.* She'd ridden her bike up the driveway of the house across the street past midnight; the memory of it etched his forehead. It had upset him then. His mother had come running into his room to find him pounding on the windowpane.

He'd worried for several nights that spring that the girl was out there when he was sleeping, with only the empty windows keeping the watch.

Aghast, Benny watched her guide the bike into the six-foot-high hedge of bushes across the street, a bigger house looming darkly behind its trees. She reappeared on the sidewalk without the bike. *That's not right.* He scowled, fists clenching. *Bikes don't go in bushes. Bikes don't go in bushes. Bikes d—*

A tall figure appeared on the sidewalk in front of her. It was a man from the size of it. Tall. Thick. Dark hair. Big jacket. He'd come from the driveway. She seemed startled to see him, her body shrinking and backing away. The man grabbed the back of her neck. A high-pitched scream launched Benny from his chair.

He stumbled back against his bed, incoherent thoughts flashing in his eyes. *Bike. Bushes. Girl. Bad Benny!* He shouldn't have been watching. He shook his head back and forth, nearly wrenching himself into a knot. Another muffled scream hit his windows. His eyes swelled in his head. He forced himself upright. The watcher knew that grown-ups should do something. The grown-ups should call for help. He waited a moment for the sound of his mother running, for the explosion of sirens that would make him scream as they pummeled his ears, but he heard nothing but the house, aching under its own weight.

Help us! Someone, please!

He lurched up and ran stiffly to his door. Frannie never locked it overnight. It was a fire hazard, and she knew it. He pushed through it and lurched down the hallway and then the front steps, knees locking and unlocking in awkward cadence as the screams in his head grew louder.

Fumbling with the front door locks, he struggled to make his fingers obey as the muscles in them tightened. A low groan escaped the snarl of his mouth when he finally managed to get the dead bolt to turn.

The night's chill rushed in through the doorway as he hurled himself down the front walk. Beneath the screams replaying in his mind, he could hear something worse. Grunting. A muffled drowning. A high-pitched shriek cut short.

In the distance, a red car headed east down South Woodland, but the rest of the street was empty. Benny forced his locked legs across Lee Road toward the spot he'd seen the girl, trying to yell, *Stop! Help!* but only managing a strangled yowl. "SOWWWW!"

The sound of two bodies struggling against the bushes shuddered through the air. Terrible wet thumping sounds followed. An inhuman grunt. A choked gurgle. Then nothing but the muffled drum of two feet running over the wet grass and away.

Benny stood there frozen, his back to his own house, his head dipped low. The street had gone silent with an exhale of air. The acrid smell of stomach gases hung all around him. *Dead,* the watcher whispered from the attic window behind him. *Dead like Darwin the fish.*

He contracted into himself. Helpless. Seizing. The shape of him crumpled to the pavement. *DEAD! DEAD! DEAD GIRL!*

"Benny!" his mother called from the front door, a note of panic in her voice. *"Benny!"*

He couldn't answer. He was gone.

She didn't see him right away convulsing on the sidewalk, a shadowy lump rocking back and forth, knocking against the cold concrete. The world sparked red and white as she ran across the street. Blood seeped out of his hair and onto the pavement with each crack of his skull.

Scooping Benny into her strong arms, she whispered through panic and tears, "Benny! What are you doing out here?"

She didn't hear the girl dying ten feet away on the other side of the bushes. His mother didn't suspect a thing until a young police officer knocked on the door the following day.

62

"It was Katie Green, wasn't it? Who do you think did it?" Hunter finally asked after reading Benny's broken account of the events a second time. The man took a few minutes to type out the answer.

> Ben33: A man. Big and tall. Older. Not a neighbor.
> Not that boy they put in the papers.

"Did you ever tell the police what you saw?"

> Ben33: I tried. When I learned to type I sent letters.
> No one ever wrote back. They must have thought
> I was crazy or a liar. It is hard when you look and
> sound like this.

Benny flashed his crooked grin and held up his curled hands.

"Wow. I'm sorry." Hunter shook his head and glanced out Benny's window, then back to the contorted face on the screen. The man's own mother had thought he was a killer.

Ben33: Don't be sorry. I like it here. I like my new
window. I see the sun set every day. A machine
helps me talk. A machine helps me read. There is a
tank full of fish. The fish are happy here.

Hunter glanced at the nurse over Benny's shoulder, who was
smiling at the sunny message. "Do you ever wish you hadn't seen
what happened? Do you ever wonder what your life would have been
like if you'd just stayed in bed that night? Or if you'd never lived in
this house at all?"

The older man frowned at him. Beneath the jagged scars on his
face and the gray hair, Benny was still mostly a boy. Inexperienced.
Sheltered. Shut in. Naive.

Ben33: Why wonder?

"I don't know. I guess I'm just . . . sort of hating the world right
now." Hunter felt ridiculous for complaining to a man with so many
problems. He hesitated a moment, then figured, *What the hell.* He
proceeded to tell Benny all of it. The history of the house. Ava in the
attic. His father and the drugs. His mother with the gun. The bones
they'd found in the backyard.

Benny took it all in, wide eyed, processing and calculating and
nodding. Then he didn't move for several minutes, and Hunter began
to worry the nurse would pull the plug on their conversation. Finally,
Benny started typing.

Ben33: Wow.

Ben33: Where is the girl? Ava?

"I don't know. She left. I woke up this morning, and she was gone."

Ben33: You have to help her.

"How?" Hunter threw up his hands, exasperated. "How am I supposed to help her? I'm just a kid. I don't know what to do. I mean, I like her. I like her a lot, but I don't really know her. I don't know what she needs. I think she might need professional help. Squatting in a haunted house waiting for a dead brother to come back isn't exactly normal, right?"

Benny leaned into the camera, his enlarged face glaring into Hunter's. He no longer looked like a boy trapped in a man's body. He suddenly looked older than his years. His dark brown eyes deepened into black hollows, forever haunted by the sound of a girl dying ten feet away. A girl he couldn't save.

Ben33: She needs you. You have to help her. For me.

Hunter shook his head at the camera. "It was really nice talking with you, Benny. I'm really glad you like your window and your fish. Maybe I'll ring you again sometime. Would that be alright?"

The man nodded at the camera, but his eyes stayed fixed on Hunter. *Help her.*

After the call disconnected, Hunter sagged back in his chair a moment and listened. The attic was still. The second floor lay silent outside his door. Down in the kitchen, he heard footsteps and then the opening of a cupboard.

He followed the sound down the stairs to find his mother standing at one of the counters with a mug of coffee. She looked like she'd aged ten years. The lines on her face ran deeper. Her skin had gone pale and thin. Her hands seemed frail and unsteady.

"Good morning, sweetie," she said with a pained smile. "How are you feeling? Are you okay?"

She wanted to scoop him up and hold him like a little boy. The palpable urge made him shrink away ever so slightly. "Yeah, Mom. I'm fine. Have you seen Ava?"

"No. Did she leave?"

"I'm not sure. She wasn't there when I woke up."

Margot pressed her lips together to keep from scolding him about a girl sleeping in his room. She allowed herself only one of a hundred questions. "How long have you been seeing her?"

"I don't know. We're not really . . . I mean, we're friends, but . . ." He blushed a little at the thought of what he wanted them to be.

The blush told her everything she wanted to know. *So sweet,* Margot thought to herself. "I'm really sorry she had to see what happened last night, but I'm glad you weren't alone. She seems like a nice girl."

He nodded and shuddered to think what might've happened if she hadn't been there to pull him out of the room. "Yeah. She is. I'm kind of worried about her."

"Worried?" Margot set her mug down and picked up a white cat that had curled itself around her ankle.

The animal distracted Hunter enough to give his mother a quizzical look. *We have a cat now?*

"Why are you worried about her, sweetie?"

He watched his mother pet the stray cat, debating whether to tell her everything about Ava living in the house and her brother, Toby. The sound of running water overhead stopped him. "I think that's her. I'm going to go check, okay?"

"Sure. Let her know she's welcome to stay for breakfast."

Hunter took the back stairs two at a time and followed the sound of running water down the back hall to the guest bathroom over the garage. The door was shut, and the tub was running.

"Ava?"

She didn't answer.

Hunter knocked on the door. "Ava? You okay?" He pressed his ear to the wood and heard a faint voice humming. It was one of her creepy Shaker songs. "Ava, open up."

He tried the doorknob only to find it locked. Crouching down, he peeked in through the keyhole and caught a glimpse of her sitting on the floor in his T-shirt. The glint of a straight razor flashed between her hands.

"What are you doing?" he whispered.

She didn't look up at him. The razor turned and turned in her hands as she hummed.

An angel whispered in my ear.
The dead, they know, they know you, dear . . .

"Oh, shit," he hissed as it became clear to him what she meant to do. "Ava! Don't!"

He banged on the door again, but she didn't even look up. He took off running back down the hall.

"Mom!" he shouted down the steps. "I need help. I think Ava's—she's got a razor—the door's locked!"

"What?" Margot stood up, alarmed at his panicked voice. "Slow down. What's wrong?"

"I think she wants to be dead. Like her brother. I think she's going to kill herself." *DeAD GiRL* flashed through his brain. "I need help!"

Margot ran up the stairs. "Where is she? The guest bath?"

"The door's locked. I can't get in, but I saw her. I saw her with a razor."

"Go talk to her. Keep her talking." Margot raced to her room to get the skeleton key off her nightstand.

Hunter ran down the back hallway and yelled through the door, "Ava. Don't do this. You don't have to do this. Toby doesn't want you to die."

Through the keyhole, he watched her study her reflection in the mirrored edge of the razor. *What do you see? Do you see them?*

Margot pushed past him and rattled the key into the lock.

"Ava?" she shouted through the wood. "Drop the razor, honey. Just think about what you're doing. This isn't the answer."

The door swung open, and Ava shrank against the wall, still gripping the steel.

"Hey." Margot stood in the doorway a minute, then turned off the running water. The tub was full and spilling into the overflow drain. "Ava. Look at me."

Ava didn't take her eyes off the blade. "I don't want to be here anymore," she whispered.

"I know." Margot crouched down and crawled halfway to where the girl sat curled into a corner. "I know how that feels. I do. But there are other places you can go. This isn't the only way out."

"I don't have anywhere else to go." Ava's empty gaze drifted over to Hunter's feet standing in the doorway. "I miss him so much."

"I know you do." Margot nodded, taking inventory of what Hunter had said. *I think she wants to be dead. Like her brother.* "I know it hurts. I lost someone too. And it hurt so much I wanted to die."

Ava finally looked up at her. "Why didn't you?"

Margot breathed a laugh as tears welled up in her eyes. "I tried. I was thinking like you are now. That it would be better to just go away. That it would be better to go and be with Allison, wherever she was. That I couldn't stand to live without her."

Hunter gaped at his mother. It was the most he'd ever heard her say about it.

"What stopped you?" Ava asked, still holding the weapon. She was within slicing distance of Margot's throat. She eyed the vein pulsing at the base of the woman's neck.

"Hunter did." Margot smiled through tears. "He knocked on the bathroom door. And I realized I couldn't do it. I couldn't. And not just for him, but for Allison too. It's not what the dead want."

These words struck a nerve, and Ava looked up at her like a lost little girl. "What do they want?"

"Why don't you give me that razor, and I'll tell you what I think they want." Margot held out her hand.

Ava narrowed her eyes at the woman and gripped the handle tighter for a moment. It felt like a trick. Margot sat there in her yoga pants, just a sad middle-aged mother who'd lost everything. Her husband. Her daughter. Her home.

"I know what you're thinking, but what do you have to lose? If you really want to die, Ava, you'll have a million other chances. There's a thousand ways to end this." Margot's voice was no longer that of a lonely and unsure woman. It was the voice of a mother. Firm. Loving. Unyielding. Relentless. The sort of voice that had been missing from Ava's life for years. "Now give it to me."

Ava handed Margot the blade. She looked so small and alone in that moment that Margot forgot she hardly knew the girl. She folded the blade and slipped it into her pocket, then held out her arms. "Come here, sweetie. Just come here."

Ava didn't move.

Undaunted, Margot picked up the girl's hand and held it between hers the way she couldn't hold her own daughter's. "It's going to be okay. We'll figure this out."

Ava wanted to pull away and run, but she closed her eyes and made herself feel it. The pain flayed her skin and stole her breath.

"What do the dead want?" she whispered.

63

A week later, Myron was released from the hospital and moved into the suite over the garage while Hunter and Margot packed. They were going back to Boston without him. Myron had agreed to not press charges for the gunshot wound in exchange for a nondisclosure agreement.

> Neither party shall speak publicly or privately or give any written testimony regarding the alleged drug use or any alleged drug paraphernalia found on the premises . . .

Margot, for all her faults, felt sorry for him. The divorce filing cited "irreconcilable differences." Myron did not contest custody. It would take years for his son to forgive him. His attempts at conversation with Hunter since that night had been met with curt one-word answers.

Fine.
Sure.
Okay.

Hunter sat on the edge of his bed next to Ava. His entire room had been stuffed into boxes. The moving truck was coming in the morning. "You have to come with us. I mean, where else are you gonna go?"

"I don't know." Ava studied her hands. She'd spent the week in and out of different doctors' offices and government buildings, following Margot from one place to the next. Each one was a dead end.

"No one else will take her, Mom." Margot spoke softly into her phone down in the den where the kids wouldn't hear. "What am I supposed to do? . . . She needs extended therapy. Do you think Medicaid will cover that? . . . But there are no beds available . . . I know I did, but that cost us nearly fifteen thousand dollars. If we hadn't had the money, I have no idea what we would've done."

Margot set the phone down and turned on the speaker. She reached down and pulled the white cat onto her lap. *Coco*, she thought, scratching behind its ears. *I'll call you Coco.* Coco had become her worry stone and constant companion.

Her mother's nagging voice went on, "But what do you even know about this girl, sweetheart?"

"I know she needs help. I know she's been on her own for years. I know she's nineteen, and no one will take her in. I know she's completely traumatized. She's a sweet kid and smart. She's just a little messed up."

"What about Hunter? Have you thought about him?"

"Of course I have, Mother. Hunter is the one pushing me to do this." Margot gazed out the window into the backyard. Outside, the police had taped off a grid and were digging trenches. The skull of a baby boy watched over their progress from inside a clear plastic bag resting in the flower bed. It had taken three hours of digging to find him, but Hunter had been in a state that terrible night. His father had turned on him. His mother had shot the man in the foot. Margot shuddered at the memory and stared in disbelief at the bullet hole she'd made in the far wall.

What good is all this money if we don't use it to help someone?
Hunter had demanded three days earlier. *Did hoarding money make the
Rawlings happy? Did a big house ever solve anyone's problems? I mean,
look at this place. It should be the happiest place on earth, right? But it's
not. It never was. Is this the sort of life you want for me? Private schools?
Ivy League? For what? To get rich and ignore what really matters? We
have a chance to do something good here. We have to help her, Mom.*

"Hunter is still so young. He doesn't know what's best. What's
safe," her mother chirped from the phone.

Margot smiled ruefully at her son's altruism. "It's just for a little
while, Mom. Until she gets on her feet and figures out what to do. If
we leave her at the mercy of the welfare state . . . I really don't think I
could live with myself."

"What if she robs you blind? What if she gets pregnant, for God's
sake? I'm not saying she will, but you have to consider what this might
mean for Hunter's future," her mother protested. "He's been through
so much. And now this?"

"He'll be fine, Mom. I don't doubt that there'll be complications
along the way, but he's a smart kid, and everything else is just . . . stuff.
This is something I need to do for me and for Hunter." Margot looked
down at the cat in her lap. It gazed back with those unearthly eyes. "I
know it sounds crazy, but I think Allison would want me to do this."

"Allison?" The name came with a held breath of air. There was
a long silence and then, "Okay, sweetheart. If this is what you need
to do. Just promise me that if it doesn't work out, you'll make other
arrangements. What about you? Are you taking care of yourself? I'm
so worried about you . . ."

At the other end of the house, Hunter reached for Ava's hand.
"You can't stay here. You know that, right? It's not good for you to
stay here. Not anymore."

"But why would your mom let me stay with you? It doesn't make
sense."

"I dunno. Because she's not a total monster? Because she wants to help? Because I'm making her? Does it matter?" He scanned the room. The only item not yet packed was the photograph of him and his sister. It sat on the floor next to the closet. The two cherub-faced children watched them both from behind the glass.

"What if she decides she doesn't like me? I wouldn't like me," Ava whispered. "This won't work, you know. I've been here, trespassing, all this time. She'll never trust me. Anytime anything goes missing, she'll think I stole it . . . she thinks I'm crazy. And she's probably right."

"And she's not?" Hunter sighed. "Who cares what she thinks? They're both so completely messed up. I just . . . I want you to come. Okay? Will you? Come stay with us awhile. Think of it as a free hotel until you can figure something else out."

Ava considered his face a moment—scruffy and awkward but soft. The sweetness of it hurt. "But I don't know if I can. I've been here for so long. This is my home."

"It's just a house. Wouldn't you rather be with people? People who care about you? Friends? All this place has is bad memories. Ghosts. Just—please. Come with us. If you don't like it, I'll drive you back here myself. Okay?"

"Your mom doesn't like me," she insisted. "And she wants me to go to therapy."

"My mom thinks everyone needs therapy. She wants *me* to go to therapy. So what? I mean, she's a basket case, but at least now she's not just sitting around obsessing about nothing anymore. She's going to get her old job back, and she'll hardly be around anyway. Besides, I think she really wants to do something right for a change." He cocked a goofy grin. "Can't you just let her?"

He hadn't noticed the way Margot looked at Ava, a girl the same age Allison would've been if she hadn't died. He only heard her nagging voice asking, *Are you in love with this girl?*

"What about your dad?"

"What about him? He's a junkie in denial. He's staying in Cleveland. They're getting divorced. I'll probably see him once a year or some shit just like every other kid. Right?"

She frowned at the venom in his voice. "You know he isn't all bad, right? Like, addicts aren't bad people. He's just messed up."

"Yeah. Tell that to Abigail Marty's family." Hunter blew out some trapped steam and softened his tone. "I just really kind of hate him right now."

"I know." She leaned her head against his shoulder.

He wrapped an arm around her and felt her stiffen.

"Um, Hunter? I like you." She eyed him cautiously. "I mean, I really like you. But if I'm staying with you and your mom, it would be weird if we . . . I mean, I'm just so messed up right now, and . . ." She couldn't put the rest into words.

"Hey. I get it." He squeezed her shoulder and let her go. He didn't dare let his smile slip or the hurt of her words show through. "We can be friends, right?"

"Right." She nodded, feeling both bad and relieved.

"So you'll come with us?"

She shrugged. *If you don't like it, I'll drive you back here myself.* "Okay."

"Good. Because if you don't come, Caleb will never fucking believe any of this."

She broke out laughing. The sweet sound of it drifted out Hunter's door and down the hallway past the empty rooms, flitting like a trapped bird into the attic.

64

House for Sale
April 2, 2019

"Wow. This is beautiful!" the young woman cooed from the front stoop. Her pregnant belly looked ready to burst.

Her husband squeezed her hand and shot her a look that said, *Don't let on how much you like it.*

"Wait until you see the inside. The renovation the last owner did is stunning. Brand-new kitchen. Remodeled bathrooms. Fully restored wood floors. You're going to love it." The real estate agent opened the front door and strolled inside. The cherub-faced door knocker watched as the couple crossed the threshold hand in hand with their two children, a toddler and a six-year-old.

"Oh, my!" the wife gasped in the two-story foyer, her voice echoing off the ceiling high above. "I love the chandelier!"

"It's original to the house," the agent purred, handing them each a flyer. "We have over four thousand square feet here, not including the basement or the third floor, nearly all of it renovated last year, including piping in central air-conditioning. It's a perfect family home and plenty of space for all three of your children."

"May I ask why the sellers are leaving? I mean, they bought the house less than a year ago. Were they flippers?"

"Messy divorce. It happens all the time. I can assure you they spared no expense on the renovation." The agent led the tour through the empty living room and the den and into the kitchen. "I believe the seller has already moved back to Boston with her children."

The young wife stopped at an enormous marble island, not believing her good fortune. "It's gorgeous! This is exactly the sort of kitchen we've been looking for, right, honey?"

"It is nice," the husband conceded, taking in the top-of-the-line appliances and high-end finishes. He did a slow turn, searching for something to dislike.

"Nice? It's perfect!" his wife whined. "Wally? Watch your sister, okay? Don't let her climb the stairs."

The six-year-old groaned. "But Mom! I want to see the house too!"

"Okay, kiddo." Wally's dad hoisted the little girl onto his hip. "Let's all go."

Sunlight shined in through the large windows, casting a warm glow in the solarium. Despite his best efforts, Wally's dad found himself picturing Thanksgiving dinners and Christmas mornings and barbecues on the back patio.

The real estate agent hid a knowing grin as she led them up the back stairs. "Now, if you're seriously considering putting in an offer, I should let you know that the house has a bit of a history."

"What history?" The man scowled, stopping the tour in the long hallway outside Hunter's old room. Wally ran past him into the bedroom and started spinning in circles by the fireplace. The little girl squirmed until her father set her down to join her brother.

"They recently found evidence that suggests that this site may have been a stop on the Underground Railroad."

"Really?"

"It's up to the scholars to debate it, but they discovered human remains buried in the backyard last summer. The medical examiner determined the bones to be over a hundred and fifty years old and of

African American descent. Did you know that Chagrin Road, just a few blocks south of here, was a known route up to Canada?"

"That's amazing!" The specter of the dead bodies didn't seem to chill the woman's enthusiasm in the slightest.

The husband was less enthusiastic. "How did they find them?"

"Digging in the backyard." The agent waved her hand. "Must've been quite a shock. Of course, they called the police right away when they found bones."

"What did they do with them?" The husband cast a suspicious eye toward the backyard. The two children went tearing down the hall into the next room. "They're not still out there, are they?"

"Of course not! Everything was done by the book, I assure you. It was quite a process, really. The police brought in the anthropology department of Case Western Reserve University to perform a full site investigation. It turns out that the old foundations of one of the North Union Shaker Settlement buildings is located on this site. They spent three months digging around back there, preserving what they could. They gave the remains a proper burial at Lakeview Cemetery, from what I understand. They wrote all about it in the paper, so in a way, this house is famous!" The real estate agent grinned like she'd just handed them a prize. *Sell it as a positive.* That's what her boss had explained weeks earlier in the foyer. *It's not a stigmatized property. It's a landmark.* "You may want to look into getting the house registered as a historic landmark."

The husband nodded slowly. "Interesting."

Relieved to have the explanations over with, the agent continued the tour into the first bedroom. "Now keep in mind when you look at the bedrooms that the closets are smaller than you'll find in newer homes, but I think the extra space here more than makes up for it."

Hunter's old room basked in the warm sun streaming in through the window sheers. The two children came squealing back, chasing each other and then their own shadows, which danced on the floor.

The two parents moved on to the next room. "Wally, watch your sister."

Wally nodded his little head and stomped on his sister's shadow. Once his parents were out of sight, the boy spun slowly in the wondrous room. The fireplace stood at one end, then windows, built-in bookshelves, and the closet door. Curious, the boy walked over and opened the closet with his little sister in tow.

Inside, Benny's angry pencil marks had been painted over in a tasteful gray. Hunter's mother had insisted it was the only way they'd sell the house. The *DeAD GiRL* lay buried there under the latex along with Ava's lonely musings.

Wally stared up at the towering walls. "Look, Annie, look," he whispered. "There's a secret message."

The toddler stumbled in. "Where?"

"Here." He pointed to the inside wall next to the door. The boy couldn't read all the words just yet, but he ran a finger over the letters written in thin black ink with reverence.

Welcome to our Rawlingswood
Please fill this house with life and love
And forgive the ghosts that trespass here
For this was the home of Believers and runaways
And it does not belong just to you
It belongs to the Rawlings, Bells, and Klussmans
It belongs to the Turners and Spielmans
It belongs to the dead and the moved away
So if you see Walter in the attic, tell him you're sorry
If you find Benny in the closet, tell him you believe him
If you hear Toby in the night, tell him you love him
We welcome your ghosts, so be a good host
And perhaps we'll all meet in the end.

AUTHOR'S NOTE

No One's Home is a work of historical fiction, and as such it contains several true events, places, and people that form the backdrop for a fictional story. Two real murders in Shaker Heights, Ohio, inspired portions of this story. However, the events contained herein, including all characters, are figments of the author's imagination.

Rawlingswood and its inhabitants never existed. The fictional house is a composite of many beautiful century homes in Shaker Heights, Ohio. A vacant home the author toured in 2008 inspired much of the story. The previous owners were rumored to have fallen victim to an untimely death, drug addiction, and insanity. The home was badly vandalized, stripped of copper, and an unopened college acceptance letter lay on one of the steps up to the attic.

The following is an index of true events, places, and people that give historical context to the novel. Any characterization or dialogue involving real persons are fabrications invented by the author to enhance the story.

Shaker Heights, Ohio—The affluent suburb of Shaker Heights was built on lands purchased by the Van Sweringen brothers in 1905. Located approximately seven miles east and south of downtown Cleveland, Ohio, the city was named for the religious commune that occupied the land from 1822 to 1889. In 1921, the Van Sweringen Company real estate brochure for "Peaceful Shaker Village" promised prospective home buyers "protection forever against depreciation and unwanted change."

Lee Road, South Woodland, and Van Aken Boulevard are real streets in Shaker Heights; however, none of the homes there formed the basis for this story.

United Society of Believers in the Second Appearing of Christ (Shakers)—A religious order began in eighteenth-century England that practiced celibacy and asceticism in the belief that Jesus Christ would soon return. Mother Ann Lee was a founding member of the United Society of Believers, and the group came to be known as "Shaking Quakers" or "Shakers" for their exuberant prayer dances.

North Union Shaker Settlement—A group of Mother Ann's Believers settled in northeast Ohio in 1822 and dubbed the land given to the commune by convert Ralph Russell "the Valley of God's Pleasure." At the height of the movement, over two hundred North Union members divided themselves into the Center Family, Gathering (East) Family, and Mill (North) Family.

The North Union Shakers took in anyone seeking shelter and were known to house Native Americans and at least one African American member. Other Shaker settlements in the US reportedly harbored "fugitive" African Americans seeking refuge; however, no direct evidence was found linking North Union to the Underground Railroad.

North Union Shakers were the victims of mob violence more than once, and written evidence suggests many Shaker buildings were burned to the ground between 1848 and 1854. Membership dwindled after the Civil War due to a lack of new converts. The commune disbanded in 1889, and the land was sold off in 1892.

The Holy Grove—The North Union Settlement experienced an intense period of mysticism between 1840 and 1852. In 1843, they believed Jesus Christ came to stay with them for three months. In 1845, they constructed a "Holy Grove," or outdoor cathedral, also called "Jehovah's Beautiful Square," where they believed they could speak to angels and experience supernatural visions. The location of the Holy Grove was at the corner of Lee Road and Shaker Boulevard and less than two blocks from the fictional Rawlingswood.

Fugitive Slave Act of 1850—Congress passed legislation in 1850 that allowed slave hunters from the South to capture "fugitive" African Americans seeking refuge in northern states such as Ohio. It also made harboring "fugitives" illegal in the North, although abolitionists and many others of good conscience ignored the law. The act was officially overturned with the Emancipation Proclamation in 1863.

Underground Railroad—According to Cleveland historians, African Americans seeking freedom from slavery traveled along Chagrin Boulevard between Shaker Heights and Chagrin Falls on a path north toward Canada. This Underground Railroad passed along the southern border of the North Union Shaker Settlement (approximately four blocks from the fictional Rawlingswood).

Angelo Lonardo—Several Cleveland crime families were known to be involved in the illegal manufacture and distribution of liquor during Prohibition (1920–1933), which included a loose network of small residential distilleries. The character Big Ange was named after Angelo Lonardo.

References to the supernatural and unmarked graves in the story were largely inspired by my research into the North Union Shaker Settlement, the Society of Believers, and the enigmatic culture of the Romany people. Romany words and phrases vary in spelling and usage based on dialect and region. Any errors or omissions are my own.

The Shaker song "Simple Gifts" was written in 1848 by Elder Joseph Brackett, and its lyrics were transcribed from "Force and

Form: The Shaker Intuition of Simplicity" by John M. Anderson, published in the University of Chicago Press's *The Journal of Religion* 30, no. 4 (October 1950): 256–260. All other song lyrics and poem verses were inspired by Shaker traditions and written by the author.

For more information on the history of Shaker Heights and the North Union Shaker Settlement, consider the following sources:

Conlin, Mary Lou. *The North Union Story: A Shaker Society 1822–1889.* Shaker Heights, OH: The Shaker Historical Society, 1961.

Molyneaux, David G., and Sue Sackman. *75 Years: An Informal History of Shaker Heights.* Shaker Heights, OH: Shaker Heights Public Library, 1987.

Piercy, Caroline B. *The Valley of God's Pleasure: A Saga of the North Union Shaker Community.* New York: Stratford House, 1951.

ACKNOWLEDGMENTS

I owe an enormous debt of gratitude to Shirley Jackson and her quint-essential gothic novel, *The Haunting of Hill House*. I also owe a heart-felt thanks to the friends, family, editors, and historians who made this story possible. Local history librarian Meghan Hays of the Shaker Heights Public Library offered her help and insight as I researched the North Union Shaker Settlement. Ware Petznick and the staff of the Shaker Historical Society opened their collections and archives as well as their personal expertise to me as I researched the mysticism of the Society of Believers and the development of Shaker Heights.

A team of editors guided this tangled story through the deep, dark woods. Thank you, Jessica Tribble, Andrea Hurst, Carissa Bluestone, Riam Griswold, Leslie Molnar, Yishai Seidman, and all my friends at Thomas & Mercer and Amazon Publishing. I would be lost without you.

Jen and MK, your thoughtful feedback led me to the final draft. Mom, I wouldn't have made it without the love. Dad, thank you for my first home and the will to leave it. Jo, thank you for being my compass whenever I feel lost. Brac, thanks for being my friend in dark places. Hugs to my boys for finding the missing pieces of my heart. Irv, you're my home, and I'll never outgrow you.

ABOUT THE AUTHOR

D. M. Pulley lives just outside Cleveland, Ohio, with her husband, her two sons, and her dog. Before becoming a full-time writer, she worked as a professional engineer, rehabbing historic structures and conducting forensic investigations of building failures. Pulley's structural survey of a vacant building in Cleveland inspired her debut novel, *The Dead Key*, the winner of the 2014 Amazon Breakthrough Novel Award. She is also the author of *The Buried Book*.